THE PIRATE KING

THE PIRATE KING

TORI QUINN

To my cat, who has been a witness to my sinister giggles in the middle of the night

PROLOGUE

The breeze settled in, and I shivered beneath my mother's warm embrace. The towel she wrapped around me was too small; my bony legs peeked through the worn edges. My toes, wrinkled from the lake, pressed into the green grass, wiggling with the dirt that clung to my soles.

Sunlight shimmered across the water ahead, and with every tug of my naive being, I yearned to leap back into it—to surround myself with the water I longed for.

And back into the memory that haunted me.

Over and over again, I wished that this moment might outlast my decaying, failing heart.

CHAPTER 1

CoverGirl Lash Blast mascara slipped flawlessly into the hem of Ethera's sleeve. Her eyes lowered on the price tag— *'Now $8.43'*.

The air around her felt colder, the AC biting down one side of her face, briefly brushing her shoulder. Her heart jolted, thrill flowing viciously through her veins despite the countless times she'd done this. The short brown baby hairs brushed her pale cheeks, but her expression never faltered.

It was as easy for her to steal as it was to take a breath.

The movements came naturally now, polished with constant repetition. A performance she could slip into without thought. To anyone watching, she was just another customer standing too long in front of a shelf, weighing a choice that never really existed.

Was the product really worth the money or not?

It was a facade truly worthy of an Oscar.

When she finally stepped away, the shelf looked untouched. Nothing out of place, and nothing amiss. At least not to the naked eye.

Ethera never rushed. After all, panic was louder than guilt, and *guilt* was something she didn't have the privilege to feel. Walking away was always the real test. Strolling down the aisles with the innocent batting of her eyelashes, the slow burn of anticipation to see if she'll make it far away from the crime scene without getting caught.

Her heart thumped loudly against her chest—*was today the day she'd make headlines?*

But much to her pleasure, she was never caught.

It hadn't always been this easy. Some things carried weight beyond their price, risks she no longer bothered to entertain. She'd learned where to draw her own lines, even if the rest of the world blurred past them, especially with the constant peering eyes that followed a girl like her.

Ethera Heart was undoubtedly beautiful, just in her own unique way. Her sharp, strong features suited her sullen face with a set of full and dark brows that rarely matched in color. Her hair resembled that of an empty bird's nest. Messy, and lifeless with split ends that curled in all sorts of directions. It was the perfect shade of dark brown that didn't glow in the sunlight but instead seemed to darken even more than her constant stern expression.

It reminded her of her mother—and she hated it.

But that was not why they stared. It was the pale streaks threading through the roots that touched her forehead, ghost-white like strands born from a body that ran out of color.

She learned early on that the rules bent easily even when she balanced on the edge of the world. The once wild jungle had turned into a child's playground with a flick of her bony wrist. Her fingers knotted around invisible strings, and the little marionettes danced in her never-ending play.

Stealing had proven to be a wretched art.

And Walmart made it easier to disappear with the chaos. She wasn't the only one who *borrowed* from there. She just happened to be better at not being remembered.

But this hidden skill didn't apply everywhere.

High school wasn't kind to Ethera. She stood out, no matter how hard she tried to disappear. It had become almost as unbearable as walking out with a gallon of clean water.

The kids laughed and pointed, hands too quick to push her, with words as sharp as daggers. They knew exactly what to say to trigger her aggression to get her in trouble.

It was more than bad blood; it was the modern replica of war. Except Ethera learned early how to fight back. Fists came easier than mercy, and survival could barely keep up with her speed.

She never lost, but trouble always followed.

The air outside remained crisp, and a see-through cloud escaped her chapped lips as she hurried to turn the corner. Gray clouds scattered the sky; the sun was nowhere in sight despite spring drawing near. The thickness of her hoodie was more than enough to shield her from the morning cold.

She shook her right hand, the mascara falling out into her other palm. A smile tugged on her lips as her frozen fingertips struggled to open the packaging.

A few stores down, in the reflection of a window, she caught a glimpse of her face and there she applied the makeup, fanning her eyelid rapidly as her heart slowly settled.

꙰꙰꙰ ꙰꙰꙰ ꙰꙰꙰

The bell rang against her ears, causing Ethera to glance towards the teacher from the wall that she had previously zoned out.

She rather liked that wall. Oftentimes, she would imagine people's faces carved on the designs of the oak wood, and sometimes, it would be animals.

But today, specifically, the aliens' little scribbled mouths were pulled wide, revealing their toothy grins. She scoffed at her vivid imagination, getting up along with the others.

A thud shook her table as she closed a textbook, shoving it deep into her weary backpack. She swept her scattered supplies inside without a care in the world. There was no point in being organized, it wasn't like she owned a lot of things anyway, and everything seemed easily replaceable.

Her eyes lingered on the clock, hands zipping up the bag before throwing it over her shoulder.

Due to her unforeseen bad luck, detention had become a new addition to her not-so-busy schedule.

It seemed that not every battle could be won.

Every Friday after school, she would stay behind and volunteer to help in different departments for roughly two hours. Or as Mr. Harris loved to spew, 'for however long necessary'. No one really knew what that meant; after all, this was his brilliant idea to take advantage of the 'rascals' of the school and to make them work to redeem their freedom.

The study period was no more. It had become labor with no fruit.

It didn't take long before she reached the library, today's meeting spot. Ethera could only assume she'd be forced to sort old, crusty books and dust the shelves that no one was interested in. For a moment she hesitated, the thought of turning tail flashed in her mind.

The door she briefly stopped in front of was dark in color, almost like the wall of carved faces. The handle was coated with a fake golden metal, lukewarm against her fingertips. A sudden gush of air followed as she pulled it open, it was almost enough to force her to retreat.

The windows inside were swung wide, exposing fresh winter air. But the scent of musty books overtook their rightful home, she scrunched her nose at the stench. The best way to describe it was the scent of old folks, and the wind would never get close enough to air out this horrid room.

It was the size of the town hall's public library. Two floors high and filled to the brim with books, more than this small town could read in a lifetime. A broad brown staircase of twisting metal curled upwards, its rails tracing the edges of the second floor. Even the steps themselves were crafted from books, although Ethera knew for a fact that those were fake.

There was no way the library hags—who valued knowledge above all else—would allow it.

The door had begun to squeak past the halfway point, and the figures who occupied the empty tables glanced up, a half-assed smile drawing on one of their faces. "Juno, it suddenly smells like fish," a girl named after the flower of love pondered. "Don't ya think?"

Contrary to her name, her personality was quite the opposite. Ethera groaned underneath her breath, not expecting the two girls to already be inside.

There was a story behind that comment, but no one knew of it. It has been a while since Ethera learned the proper way of personal hygiene and how to use the countless stolen products that were at her disposal. But despite the perfumes, deodorants, lotions, toothpastes, scented hair oils, and so many other things she managed to get her hands on, it was never enough to mask the stench of fresh water that followed her.

"Oh! Whoopsies! It's just our dear Ethera!" Rose cheered with a fake snarl, putting her phone screen facing down on the table she sat on. Her legs swung excitedly at the intrusion. "I'm surprised you didn't slither your way out of this one."

Her strawberry blonde hair sparkled from the Bath & Body Works shimmer mist that she sprayed on every inch of her body. Ethera smirked, opening her mouth to say something sparkly.

Rose's friend, who sat right across her on a chair, interrupted. "Don't tease her, Rose," she warned, her dark almond eyes glued to her phone screen. "You know how violent she gets."

Rose's glossy lips pressed together to form a small smile, and her taunting gaze squinted with a daring blue hue. "Yeah, yeah, *sure.*"

If a fight broke out, Ethera would have won in seconds, and that much she knew, after all, Rose wasn't one to risk the expensive cost of her freshly done nail spring set.

Juno was Rose's sidekick, or as Ethera loved to point out. Best friends since birth with a familial bond that dated back for generations. The two were inseparable, always stuck to each other like gum on hair. Whenever Rose was around, Juno would act as if Ethera was nothing more than a pest that deserved to be crushed beneath her black Dock Martin boots. But on the rare occasions where they found themselves apart, the raven-head wouldn't think twice to spare Ethera even a spec of attention.

She scoffed, her eyes rolling as she strolled in. "If you know how violent I am, then you should know to watch that little mouth of yours," she hissed aggressively, eyes drawing back to Rose. Juno looked up, her dark brown orbs watching the passing figure as if the threat itself was alarming enough.

Two rows of three tables were spread out evenly in the middle of the open space. In the back, another student sat nearest to the window; a book lay open on the table, its pages threatened to flip with the light breeze that followed.

Ethera's eyebrows rose in surprise. There was no way that Hugo Blake—a star student—would end up in detention. She could only assume that it was not of his own doing.

The name alone was enough to aggravate Ethera, more than she already was. She couldn't stand the thought

7

of being in the same room as him, and much to her observation, he felt the same. His brown eyes had already peered over her from above the squared frames of his glasses. His eyebrows furrowed, mirroring her own expression.

She was positive that somehow, during their younger years, he became the reason for her harsh bullying. Ethera was an easy target, even she could admit that. The lack of melanin within her body had given her two-toned hair, and the drastic shift in her personality in middle school became a magnet for trouble.

After all, who wouldn't pick on a girl with a vulgar tongue and fiery fists?

The blame could not entirely be placed on Hugo, but the sweet sound of revenge—or even one punch in his stupidly smug face—could perhaps spark her path to redemption.

The door opened simultaneously as Ethera dropped her bag on the table. Two more figures strolled in.

The principal, Mr. Harris, gripped the fabric of a black backpack as he dragged a student into the library. His round glasses sat on the mountain-like bridge of his nose, and a French mustache curled upwards in glee. "I found this one trying to escape," he broke the silence. Mr. Harris's chest proudly puffed upwards; no doubt he had been hovering outside the boy's last period with speculation of yet another attempted detention escape.

Hugo's brother and twin, Reymond Blake, sighed in defeat. The boy's face twisted with annoyance but quickly turned into a tight-lipped stare upon receiving the wrath of the principal's piercing eyes.

Mr. Harris let go of the student's bag, lightly giving him an encouraging shove forward. Ethera rolled her eyes, placing her face in the palm of her hand. Her luck had gone from zero to non-existent. Detention with her enemy, her enemy's best friend, her other enemy, and the other enemy's stupid twin.

Finally, the concept of karma had settled in the back of her mind.

Reymond rushed in, sitting by his brother, his bag still on his shoulders. Without warning, he let out a loud, disturbing groan as Hugo smacked him on the back of the head. "Ow—what the fuck, lil bro?"

"Language," the principal warned. "Now that all of you are here," he paused, his eyes scanning the miserable faces of his students. "I have exciting news for you. Instead of sleeping, or talking, or rotting with those devices you call phones…you will have to work together to sort out these books in a timely manner, or else you will be staying in the library throughout the night. Whenever you finish, ring the front office, and I will come to let you out. Any questions?"

Juno raised her hand, the sleeve of her long white tee coming down to her elbow. "Sir, is that even allowed?"

"You'd best get to it, or it will be an unforgettable sleepover," he grinned, completely ignoring Juno's question and motioning with his hands at the countless trolleys overflowing with books.

The students remained quiet at his strict announcement, trying to catch the bluff on his expression. "Oh—! And naturally, none of this brilliance would exist without Mr. Alden. What a stroke of genius to teach students to get along better!" He mumbled something on the way out, but the

9

screeching of the door muffled the words completely. The sound of the lock twisting seemed more intense as the unusual group remained still.

The two girls groaned in sync, picking up their phones and resuming their conversation. Hugo and Ethera got up at the same time, each grabbing one of the carts that lined the spaces between the tables. It rolled with ease on the maroon carpeted floor despite the weight it carried. Self-aware of their proximity, they turned on their heels and rolled in separate directions without a word.

Reymond, on the other hand, began inspecting the windows, one hand pushing against the delicate glass. The rusty hinge struggled against the force of his palm as his eyes measured the fall from the second floor, along with the possibilities of injury.

Hugo's twin senses went off; he turned around and shouted angrily at his brother. "What the hell are you doing?"

"Looking for a way out…" His eyes moved towards the ceiling, scanning it for vents. Reymond scratched the back of his head, a dumbfounded expression on his face. It had pained Ethera to see his smart looks not pair well with his lacking brain.

"Don't be an idiot and come help. I'm in this mess because of you."

"But I have practice! Coach will kill me if I'm late again!"

There were many differences between the twins despite their almost identical appearance. Both of their hair was a golden curly mess, taking on a personality of its own. Hugo was the only one who bothered to style it on the side, attempting to control it to match his intellectual image, while the other twin let it take its own unique shape.

Hugo was slightly blind in his right eye; rather than wearing a prescribed contact, he begged his mother to buy him a bulky pair of glasses for his 12th birthday.

Both brothers had brown eyes; Hugo's were more furrowed and serious than Reymond's, which often were relaxed with a clownish glint of mischief. Just a year prior, Reymond had spontaneously decided to shave a split in the middle of his right brow and had kept it ever since, pairing it with another one of his bright ideas—an ear piercing. It was divine intervention from above when his mother had walked in on her son holding a lighter with a needle; if it wasn't for her, then there would have been nothing stopping him from customizing himself everywhere else.

The twins were the same height, rounding up to six feet two. Reymond had become bulkier after joining the football team; it had become obvious to all the high school girls in the perimeter by the way his muscles fitted his shirt perfectly, and the defined sculpture of his freckled face— what they had now referred to as 'the jaw of the century'.

Ethera simply called it puberty with a crazy amount of exercise. After all, he ran for miles every weekend.

But unknown to the simple-minded boy, it was also the cause of his rise in the school's hierarchy. From skater-pot head to the future team captain, based on the set predictions for the following school year.

"The hell are you looking at?" Hugo cursed in Ethera's direction, who quietly listened to the bickering without any self-awareness. She glanced at Hugo; his brown eyes darkened underneath the shadow of his thick brows.

11

"Am I not allowed to look at zoo animals? Since when was that a school rule?" She snarled, tilting her head with a sarcastic smile on her face.

Reymond butted in, sensing an argument stirring. "Come on, guys. Not again! You used to be besties like a year ago, what happ—?"

"*Elementary!*" They snapped back in unison, exploding with offense. That had pretty much broken any sort of restraint they held to keep civil. Ethera couldn't stand it when the boy copied her as a kid, and Hugo came after her inhumane nature of a wild, rabid dog.

Reymond sighed, ignoring them as if this wasn't the first—or the last time the two would bicker. His eyes scanned the numerous carts; the hope of finishing in thirty minutes was completely crushed at the sudden realization of how much had piled up throughout the week. Spending the night at school was definitely a no-go.

He dropped his bag onto the nearest table and turned to look at the other two girls, who giggled among each other. "Are you guys going to help us or what?" He called out in their direction.

They didn't turn around, not paying attention to anything but their phones. Rose lifted her hand, waving it in an attempt to tell him to piss off. "Yeah, yeah. Give us a sec," Juno answered for the blonde.

Whatever was cheery and happy on their end had completely snapped Ethera in two. "Hey, idiots! If you don't get off your asses and help, we'll never be able to leave on time. Unless you want to spend your night with the roaches, you better hurry and get to it." Her loud voice shook the windows in anger. The thought of walking home in the dead of night sounded extremely unpleasant. "And as for you—go back to ignoring me, you twink."

"Twink?! You—!"

"HA! Hey, I also call him that!" Reymond burst out laughing, and with it, the invisible string of patience finally snapped. All their voices overlapped with each other, creating a chaotic pile-up of loud chatter and hate.

It took five whole minutes of throwing meaningless words back and forth before they finally ran out of insults—or breath. Realizing the work at hand, they finally quieted down, each grabbing a cart.

After a while, their motivated speed, fueled by anger and discomfort, finally died down. And no matter how fast they worked, it seemed that the number of books was barely declining.

It wasn't as easy as it seemed; not all books were sorted in their corresponding trolley. They had to match the genre and author name in alphabetical order, which forced a few of them to hop from aisle to aisle just to find the correct spot.

Ethera and Hugo ended up in the same section, their eyes trying their best not to look at each other and not give in to the satisfaction of breaking the pretense that the other did not exist.

Ethera found it rather odd. Standing next to someone she used to be close with, a past that had now turned into a long-forgotten fragment of her imagination. Perhaps once a bittersweet dream that faded away with each passing day.

Her head almost turned to look at the boy if it wasn't for a jolt that startled her. She quickly looked back at the electric-like feeling that rippled through her, touching every inch of her skin. From the tips of her fingers to the shiver down her back and the jittery itchiness in her toes. Her entire body froze as if the phenomenon had paralyzed her. Her fingers glowed a bright white light as they brushed the hard spine of a book that sat upright on the shelf.

In that moment, everything was gone; the books around her vanished as if they never mattered to begin with. The enticing energy charged through the blood in her veins, traveling at lightning speed and igniting the book. It sparked a goldish-yellow flame so bright that the shock of it all was enough to finally snap her mind out of it. Her fingers gripped the edges of the book, pulling it out along with her body, which jumped backwards.

Ethera's eyes widened, the fire died down, and the sound of her heartbeat rang in her ears. Hints of white outlines filled the cover, moving like a mouse on a computer screen. Words of a language she could not read slowly began to dim.

Her hand twitched in a futile attempt to let go. "H-Help," She cried out, her eyes wide with fear. The book would not let go, no matter how hard she shook her arm.

It was stuck to her.

Without much thought, she grabbed it with her free hand, attempting to pull it off. The bizarre feat only managed to capture her other palm. The book moved on its own, opposing her own force and pulling her wherever it seemed fit. "What the f-."

"Quit messing around and get back to work," Hugo interrupted her, shooting her a dirty look. The brown waves on Ethera's head obstructed her vision as the book yanked her forward and backward. Her mouth opened to ask for help but was greeted with a lock of hair. Hugo looked confused, watching the girl as her legs shuffled about.

A smirk naturally fell on his face; he was about to make fun of her if it wasn't for the girl's body bumping into his own. He stumbled backwards, his back touching the metal bar of his book cart.

"I-I can't get it off! Don't just stand there, help me!" Ethera yelled out, spitting out hair in the process. Hugo looked at her as if she had lost her mind.

Everyone knew that Ethera Heart was crazy. But even this kind of crazy was way above her efforts.

He would have disregarded her pleas if it weren't for the book she held in between her palms. Like a dimming light that was slowly turning on, the book began to glow brighter now that the boy was closer. Hugo was quick to jump into action, helping by any means necessary. His displeasure with her presence had vanished, and the unexplainable situation had taken over his mind.

His hands gripped her own, trying to pull them off. "What the hell…"

She really was glued to it. "Stop! You're stepping on my toes!"

"W-Wait—I can't take my hands off!" He complained, and the two of them almost tripped over each other, trying to maintain their balance.

His hands were stuck right on top of hers, and Ethera was furious. "Get off me before I scream!" He opened his mouth to protest, but Reymond's unwelcome laughter filled the air around them.

His head poked from the other side, a hand gripping the bookshelf for support. "Aww! Have you two made up, finally?" He cheered supportively in between laughs. The stuck pair yelled in sync; their mission had lost its goal.

Instead of attempting to get the book off, they pushed each other until they ended up on the floor. Ethera lifted her leg, kicking Hugo off her before rolling on the side. She brought her knee up, pushing herself up, only to fall back down. The 150 pounds of meat that was Hugo Blake was making it difficult to get off the ground.

Ethera's eyes widened dangerously; the joke had sailed without her. "Let go, you fool," she gritted her teeth, a dangerous expression crossing her face.

"I've been telling you, I can't," Hugo shouted, hoping that if he rose his voice, then the brunette would finally hear him.

Reymond had walked closer; his laugh was replaced with a dry and serious tone. "Quit fighting, you two. What the hell are you guys even doing rolling around like dogs? You guys do realize that they haven't washed these carpets since like forever, right?"

Ethera sat up on her knees, which burned from the friction caused by the carpet and her pants. Hugo took this calm opportunity to sit up; his back ached from the tumble he had taken. "It won't let go! Reymond, help us!" Ethera yelled, her voice just as disoriented as her appearance. Hugo's eyes narrowed; the pain from the recent memory of being kicked in the garage was sparking another possible incoming argument. He silently swore to himself to never—EVER—help his nemesis.

Reymond bent down in front of them, glancing at the book. Two other female figures appeared at the end of the aisle, getting curious at the sudden disturbance.

"Don't touch the book, it has some kind of glue on it," Hugo yelled out suddenly, trying his best to warn his brother in time. But Reymond had already grabbed it with one hand, his fingertips locking in on its hard shell. He jiggled his hand; Ethera's and Hugo's arms followed.

Reymond gasped, eyes widening as a smile crept through. "Whoa! You're not kidding!" He said, getting up excitedly. The sudden motion forced the other two to hurry to their feet. Juno had burst out laughing as a white light from her phone flashed suddenly, followed by the sound of an iPhone picture being taken.

Hugo took a deep breath in, trying to calm himself. "Are you an idiot?"

Ethera remained quiet, trying to shake the hair away from obscuring her vision. She stumbled forward, being pulled by Reymond, whose strength exceeded that of the book. Her head bumped into Hugo, who disgustedly looked down at her.

"This isn't funny, guys," Reymond murmured, trying to stop the other two from laughing. "I can't feel my hand!"

Both Hugo and Ethera took notice of the numbing sensation that slowly spread from finger to finger. They had been so busy fighting each other that they had not noticed how detached their hand felt—as if it was not even there. Their blood had completely stopped circulating at the point of contact with the book, but the sensation didn't stop there; it was spreading, eating at their arm with every bite.

Reymond's frustration turned into anger, and he pulled the others with him towards the only people who were able to help. Hugo and Ethera tried their best to keep up with him and refrain from falling back onto the ground. It was proving to be difficult with every foot that became a hazard; they had to be careful to avoid tripping over themselves.

"Go ahead, you try it. See if I'm playing around."

"Rey, no—Rose, don't do it!" Hugo shouted, his voice overlapping with the others. The warning never made it to Rose's ears, and with a single fingertip, her daisy-green nail touched the golden-white cover. The book showed no mercy; it took her hostage as well.

The light illuminated even brighter with Rose's capture, glowing vividly and clearly with every person it seized. Ethera seemed to be the only one paying attention to its bizarre behavior.

A high-pitched screech left Rose's mouth. Everyone winced, not being able to cover their ears to save themselves. She turned to Reymond, using his back as support for her free hand. Her attempt to pull away was futile.

Hugo took it upon himself to calm and reassure the group. "Okay...it's okay! Let's not panic now."

"Wait, are you guys like pranking me, right now?" Juno wiped the tears in her eyes with the sleeve of her long tee. Her thumb hovered over phone, a white flash went off again.

Reymond shook his head in response to his own thoughts. "On three. I'm pulling as hard as I can," he announced. Everyone yelled for him to stop, but his mind was already set. "Fuck it. Three!"

He took them all by surprise, yanking at his hand, the book, and the three figures that came with it. They didn't have the strength to match him, so they accepted their fate as they stumbled forward. Juno stood there, with all her innocent glory, as the four of them inched closer, colliding in an instant.

Ethera closed her eyes, feeling herself falling. However, when they finally landed on the hard dirt, the book let go, freeing all of them from its temporary captivity.

Juno had it bad. Being squashed by four people, she couldn't comprehend how she was still alive despite the throbbing sensations of unmistakable pain in different parts of her body.

Her oval eyes fluttered open, confusion overcoming pain, for what stared at her was the bright blue sky.

CHAPTER 2

"Am I…dead?" Asked the raven-head, fear flashed across her face as the question settled in her mind. It wasn't the blue that threw her eyes into a whirlpool but the shimmering green of the very-much *alive* trees. The leaves rustled through the chaos, slowly waving down towards her. She quickly brushed her hair aside as the grass tickled at her olive skin.

Juno immediately sat up, her head turned from side to side. Relief suffused her features when her eyes landed on her best friend, who lay still on the ground.

The sun was charming, shining brightly on Rose's side, warming up her aching body. It felt weird and odd, considering it was the end of February.

Juno jumped to her feet, ignoring the pain that radiated through every moving limb. "Get up! Get up! Oh my god!" She pulled Rose by her arm, yanking the girl upwards. Her blue eyes fluttered open in annoyance, the enchanting warmth disturbed with the harsh tug. Nevertheless, she allowed herself to be pulled up to her feet. A yawn escaped her mouth as Juno dusted off the back of the blonde's hoodie with haste.

Ethera stood frozen in the distance, eyes scanning the unfamiliar landscape. The hair on her bare arms stood up against the long sleeves of her sweater like an unmistakable warning.

The library was no more.

Obnoxiously tall trees scattered the forest around them, the brown bark stretched high into the sky like palm trees in the Caribbean. Sunlight fell through the millions of bright green leaves, contradicting their dull Oregon weather, and the winter that had wiped everything for miles. The air around them held the faint glow of light, suspended and frozen like a painting.

The wind had paused, disappearing as if it had moved away. The forest did not make a single sound, and that haunting fact felt queasy.

This was not home—this was someplace else entirely.

The wheels in her brain were turning at an alarming rate that was faster than that of the smartest boy in school. Hugo remained seated in the dirt in shock, his long fingers gripped the soil, as if pinching it would settle the confusion in his head. His twin brother rubbed the back of his own, trying to make sense of this situation.

Reymond's eyes drifted down to his arm, the very arm that seemed to be the cause of this...*situation*. "Oops..." He muttered to himself, eyes looking back at their surroundings.

Rose's sharp hearing caught on to him. "*Oops*?" She repeated louder so everyone else could hear it. "*Oops!* Where in the hell are we?" She shook with fury, grabbing Reymond by the collar of his shirt. Juno leaped towards them, both hands reaching for her best friend's shoulders.

The boy shrugged in reply, his hands rose defenselessly. "Well, as you can see—we are in a forest." Their conversation faded into the background as Ethera turned around, eyes landing on the dazed twin. Hugo's brain seemed to have stopped working; no doubt his rational mind had been overloaded. Seeing him in such a state almost brought Ethera to tears.

Tears of happiness.

He always acted like a know-it-all, and right now, he half-heartedly convinced himself that this was nothing more than a mere fragment of his imagination. Probably caused by the stress induced by his brother.

It was like they had teleported. *Yeah, right, as if.*

"Guys, I think we teleported," Reymond pitched in, reading his twin's thoughts aloud. Hugo's head snapped to his brother, rising to his feet. He fixed his crooked glasses, his finger pushing up the taped bridge on his nose.

Dirt. They landed on dirt. Well, some of them at least.

Hugo scoffed; his brother's suggestion was quickly debunked by science. "Don't be an idiot." His hands quickly dusted off his soiled clothes, the smell of dirt lingered on his fingers.

"Unless we all smoked the same shit-."

"You smoked in the library?" His brother's temples throbbed with rage as he paused mid-action. Ethera's brows shot up, lips pressing into a thin line.

"I needed motivation?"

They stood frozen in silence, all eyes on Reymond as if expecting his words to be nothing more than a prank. "Are you out of your mind? You could get expelled!" Hugo snarled through gritted teeth, second-hand embarrassment flooding him as he leaped at his brother. Rose had finally let go of Reymond's collar, not wanting to get in between a family dispute.

Hugo grabbed the wrinkled fabric, yanking at it as if the earthquake would force his twin's brain to fall into place. Reymond clutched his brother's hands, pulling them off him with ease.

Ethera let out a long sigh, turning around and walking off into the distance just to give herself some space to breathe. Their voices piled up from behind her as her eyes landed on the disturbed patch of dirt ahead.

In the distance a large paw print sat across the ground; the animal responsible must have weighed a ton to be able to carve such a mark. It was a fierce print with long claws that dragged outwards, its frightening size was half her height. She stared at it, her mind seemingly going blank as the vicious possibility stared back.

Her throat tightened, lips parting. "Do you guys have your phones? I-I don't think these are ordinary woods." The shock was audible in her words; the stutter somehow caught the attention of the rest of the group. Footsteps shuffled behind her; the rest of her classmates appeared, surrounding the animal print.

"Bears…" Reymond muttered to himself again, and Ethera cringed at the thought. "Fuck, we really need to get out of here. Like now. Or else we'll be bear food."

Ethera shook her head, her throat feeling dry. "That's no bear," she announced after a moment of uncomfortable silence, as if her pitch of information would provide any sort of comfort to the group. They erupted into a panic, hands patting down their pockets in a hurry.

Rose was first to pull out her cell from the pocket of her denim skirt. "Huh? It's dead?"

"What? Let me try mine—." Reymond stuck his hand deep into the cutouts of his cargo pants, shuffling through the contents before pulling out the device aggressively. It was covered with cracks from top to bottom, but it too wouldn't turn on.

Rose's breath shook. "I had literally just used it." Everyone looked at Juno with hope.

"I must have dropped mine when you guys tackled me."

Everyone looked at Ethera with hope. "Oh—I must have left mine in my bag," Ethera quickly said, embarrassment stirred in her as her eyes averted from their gaze. Disappointment crossed everyone's faces. Heavy silence hovered in the air, and the soft hum of the wind resumed, dancing through the leaves of the trees that seemed to cave in on them.

Hugo lightly jogged from behind them, his eyes wide in panic. Everyone was so concerned that they hardly noticed his absence. "Guys…that book," he pointed out, "I can't find it anywhere." They all broke out, checking out the surrounding area and peeking into every bush with the hope of locating the answer to one of their countless questions.

But much to their disappointment, the mysterious book was nowhere to be found. They dragged their feet in despair, meeting up in the middle of the clearing. The dirt crunched underneath their feet, and the trees began to whistle in the background.

"W-We can't stay here."

"Alright—then let's just keep moving. We'll go the opposite way, so we don't walk into wherever that thing went," Hugo suggested after catching on to the lack of thought in everyone's mind. They all shook their heads, buzzing with agreement. Even the sunlight, once warm and comforting, had sent chills down their backs.

"Wait," Rose quickly stopped. "Aren't you like a forest expert or something?" Her round eyes landed on Ethera.

Her heart skipped a beat, eyes looking back at Reymond.

"I-I mean…kinda, I guess?" She punched the air and cursed her mind for stuttering, but the nerves on the back of her neck were making her fidgety.

"Then lead the way," Rose ordered. Everyone nodded urgently, and Ethera walked off first to lead the group, every step as robotic as the last. She wanted more than anything to be in the back of the line, where she presumed was safer.

Suddenly, she jerked to a stop, partially turning around. "Well—if we just follow this dirt trail, I'm sure we'll be able to find a road or something," she cringed at her delivery. They all came to a stop, everyone watching her intently. "I hike a lot." She added before telling herself to shut up already.

"Okay, we don't need to know your life story—OW!" Rose yelped suddenly.

Juno's hand gripped her friend by the arm, pinching through the fabric of the hoodie. *"Play nice."*

Rose rolled her eyes in response. "Yeah, whatever, *mom,*" she muttered under her breath. Ethera ignored the girls; her mind and eyes were busy gathering confirmation.

These were not the friendly woods of their hometown. And those prints were definitely not those of a bear. After all, she lived in the woods and could wholeheartedly say that she knew her way around quite well.

But that was a secret not worth revealing. There was no doubt that the girls would jump at the opportunity to spread this information for the sake of revenge, and other kids with nothing better to do would come looking for Ethera on their days off.

The silence could not be helped; after all, the unlikely group had nothing in common except the unexplainable change in scenery. They followed one another, both Rose and Juno fell behind everyone else, their hands intertwined with each other, sharing comfort and fear. Reymond walked closely next to Ethera, his head twitched towards the sky making the brunette nervous. Hugo fell behind his brother.

The trees fed into Ethera's imagination as they stretched out longer, their limbs and twigs falling forward towards the group. They grew taller and wider with every step, hovering in front of the sun, covering their path with dancing shadows that howled in the wind.

It had become dark and scary. The dirt road was so narrow that they trailed behind one another one by one. Eventually, the wind relaxed, falling still as if listening to their footsteps.

Ethera kept glancing back, each time holding eye contact with a different person. She half expected something to pop up from behind and devour them all. An uncomfortable feeling settled in her stomach; her mind was not able to tell if this was a dream or reality.

Rose suddenly jumped to the side, pulling on the back of Juno's sleeve. The short girl stumbled backwards due to the surprisingly strong pull of her friend. "Did you hear that?" Rose's voice trembled. Everyone stopped in their tracks; no one dared to make a sound. "P-Please tell me someone heard that?" Rose spoke again; this time her voice was reduced to that of a whisper.

There were sounds coming from behind the trees. Unidentified whisperers flooded their ears; they were almost as loud as the thumping of their own heartbeats. Ethera didn't want to admit it, but she was scared shitless; she didn't have anything to hold to remind herself that this really was happening to her. "L-Let's just keep walking," she cried, her stomach knotted. She took a step forward, but the sound emerged again, this time louder than before.

It was unmistakable. A low, deep growl pierced through the air around them as if the creature in question was alerting the humans of its presence.

Ethera shivered, her eyes scanning the faces of her classmates. She had no idea if she was leading them all towards safety or to their deaths. The creature didn't wait to build suspense; it growled again. This time, the forest reacted to the sound.

The ground shivered at the noise, pulsing with a warning like a quake about to submerge. Their eyes locked onto each other, and a telepathic agreement sent them bolting in seconds.

They all broke into a sprint, promising to keep running forward no matter what. Whatever was following them sounded more gruesome than a bear.

The loud drums of their hearts fueled the rush of adrenaline that clouded their judgement. They managed to jump over roots and rocks, cross a small stream of water, and somehow miss a hidden sign, all together. With the world turning blurry and their desperate attempts to get somewhere less intimidating, they failed to realize that a wooden sign was nailed across a thick bark of a tree, its words capitalized to emphasize the danger. *WARNING* was written in burgundy faded letters—but even if one of them had noticed the sign, the foreign language was not something they would have understood.

Once tall and mighty trees shrank down to a humble, earthly form. The wood bark had disappeared behind the branches that brushed past their shoulders and arms.

Their run had slowed down to a fast-paced walk, trying desperately to make their way through the forest as quickly as possible. The loud breathing was a giveaway, and the hurried footsteps had made up the mundane sounds of the forest.

The figures moved the thin branches out of their faces, bending down, when necessary, just to get by. Eventually, they had to slow down even more, finding themselves getting tangled in the hanging leaves that resembled those of the weeping willow.

Except these ones seemed to be weeping too much. Their leaves like tears, hundreds upon thousands brushed the unrecognizable road below them. Small pink flowers sprouted from the leaves. No one stopped to observe their beauty, fearing that whatever was following them might just turn this forest into their gravesite.

"Let go! Let go! Ew, ew, ew!" Rose cried out loudly, startling everyone once again. Ethera spun around, and anxiety swirled around her, hidden behind the flowers and the leaves. The blonde fought against the vine-like branches that tangled themselves around her. Juno's hands ripped through the leaves, whispering for her friend to stay still as the branches cling to Rose's arms.

In an instant, Ethera tripped over something, falling backwards on her butt. She flinched from the contact, tiny pebbles digging into the palms of her hands. Suddenly, something brushed against her pinky finger. Her heavy breathing soon froze, her brown eyes scanning the ground behind her.

A root had emerged from the ground. A moving root. It slithered away like a snake. Made out of brown rock and dirt, it blended in with the path below. Cracks formed with

29

tiny bits of moss and mushrooms grew from between, spreading farther away from what her eyes could see.

Why was it moving?

She turned around, crawling behind it on her knees despite Reymond's whispered protests for her to stop. Quickly turning around, she held her finger up to her lips before turning back. The sound of crumbling leaves blended in with the sound of dragging dirt.

Every second, she had to pause to move the hair out of her eyes; the twigs and vines had made it almost impossible to keep her hair at bay. Reymond had followed her, along with Hugo, who silently protested against it.

A grunt rumbled in the distance, and the slithering root came to a stop along with Ethera. There was movement past the hanging leaves; something was surely out there.

Something big.

She gulped nervously, mustering the courage to get a closer look. Very quickly, still down on all fours, she moved the leaves out of her line of sight, and just as soon as she did it, her fingers scrunched up, letting them all fall back to their natural flow. Hiding herself from the creature in front.

She was smart to do so, for the creature was not familiar with mortals of any kind. No one was stupid enough to venture deep into the forest, not until now.

This creature was made entirely of hardened dirt, almost like it was glued to its bare skin, which was found deep underneath its rocky exterior. It moved on all fours, its long tail dragging on the ground beneath it. The cracks on his shell were created from growth and flexible movement, and with the touch of the sun grew moss that spread all around the creature's back. Tiny little mushrooms poked out, making their way down to its long and thick tail.

Ethera didn't seem to look at his face when she first laid eyes on its enormous body, but this thing had quite a big nose that was good at sniffing out nearby food. His eyes were hidden in the cracks of hard dirt, in a place where moss could not reach.

The moment she had touched the vines, it had noticed her too, and without her knowledge, it was lying in wait—*watching*. Ethera's hands shook against the dirt, her mind pulling a blank. Fight or flight instincts kicked in, except fight was out of the question, and the flight seemed to nail her down to the ground.

This was an animal. A not-so-ordinary creature. A beast she had never seen before. Not in her forest, not in the books.

Not anywhere *human*.

She wondered if it knew she was there. She wondered if her fear could be smelled in the air around them, escaping through the cracks of the leaves.

What if it had ears? Ears as big as elephants? Would it hear if she backed away? Or should she wait for it to move on its own?

It was her foolish mistake to follow it. After everything she'd seen, after what she had witnessed. Why would she do such a thing? It was a fool's funeral.

Ethera was so deep in thought that the creature began to get restless. A hot, small breeze rustled the leaves. Ethera gulped. That was no wind.

She glanced back at Reymond, whose face had gone blue. He had seen it too and had been frozen ever since. Hugo, who was still crawling behind, had finally caught up, meeting the shaking eyes of Ethera. In a second, he understood and began to crawl backwards.

A pale white hand grasped Reymond's shoulder, causing his eyes to meet hers. She nodded in false reassurance and motioned with her eyes for him to go, but before he could, the rustling of the vines was heard, and light illuminated Reymond's already frightened face.

The creature had moved its tail upwards and used it to move the leaves out of its way, just so it could take another look at these unknown entities in front of it.

Its hidden eyes landed on Reymond. His body shook, eyes staring right at the beast. It let out a loud growl, shaking the ground, the leaves, and the hearts of the humans, snapping them all out of the frightened trance.

They were staring death right in the eye—wherever it might be.

Before Ethera could turn to look at it, Reymond had grabbed her by the arm and dragged her away with force that ripped through the vines and leaves that tugged at their clothes.

Branches scratched at their faces and hands, and they had no choice but to endure the pain or face the wrath of the beast they had awakened.

CHAPTER 3

"GO! GO!" Reymond yelled out, one hand fighting the vines and the other dragging Ethera by the arm. No one stopped to question the situation. That chilling growl was heard by everyone, and unknown to the humans, other entities of this world had heard it too.

The figures dashed through the forest, half of them not knowing what it was they were running from. The beast kept flashing in Ethera's mind and sweat rolled down her spine. Her side ached with pain, the muscles in her legs burned from the sudden movements, and despite the amount of strain her body was receiving, she kept going.

The vivid image of them all perishing by its rock-like fangs had haunted her mind, and Reymond's too, fueling their thirst for survival. The twin had long outrun the rest of his friends, leading them back to where they had originally come from.

Juno was hot on his tail. Her arm reached out and pulled the muscular boy to a stop. "We can't go that way! T-

That thing went there, remember?" She screamed, her chest rising abnormally.

"Fuck," Reymond paused to breathe. "Fine—that way!" He pointed through the trees. By the time Hugo, Rose, and Ethera caught up, the leaders broke into another jog.

Ethera paused, her mouth agape, begging for oxygen. Her eyes stared deep into the forest where a trail was not visible. There was no time to protest, to calm down, or to discuss an actual plan for survival. The others didn't wait for democracy.

Reymond, ahead of everyone else, suddenly came to a halt. He raised his hand, grabbing onto the sleeve of Juno's shirt, pulling her back. She turned her head, ready to cuss at him and everyone else for being the reason for her haggard expensive fabric, but his expression had completely taken her by surprise.

The boy thought he'd seen it all. From magic books of teleportation to beasts the height of a soccer goal net. But it appears this world was not done surprising him. In a split second, Juno's expression mirrored his.

Rose arrived behind them, followed by Hugo. "W-What the hell guys—." She was wheezing loudly, trying to gasp for air. Her lungs burned from the exercise. Her eyes caught on to the situation instantly, and just as quickly, her breath hitched in her throat.

"Fuck, I think we lost Ethera," Hugo stumbled behind them, his head turned towards the path they had come from. The forest was colder in this region, whether it was the lack of sunlight or the roughness of the wind that was almost strong enough to sway them side to side. Hugo had turned to face his group, ready to convince them to retrace their steps. Instead, he too froze, blinking rapidly as if the action would make the fantasy disappear.

Three figures stood in front of them, towering over. Tall was an understatement; these people were giants like straight from a basketball recruiters dream. The sun parted in their honor, shining down from above, illuminating the muted greens and silvers that glimmered in the light. Their garments resembled armor made of layered leather and leaves, a perfect blend of green and brown that matched the color of the trees, as if intended to camouflage them.

And so, it did. There were more than three; countless others were hidden within the branches, out of sight, watching as they lay in wait. Their eyes were narrowed and sharp, matching the ornate spears that pointed at the group of intruders.

What scared the mortals wasn't the weapons or the hostile looks, but the braided white hair that paired well with their pointy, long ears.

Much, much different than those of humans.

Whoever these people were, they were not from Oregon. Hugo took a step back, not realizing that his body had moved on its own. He bumped into someone, flinching and jumping away. Ethera stood beside him, not sparing her nemesis a single glance. Everyone's eyes were glued to those of these *people.*

In an instant, loud thuds appeared behind them. More of them spawned all around, long vines hung lowly from the trees, some gripped by the pale white creatures. Their weapons prevented any escape.

Reymond choked on his words, breaking the silence. "Whoa…what the hell did I smoke?" He felt delirious, much like the rest of his friends. His grip on Juno's sleeve had loosened, finally letting go of the petite female. He smacked his forehead lightly in an attempt to wake up. Nothing happened, they were still there—or rather he was. He shook his head, brushing the loose curls out of his face.

"Rey, let's be real," Hugo couldn't help but whisper, "You're not smart enough to use your imagination like this." Reymond's face twisted in annoyance at the insult despite the new danger they were presented with.

"Shut it, you idiots," Ethera immediately urged, pushing through the group to stand in front. Her eyebrows scrunched together in the middle, eyes still looking up at the unfamiliar faces. Her hands immediately shot up, a humane indication that she meant no harm. "I'm sorry to bother you guys, but we are lost. Would you be able to help us find our way home?" She spoke in a loud and clear voice.

The group didn't budge; the only visible movement was in their eyes. Ethera thought of herself as brave in that moment; she had the guts to take initiative despite the shakiness of her fingers and the fear that slithered through her. One by one, the mortals followed her example.

The people in green lowered their spears, glancing at their leader. An unreadable look crossed one of their expressions, and for the first time, Ethera could not interpret it.

Their hostility never faded. She gulped nervously, her throat closing in.

The one in the middle tilted his head with curiosity. "Come." His voice echoed through the forest like distant thunder. The mortals exchanged uncertain looks. There was not much that could be done in this situation; they were out-numbered and defenseless, somewhere that did not resemble their planet.

The tall pale-green creatures parted to the side, watching as the impostors slowly walked forward. Their spears never lowered, half-expecting the short humans to at-tack any second.

"They're kinda buff," Rose whispered shamelessly towards Juno's side. Her dark eyes widened, a clear indica-tion to shut up. Rose wasn't entirely wrong; beneath the cape, the leather, and the tunic of their shirts were mountains of muscle from centuries of brutal training. The forest had gone quiet, the wind dispersed as if it was no longer needed. The unseen danger dared not show itself before the forest folk.

Ethera was not oblivious to the myths and stories that paraded through the children's books on Earth. However, her eyes refused to deceive her rational mind.

These people were elves, no doubt about it.

Seven of them followed them on the ground, and more hovered and hid within the trees. Ethera glanced up; her eyes were not adjusted to the quick movements of those who leaped soundlessly through the branches. There was no sign of them, but the vines flowed lightly to the rhythm of their jumps.

"Excuse me?" Ethera called out, eyes still hovering above before glancing down at their supposed leader. "But what are you?" She asked all of a sudden. The man in front of her tilted his head, and the green of his eyes looked down on her.

His expression was cold, blank, and for a second, Ethera thought that the man was going to ignore her. "Children of the sun, the root, and the wind. We are of Elderkin." His words froze mid-air, and even the leaves shuddered in anticipation.

Reymond tilted his head, eyes squinting. "I think you guys kind of look like elves?"

"I think that's what he said. Just in a weirder way," Rose whispered towards the mortal boy, nudging him on the side. The elf did not look at her; his eyes hovered on Ethera, particularly the white that resembled his own.

She quickly turned her head, shooting her classmates a nasty look. Her one-way ticket to getting information was now being threatened by the sound of giggles. Juno averted her eyes, but she couldn't hide her creeping smile. Hugo was the only one with a stern poker face. Ethera could only assume that the boy was dissociating from shock. Rose snorted, eyes meeting her best friend before muttering a quick apology.

"Does laughter stir so easily at the mercy of danger?" The elf questioned, a dangerous expression crossing his face. He did not sound pleased.

The elf was about to turn around, but Ethera's hands waved in front. "Oh—well, it's just that there aren't many of your...*kind* where we are from. Sir, if I may ask, but where are we going?" She stuttered, words not registering in her mental dictionary.

He faced forward, his intimidating, hostile look returning. "You shall stand before the chief. He will decide what becomes of you." And that was the end of the conversation. Ethera did not dare press him for answers any further in hopes that this elf might put in a few good words to this chief of theirs. Either way, annoying him would do neither her nor the geniuses behind her any good.

Walking through the forest in silence, the mortals' footsteps were somehow louder than those of the elves, which was odd considering they were bigger and taller. Even their breathing became frightening. Too loud and coated with fear that perhaps it would snap the invisible sting of momentary peace that hung between the two species. There was nothing to put the human mind at ease except the loud thumping sounds of their heartbeat and the conscious presence they had of each other.

It still felt like a dream. Except they seemed to question each other more than the world that surrounded them.

There was magic in the air; beams of sunlight fell through the leaves, casting all sorts of otherworldly patterns on the green and muddy ground. Flowers of all shapes and sizes grew along the path. Some of them were even as tall as the shortest in their group, Juno.

Strange creatures lurked behind the trees. Their movements were concealed by the shadows, moving from each bark in order to stay hidden from sight, but their presence could not escape the keen senses of the elves. Their ears twitched in response, hearing even the faintest heartbeat.

Elvenwood was a hidden village nestled high and deep within a dense woodland that had been claimed by the elves. It was hard to come across; many trails were purposely made to lead the impostors back to where they had originally started, or worse, deeper into the forest where dangerous animals awaited their next meal.

The humans were no exception, but this time, it seemed that the forest had spared their lives. The village itself was surrounded by towering trees, their houses mounted in the middle of the tree's bark, inches from the ground to protect them from those who meant them harm.

Each house was crafted from living wood with the use of magic that melded with the bark of the tree, with a harmonious blend of leaves, flowers, and vines. There were little windows overlooking the forest with no glass protecting the inside of the house. Elves did not need such a thing; they were one with the forest and everything that resided in it.

That included bugs, wind, and on some days, rainforest rain.

Twisted branches formed wooden doors, decorated with moss and a wide variety of flowers. On nearly every elven door hung a yellow blossom, a symbol of happiness and warmth, tinted with gradient green that leaked through the middle of its petals.

Each house in Elvenwood had crystals that grew on the ceiling, and when the sun fell beyond reach, they would glow ever so lightly to help the lost elf find its way back home.

Their houses were spread out all around the upcoming trees, and the small village that Ethera was expecting turned out to be a hidden colony. As they drew closer, she began to realize more of their artistic side. Many doors were also hand-carved with different designs, swirling with shapes and words that she could not understand.

It was a pleasant sight, never to be seen by the human eye.

The elves were quite a working bunch, from what the humans noticed. They gawked at every little thing, trying to take in as much visual appeal and information as they could, but the new world that they were slowly introduced to seemed to be increasingly confusing than fascinating.

"Whoa," Reymond whispered breathlessly. He wasn't the only one who was left in awe by the scenery. Both Rose and Juno had finally let go of each other, their attention drawn to different sides. Juno's eyes hovered at what looked like a weapon construction station. Different sizes of spears lined the trees, with them, numerous arrows were polished by an elf who was yet to spot their presence.

Rose glanced at the dancing little elves with flower crowns and long white tunics decorated with green outlines and swirls. They sang a soft melody with words that almost sounded English. It seemed like the village had lived in harmony until the mortals arrived.

The little elves who ran around with wooden swords in their hands had completely stopped, looking at the large group that strolled in. With one glance, they ran off, some jumping on vines and hiding inside their houses. Their big eyes and little ears peeked through the windows with curiosity.

Other elves who were crafting weapons, sewing clothes, or cooking food had also stopped. They stood up,

41

hovering around and waiting to see what was going to happen. Their eyes narrowed with suspicion, large hands clutching weapons, brooms, or appliances.

"Pray, by the stars, what have you brought here?" Everyone flinched at a hard and rough voice that emerged from beneath the bark of their biggest tree yet. An elf came forward, his white hair had not been braided like the rest; instead, it blew lightly with the wind. He wasn't dressed like the others; his clothes were loose and with no pockets or leather belts.

His pale, wrinkly hand clutched a large bow, and over his shoulders, a leather quiver held about a dozen arrows. Hostile was an understatement. This elf was ready to put those shiny arrows through all of their heads, including his own kin, for daring to bring such disgrace to his village and his forest.

The humans exchanged glances, a chill swooshed through the air.

"Honored chief, the forest in all its wisdom, has drawn us towards these wandering mortals." It was no surprise that they were found, maybe even rescued. Who knows what would have happened if they had kept running around screaming at every cracking twig?

The chief remained quiet, his eyes slightly widened upon hearing this news as if it meant something deeper than 'Hey, we found these things running around screaming!'. He walked closer, his eyes scanning through every one of their unfamiliar faces. "This one—bring her forth, let the rest be cast below," His long white finger rose, pointing at Ethera.

She quickly took a step back, raising her hands in surrender. "Wait a second—." Her path was blocked immediately, hands seized. She cursed aloud, struggling under the rock-like grip of the elf behind her. The rest were also restrained.

Hugo fought against an elf's grip, shouting for Ethera. His eyes were wide with worry, which caused Ethera's own brain to shut down. She let her body get dragged away; it was pointless to challenge the strength of an elf. Her frame was frozen in shock, contemplating whether her eyes were deceiving her.

Was Hugo Blake *worried* about her?

Her classmates put up a decent fight, arguing back and fighting against the spears that were drawn on them. Hugo seemed to put on quite a fight despite his lack of *everything*. They eventually faded out of her view, being pulled in two different directions.

Ethera didn't see this coming. She had made an assumption that even though the elves were showing wary signs, they wouldn't be violent. Perhaps she underestimated them; after all, the stories could differ from reality.

Eventually, her brain finally awoke, survival instincts kicking in, but not before her temper. "You know I have legs too, right?" She snorted, attempting to get up on her feet. The grip on her tightened, but the two elves who had accompanied her gave in, allowing her to at least walk. With both hands seized, escape was impossible, but at least she wasn't dragged around in the dirt. But if someone were to find a way out of this mess, it would be her.

She was sure that somehow, if there was a way out, she would figure it out.

They had descended deeper into the opening underneath the grand tree, its roots forming a ceiling with cracks and holes that proved to be the only source of light.

Ethera's face scrunched with worry. The ground could collapse on them with a single earthquake, or at least that's what it looked like. But the deeper they walked, the smaller those holes became until they had completely vanished. It was dim, and the walls were made out of dirt or clay that curved upwards.

It was hot—*too hot.*

Ethera had begun to sweat uncontrollably. Not to mention the suffocating feeling that washed over her. There was no circulation of fresh oxygen, and if it wasn't for the dire situation, her mind would have thrown her body into a fit of anxiety.

The rough hands of the elves that captured her were now loosened; they were wise enough to understand that even if she attempted to run, she wouldn't be able to see in the dark. The light could not reach her anymore, and the more they learned about her, the more she began to understand them. Theories, but hints, no less.

Finally, something came into her vision. Up ahead, the tunnel opened up into a wide underground clearing, a room made of stone and hardened dirt.

The ceiling was opened above, allowing the sun to completely descend towards them and onto the only furniture in the room. In the middle stood a large table adjusted well to the height of the elves. Its legs were made of roots, while the top was a carved piece of ancient wood. On it was a map of some kind with words that Ethera could not read.

Even if she tried, the sudden light had taken her a few moments to regain her composure. Vines had slid through the cracks and hugged themselves against the stone walls. Small flowers that were yet to bloom clung to the curving stems.

The elves roughly let go; her arms instantly felt sore from the rigid posture she maintained. Ethera stumbled a little bit, her eyes scanning the area to find a possible escape route. She hadn't even noticed the chief standing in the shadows until her eyes passed him and double-backed.

They both watched each other cautiously before he stepped into the light, where she could get a better look at him. His eyes were a dark emerald green with defined deep wrinkles. He wasn't the only elf in the room; the other two who forced her in were guarding the entrance.

Her eyes glanced back, rolling her shoulders and allowing herself to stretch her arms. She wasn't going to speak first, that was certain. "I would like to ask thee a question." Ethera nodded, not wanting to let his intimidation affect her.

"As do I."

The chief's lips curled into a little smile; it seemed he liked her guts. Or as Ethera would call it, fake confidence. But guts alone were not enough to get her out of this situation. "Your hair—are thee of elven origin?" His question caught her off guard, and Ethera fell silent. Her cheeks puffed up as she tried her best not to smile in this very serious situation. The elf behind her had stepped forward, ready to

45

defend the honor of the chief from a snort that escaped from her lips.

Her hands immediately shot up, something she found herself doing a bit too much lately. "I meant no disrespect. I'm not of elven origin," she said, a smile still on her lips. "This is simply a medical condition, but it has nothing to do with your kind." Her brain yelled at her to stop smiling.

The chief stepped closer to her, gazing deep into her eyes. He reached out, lifting her head by grasping her chin. Ethera flinched upon the icy contact of his fingers.

He was cold compared to the other elves.

His hand was big enough to cover Ethera's entire face, the difference between the two species was becoming clearer with every passing second. Despite the discomfort, Ethera didn't try to pull away but awkwardly averted her eyes elsewhere.

He was observing her, his grip digging into her delicate, human flesh. "She is not the child foretold by the prophecy," he finally announced, letting go of the girl's face. "Her eyes are of one color."

Ethera was frozen in her tracks, her breath stopping halfway through her body. She didn't dare move for the fear that perhaps that little facade that is saving her skin right now would somehow reveal her lies. Instead, she averted her attention to her own questions. "What will happen to me and the others?"

"Time is not on our side. War is approaching, your kind will remain in the cellar until it is over," he answered, his eyes scanning the large map.

"And when will that be?"

"Only the red moon shall tell. Place her among the others," He waved his hand, dismissing them, and not paying the mortal any mind. The soldiers nodded before stepping towards Ethera, their hands reaching out to her.

Her body swayed, dodging their grip. "I can walk by myself," she barked, not wanting to be unnecessarily dragged around again. The elf narrowed his eyes, displaying a warning. He glanced at the other before nodding in response. His head tilted, motioning for her to walk after the other, who led the way.

Both routes of escape were blocked yet again, but at least this time she was free to walk by herself, her fingertips brushing the wall to maintain balance.

The elf in front of her walked slowly, leading the way. It was hard to see even with Ethera's squinted eyes. As soon as they emerged from the underground, they ended up entering another one. This one without an ounce of light to guide her. She could only assume a prison awaited her on the other side.

It wasn't long before she tripped over her own feet, grabbing the lower back of the elf in front of her. He hissed at her touch, and she pulled her hands away with a squeal. "S-Sorry, I literally can't see," she muttered embarrassingly. She didn't mean to grab him that roughly, and she could only hope that her words could reflect the look on her face.

He brushed the place she touched in disgust, not saying a single word. Her freedom was stripped away, and so was her arm. His fingers gripped her left hand harshly as he led her slowly down the stairs.

She barely noticed the specs of light that appeared to be dancing in the distance, followed by the light breeze that howled through the thin hallways. It seemed that the passageways weren't as deep underground as she originally suspected. Undoubtedly, this was like a maze carved with an awfully slim chance of escape.

The cellar was lit up with a burning flame in between each barricaded block, and Ethera couldn't be happier to finally be able to see.

But the cells were small, and seeing all of her classmates shoved into one at the end of the large underground opening made her nose scrunch in displeasure.

They all stopped in front of the wooden doors. Ethera turned around, glancing at the elf in front of her. "Pretty please, can I have a cell to myself?" The elf's irritated expression turned into a nasty smirk as the one behind reached out to unlock the door. His expression only darkened, as if he was casting revenge on her. "No," He grunted, shoving her inside. Ethera shook the door as they locked it, her middle finger stuck out instinctively with a grunt.

She turned around after making sure that they were out of sight completely. "Are you okay? Did they hurt you?" Reymond was the first to speak; he had gotten up from the ground and appeared in front of her. His brown eyes scanned her to make sure she was still intact.

Ethera's eyes lit up maliciously, and a wide smile spread across her flushed cheeks. Everyone looked at her in confusion, assuming that she had been hit on the head or tortured for information. Slowly, she lifted her index finger, pressing it firmly against her lips.

On the other hand, a pair of keys silently sat against her palm.

CHAPTER 4

They all exchanged astonished looks until a smile crept up on their faces. "I'm so happy right now, I could hug you!" Rose cheered, jumping on her feet with her hands extended.

Ethera shrieked at the thought. "Please don't do that."

"What are you waiting for? Let's get outta here," Juno hurried towards the door, ready to bounce any second now. Her hands gripped the wooden bars. Polished and sturdy.

Much to her surprise, Ethera shook her head. "We can't go. Not until nightfall. These people...they'll catch us the moment we step out," explained Ethera.

Much to their tenacity to jump into action, the group stepped back. Some took a seat on the hard ground; others leaned against the walls. They all fell silent, cramped together so close that they listened to the desynchronized sound of each other's breathing.

"W-Were you able to find something while you were out there?" Hugo spoke for the first time since she had entered the cell. Ethera's eyes hovered on him, the cold expression on his face was different from her prior memory.

"Yes. They said they will not let us leave until the war ends."

"A war?" Repeated Reymond. All eyes had focused on Ethera, begging her for more information.

She nodded. "Yeah, based on what the chief said, it won't be ending any time soon." Her back pressed against the hard wall as she slid down into a sitting position. Her head fell back, eyes closing. "That could mean being locked up for weeks or months?"

"Or years!" Rose shuddered at the thought, her hand pressed against her lips, muffling her gasp.

"That's why I took a little souvenir. We won't be locked up here like some criminals for God knows how long. So, get some rest, guys. We will most likely be going for a midnight run," Ethera breathed out shakily, her memory flashing back to that beast in the forest. She only got a single glance, but it was more than enough to contemplate her whole existence.

Hugo's eyes remained on Ethera; a nervous chill crossed his body. His brows furrowed, trying to read the expression on the girl's face. Everyone else shuffled around to find a comfortable position to get some sleep. They were all tired, drained from what had happened earlier, and stressed at what was coming.

Even a few hours would be more than enough to relax their aching bodies and prepare their minds. At night, the monsters will undoubtedly come out from behind the shadows. The thought alone was unbearable. How will they manage against them?

Would it be better to remain a prisoner in this cramped cell than die at the fangs of some unknown beast?

If the elves wanted to kill them, they would have already done so. Unless their preferred method of execution was starvation. But it was to no one's surprise that they lacked appetite. Everything felt like a dream. They took on useless roles, armed with nothing but sheer will—and Reymond's jokes—left to guard themselves from the danger lurking about.

Ethera tried her best not to overthink the situation and the million things that could go wrong. She seemed to have no power over her mind today, so instead she focused on everything that could go wrong and exactly how she would overcome every situation.

As for the beasts…well, the only option was to run.

Rose broke the silence by clearing her dry throat. "You know…" she began, "if we get out of here and make it back alive, I'll try to stop picking on you." She somehow felt that the brunette was awake. Ethera broke into a smile, opening her eyes and looking at Rose's expression dimmed in the lack of light. The shadow flickered over the blonde's face, but her lips curled into a teasing smile.

"Gee, thanks," Ethera let out a light laugh although the doubt in her mind didn't cloud her judgement.

"Guys, if we do make it in one piece, I promise to stop smoking pot," Reymond pitched in, his seriousness had cracked the quiet atmosphere between them. His hands were interlaced on his stomach, his head lying on the hoodie that he had taken off, and his blank gaze stared forward. The inky shirt blended in with the surrounding darkness, almost swallowing him whole. She couldn't read the words; the light forbade her.

He turned over, prompting his head on his arm. "No, I swear on our mother. I still feel like I'm having the trip of my life. I've already pinched myself fifty times, and we're still here." Disbelief crossed his face. They laughed together before falling into silence yet again. It's been a while since she had laughed so lightheartedly. Reymond had that effect on her and she hated it.

The joke was stupid. Everyone knew it. Still, in the middle of a crooked smile, a snort, and a sigh of disappointment, made them feel like they weren't alone. "Well, what about the rest of you?" Asked Rose, the silence had become frightful, and the darkness had made her nervous enough to want to hold onto the conversation longer.

Even with their eyes adjusted to the little light they had access to; it was still difficult to make of everyone's sincerity. "I guess I'll also promise to be nicer to Ethera," answered Juno, her silhouette slightly adjusted her sitting position.

As for Ethera, there weren't any self-revolving promises she would stake, none which she was comfortable to share. Another snort followed. Ethera tried to mask it by crossing her feet. "Wow, you guys. I'm so honored."

Hugo was next, his voice steady and clear. "I guess we can all promise to be nicer to Ethera." Now hearing him say it gave disbelief a new kind of meaning.

Ethera sighed, regaining her shocked composure. "You do know that I will leave your asses if the situation calls for it, right?"

They fell quiet before shaking off her statement as a joke. "Yeah, right. I'd like to see you try. If I die, I'll come back to haunt you as a ghost," Reymond wailed from the shadows. It sounded convincing enough now, but his attention span would surely give up after a day or two.

"Yeah, yeah. Get some rest. If you pass out from lack of sleep, I am not carrying you out."

� symbols⟩ ⟨writing symbols⟩ ⟨writing symbols⟩

Not everyone fell asleep, but those who stayed awake managed to get a good amount of rest for their bodies. That was more than they could ask for. The rushing beats of their hearts had awakened the mind, and the unsettling adrenaline had left an unmistakable trace.

Ethera stood in front of the door, her hands reaching over with the numerous keys that lines a metal ring. It took her three tries until the door had clicked open against the metal lock. The wood creaked loudly in the silence, and the group hovered in front of it, peaking into the dark hallway as if expecting someone to come running in. The walls were lit up brightly with a yellow and red flickering light that had not once dimmed throughout their stay.

Ethera turned around, blocking the way before they could take a single step forward. "Okay…this is the plan,"

Her eyes scanned the serious faces of her classmates. "We stay quiet and we move as silently as we can. They have sharp hearing, if you so much as whisper, we will get caught in no time. We'll grab the torches and go in a single file line. I will lead." Ethera instructed quietly. They exchanged encouraging glandes before nodding in sync.

"And put your hoodies back on. Zip 'em up and put the hood over," Juno added, and the rest followed suit. It was hot in the cell, and the air circulation was mild, so to be comfortable, they had stripped off any thick layers that protected them from the Oregon cold.

Reymond walked away first, hands interlacing the wooden torch. He pulled but it didn't budge. "We've got a little problem...the torches don't come off?" He whispered, his leg was plastered against the wall, using all his strength.

Ethera jogged towards him, sliding her hands through the sleeves of her hoodie. Her eyes examined the wooden stick as she pursed her lips. The torch was warm under her touch, but it wasn't the kind that came off. She had no idea how the fire remained burning—it did not look like it had a wick.

"Forget it, we'll just walk through."

"But it's pitch black, how will we know where to go?"

"There are four corridors on the right side coming in. Then a left turn, passing two more. Another left turn. Stairs. Two more corridors and a right turn with three. So just reverse that and we're out of here," She zoned out, rambling to herself, trying her best to remember. Her dirt-stained index finger traced the numbers on the palm of her other hand.

She went over these numbers about a dozen times, the fear of forgetting them had kept her awake, much to her displeasure.

They exchanged looks, hovering around the fire. Their faces looked almost sinister with the shadows of the flame. But at last, they could see each other. Juno's beauty mark under her right eye had begun to show under the layer of smudged concealer.

"What?"

"How the hell do you remember all that?" Reymond raised his voice in shock.

Rose tilted her head, arms falling to her hips. "Wait a sec—are you the one who stole Mrs. Morris's keys to that stupid fridge she installed in her classroom?" Rose asked suddenly, a baffled expression on her face. Ethera grinned, quickly looking away.

Not her proudest steal, however, the dread that the classroom suffered started to rob off on her.

Juno gaped in shock. "No way." The boys stared at each other in confusion, not understanding the direction in which the conversation was leading. They were not in the same history class.

The girls stood with their mouths on the ground. It seemed that Ethera Heart was not just some delinquent—but a savior in disguise.

She cleared her throat; her thick hair hid the crimson color of her cheeks. "That's a story for later. Remember, no talking unless it's necessary," she quickly reminded them, making sure that they all understood. They followed her, stopping short of the dark, empty passageway. A light breeze carried itself, inviting them to dare solve the maze.

It was no surprise that Ethera could remember the numbers. After all, she too excelled in most of her classes, and exceeded with her keen understanding of mathematics. She had found English to be boring and history to be an amusing class, all thanks to the teacher.

They all lined up in a single line, Ethera stood in the front. A gush of fresh air made her shiver, nerves knotting at her stomach. A weight suddenly pulled the back of the girl's hoodie causing her to jump.

Rose gripped the bottom hem of the sweater, her nails digging into the fabric. "Sorry…I'm kinda scared." Behind her, a trail had formed, each of them holding on to the person in front.

No one had bothered to remember the numbers and the tunnels; that information solely lay in Ethera's mind.

She took another deep breath, her shaky hand trailing against the wall as she dropped down to a slow pace for the sake of the others. This was by far the most nerve-wracking thing they had ever done.

Who knew that they would be escaping an underground cellar in some unknown world run by elves and monsters? And considering the map that she had seen, there was no doubt other species existed. Perhaps some friendlier than others?

Ethera pushed away all unnecessary thoughts, focusing on counting in her head. Getting lost would surely kill them. She could only imagine how many people died in these hallways, the gruesome mortal bones displayed against the walls that they could not see.

It was easier for their imagination to run wild in pitch darkness with the low howling of the wind that sang between the gaps of the walls. The air had gotten colder, but their winter attire had kept them prepared.

For every hole between the walls, Ethera's heart skipped a beat, and she jumped ever so slightly. After a few torturous minutes, they finally began to see a speck of light. The sun had long hid below, and the beautiful bright sphere was rising above, a light blue cast shining down on them.

Once they were fully out, they hid behind a tree, taking a moment to breathe and relax, sluggish smiles tugged on their faces as they exchanged happy looks. They knew they had to keep moving, but the sight was truly like a wonderful dream.

The calm after a storm. Even the moon seemed to smile at them.

A sigh of relief escaped their mouths. The moonlight had illuminated the path before them. Even with the tall trees and the millions of leaves, it had found its way down to greet them. It had become easier to see, but despite their vision returning, the road ahead was still unpredictable.

They had to play their cards right in order to be able to escape in one piece. Ethera took a step forward, her eyes scanning the trees ahead. She shoved a piece of hair behind her ear before motioning for her classmates to wait.

Swiftly, she ran alone towards the nearest tree, staying close to the ground. She paused, her back pressed against the bark and her eyes scanning the area.

It was quiet. Too quiet.

She had made an assumption that maybe there would be guards or something looking over the village, and yet, there was not a soul in sight. Almost as if everyone was sound asleep, or so she hoped. Whether it was a good thing or not, she did not wait around to speculate.

Glancing back at Rose, her brighter hoodie glowed in the moonlight, standing out like a sore thumb. Their eyes met, and with a single nod, she, too, ran towards her.

One by one, they moved quietly through the village, always looking upwards to make sure that they were not being hunted. It was easier for Ethera when it came to direction; she had picture memory and trusted her gut if something felt familiar or different.

After all, she grew up in the forest.

It was simpler to move through the village, but the forest worried her. She had been too preoccupied with the chatter with the elf that she had not paid any attention to her surroundings. The way through was a complete blur.

Hugo's eyes couldn't help but hover on Ethera. The way she moved, the way she thought. He could see it all, even in the darkness. It was pure instinct. Pure survival. He could barely recognize the girl in front of him, but a person doesn't just become different overnight. Despite growing up beside her and watching her for years, it finally struck him how little to nothing he truly knew about her.

Suddenly, Rose tapped on Ethera's shoulder aggressively, causing her to jump from fright. Her mind had instantly gone towards plausible danger, but Rose's expression had indicated otherwise. Her blue eyes were wide, one of her hands frantically moving around trying to signal something that Ethera could not understand.

A large spider had made its way up the sleeve of Rose's hoodie, sitting still as if it were also watching the charade displayed by the blonde. Ethera's eyes widened in amusement, a smile instantly growing on her face. Rose's possible savior had turned into her persecutor, and the girl before her was not planning on helping anytime soon.

Her blue orbs darkened, turning from fear to anger. She mouthed with gritted teeth, something along the lines of 'I will scream,'. Ethera rolled her eyes at the immaturity. She pulled the sleeve of her own hoodie and, in a quick motion, used it to slap the spider away.

It didn't go flying like she had hoped; instead, it stuck to her own sleeve, dangling upside down and holding on for dear life. Ethera jumped to her feet, swinging it around and trying to force it off. The other's eyes widened in shock, and Rose had burst into a silent battle concealed laughter.

Ethera hopped around in panic, seeing how its tiny, hairy legs had begun walking forward and disappearing into the hole of the sleeve. She immediately threw her head back, throwing the hoodie off her and tossing it on the ground. She stomped on it aggressively, trying her best to kill it.

The spider was one lucky fellow; it survived and crawled out of her sweater, running off into the distance.

Ethera fell silent, eyes staring off into the distance where the insect had run off. She bent down, picking up the sweater, before dusting it off. Her back was turned towards the others, masking the blush that had overtook her pale features.

Rose remained quiet, but her face had said it all. If it wasn't for the invoked rule of silence, she would have spoken up, possibly saying something stupid. Ethera quickly dressed, leaving the hood on out of sheer embarrassment. She had almost broken her own rule of staying quiet, her throat itched to scream and shudder at the memory.

Rose had patted her on the back again, and Ethera ignored it, if it wasn't for the trembling hold on the middle of her sweater, the brunette wouldn't have turned around.

Rose's face was petrified; the mocking expression was no more. All color had been drained from her soft features, which now resembled that of a blank canvas.

A few feet away, another creature blocked their escape. Smaller than the beast they had encountered in the forest, yet somehow more dangerous. It crouched low to the ground, green scaly legs bent sharply at the joints, its body coiled towards the soil, like it was ready to spring at a moment's notice. Claws hooked into the dirt beneath it, tearing at it, as if digging for something that had escaped its clutches.

The thick tail wasn't just for show; it hovered above its body and jerked at every sound. Every rustle of the leaves or a coo of an animal. Spikes lined its back, gleaming in the light, moist with something that glittered like poison.

Ethera's breath hitched. Her palms pressed into the dirt, trembling. Her body refused to obey her mind, as if there was nothing, she could do to escape it.

To escape death.

She knew—one wrong breath, one wrong step, and it could rip her apart before she had a chance to scream.

It was the embodiment of fear. She had never seen such a beast before. Not in the books. Not anywhere.

They pressed themselves against the bulky rock. Only Reymond and Hugo were spared from the sight of what lurked beyond it and judging by the girls' faces, that, in itself, was this world's mercy. For a fleeting moment, they all had the same thought: turning back might be worth it, even if it meant waking the elves and facing their wrath.

Ethera turned robotically, her gaze landing on Rose and Juno. Their faces had gone pale, as if their souls had fled leaving their frail bodies behind. Ethera grabbed Rose's hand and gave it a sharp shake, pulling her back from whatever terror had seized her eyes.

Then Ethera looked at Reymond and motioned silently, urging him to move backward, around the far side of the rock, just enough to be out of the beast's eye. If they were lucky, they could wait it out. But first, they had to move out of his line of sight.

The beast began moving, sniffing the air, its head tilted upwards. Rose's glossy eyes looked back at it. Ethera quickly shook her head drawing the blonde's attention back. It let out a half-growl.

Could it sense them?

No. If it did, then it would have attacked already.

Rose shook her head, tears threatening to fall. Fear had taken over her body and despite the encouraging grip of the girl in front of her, she dared not move.

The boys had slowly crawled backwards, moving silently with every step, but it was too late, the creature's head snapped towards them as if the sounds of their hearts had betrayed them.

Juno reached out to grab Rose by the arm. "Run!" She alerted the rest of them. Her hand slipped with a loose grip; her best friend did not budge. Ethera instantly intertwined her arm with Rose's, forcing her aggressively to her feet.

They all broke into a sprint, their lives on the line. They tried not to scream but the beast seemed to be making the sounds for them. It let out a hungry screech.

Ethera's eyes darted from every tree and elf-built-structure, panic flooding her mind. "Fuck, fuck, fuck!" She cursed out before shoving Rose in the opposite direction. The blonde was running too slow; they were going to get caught in no time.

She took a deep breath. "Split up, guys!" She yelled out loud enough to draw the beast's attention onto her. It leaped in the air, excitedly, to have found pray to hunt. Its back legs kicked upwards, trying to gain speed, and the long pink tongue hissed in her direction, almost salivating at the thought of fresh meat so soon.

Ethera knew screaming would attract the attention of those whom they were trying to escape—or worse, something else lurking in the dark. But reason was not going to save her. This was their only chance to survive.

None of them could take the beast down. That much was certain. And outrunning it? Even if they could somehow get away by running in different directions, they would only fall prey to something else. Swallowed by the forest one by one.

Sticking together was the only choice that made sense. When the beast's footsteps stopped, Ethera nearly stumbled. She came to a halt, bracing herself against a tree as her lungs burned. Her heart violently pounded in her chest, her vision pulsed as she listened, head snapping in different directions.

Where did it go?

Her eyes widened. Ethera dropped low, snatching a few rocks from the ground as she carefully retraced her steps. The forest was silent; her classmates were nowhere in sight. Just as she was about to turn back, she spotted it. It circled a small open stand made of wood and green leaves.

Someone was inside, no doubt about it.

Ethera sprinted toward the monster, coming to a stop a few feet away. She launched the rocks at it one by one. The creature slithered side to side, its movements were unpredictable, making it nearly impossible to hit. Eventually, one rock finally struck the bullseye.

Its golden gaze snapped toward her.

Ethera bolted. Her muscles screamed as she ran, breath tearing at her lungs. She sucked the midnight air and screamed as loud as she could, drawing all the attention to the chaos.

Her eyes flicked to the trees above. Any second now, they would come, she just had to hold out just a little longer.

The beast slowed, almost studying her, before its long sharp tail whipped toward her. It missed by an inch. Ethera jumped to the side, shock almost throwing her off balance. Suddenly, she stumbled forward, her ankle twisting over something that she had thrown herself.

64

She crashed to the ground, rolling onto her back. She had to get up. Now. Or it would attack again. And this time, it would not miss.

Rocks suddenly flew past her.

Hugo appeared behind it, his hands throwing pebbles of all sizes. His glasses reflected the white glow of the moon, and his mouth was moving but the sound did not make it to Ethera's ears.

The beast ignored him, not falling for the same trick twice. Its spiky tail braced itself for another attack. Ethera's body jerked upwards but before she could attempt to get away, an elf fell from the sky.

The spear dove straight through the beast's skull, pinning it to the earth beneath it. Its body collapsed with a heavy thud as dark blood spilled onto the dirt, the foul smell curling into the forest's air.

Ethera scrambled to her feet, backing away as she scrunched her nose. The young elf stood atop the fallen creature; dark eyes locked on the mortal. He gripped the spear and yanked it free in one smooth motion.

The beast twitched once, then went still.

"T-Thanks?" Ethera stuttered, adrenaline still racing through her veins. Another brush with death. At this rate, she was sure the grim reaper was growing tired of her shit.

More elves emerged from the trees, their movements swift and silent. Some already had seized the other mortals, dragging them from their hiding spots with ease. "Spare them not," the elf announced coldly. "We have no time to tend to mortals in the heart of war." Horror surged through Ethera's body, forcing her forward. She lunged at the elf, grabbing his arm. In a blink of an eye, his spear was at her throat, stopping just a hair away. She froze, forcing her grip to hold on to him as her mind scrambled for something.

Anything

A weak smile escaped her parted lips. She had one card left to play. The truth she'd hid from everyone. "I wouldn't do that if I were you," she drawled drily, her throat was clogged with a pound of dirt.

It bought her a second. Doubt and curiosity piqued his narrow eyes. The elf seized her by the collar of her hoodie, yanking her up an inch, until their eyes met. The spear's edge pressed cold and sharp against her skin—close enough to promise a painful death without a proper delivery. "What game do you weave now, mortal?"

"I am the girl in the prophecy," she hissed, wincing in the pain. Her tippy toes barely brushed the dirt beneath. His grip tightened, a warning to not spew nonsense.

She had released his arm which had left a wrinkle on the sleeve of the pure white tunic. Ethera slowly raised her hand to her face. Fear and instinct guided her now. Her dirt-stained finger dug into her left eye, pinching at something thin.

She pulled it free, blinking rapidly. A brown lens had come off.

Her right eye stung as tears welled inside, dust catching in the moisture. The elf leaned closer, his eyes squinting to get a better look.

Blue

Her eye had revealed its true color. A deep, raging blue.

His grip loosened. Shock flickered across his face, clouding his thoughts.

Ethera swallowed out of habit, steadying her shaken body. She held her head high, a smile reemerging yet again. "Now," she sneered, the tear-stained trail on her cheek sparkled in the moonlight. "Shall we have a proper conversation?"

Not today, grim reaper. *Not today.*

CHAPTER 5

The atmosphere had shifted. The elf's eyes softened as if something that was lost had finally reappeared.

Hope

He finally let go. The shock on his pale face had caused his ears to rise with a shiver. His long fingers immediately grabbed at her arm, as if she was going to disappear at any moment. The mortal's eyes hovered on his grip that trembled against her elbow. She quickly blinked away the tears, trying to regain her vision. She wiped the excess water on the sleeve of her hoodie.

The moon was high above them, casting shadows on the unpaved dirt below. More elves appeared, surrounding the body of the beast, getting ready to remove it. "Wake the chief. This shall not wait," the elf soldier ordered, eyes drifting back to the mortal. "Come."

"They are coming as well," Ethera quickly added, motioning to her classmates. He remained quiet, contemplating her order. The tone of her voice had irritated him, but despite his unsettling feelings, he nodded his head, and the rest of the mortals were let go. They quickly reunited in the middle, their faces gone white with anticipation.

The elf, who seemed to be one of authority in this village, led them down a familiar path. The man-made tunnel ran straight underneath the ground, and it was much darker than before. Even the moon's light could not help the mortals maneuver through the passage.

Someone had tugged on Ethera's hoodie; the touch was harsh. It was too dark to see, but she was certain it was not Rose. The elf's grip had lowered down to her wrist, dragging her along with his unsettling speed. He had no consideration for the mortals who were much shorter than he was. The urge to discuss this new development had clouded his judgment. The humans were forced to awkwardly half-jog just to not get left behind.

The room at the end of the tunnel was lit by torches mounted along the walls. Everything was still the same, except this time, beautiful pearly white petals bloomed from the vines that traced the walls. They came to life, kissed by the moon, and if Ethera's eyes weren't playing tricks on her—she could have sworn they glowed.

Moonlight spilled across the long tables at its center, tracing the carved lines of the wooden map. Ethera's gaze lingered along the drawing, searching for any clue that might reveal exactly where they were.

She couldn't read the map. Along with the familiar carvings there were shiny scribbles and doodles that revealed under the light, something she didn't notice before. Mountains caught in silver flames, waters with dolphin tails, and skies filled with flying beasts. Ethera shivered at the thought of what else could be out there.

The young elf had long since let go, while the chief remained hidden in the shadows, watching the room fill up with more mortals than his own kin.

The humans almost jumped from fright, not expecting the chief to appear beside them suddenly. His green emeralds bathed in the fire, staring at the dual-haired mortal with eyes that were of dirt and sea. "At last, you stand revealed...but how came the truth to light?" Ethera dumbfoundedly stared at the chief of elves; his tongue sounded foreign in her ears.

The younger elf opened his mouth to speak, but even he could not explain the spell that she had used.

"Oh—they are called contacts. I use them to hide my condition," she said in a hurry, not appreciating the sudden attention from everyone. Her classmates also seemed to be bewildered; half of them had not known about this, while the other half had long forgotten. The color defined itself more vibrantly the older she got; only now did it seem to finally settle down as an ocean blue. The room had gotten silent. It seemed that contacts did not exist in this peculiar world. "So, this prophecy," she continued, heart jumping, "I want to know more about it."

The attention lingered on her, giving her the chance to finally find the answer to the question that had followed her through the night. The chief moved forward, his eyes lowered onto the map. "From the depth of the Wishing Well rose a song of prophecy of a maiden with eyes that meet on shore and hair strands kissed by the moon. She shall cross the Crimson Waters beside the Pirate King, leading to time-less victory and forge the world's true name," his eyes lifted to meet the others in the room. "Never was it spoken that the maiden bore mortal blood—we merely claimed her flesh as our own."

The humans exchanged confused looks with each other. When no one had given a satisfactory expression, they all looked at Ethera. But only her blood ran cold; the thought of being destined to do something, *anything,* was laughable. She was no hero, and the shock of this ridiculous prophecy had left her body paralyzed. "W-Who exactly are we up against?" Images of little monsters or faeries crossed her mind. She was in fairyland after all, and the gruesome thought of her predestined belonging in this world had completely spiraled into a new thought process.

Perhaps she had gone mad, imagining things in a state of schizophrenia. More than anything, she dreamed of being wanted, being seen, and now, suddenly, she was destined to play the role of a hero.

It was *suspicious.*

If not, insanity.

"The Enchanted Forest has fallen to evil. Demons walk its withered paths, and we call it not by its old name, but what it has become—the Land of the Dead. Cursed armies rise, their souls enslaved by dark sorcery, eternally bound to war. All has either fallen or faded, and still they come. They will not rest until everything decays into history. The war we once hoped to outrun now marches upon our soil of sanctuary."

Ethera remained quiet, her brain lagging in an attempt to decipher the words of the chief. Her eyes drifted off, not wanting to see the hope that was suddenly thrown at her.

"Your hand will lead our army, and what once lost shall be restored. So spoke the prophecy of the Wishing Well."

Ethera snorted. "No offence, but I think someone as strong as the guy behind you is more suited to lead the army you speak of," she noted, her hands defensively waving in front of her.

Behind the chief stood the young elven soldier, the one who had slain a beast of such terror. The elf remained silent, his ears twitched to every word, his eyes looked cold and distant. He had heard the prophecy countless times, repeating it over and over again in case some crucial detail had slipped through their long, slender fingers.

But alas, no matter how many times they heard it, the answer never revealed itself.

Until now. And it came in the form of a human.

"It is what must be," the riddled chief replied, his composure unwavering.

Hugo and Reymond exchanged uneasy glances. The idea of Ethera playing the hero was...*concerning*, given her personality. Yet this strange journey had begun to reveal something neither of them wanted to fully acknowledge—a possibility.

"So how do you suppose she—*a high school girl*— is supposed to fight demons and the walking dead army? Does the prophecy mention something about her having superpowers or...?" Ethera was surprised at Rose's piercing

72

voice, jumping to nitpick at this so-called prophecy. She had also appeared beside her, arms crossing her chest.

"Nothing of what you speak of."

It was Reymond's turn. He, too, shifted closer. "Wait a sec...why would you need a human to sail the sea? Can't you just gather your army of giants and get on a boat or something?" The support was uncanny, and Ethera was glad she was not alone on this train of reasoning.

"Dare we not! The Crimson Waters are cursed with beasts that tear through all who dare touch the sails. To cross such a sea, we must seek the favor of the King of Pirates. Only with his guidance and aid will we endure the storm." The chief walked forward towards the map, his wrinkled finger gently touching the wooden carvings.

Little, cute monster-like creatures were carved in the middle of an open space of what they assumed was the sea. The humans all examined the map, exchanging looks. It was definitely not Earth.

"And you guys haven't tried to talk to him?" Juno asked, eyes drawing back to the chief. She stood next to a fire, the heat felt comforting against her cheeks, reminding her that this feeling and this world just might not be a dream.

"We are not welcome in the Pirate's Lagoon. They draw their blades the instant our shadows touch their shores."

She scoffed, eyes widening in Rose's direction. "Well, sounds like a personal problem," Juno whispered under her breath. The elves heard her, ignoring the comment without an ounce of understanding. It seems the barrier of the tongue came from both sides.

Ethera fiddled with the hem of her hoodie. "Yeah, sure. I'll sail hand in hand with a thug across the sea of monsters to go help you guys kill more monsters and restore the Enchanted Forest 2.0? Did I get everything right?" She didn't wait for an answer; instead threw her own. "Yeah, I think I'll pass."

Her classmates let out muffled laughs, trying to conceal their unseriousness in the heat of the moment. Their minds were just as tired as their bodies; it was too much excitement, or rather fear for their lives, in one day.

"Innocent lives will perish. Blood of youth that is yet to learn the way of life," the young elven soldier snapped, his anger directed towards Ethera as if she were the leader of their group.

"People die every day, so what? How can a bunch of humans help you fight a war of the supernatural?" Ethera spat back, ready to bump heads with the spear-wielder.

Hugo stood in front of the two, attention directed towards the chief. "How do we get back home? This isn't Earth, right?" It was wise to dispel an argument, especially if it involved Ethera. It seemed that the most important question had been lost in the pages of fantasy.

The elf paused in thought. "How have you come into our lands?" The chief asked the boy with specs, ignoring the heat radiating off the two opposing forces behind him.

The mortal boy fixed his glasses, his face flushing. "We came through a book?" Saying it out loud sounded sillier than the thoughts within their heads. "It kinda teleported us to here." Hugo quickly added, as if that fact could make a difference.

"Many portals dwell in this place—some leading to distant realms, others linger in between times. Heed that the way you return must mirror the path you come. Should a book be your doorway, then a book must be your way back. Stray from the path, and you may wander lost between worlds," the chief's warning was clearer than the raspy tone he spoke with, but everyone's mind drifted to the discovery of other places just like this.

How many stories that they thought were nothing more than words scribbled on paper held some truth in them?

"And where can we find a book portal? I don't suppose you got one on you?"

He shook his head. "No books lie hidden within the Thalorin Forest. If one yet remains intact, it is most likely in the Enchanted Forest in the palace bathed in sunlight, where the veil between worlds runs thin."

Ethera groaned out loud, turning away to hide her pissed expression. The young elf shrank back, his flaming eyes still eyeing the mortal girl.

Rose sighed heavily, eyes looking at Ethera. "Of course, the Land of the Dead," the blonde muttered. The uncomfortable silence filled the spaces between each of them. The prophecy couldn't be avoided. To get home, they had to find a way to cross the sea filled with more beasts. But the answer was clearly handed to them on a silver platter.

They had to find the King of all pirates.

A shiver ran down Ethera's back, as if the thought of him was somehow forbidden.

Reymond clapped his hands together, drawing everyone's attention. "Alright, easy. Done deal. Convince the king to help us, sail across the sea, defeat the zombies, and win the war. Find the book. Go home," He recited out loud, like a memorized poem that sang in another language. It sounded easier coming from his mouth than from the chief.

The young elf sighed heavily. "They are no mere zombies, you fool. These are remains of those who have long passed, skeletons that crawled out from the darkness, risen by dark forces." The idea of these *humans* holding the torch of his people's destiny in their feeble hands was a cruel twist of fate.

The mortal boy flashed him a smile. "Even better. What could a lump of bone do against real weapons? We get weapons, right? Lighten up, guys," he cheered, bringing forth torture to the young elf's ears.

The chief didn't seem to care; he knew where his faith lay, and it seemed the dual-haired maiden in the prophecy already had her clutches on it.

"You do realize that it's Ethera's prophecy, right?" Rose asked, her hand firmly pressed on her temples. Her nails mirrored the dancing flames.

"God forbid a guy tries to encourage his friends to save the world."

"Yeah, since when are you so motivational? Nice try, though."

"It's not like we have a choice, anyway, so it's better to be optimistic." Ethera nodded, briefly agreeing. The depth of the situation felt unsettling in her stomach.

The young elf, who went by the name of Dilian, had escorted them out with the chief's order. They were given a place to rest, and thankfully, it was not the cellar.

Their room was located above ground, embedded into the bark of the tree. The mortals did not use vines like their hosts; instead, they climbed up the ladder located on the other side, built for special occasions such as this.

The inside of the tree cove was much different from the elves' personalized homes. It was like a large nest filled with hay scattered across the wooden floor and on top, soft, silk-like fabric stitched together with green string. Pillows overflowed in every corner, more than their tired eyes could count, and tiny feathers poked out from the cotton fabric.

There were no doors. No windows.

It felt like a resting place for travelers, yet in Reymond's mind, it looked unmistakably like a nest. "A bird won't fly in and squish all of us to death, right?"

"God, shut up, already," Juno sighed heavily, the drowsiness suddenly rushing through her body like a button being flicked off. They all got comfortable in their own corners, putting as much space between each other as they could. Even the twins didn't think twice about the distance. Their aching backs felt relieved as soon as they hit the comforting silk.

"No, but seriously, if I wake up and see some bird's ass in my fa-."

"SHUT UP!" Everyone yelled in sync, achieving the near impossible all together. The room had fallen silent, the cold night air clung to their skin. Stillness pressed against them, trapping every sound that they made in its grasp.

No one dared to speak, yet their mind drifted to the ongoing war, and the looming possibility of disaster played on repeat like a cursed record.

After all, they didn't belong here. Ethera did not have any magical powers that would save the day. None of them stood a chance of outrunning a beast—let alone killing one.

A mortal had no place in a war of the supernatural, and that was the truth.

Ethera lay there for what felt like hours; the words seemed stuck inside her throat like glue, haunting her, and refusing to let go, not allowing her to rest. Hope and expectation weighed heavily on her. All she wanted was for everyone to make it home in one piece. But going through this war was not the right way through.

They wouldn't survive. How could they?

The pressure pressed in on her, almost suffocating, yet she couldn't let them down. The feeling was foreign, but hauntingly familiar. A memory etched into her bones.

Fear. Anxiety. Uncertainty.

She opened her mouth, lips trembling as they parted in a low whisper. "W-We'll get home. I'll get us across the sea, that much I can do, right?"

With that, she closed her eyes, letting sleep take over her before the thoughts could consume what remained of her sanity.

CHAPTER 6

"Rise, mortals!" Dilian's loud voice echoed in the dim co-coon. The irritated expression never faltered, as if he had slept with it overnight and came back to haunt them. The mortals didn't budge; their eyes remained closed. It wasn't until he decided to use physical force, pulling a bulky boy by the leg.

Reymond awakened instantly, screaming and kicking at his feet. His half-asleep mind made all sorts of assumptions. Birds, dragons, more birds, even bigger birds...he had fallen asleep praying he wouldn't wake up dangling in the clutches of a giant *thing* flying in the sky.

Hugo was the first on his feet, his fists defensively rolled up in front of him. His glasses had gone missing in his sleep, and his good eye wasn't quick enough to understand the situation. The girls remained still, barely even twitching.

The elf stared in astonishment, wondering how they could be sleeping so deeply in a land that was not their home. "Make your way below. We depart with the coming light," The elf announced, his eyes focused on those who were already standing. He grabbed a hanging vine in the opening and jumped off with a swift motion. Hugo tilted his head, looking for his glasses with his good eye.

"Wait…where are we going again?"

"To save the world and stuff, remember?" Juno lazily lifted her head; she had heard everything but didn't bother to move. They hadn't slept that soundlessly in what felt like years, and it took them another ten minutes to wake the rest of their friends before finally descending downstairs.

Climbing down proved to be far more difficult than going up. They paused constantly, looking below to make sure each step was not missed. Still, despite their aching muscles and heavy eyes, they reached the ground safely.

Ethera's hair was a nest of its own. Brown curls twisted at the ends, and strands of hay poked out in every direction. She wasn't the only one; everyone seemed to have woken up with a new hairstyle. Rose's makeup had smudged underneath her eyes, and Ethera could only assume hers looked just as bad. Juno, however, appeared untouched by the night. Her round face was bright and refreshed, as though the day ahead was something to be excited about.

The elven women guided them to a small stream on the far side of the village. They were dressed differently; the long skirts of their tunics were draped loosely over their frames, embroiled with traces of leaves and vines along the sleeves and hems. Braided leather clung to their waists, decorated with small charms of wood, feathers, stone, and bone.

These women were not warriors. The flowers braided into their hair had told as much. Yet the skill with knives was unmistakable; their hands moved steadily, carving shapes out of wood. All the while, their eyes never left the humans. They hovered nearby, giving them space while quietly guarding them—or ensuring they didn't run.

The water from the stream was ice cold. The sun had barely begun to rise, and the air around them hadn't had the time to warm up properly. Ethera sat on the ground with her knees folded, leaning over the edge to get a better look at her reflection. She was indeed right, black panda-like smudges mirrored each other on both of her eyes.

She cooped the water in her hands, splashing it against her skin. It was something she was already long used to, but the girls on her right had squealed from the cold contact. They had to scrub hard to get their makeup off, and Ethera was no exception. She rubbed her eyes roughly until the black stains appeared on the tips of her fingers, but the mascara still stained her lids.

"You missed a spot," Rose noted. She was already looking at Ethera before pointing beneath her own eye to mirror it. "Jeez, let me help you. Why are you scrubbing so hard? You're going to lose all your lashes. Here, close your eyes for a second."

She lifted the sleeve of her hoodie, still damp and darkened with water, and gently wiped it over Ethera's eyes. The brunette was as rigid as a log. It had been a while since she experienced such casual closeness that didn't end in a take-down. It was almost unsettling, like something she'd long since outgrown.

Rose kept repeating the same motion with a surprisingly gentle touch. "It's easier to take off with cloth," she said lightly, glancing down at the black smudge staining her sleeve. "Whoa," Her voice trailed away. To her surprise, when Ethera opened her eyes, both girls were staring at her, wide-eyed, fixated on the left side of her face.

Ethera's fingers twitched; the sudden urge to cover it overwhelmed her. "It's—uh—it's called poliosis," Her throat clenched, heat creeping into her cheeks. "It affected my left eye and eyebrow, too. Just…not all of it. Oh! It's not contagious, so you don't have to worry about it."

It was always hidden beneath mascara and brown eyebrow gel, but now it seemed to finally be out on the table. She felt stripped to the bone, as if she was completely naked. Her secrets and imperfections were out for everyone to gawk at.

"Aye, that's kinda cool. You got white eyelashes like a husky," Reymond excitedly exclaimed, earning a mighty hit on the shoulder from Hugo. They had ended up coming shortly after washing up a few feet away from the girls. The boys had long forgotten about this phenomenon. When Ethera was young, her lashes and brows were much lighter than the dark color they had settled into over the years.

Hugo shook his head, giving his twin a disappointing look. "A dog? Really? You compare her to a dog as a compliment?" Ethera awkwardly smiled; she didn't care much to be compared to a husky. They were cute.

"What? I was just being honest. What do you want me to say? Oh, sweet Ethera, your beauty is that of a wilting flower." This seemed to earn him another smack from his brother. Mr. Alden would have given him an A for such a poetic assessment.

She had gotten up, stepping to the side to dust off her leggings. "Well—anything is better than being called old."

"It's very pretty and unique," Juno commented. It wasn't long until they returned to the village, quietly following the elves with limited chatter. Dilian was already there, although spotting him had become much easier.

He was dressed differently, more casually. His hair was unbraided, light waves fell loosely to his shoulder before being tied into a low ponytail. It concealed his ears so well that, at a glance, one might have mistaken him for a human.

But his garments told another story. He wore a loose white tunic that nearly blended with the pale strands of his hair, paired with high black trousers and heavy-duty leather boots that chipped at the front. Around his waist, a leather belt attached a long sword with silver hilt.

He looked awfully like a pirate.

They had agreed beforehand that anyone traveling to the Pirate's Lagoon would need to dress for the occasion. The mortals' modern clothes would have drawn all sorts of unwanted attention.

Hoodies and leggings didn't exactly exist here. So, instead, a change of clothes was necessary, and what better way to blend in with the pirates than to dress up as one?

A large wooden chest sat in the center of the clearing where Dilian stood, his foot tapping impatiently on the grass. Once the elf spotted the slow bunch, his boot kicked the box open. It was full to the brim with all sorts of fabrics, tunics, dresses of old colors, accessories, hats, and a bunch of other trinkets. "It feels like Halloween all over again," Reymond cringed, his hand in the crate lifting what looked like a red velvet corset. "Where did you guys even get this stuff? Spirit Halloween clearance section?"

"Out of necessity, we *borrowed* a few from their village late last night," the elf admitted, which took the mortals by surprise. They didn't think elves were capable of such deeds; they seemed to be too noble.

"Do you mind if I take my pick first? I need something flowy with big sleeves so it's easier for me to...take stuff," Ethera admitted embarrassingly. She glanced back at the elf, her hand digging into her pocket. "Oh yeah, I forgot about these. I held on to them just in case."

She threw something in Dilian's direction, and he caught it with ease. His eyes widened when he opened his hand. The bundle of keys that had gone missing was finally returned. He opened his mouth to say something but decided against it; his eyes lingered on the female with an unreadable expression.

The mystery of how a bunch of humans escaped the prison maze had been solved in the most shocking way. She was calculating for a mortal, that much he could admit.

Without wasting any time, Ethera dove in, searching for something that would not only suit her taste but also the mission.

She slipped behind the bushes and began changing out of her comfortable mortal clothes, trading them for something that would help her blend in.

The linen blouse she chose was loose, with long, puffed sleeves, and a deep, open neckline. She had no choice but to tie it closed; otherwise, her bodice would have been far too exposed. Beneath the skirt, she put on a layer of white breeches, clearly this world's undergarments. They allowed the deep red skirt to flare outward despite its many ruffled layers. A hidden slit ran up the right side of the fabric, making it obvious why the breeches were necessary.

It was uncomfortable and heavy. Ethera made a mental note to lose the skirt as soon as she was free to do so.

If not for Rose's impressive knowledge of clothing, even styles from such distant places, Ethera would have been utterly lost. Rose helped her pair the perfect blouse with a striking skirt, carefully selecting accessories that matched both color and aesthetic.

It felt like she was playing dress up, and Ethera had become her victim.

She tucked the blouse into the skirt and fastened the corset Reymond had previously fiddled with. It was stiff and rough against her ribs, but the deep red complemented the skirt beautifully, while the white trim matched the blouse. She kept her old sneakers since none of the shoes in the chest fit her small feet.

The accessories Rose chose were unusual. A black leather sash wrapped around Ethera's lower waist, hanging on her hips, packed with countless pouches and compartments—practical, clearly meant for weapons. It had more space than she could ever use. Another, smaller pouch was strapped beneath her skirt along her lower thigh, just where the small ruffles of the breeches ended. It hooked on to the breeches lightly.

It was the perfect place to hide a knife. The thought alone thrilled her, making her feel like a real pirate. The slit in the skirt allowed her to move freely without being repressed. She jumped, stretched, twisted side to side, to ensure the comfort of her new attire. She bit the inside of her mouth, concealing a cheeky smile that threatened to spill through.

The final piece of the costume was undoubtedly the worn, three-cornered hat of faded black. It reeked of alcohol and something old, but it was a necessary accessory if she wanted to hide the streaks in her hair.

Ethera returned towards the half-empty chest, her modern clothes in her arms, and tossed them inside. She excitedly bounced around, testing out every seam, afraid that it would give out any second now.

One by one, the others came out from behind the woods.

Hugo and Reymond had matching blouses, ruffles spilling from their chins down to their chests. Reymond's hung untied, claiming that it was itching the top of his neck too much. The sleeves fell loose at the wrists, unlike Ethera's tied cuffs. Both of the twins wore loose brown trousers with mismatched patching. Reymond's were tucked into tall brown boots that clearly did not belong to him.

He was the only one of the boys who had a hat. A grand tricorn with feathers that stretched towards the sky, making him look like some sort of peacock. Hugo's head remained empty, but a medium dark cape with a few missing buttons and holes rested on his shoulders.

Rose came out shortly after. Her blouse mirrored Ethera's, though the neckline was far more modest. A tightly laced corset hugged her waist like something straight from the eighteenth century. Her deep emerald skirt reached just above her ankles, layered with ruffles that matched those on her sleeves. Rose's grey-stained Adidas sneakers blended surprisingly well with the outfit. A matching bandana framed her strawberry-blonde hair, making it glow against the contrast.

She felt giddy, as if looking like a mistress of a rich noble had just been crossed off her bucket list.

After Rose finished twirling, Juno stepped out, looking less like a pirate and more like an assassin. She wore dark brown trousers with suspenders stretching over her shoulders, disappearing beneath her shoulder-length hair that was tied half into a bun with a loose string she found within the treasure. She quickly threw over a black cloak as she danced around, playing the role of a dark wizard.

The mortals buzzed with excitement over their new identities. Nearby, Dilian glanced down at the sleeves of his tunic, clearly wondering whether he, too, should embrace what it means to be a pirate.

"Aye, aye, captain," Ethera joked, pretending to draw a sword. "Ready your sails, ya filthy peasants."

"Say something like that," Dilian began, appearing closer, "and you'll surely get hanged. Best leave the talking to me."

CHAPTER 7

Dilian was the only elf who decided to accompany the mortals to the Pirate's Lagoon, and fear had nothing to do with it. Elves were very proud creatures, with their tendency to run into a fight blind if it meant defending their home, their people, and their land. However, they didn't quite have enough clothes that could fit a seven-foot-tall elf. In fact, it was a miracle that the boots that they had found fit Dilian perfectly; otherwise, his short trousers would reveal the light hue of his pale, almost green skin.

His dark cloak cast a dark shadow over his face, just enough to trick the pirate's eye. After all, pirates were human too.

The trip to the Pirate's Lagoon wasn't as long as the mortals had originally thought it was going to be, it lasted only six hours.

For Dilian, those six hours were a piece of cake. He itched to finally leave the village, even if it meant as a guard to mortals he could not stand.

But for the humans, it was a different story. They had the urge to sit down every twenty minutes, gawk at every small animal, and refused to control their large, hungry stomachs. The elf had to remind them countless times to restrain themselves, for they didn't know exactly when they would be returning back and the rations would only last them for a few days.

Of course, they did not listen to him and did as they pleased. He could only wish that he could dispose of all of them.

Only when they inched closer to the lagoon had they finally realized how thick and dense the air had become, despite their coming closer to the waters and the never-ending sea of monsters.

The air had dropped a few degrees, and Ethera ended up feeling thankful for the mountains of layers that the skirts were made of, which had kept her legs warm despite the extra pounds it had added to her already tired body.

The town was shabby, and the ground had turned from hard soil to a mud-like texture, sometimes even sinking a whole two inches under. There were more houses than they had originally thought there were going to be, and the pirates were no other than humans dressed up, their blood toxic with alcohol as they ran around, pointing their swords at each other every opportunity that presented itself.

The boys were disappointed, thinking they were going to see something more exciting than flying empty bottles, swords clashing at every corner, or wild running animals, like horses and donkeys. The girls had the opposite reaction; their fear had urged them to stick together like glue, horrified at the thought that one of the big, bearded men was going to snatch them off and sell them on the black market.

That is, if they had one.

Contrary to their fears, the pirates did not pay them any attention.

Ethera's hand seemed to rest close to the hidden satchel on her thigh, and the thought of the small dagger carried the weight of slight relief. On her hips was a long, rusty sword that belonged to a pirate. It was only for display; she couldn't actually pull it out of its sheath. The rust had rotted it beyond recognition. It had become nothing more than a mere decoration.

Everyone in their group carried some kind of weapon, either knives or swords. Both Hugo and Reymond had swords. Dilian had his spear hidden under his cloak and a sword on his hip. Rose had a pocketknife, and Juno had a lightweight, thin sword mounted to her hip.

Despite it being in the middle of the day, almost every pirate was already drunk or in the process of drinking.

Ethera doubted they could tell the time between day and night, for darkness had swallowed this little town, casting shadows over every house.

She found it easier to deal with drunks who could barely stand than sober, ruthless pirates with no fear for their own lives. That seemed to shed some light on the uncomfortable path that they were walking towards.

Their first stop was a tavern, a pirate bar that provided lodging at the cost of one silver coin. It was a place of vast information that travelled throughout the land from the many visitors who would stop to rest there. Except the

Pirate's Lagoon rarely had visitors, and the lodging upstairs proved to be useless.

And it was also a mess, empty bottles and broken glass lay all over the wooden floor inside. There were some chairs with missing legs and tables here and there. It smelled of beer and food. Bits of chicken and bone lay on the intact tables, with plates that were already broken.

A large chandelier hung from the middle, tilted to the side as if the ceiling above it was slowly giving in. The mortals were frozen in shock, gawking at the inside of the tavern without taking a step. The sweaty stench in the air had made it impossible to want to come inside. It was surprising that this place was standing, for it looked like it was going to collapse any minute now.

Dilian pushed through Hugo and Reymond, who blocked the doorway. They glanced at each other before following after him. "We shall part ways to cover more ground. Let no stone be left unturned," Dilian nodded in what looked like encouragement and split passed two drunk maidens.

In the blink of an eye, he was gone. So much for being their guide. The group awkwardly shuffled at their feet, trying to figure out how to split themselves evenly.

Reymond cleared his throat. "Alright, ladies, you two are coming with me. Hugo and Ethy will stick together," he uttered quickly, putting an arm over the girls' shoulders.

Ethera and Hugo, much to their surprise, didn't have time to protest or react to the last-minute decision. The unlikely pair was left standing in the middle together, simply staring at each other.

Ethera broke the uncomfortable silence by taking a step towards him. "Let's ask around," She quickly mumbled, her shoulder brushing past his. He shook his head in understanding, knowing the chaos in the room would only drown his voice.

She walked slowly, eyes scanning every possible target, none of which she wanted to approach. Men and women yelled loudly in heavy accents; their faces flushed from the heat and the alcohol. Ethera jerked her head towards a little redhead sitting with a passed-out man. The woman twirled her wooden mug, eyes spaced out.

"Excuse me…" Ethera began, not even knowing how to start. "I'm looking for the Pirate King."

The redhead's eyes slowly drifted to the girl with a vibrant red dress. Silence fell among them before the woman let out a small laugh that was muffled by her hiccups. "Well—good luck, little girl," she muttered, her body swaying to music playing in the background. "Last I heard, the Pirate King sank with his ship and never rose. If yee lookin' for his bones, go sail, and yee shall find 'em."

Ethera remained quiet, eyes darting to the woman's passed-out friend who twitched in his sleep, as if the mention of the Pirate King was daunting.

The redhead leaned in, lowering her voice. "If yee a smart little girl, stop lookin'. Men like him ain't meant to be found."

The man beside her suddenly rose. "T-The King? Hah! Heard he's off cuttin' deals with the Demon Lord— aye, sellin' souls like they're see—seashells!" His tongue stumbled at the last word.

92

The woman kicked him underneath the table, not wanting the others to hear. "Shhh—you fool. He ain't...but word on the streets is those demons are coming and he sure as hell ain't comin' back for the likes of us."

The man grumbled, eyes half closed. "Aye...aye. The likes of us—." His head fell back on the table with a bang.

"Best pray yee never find him. Now be gone, little girl. Before trouble finds yee."

Ethera didn't answer but nodded her head in reply before moving away, trying her best not to show off the irritated look on her face. That was the first time she was called a little girl by someone who seemed only a few years older.

Hugo walked alongside her as they moved a few tables down. A big, bearded pirate sat at a table alone, smoke surrounding him and his pipe. The scent was suffocating. "The King of all Pirates..." He breathed out the smoke in Ethera's direction, reminiscing on the once victorious time. "We waited for years, y'know? Thought he'd sail back for us all and drag us out by the hair. Curse us all for gettin' soft." A light laugh escaped his lips. "But he never did. Folks say he's dead. Eaten by the monsters."

They moved on to another pirate. "Eh? The King of the Sea? Well, if ya do come across him, do let me know—," the Pirate paused, lifting his arm. A silver hook replaced where his hand once was. "I outta pay him back for this." The pirate laughed loudly at the kids' grim expressions; his hand dropped on the table, his drink swayed, spilling out the edges. Contents of it already coated the table, as if this was not the first time his excitement had gotten the better of him.

Hugo grabbed Ethera by the arm, dragging her away.

"Did your momma not warn yee of asking around for *him*?"

"He stole my sister's boots once."

"Cursed."

"*Dead.*"

"Became a demon."

"Shhh, best quit asking—word already got around yee lookin' for him!"

Ethera walked away quickly; they were getting nowhere, and this information was absolutely useless to them.

The drunk pirates could not see straight. Despite their wobbly appearance and sloppy tongue, they were still in their right minds to answer the question they had been asking for almost an hour: Where was the Pirate King?

But their luck had run thin. No one knew of his whereabouts. Those who dared to speak of him had nothing nice to say, while the others shushed in fear for their own lives and scrambled off.

But the rare few who were not as frightened simply said that the man in question had not been seen in a decade. Presumed dead at sea.

Even across the battlefield, Rose's group was having just as much difficulty. The impatience was getting to Ethera. The lack of answers was just enough to drive her over the edge. She assumed this would be easy, but with every passing minute, she realized how wrong she was.

Perhaps she was looking in the wrong place. She glanced in the direction of the man who guarded the bar, pouring drinks for fellow pirates who could no longer stand.

The keeper was in his thirties; his hair tied back into a thin bun. He wore a yellowish tunic reflecting the dim lights in the room, and his sleeves were rolled upwards. Tattoos covered every inch of his forearms like a coloring book that was yet to find color.

Ethera looked at Hugo, giving him a glance and a nod towards the pirate's direction. Together, they strolled to the other side of the chaotic room, where the noise was slightly quieter. "I want to know where I can find the King of Pirates," Ethera stated, her voice tight with restrained anger. She took a seat on one of the tall wooden chairs in front of the brown counter, her arms resting on the chapped wood. Hugo hovered next to her, fixing his glasses uncomfortably. The man did not look up at her; he continued pouring beer into wooden cups that seemed as big as Ethera's head. His lack of attention had irritated her so, causing her brows to furrow.

Finally, the man lifted his eyes, darting back between Ethera and Hugo. He scoffed after a moment of silence and turned away. "I do not know."

He shook his hands, mixing something before sliding the mug down the long table where another pirate had the pleasure of catching it. The short man lifted the mug, downing the liquid with violent gulps. Half of it spilled across his clothes as he used his soiled sleeve to wipe his orange mustache. With a bang, he threw the mug onto the table and laughed to himself. Ethera narrowed her eyes, looking back towards the keeper, not giving up despite how desperately she wanted to leave.

Her hands pressed against the table as she leaned closer. "But you do know, and I pray you tell me. It is for the benefit of our King, of course," she proclaimed in a quiet, much calmer tone.

Hugo couldn't figure out where Ethera got the confidence to lie in the face of danger. The man was five times their size with muscles spilling out from the middle cut of his tunic. His dark brown orbs were haggard; not even the fiery lanterns hanging from the ceiling were enough to cast light into them.

He scoffed, inching closer. "What would a little girl, like you know of our King?" He paused in front of them, his arms resting on the wooden counters, awaiting the next order and entertaining his new little friends.

Ethera looked around before leaning in a bit closer. "I hear whispers. The dead are bound to sail the seas. Do you think they will spare us or turn on our King instead? Pray tell, is the captain really negotiating safe passage for the demons?" The fire lit within the man's eyes, as if that baseless rumor was nothing more than an insult.

He grunted, leaning backwards. "The captain will not put us in danger; he is a noble leader." He reached underneath the counter, pulling out a greyish-white rag. His arm darted across the already clean table, eyes never leaving Ethera. Her eyes fell to the sudden movement, his right hand showing off flawlessly drawn tattoos.

The man's eyes lingered on her, his hand pausing deliberately. "May you find what you are looking for."

He retraced his steps, tossing the rag away as he disappeared to the other side, grabbing the empty wooden mug.

The background noise had faded to oblivion, and Ethera's mind ran in loops, trying to tie something together. Her index finger tapped against the table, and the presence of Hugo standing next to her had vanished as a bright light lit up the inside of her brain.

She turned around, jumping off the chair. "I got it. Let's go find the others," She raised her chin excitedly, trying to hide her satisfied smile. Her eyes peered back to the keeper, whose gaze was hovering on her like a confirmation. The pirate nodded to himself, looking away.

Once they dragged the others out of the tavern, Dilian didn't hesitate to bomb Ethera with questions as to why they were leaving. It was clear that they had no luck on their side either.

"A ship, is it not a meaningful symbol for a pirate? As far as I know—which is not much, but a pirate only tattoos the ship they have sailed on, right?" She thought out loud, mumbling to herself. The elf's keen sense of hearing picked up on everything. He nodded, answering her rhetorical question. Hugo tried his best to keep up, but he could not tie the knot properly.

Ethera definitely realized something after looking at the tavernkeeper's tattoos. But what was it that she had seen that he hadn't? "There was an octopus...and mermaids. A sea dragon, perhaps?" He chimed in, pausing to think back to what else he missed.

"A leviathan," Dilian corrected.

"Don't you think it's odd the way the tattoos are positioned? How all the monsters are lurking beneath the ship, almost like they are looking up at it and avoiding it. Could it be that the reason why the Pirate King's ship never sank was because it's being guarded by something?"

"It would make sense why the other pirates can't sail past the lagoon. The King's ship might be different, but it's hard to know since he's the only one that sails in it."

"Lagoon…that's right. The Pirate Lagoon. There were fins on that map—the one in the elves' village. The lagoon refers to mermaids. But why are the two connected? Even the pirate had a tattoo of a mermaid. You saw it too, right?"

Hugo nodded eagerly. "It was surrounded by a yellow glow. The only tattoo that had color."

"I'm not following," Reymon whined, scratching the back of his head. His group only managed to receive snarky remarks and threats.

"I believe that the King has control over the sea monsters. It would make sense why they call him the King of the Sea. He can sail through the Crimson Waters because he has the power to control them, so they won't attack him. And the mermaids might just act like his messengers, right?" Ethera's eyes lit up brightly.

Dilian's eyes widened, and his head nodded with approval. "If your hutch is right, then we might be able to find a mermaid beyond the cliffs of the Pirate's Lagoon."

"But what kind of king sinks his own ships?" Rose wondered aloud.

Everyone fell silent, exchanging looks. "The king who wants to stay in control of the sea," Dilian replied coldly.

CHAPTER 8

It was refreshing to get away from the booming town of drunken, smelly people, or as they referred to them in this world—*pirates*. They hurried along the street, making their way through the thick, condensed fog that mysteriously sat around the little town, completely hiding it from sight. One would have thought it was cursed.

The streets had come to an end, turning right and leading elsewhere, but the path that they sought was hidden behind a wooden, run-down house. There was no light in sight, and the grass had long overgrown it.

Dilian had taken his sword out, leading the way as he sliced through weeds and forcing his tall body through. His cape had fluttered in the light wind, catching on the twigs that poked out.

Rose and Ethera lagged behind, hoping to shield the elf's actions from any passersby's with their long skirts that tripled their frames. Reymond had stayed close to the elf, watching the flow of the sword with envy. He was going to say something, but the view ahead completely shut him up.

It was a short hike down that hugged the side of the small hill on which the town was built. The beach stretched out farther than the eye could see, leading down towards a cliff with dozens of giant rocks below it.

The famous Crimson Waters were nothing more than a vast, beautiful ocean that sparked with the touch of the sun above it. Their vision burned at the sudden light that shone through the small clouds. Some of them reached out to shield their eyes as they walked down, while others simply looked away.

It was breathtaking and sparked yet another pit stop for the humans to admire. Dilian urged them to hurry; the sun was to set in a few hours. It was a long walk ahead of them, and he was desperate to make it before sunset. They advanced in silence; their shoes sank into the sand with every step.

Large pebbles and seashells decorated the golden sand, with not a footstep in sight. Little animals hid themselves below the ground, away from the people who had suddenly shown up. Flashes of red and pink had crawled away in a hurry, refusing to get caught.

It took the group a whole hour to walk to the other side, where large rocks the size of single-family homes were stacked up between the crushing waves. They came in fast with violent roars, hitting the rocks and shooting the water high up into the air. Tiny specs of water left their faces feeling refreshed, but the haunting thought of crossing through had left them hesitating.

"Come. We must not idly linger," Dilian urged them, his long legs allowing him to climb up the rocks with ease.

He glanced back, the mortals slowly making their way towards him. They began to climb in an ant-like stance, their hands looking for grip. At this rate, they were going to be here all night.

Dilian reached his hand out, not saying a word. Ethera grabbed on, one hand gripped her skirts that dangerously pulled with the wind and threatened to tangle her legs together.

She had taken her cape off and left it close to the edge, along with Dilian's and Juno's. They also left their swords behind, hoping they wouldn't need them.

One by one, the elf helped them up and continued assisting them with every high rock they encountered. The boys struggled just as much as the girls did. Moss coated the rocks, making their journey far too slippery.

Ethera let out a loud yelp, feeling her shoe slip. "How far are we going?" She asked their leader once she regained her composure.

Her eyes scanned the area ahead. There were too many rocks, and the water was rising at an alarming pace. It would have been suicide to keep going further, not knowing if they would be able to turn back in time.

Dilian sighed, knowing that time was not on their side, especially with the heavy baggage that was dragging him down. "Let's stop here." His green eyes focused on the shallow water ahead.

Ethera motioned for Reymond to come over. "This is a very dumb idea. Why can't we just call for one to pop out?" He complained as he hopped over a few rocks, following the girl's instructions. The area ahead might have been the deepest part of the Rocky Tail, deep enough for a siren to slip in and out with ease.

It was also deep enough for them to catch one.

There was a reason the name hinted at a tail. Mermaids were often seen basking in the sun, and whenever someone tried to get near, they would jump in the water with only a glimpse of a tail to be seen.

Reymond tapped his foot on the sturdy rock below him, nerves tearing his stomach apart. "Why must it be me?"

"Dilian is the muscle. Hugo is the brains," Rose mocked, she was also the first to agree with throwing the lesser brother as bait for a mermaid. They were known for bewitching sailors with their sweet nothings before drowning and devouring them whole.

"Ethera is the brains, not Hugo, first of all. I'm more useful than he is, so can't we just use him?" He continued whining; the thought of being whisked away by a mermaid and murdered had made his body go rigid.

The others ignored him, helping the elf untangle the net. "Well—you're a better bait. A muscly bait. Hugo's too skinny for that. If I were a siren, I'd go for a bigger guy with more meat on his body." Juno didn't make the situation any less justified, but Reymond seemed to agree for a moment. He waited patiently for them to set up a trap, something he had to blindly trust.

"Okay…right there. Just remember to be vocal about it, you know? Like, whine loudly—you're pretty good at it," Ethera nodded, giving him a thumbs up. "Oh, and pretend you slipped and can't walk or something." Juno and Rose gave him an encouraging pat on the back. He glared at them without saying a word, climbing down and getting closer to the water.

The sea had hit his leg, sending a trail of shivers up his spine. The water was cold, but his heart was colder. He mocked Ethera's sincere expression and muttered curses to himself all the way until he reached the rock that would act as a prop on his pitiful sailor act.

How would this even work? What siren was dumb enough to fall for such an obvious trick?

Reymond let out a loud scream, purposely slipping. "Oh no, my leg! It hurts! Ow!" His bottom landed roughly in the cold water, and the splash sent ripples in the ocean. He shivered and almost screeched, biting his tongue in the process before continuing. "I can't seem to walk. I really hope my leg stops hurting before these waves lure me into the water. I'm. Such. A. Pitiful. Yummy. Sailor."

Ethera almost face palmed. She didn't know which direction to peek from, just so she could exchange looks with the others that were hidden nearby. It would be a miracle if this worked with Reymond's horrible acting. They should have disregarded reason and just sent Hugo instead. Although even that would have been no different.

What kind of mermaid would fall for that fool's trap? Maybe a hungry one beyond any reason?

"Oh no, cries of a pitiful young man! Someone help me, I can't walk!" He shouted even louder, getting impatient. Rose and Juno were shaking with laughter, their hands gripping their separate rocks in an attempt to hold on. Hugo was undergoing second-hand embarrassment, which was a given.

This plan was an absolute disaster.

It was hard to keep their focus with Reymond's pitiful wails that sounded like an animal being choked to death. Despite the pathetic act, a mermaid did show herself. When the water seeped through a rock, a siren climbed on top of it, her glowing orbs landing on their friend, who was still blinded by his act.

A pair of curious eyes stared at him, wide as if it was ready to pounce on the mortal any second now. It was a siren, no doubt. Her eyes resembled the color of a pale blue sky with specs of white. Her skin was coated with a shiny green, camouflaging her in her environment. Long black hair gave her way; it stretched out way past the water and disappeared in the foam that surrounded the rock when the water receded.

Her wide eyes stared at Reymond with curiosity and excitement, the stench of live human meat filling the air. A smile pressed itself firmly on her lips, but its innocence did not match the look reflected in her eyes.

How exciting must it have been for her to catch such a meal right before her very own pale eyes? Almost as if it had been a gift that crawled its way from below, a gift for all her hard work. It took Reymond a while to notice another presence near him, and for a second, Ethera thought he might have been blind.

But Reymond wasn't blind; he was a little slow when it came to his surroundings, so when his eyes had finally landed on the sea creature, his soul had almost fled his body.

He regained his composure quickly with a nervous laugh. "Oh? Hello there! Are you also lost?" He asked, his brain filling itself with water. Rational thoughts had jumped through his ears, leaving him to fend for himself. The woman smiled widely, displaying her sharp, pearly white teeth, as she tilted her head. He gulped in fear. "On second thought, I think my leg is perfectly fine now. Reymond is out!"

"Swimming away so soon, my sweet feast?" The siren leaped at him, catching the mortal off guard with the sudden movement. Reymond jumped as far as his body could let him, splashing water into her open, toothy grin. He had screamed along the way, chills running down his frail body. The woman paused, coughing up the water that went through the wrong hole.

The elf seized at this perfect opportunity and jumped from his hiding spot. Before the siren could react, a big fishing net was thrown on top of her scaly body. The elf appeared on top, pinning her down with a wide smile on his face.

Her sparkly silk, green tail flopped in the shallow water. "Well, well, well. If my eyes do not deceive me on land...an elf tangled with a pirate. It seems land has its own wonders," the siren sang, her voice dripping with honey. The elf tightened his hand around her neck. The siren's song did not work on him.

Her eyes sparkled with the setting sun that had just come out from behind the clouds. It peeped at the commotion and just as fast, hid behind another set of grey.

The rest of the mortals came out, some rushing to Reymond's side, who sat frozen in the water. Shivering from the fear and the cold. Despite their bodies going to their friend, their eyes could not look away from another tale that had been revealed to be true.

"You will carry word to the Pirate King—." The mermaid giggled, cutting the elf off. Her tail splashed in the water, and her body shook with amusement.

"The *who*?"

She played dumb, and it irritated the elf. "Your master. The King of the Sea."

"Oh? And pray, what do I tell this master?" The siren's gaze lit in a joking way. Ethera's breath hitched, did she get it wrong?

Dilian pulled his spear out, he jabbed it right next to the siren's abnormal ear. Her pale eyes widened, glancing back at the merciless elf. "A message for your life. How about it, siren?" He spat; his cold tone gave the mortals chills.

"If you answer my riddle, I shall carry your word across the sea."

The elf paused, giving it some thought. He nodded. The water slowed, pausing deliberately for the siren's riddle:

I sleep beneath the sea, yet I am not found,
I walk on land, yet I make no sound.
I am one half of a whole,
And no man shall claim my soul.

"—What am I, elf?" she snarled, baring her fangs. The elf's grip tightened.

"An Ignis Tear."

106

The siren giggled, and her tail splashed excitedly. "The sea shall sing it for eternity—."

"Enough of these games."

"Fine, what is your message, elf?" The siren's gaze narrowed, the playful smile disappearing, but beneath her serious look, Ethera recognized a bluff.

She wasn't going to do it; her face had said it all.

Ethera jumped closer, kneeling towards this other-worldly creature. "Listen here, siren. We don't have much time to play splish-splash in the ocean with you. You go tell the King of Pirates that a prophecy of his death surfaced through the Wishing Well, and if he doesn't get his ass over here, then he will die the most miserable death known to mankind," Ethera threatened, her eyes not wavering at all. The siren's eyes met Ethera's, watching the human in silence.

The seriousness of the situation had shifted. Words held power, and Ethera knew exactly how to utilize them. Not in the correct font, but even her vulgar language brought weight to her threats.

The siren snorted, tail splashing. "Lies told by mortal tongue. Do you take me for a fool?" She denied it, but hesitancy crossed her eyes.

"I wouldn't be here if I weren't in the prophecy too," Ethera revealed, much to her dismay.

The siren paused, eyes glancing at the elf, as if looking for confirmation. "Very well, I shall carry your words through the waters. Do not stray too far from where my song cannot reach you, or the King's word will be lost at sea, mortal," The siren hissed disobediently, her ghost-like eyes looking back at the girl.

The elf hesitated but loosened his grip, pulling back the net. Just like that, the sea creature was gone as fast as she had appeared, leaving her words hanging on their every thought.

"Why would you speak so carelessly? You may have provoked a wrath beyond your control," warned Dilian, tossing the net behind a rock.

"*Good*. It'll make him get here faster."

ᚦᚻᚻᚨ ᚦᚻᚻᚨ ᚦᚻᚻᚨ

Ethera Heart

The brunette opened her eyes, sitting up drowsily. Night has fallen already, and countless stars have swept through the dark sky above her. She scanned the area, a clearing they had found in the forest that was close enough to the cold waters of the ocean that had already swallowed all the lagoon's rocks.

The circle around them was still intact. It was a magical barrier that masked their presence from the beasts that inhabited this world. This enchantment, or ritual, required burying a magical crystal and drawing the circle around everyone in the party.

From what Ethera observed.

It wasn't like Dilian had any intention of teaching them the ways of the elven folk. One could leave and return whenever one wished, but those who were not protected by the magic could not see or sense those who stood within it.

It was extraordinary watching it come to be. Dilian was the first to fall asleep between the mortals; no one had put any trust in a mere stone despite everything they had witnessed. But eventually, their second night had befallen them, and the fatigue of the long day had caught up.

Ethera Heart, come quickly

Ethera got up on her feet, tossing her skirt aside, which she used as a blanket. Her feet stepped on the black cape that lay flat on the ground. Her eyes glanced at the others who slept soundly. She walked carefully between them, grabbing a knife as the familiar voice rang in her ears, impatiently.

Stepping outside of the circle felt nerve-wracking, but she decided to let the rest of her comrades sleep in peace. As soon as her foot touched the ground on the opposite side, a rush of chills fell across her hands and back. The magic was letting her go through, but the uneasiness had forced her to turn around.

She sighed in relief; her friends were still there, soundlessly asleep.

The soles of her feet wiggled at the touch of the cold dirt, her boots left behind in their campsite. The path ahead was short, located close to the beach. With just a few steps, the dirt road had blended in with the sand. Tiny pebbles poked at her feet; much to her surprise, it felt oddly relaxing.

The siren was swimming around in the water, her tail shimmering in the moonlight. Green scales reflected the coat of water as she floated upwards, her face turned towards the sky.

"At last, I was beginning to think boredom might drown me first," She greeted, disappearing into the water. Ethera stood by the little waves, her toes an inch away from the sea.

The siren reemerged, this time closer. "I shall reveal the King's answer, however, your kindness, if you could spare. A sharp twig has lodged itself into the curve of my spine. Unreachable as it is and painfully itches at my skin." The mermaid turned around, moving her seaweed-like hair out of the way. Pieces of extra skin hung between her bony fingers. The scaly back was paper white with dark, brown marks of her spine, which rolled from underneath the skin when she stretched like a half-dead monster.

But what made Ethera stumble at her words was a twig that penetrated the siren in between her shoulder blades. The water turned dark green upon contact with the wound.

The human winced, hand twitching as she made a decision. "Okay," she whispered hesitantly. Her toes curled into the sand as she stepped into the water, the coolness sending shivers up her legs. She walked closer until she was right beside the siren. The water had caught up to her knees, forming dots along her thighs that travelled all the way up to her arms.

Her tunic concealed the knife she hid within the waistline of her breeches. It pressed firmly against her lower back, adding weight and relief.

The siren sighed calmly. "I thank you," she spoke, her voice sounding softer. Her pearly eyes smiled, watching the shaky human's hand reaching out towards the brown log.

All of a sudden, Ethera's courage vanished in the blink of an eye as if her brain had fully awakened in the middle of the night. She wished more than anything to run back to where she came from—where she knew she was safe and go back to sleep.

But she couldn't. It would make her a cowardly liar.

And a coward she tried not to be.

The King's word—she reminded herself of what this proximity would give her. Holding her breath, her hand grabbed hold of the twig, and with all her mental strength, she pulled it out, immediately tossing it away.

The siren winced in pain. "The currents are stronger here than most. I couldn't quite reach with these poor fins of mine." The mermaid turned around, her slimy hand grabbing Ethera's arm and tugging her off balance and forcing her deeper into the water. The water stained her breeches, slowly drenching her waist. The siren let out a high-pitched laugh. "Trust is a foolish thing above the waves, not even your precious little companions are worthy of it. Had I wanted, you'd be nothing more than bones on the seafloor. But the King will sail within the next dusk—angry, he is, but not deaf to your words," the siren snared, her slimy fingers letting go of the mortal.

Ethera stumbled back, her mind thrown into an uproar for not taking any sort of action to defend herself. "O-Okay," the mortal stuttered, her heart ringing loudly in her ears. The siren jumped, sensing something stirring in the water.

111

Her eyes widened, glancing back at Ethera in a hurry. "Someone is coming. Best of luck, little mortal." And with that, she dived into the water, leaving a trail of dark green blood. Ethera didn't waste any time; she shuffled backwards, trying to put as much space as she could between the unknown imposter.

It was a man this time. He peeked from below, the bridge of his defined nose poking out of the water. His dark, long hair floated alongside him. Soulless, black glowing eyes stared back at her, not making a single sound.

The mortal stood frozen, not from fear but anticipation. Who was this thing? And what were they going to do next?

The man in question did not move, but bubbles emerged from the water as if he were blowing out excess air from his mouth. It was an immature act, that of a bored toddler. Ethera's eyebrows furrowed, her hand inching towards her back. Her eyes suddenly widened, all blood rushing towards her face.

The knife was gone.

The moonlight had guided her eyes towards the sand, illuminating the knife that she had dropped. It lay flatly underneath the water, one step in front of her.

The water returned to its steady and still surface. No one dared to make a move; they just stared at each other.

One in amusement and one in fear.

Ethera gulped, mustering the courage to speak first. "Hello, can I help you?" Her eyes glanced down at her knife that she unknowingly dropped. Without even an answer from the impostor, she had leaped towards it. Her hands reached to lift it, but before she could, a firm hand bigger than her own had pushed her palm against the blade. Ethera tugged, attempting to at least slither away, but the more she pulled, the more crushing her fingers felt against the coldness of the dagger and the sand.

His hand was fin-like, a siren? A merman? What was the difference between the two anyway?

The man in question was towering over her small frame, his long hair falling over her head. The water from the ends dripped down her arms, drowning the white of her tunic.

The mortal was frozen, not even her eyes blinking. The pale complexion throughout his large body shaded her even from the moon itself, casting a large shadow over her.

"Hello," The man spoke, his raspy voice coming from somewhere above her head, next to her left ear. It was icier than the water, sending a new violent wave of shivers through every cell. Her body would have shaken from his voice alone, but the fear of his presence had put her muscles on lockdown.

Ethera's eyes slowly looked up, their color blending in the shadows. She looked forward, trying to catch a glimpse of the stranger, her gaze met his light, green-tinted chest. Her head snapped back towards the sand, looking away in embarrassment, still not knowing how to escape this.

Never in her wildest dreams had she thought she'd see manboobs this up close, especially those of a complete stranger.

This man…he was a merman. But why did the siren flee so quickly from her own kind?

"Excuse me…I don't suppose you could move?" Ethera spat, her voice dripping with hostility. She could sense the danger that she had gotten herself into, and she had yet to find a way to dig out of this self-made grave.

The man did not move, but his wicked smile seemed to grow wider. Ethera proceeded to act on instinct; she lifted her head with as much force as she could muster and head-butted the man in the chin. His grip on her hand weakened, and she managed to snatch her knife, positioning her body back, and placing the cold blade against this creature's neck.

The waves danced in excitement, staining her back and the ends of her hair.

His teeth shimmered, eyes widening. "Oh?"

"I suggest you back off before you end up as fish food," the mortal threatened, eyes narrowing like a hawk. She silently prayed to whoever the gods were in this world for this strange merman to leave and let her be.

And to think that she bumped into another creature that could also just as easily drag her down into the deep waters was somehow ironic.

Ethera did not have the courage to cut someone's throat, nor did she wish she did. But she was a master at faking it, just like in everything else in her life.

The man leaned in, causing the blade to press deeply into his neck. Ethera didn't back off even when his smile widened with disgusting excitement. This method was not working on him; the results were different from what she had foreseen in her mind.

"What the hell do you want?"

"How will the King of Sea meet his doom?"

"I won't tell his secret to a mere servant. The King will hear it first before anyone else," Ethera announced, not backing off either. Although if this were a demonstration of body stamina, hers would run out faster.

He laughed coldly in response, not saying anything else. His throat extended with the movement of his head, eyes peered above her in the direction she had possibly come from.

A distant shout was heard in the background.

The merman backed away, disappearing into the water.

CHAPTER 9

Despite the rising of the sun, the Pirate's Lagoon was dim, foggy, and empty. It seemed that word had gotten out about the arrival of the Pirate King, despite only a select few who knew of this information. The drunken pirates had scattered, desperate to stay out of sight. Even those who spoke ill of the King with intoxicated courage were nowhere to be seen. Not a single soul was strolling in the streets, drinking at the taverns, or fishing at the port.

It was oddly quiet. The symphony of chaotic sounds from the day before was replaced with an uncomfortable stillness; even the fog seemed to conceal the sound from the forest.

Where had all those pirates vanished in such a short amount of time?

Ethera and her friends woke up feeling refreshed despite the uneasiness that lurked in everyone's stomach. Only Dilian was confident enough that this fateful meeting would go splendidly. It wouldn't be long until they sail across the Crimson Waters and take back what was once theirs.

The prophecy will come true. He glanced at the mortals' leader, whom he identified as Ethera. She was cunning, and if truth be told, he didn't trust her. There was something odd lurking behind her dual-colored eyes, something that threatened his own existence.

But the same went for her. She didn't trust Dilian one bit; the gap between their physical capabilities and knowledge of this world was too grand. At any second, she and her friends could get tossed aside as nothing but monster food.

That cursed prophecy was the only thing proving her to be of use to the elves. It was what had saved her life. If it weren't for the bigger picture at play, everything would have fallen. Dilian was no different; he was hostile and became a bundle of suspicions the moment he joined them on this journey.

Dilian paused, his eyes scanning his surroundings. "Know this—he bears the title 'King of Kings', some say the only king worth naming. Humor him if you wish to keep your head attached. Best you leave the speaking to me," he warned, his eyes specifically landed on Ethera, awaiting her response. She nodded, not thinking much of it.

"A King of all Kings, huh? That's kind of cool, I'm excited to see this guy," Rose chatted honestly. It wasn't every day they met an important figure like the Pirate King.

Dilian looked at her as if she had left her head behind at the Rocky Tail. "Keep your blade at bay, do not be lured by his face."

Rose scoffed, somehow feeling offended. "Geez, who said anything about that? You need to learn to take a chill pill. Everything is going according to plan, is it not? Lighten up, for once," she uttered, her head tilting in the elf's direction.

Dilian's green eyes rolled, reminding himself not to lose his composure. "Do not fret, I am calm—I do not need a 'chill pill'. Must you always act on impulse? It would spare us all much trouble if you listened for once."

"Okay, *boss*. Let's not forget that we literally fell into another world, and you're still the strangest thing we've come across. And aren't you people supposed to be puny?" Rose sneered, with exaggerated slowness, she pinched the air, her expression deadpan as the fingers drew nearer to each other until they were a hair apart.

"You dare to compare us to those creatures? Watch your tongue before you choke on your ignorance." Dilian had stopped leading, his body turned towards Rose, his hand resting on the hilt of his sword. Juno and Ethera both hurried to get in between them, trying to create some distance and get Rose out of sight.

Dilian had been ordered to protect the mortal from the prophecy; there was nothing in the command to entertain her other mortal friends.

Reymond appeared beside Dilian, putting a sturdy hand on the elf's shoulder. "Settle down, pretty boy," Reymond sighed, a little surprised to see an argument break out so easily. Dilian glanced back, his forest-like eyes burned with fury. He averted his sharp gaze and continued walking before his emotions could get the better of him. It seemed that the mortal's vast range of expressions was contagious, for he had never felt anger as such.

"Rose, don't provoke him. We all need to get along if we are going to make it back alive, okay?" Juno exclaimed, her hands resting on Rose's arm.

"Yes, yes. *My bad.*" They exchanged looks before following after the elf.

There were many pirate ships in the port; some had been moved to one side to accommodate the arrival of the Pirate King. His ship stood out in the distance, seemingly twice the size. The fog slowly grazed the calm waters below it, mysteriously covering the ship's dark oak wood. The sails were high, and the wind viciously blew the flag, making it wave and dance as if greeting the mortals from afar.

There was a single skull on the dark fabric of the flag, making it much different from the others, who had weapons and such. If Ethera wasn't mistaken, the skull's eyes were a glowing ruby red.

A one-man ship, just like the rumors from the previous day had spoken. It was no surprise that the King could maneuver through the ocean alone. He wasn't just the King of Pirates, but the King of the Sea—the master of the creatures that poisoned the ocean. But the question remained: why did his greediness prevent others from taking sail?

"He has come. We are late," Dilian announced, quickly rushing through the grass that he had violated with his sword the day before.

"I thought we were supposed to meet at noon?" Hugo asked, confused, as the sun had yet to reach above their heads.

Juno shrugged, hands moving a few loose pieces of grass out of the way. "Being early is a great sign. Who doesn't love an early bird?" She said with mock seriousness.

Reymond snickered behind her. "Some might say— an early fish." The humans exchanged glances. Dilian's lips curled upwards as his ears twitched at the joke. "You guys get it, right? It's like an early bird, but I said fish because well…he's the King of the fish, supposedly?"

"Yes, yes. We get it-."

Dilian shushed them hurriedly, his long finger pressed against the middle of his lips. The pirates' village had fallen deep under fog, more than they had previously encountered. The lack of foot traffic had caused it to lie asleep on the ground. It was difficult to navigate, but the one faint golden glow had led them straight to the tavern. It was the only house on the block that was not afraid to have its lights on; everything else was either shut off, fenced, or dim.

Dilian suddenly came to a stop right in front of the door, feeling the dark energy emerging from within. He glanced back at the mortals, a thousand words of 'be quiet' flashed in their minds in Dilian's voice. They nodded, flashing thumbs up in the air as a form of encouragement. The elf looked away, his eyes wide from the scene that had presented itself before him. What had they done? What did it mean? Day by day, he had come to realize how odd humans were with their mannerisms.

He shook his head, bringing back his attention to the door in front. The wooden chipped handle was crusty against his nervous grip as if it were about to break if he put too much force on it. The door flung open, creaking in the process and announcing their arrival to the two figures inside.

The tavern was spotless. Unrecognizable.

Broken glass had been swept away. The tables with scattered pieces of food were gone, the surface wiped clean. They had been pushed to the sides of the room, along with all the chairs, leaning against the walls. The room had opened up like a lobby, transforming into a large, empty ballroom big enough to host a single man.

Any trace of the madness had been erased and transformed into something worthy of human presence. The tavern keeper had looked up, his stare lingering on those who dared to come in. His eyes relaxed upon seeing Ethera's face behind the group of figures before going back to serve the man who sat in front of him.

Dilian lowered down on his knees, a bow worthy of the man before them. "Your majesty, the Pirate King," Dilian breathed out, showing respect. The humans awkwardly glanced at each other, their knees popping as they bent down in sync.

The King did not acknowledge them. This man, his back to the room, was underdressed for someone with such high standing in this world. He wore a plain loose-fitting white tunic, the sleeves wide at the forearms and tucked into little ruffles at the wrist. The tunic was partially clumsily pushed into his brown trousers; the rest idly hung out.

Around his waist, over the tunic, a piece of coral colored fabric was draped, hanging loosely over the middle part of his pants. He had no vest, no coat, no unnecessary leather pouches.

He was by no means a traveler. But he was no king either. His attire was plain for someone who was supposed to be the King of Kings.

Despite his lack of garments, he made up with his exquisite amount of jewelry. Golden rings with rubies of all colors crowned his pale fingers. His dark hair was pulled into a low bun secured with a golden pin with a skull morphed at the very top. Hanging from its mouth was a thin golden string, tied around a red crystal, glinting in the light like a drop of fresh blood.

He made no sound, no movement. The King was a statue of coiled silence that brought forth not just uneasiness but also fear. The mortals awkwardly glanced around, shifting on their feet to draw their attention from the rapid beat of their hearts. The elf remained on his knee, head tilted downwards, awaiting permission to speak.

Finally, the king spoke. "It's been some time since I last walked on something that did not sway beneath my boot." He lifted the glass, from which he drank, to his eye level. The brown liquid danced around as he tilted it from side to side. The drink dangerously lapped against the curved edges like the waves of the sea, each motion was deliberate—carrying out a message to those who idly stood behind him.

Dilian finally rose. "We seek safe passage across the Crims-."

"Do tell me…" the pirate interrupted, holding the glass still in his glamorous hand. His head turned just enough to catch the flickering light of the torch, revealing a sharp cut of his jawline and the edge of a grin. "How is it that I die?"

He waited for an answer that did not come. Dilian's head turned towards Ethera, his eyes glaring at the mortal who cowardly looked away. The atmosphere somehow shifted, as if the lack of an answer would bring death that was waiting for them right outside the tavern door.

His impatience drawing near, everyone could sense it. He turned back around, toying with his drink once again, boredom consuming him.

"That was a lie," the elf admitted, his voice cutting through the silence in a whisper. An icy stillness cast over the air; even the walls surrounding them froze in anticipation, awaiting the plausible catastrophe, the King's anger.

The king's hand froze, and even the liquid inside the glass fell still. "You dare lie to me?" The room seemed to fall silent with every sentence. Ethera took a step forward, the sole of her shoe thumping against the wood and causing it to creak in response.

She had to do something about the raging flame that was the king. "If I had not told you a lie, you wouldn't have run all the way here," she took charge, in the most disrespectful way possible. Like pouring fuel over a scorching fire.

Dilian had reached to grab her arm, but she pulled away, dodging his angry grip. The conversation was tilting dangerously towards the dark abyss of the sea, and Ethera was desperate to change the tide.

The king scoffed but answered immediately. "Run? I do not run, girl. And who might you be?" He had finally turned around, the drink in his hand pressed firmly against the table.

The Pirate King's face was carved in sharp lines that looked menacing in the dim light that cast shadows on every edge. Pale skin contrasted with his jet-black hair, and despite the warm color of the fire, his face remained cold. His thick eyebrows furrowed at the mortal's comment, casting deep shadows over his eyes as dark and endless as the sea, miles beneath the surface. A sharp nose cut down the center of his face, balanced by the defined structure of his jaw. His long lips had no color, but the little shadow on the edge had revealed his displeasure.

The girl gulped the fear down. "Ethera Heart," she answered, her eyebrows scrunched in the middle. Her head tilted down, attempting to conceal something that was already hidden.

It didn't take the king long to realize that she was not one of his. "You are no pirate." Was it that obvious? Ethera had the urge to turn away, but the weight of her hat urged her not to.

"I am not."

Then, his cold gaze turned towards Dilian. "I see an elf mothering five humans, how amusing," he scoffed, turning around and lifting his glass cup to his lips. The liquid burned his throat, and he savored every second of it until the glass was empty. He stood up, the chair creaking against the wood. He was taller than he looked when he was sitting, landing a few inches above than Hugo and Reymond, but falling short of Dilian.

In the blink of an eye, he had walked towards the door, and Ethera, much to her displeasure, took a dangerous step to block the King's path. "There is a prophecy with *your highness* in it, but it is not of your death. I will not reveal it until you grant us safe passage across the Crimson Sea," Ethera spoke loudly and clearly, trying to somehow draw his interest to the prophecy.

He let out a dry laugh. "That's very comical. The demons had also given me a bargain. Two sides at war and only me and my waters preventing the other from perishing out of existence," he motioned with his hand, his fingers fluttering in the air like deathly butterflies.

"Your majesty-."

"It is unwise for me to go into this bargain blindly. What do you offer in exchange for my cooperation?"

Ethera fell silent, eyes looking back at the elf for help. "The sea witch's heart," Dilian immediately answered, the bargain already prepared. The mortals were not informed of this, and they could only guess as to why. Ethera glanced back at the King, his expression stern, but the offer echoed in his hollow mind. Dilian continued, seeing as that piqued his interest ever so slightly. "I am aware that you have no clue of her location. She poses a great threat to your title. Allow me to take care of her in exchange for a safe passage across the Crimson Waters."

Never once had the King's eyes turned to look at the elf; his bottomless gaze looked down on the mortal before him, who also stared back. The room had suffered much silence today, but this time it was for the King to make his final decision.

The heart of his mother was tempting, and he gave in to the offer with a pleasant smile. His lips curled upwards, the face of the mortal glaring at him from underneath her tricorn was burning deep into his mind. "I shall accept the heart, and I will grant you safe passage across my water. I will lend you my troops if you so wish to have them. However, this mortal will be the one to carve the heart of the sea witch with her own bare hands."

Ethera opened her mouth in protest.

Dilian took a step forward. "Your majesty, allow me-."

"Ethera Heart, was it? Do we have a deal?" His eyes lightened but still glowed with dignified darkness. Ethera's eyes fell down to his lips, the cursed smile that told her exactly what this man was thinking. She was nothing more than an example; this was a way of punishing her for tricking him and for daring to stand in his way. "Deal, your highness," she agreed, challenging him. "However, the King will fight with us. On the front lines."

His shoulders shook, a cold laugh echoing in the half-empty room. He covered his eyes, the sleeves swinging from the motion. Loose hairs were brushed past his pale forehead, and his teeth gleamed, whiter than his pale skin. For someone who spent so much time taking sail, he was sure lacking vitamin D.

He sighed in amusement. "Deal. I will be looking forward to the day you slay my mother. Send me a fish when you're done," he waved his right hand before stepping around her and walking out the front door.

Everyone waited a few seconds before bursting into overlapped conversations. "Are you sick in the head?" Dilian's voice was the loudest, almost instantly shushing the rest of her friends. Her eyes lingered on the door, the Pirate

King's back still vivid in her mind as her anger settled down in her bones. Why was it that the way he looked down on her aggravated her so?

"Can't you just kill the sea witch? I mean, how will he know?" Reymond asked, trying to soothe Dilian's stress.

"He will know. He has eyes everywhere."

"It doesn't matter, what's done is done," Ethera's eyes squinted in suspicion, her mind trying to fill out the potholes of her unanswered questions. The King had not only agreed but went out of his way to even offer more than what was demanded. He was surely hiding something—or worse, planning it.

Juno stepped forward, blocking the piercing gaze of the tavern keeper. "Let's not speak about this here," she reached out, lightly tapping Ethera on the shoulder. The pirate was wiping the tables, his eyes watching their every move. Everyone had forgotten about him due to the overwhelming presence of the King.

They quickly stepped out, and the fog seemed to evaporate into thin air abnormally fast, as if it had followed after the King wherever he went. The girls remained silent, too fearful to say anything. Every minute or so, they would glance up at Ethera to see if she was just as scared as they were.

Once the anger settled, only fear left standing. The young girl was terrified; to kill a sea witch with her bare hands would be no easy task.

She should have thought about it twice before agreeing, but alas, in the heat of the moment, there was nothing

127

but action. If this is all leading towards the prophecy, then that's what she must do, right?

Dilian led them out of the village in silence. "I will send a bird to the chief to start preparing a poison," he announced as soon as they entered the forest.

"Poison?" Ethera questioned.

"You lack physical strength, so poison will be the most effective weapon for you. You have a knack for talking yourself into 'favorable' situations, so I'm sure you'll be able to utilize the close distance to your advantage. After everything is done, you'll just have to cut the heart out," He made it sound so easy. Ethera hadn't even thought that far ahead. What he said bore some truth in it, but now she had to worry about how she was going to trick the sea witch into letting her guard down enough to get close.

She decided not to dwell on it; overthinking wouldn't do her any good. "What kind of poison will it be?"

Dilian thought, weighing the options in his mind. "We shall see. Nothing too complicated, perhaps something that can be transmitted through blood. Do you think you can manage that?" Ethera nodded in reply. Her mind constructed a vivid image of a witch with octopus tentacles roaring in the air, her own hand penetrating the woman with a knife.

She felt mental.

Dilian sighed. "That's why I warned you to let me handle the talking. I hope this serves as a lesson to you."

They hadn't even noticed how fast they suddenly appeared inside the forest until Dilian came to a stop, digging through one of his pouches and pulling out a piece of rough paper. He used Reymond's back as a flat and sturdy surface before proceeding to write a letter.

Rose shifted uncomfortably, trying to think positively. "Don't worry too much, guys. Once we get the heart, we'll have an advantage over him. Maybe we can keep it until the end of the war?"

Juno sat on the ground, stretching her legs that had gotten sore over the past few days. "There is no use in keeping it. He just wants proof of her death. But what use does he have for a heart? That's wildly specific to ask for something so disturbing."

"Maybe he has some kind of creepy collection for the hearts of his enemies," Rose added, shrugging her shoulders.

"The sea witch may be his enemy, but she is also his mother," Dilian reminded them. The chilling thought settled in their brains; they had totally forgotten about *that* part. No one could imagine killing their own mothers, or worse, having to cut the heart out. They all glanced at Ethera, who had also completely forgotten that one minor detail. But that did not change anything.

"I should be able to receive an answer by sunset and perhaps poison with it," Dilian whistled and went back to rolling up the piece of paper, written in a language they could not understand.

After a few seconds, a green bird flew in, its feathers flapping in the wind at an alarming pace. Flashes of yellow and blue flickered in front of their eyes. Reymond flinched, hiding behind Rose who simply rolled her eyes. The elf reached out, letting the bird sit on his fingers. It secured the note in between its beak and flew off just as fast as it appeared.

The walk back to their campsite was overwhelmed by silence, heavy breathing, and the loud thumps of Reymond's boots that overshadowed their own. Dilian had walked as quietly as a feather; not a single sound emerged from him. Ethera stared at his feet, trying to understand this phenomenon and replicate it to the best of her ability. His skinny dark leather boots were big; he was tall too, not as tall as the other elves, but with his constant straightened posture, he still managed to loom over everyone else. It made no sense as to how this big man walked so quietly.

Even with Ethera's own lace-up shoes, she found it hard to even sneak around discreetly.

Ever so often, Rose would look up from the ground and glance over at Ethera. She was walking ahead, falling behind by a few steps, as her eyes stared out into the distance with a stern, blank expression on her face. But her hands trembled, her fingers interlaced with each other to hide that fact.

Rose had seen it, guilt rushing over her. To take a life was no easy matter, physically and mentally. She took it upon herself to try to reassure her friend and give some kind of comfort, but every time she'd open her mouth to say something, she froze. Words could not form themselves, and it was laughable to even find the right sentence that could lift that heavy burden from Ethera's shoulders.

Dilian broke the silence once they had arrived, pulling the mortal away. "Ethera, I will show you some self-defense moves. Just in case things go south, let's also go over the plan." The elf turned to face her, and she nodded, aching to release her body's stress in some way. The rest of the mortals split up in half; some ventured off to gather firewood. Hugo stayed behind, instructed on lighting up the fire.

ↄ┼┼┼◌ ↄ┼┼┼◌ ↄ┼┼┼◌

Nightfall was only an hour away, and the bird had not returned. After Ethera finished her training session with Dilian, she was left in worse shape than before. Exhausted, and sparks of pain shot in different parts of her body. She had not expected brutality from Dilian, especially not when learning self-defense moves. But almost everything that he had taught her was counterattacks, nothing close to self-defense.

It so happened that counterattacks were the best way of protection in the elven world.

Her body had been exhausted beyond thought, and her mind had finally gone blank. The skirt was making it difficult for her to move with ease, seeing as how much trauma her body had been through. Much to her surprise, when she reunited with her friends an hour later, the fire had already settled down despite the red sun. The girls excitedly squealed when they saw Ethera, instantly jumping to her side and linking arms with her sweaty body.

131

They had found a lake nearby, and it was Rose's brilliant idea to go for an evening swim. The girls had drawn the longer straw, which meant they were first in line for a much-needed bath. They dragged Ethera away before she could even have a chance to sit down to rest her sore legs. Without hesitation, they began taking off their clothes.

Ethera looked away, embarrassed, trying to cover her body with her skinny hands. She couldn't recall the last time someone had seen her naked. A memory of her mother's face had crossed her mind, her eyes dropping down as she untied her shirt.

She quickly dove into the water with a splash, not wanting to think about something that wasn't there. The chill of the lukewarm water felt relaxing against her scorching body. This was what she had needed, and the shyness had completely melted away.

Rose and Juno also jumped in, causing a big wave to wash over Ethera. They giggled among themselves as their raptures had almost taken Ethera fully under. "Now this is refreshing," Rose sighed, leaning over a rock and facing upwards.

The sun had hidden behind the trees, and the chilly air was only going to grow from there. A shower is what they wanted, even if it meant taking it in the cold. The sun had warmed up the lake to some extent, but the coldness of the coming night was slowly creeping in.

Juno brushed through the short black strands of her hair, her fingers getting tangled. "I miss shampoos and conditioners," she cried, her eyes scrunching with her nose. Ethera watched her, wishing she too could have short hair.

She couldn't be bothered; her hair was like a bird's nest, uncontrollable but manageable on some days. Without any product, she could only predict how frizzy it would be when she got out, and brushing through it could send her into a spiral of aggravation.

"Ugh…and hot showers," added Rose when Ethera went under the water. Her hands interlaced through her hair all the way to the top of her roots before attempting to brush it through. She gave up halfway and swam up, taking a deep breath in.

It was pointless to even try.

She was overdue for a haircut; that much was certain.

Ethera paused, resting her back against a rock. "Do you think they are looking for us?" She asked the girls, and the change in conversation had completely shifted.

Rose remained silent, and so Juno spoke up. "Yeah, I'm sure they are," She tried to reassure them. Ethera looked away into the woods to hide the sour expression on her face. No one was looking for her; no one was waiting for her back home.

But she could almost imagine the articles swarming the news, maybe even making national headlines, FIVE TEENAGERS MYSTERIOUSLY VANISHED.

Her eyes widened at the thought. If her name is written in those newspapers with her yearbook picture plastered on every news station, then maybe her mother will see it.

Would she come back then?

"The whole town is probably out looking for us as we speak. I really hope Mr. Harris gets in trouble for leaving us unsupervised," Rose giggled to herself.

Ethera looked back, a mischievous glint in her eyes. "I would have paid to see that."

CHAPTER 10

Different shades of orange and blue filled the sky. Five figures sat on the edge of the cliff, enjoying the setting sun. No words had been spoken, but the comfort and tranquility in the air were more than enough.

Rose leaned over on Juno, her frizzy blonde hair falling over the short black strands. The wind blew past them, creating shiny ripples in the steady water below as it carried the saltiness over to the land..

The twins lay on their backs, gazing over the sky that stared back, a color so rich it was bewildering. The silent appreciation for nature had befallen them. The book was to thank for the phenomenon; if they hadn't stumbled into this enchanted world, filled with elves, pirates, and magical creatures, then they would have never known the invisible beauty that lurked in the background.

It has been two days since the letter was sent via bird, and for two days, the tension and worry grew bigger with every passing minute. Ethera, whose hair seemed to brighten in the sunlight, was trying her best to keep her head high and her nerves at bay. The struggles ahead were visible, but a speck of reassurance remained in the back of her mind.

This wasn't just for her. It was for everyone. Her friends, who were eager to get home, and the elves, who desperately wanted to take their land back. The prophecy clearly stated that she would sail across the sea with the Pirate King, and it is *fated* to happen. The demons and their army were bound to fall.

The how and the whys did not matter.

However, the prophecy did not say whether Ethera and her friends would be able to make it home safe and sound. It was self-explanatory; if they succeed, then there won't be any problems getting their hands on the book that will bring them back.

She still remembered that thrill of her entire body, mind, and soul overlapping with the book's light. Not to mention the feel of traveling through the specs of time and energy.

Reymond sat up suddenly, startling the rest. His ten minutes of silence were up. "Man! If only that old geezer didn't force Ethy to kill the sea witch, then we would have been sailing home by now!"

"Old? That man was nowhere close to old!" Rose bit back, throwing everyone's minds down memory lane. The Pirate King, with his tall and mighty self, a man with no blade, was young for someone who was King of all Kings.

Ethera turned her head over, looking over at her friends. "You know…I kind of thought he was going to be older. You're right, he is young looking for a pirate," she gulped, the thought of him sent shivers down her spine. His coy smile and soulless eyes felt like they were still on her, watching her every move. The temperature was freezing, even with the sun's warm embrace.

"Yeah, I kinda imagined long black hair, a mustache, a patch on his eye...oh yeah, and a hook!"

"Rose, you're literally describing Captain Hook from Peter Pan. There is no way a Pirate King would have a hook and a missing eye," noted Reymond.

"And why not? It's their battle scars. It makes them more intimidating."

Hugo sat up, crossing his legs before chiming in. "I'd say weaker than intimidating. That man had not a single scratch visible. It just means he is not to be underestimated."

The sun was barely visible now, a speck of light peeking out from the horizon. Ethera hadn't thought of this before, the appearance that defines character and strength. She wondered what the intelligent species here thought of her appearance.

A weak mortal? Or someone whose strength reflected in a prophecy guaranteeing the birth of a new era?

"Who would have guessed that a world like this existed? I mean, really—everyone would lose it if they found out that there are seven-foot elves, crazy scary mermaids, and blood-thirsty beasts running around?" Reymond babbled, his eyes widening. No one had really thought about the possibility of spilling the secrets of this world, but that was because they were busy trying to stay alive.

Hugo smiled, fixing his glasses. "They would definitely know you'd been smoking pot, Rey," he snickered, glancing at his twin.

"Speaking of pot—I wasn't going to tell you guys this, but our stress levels are so high right now, and I might have two blunts on me..." His voice trailed off, ending in nothing more than a whisper. He chuckled nervously, looking at his friends for their reactions.

When does Reymond Blake not have weed on him?

The two girls jumped in excitement as if the world had been getting boring without any sort of substance to spice things up. Hugo groaned; he was by no means a smoker. In fact, he had hoped that this vacation could sober up his brother.

Ethera had never done anything of that sort before.

Rose was on her feet in no time, appearing beside Reymond with sparkling eyes. "Oh my god! Yes! We should smoke some today when we make the fire and eat our dinner! This will be so fun, and hey! Maybe we can even get Dilian to hit a few and spill some secrets," she snickered mischievously. This caught Ethera's attention; her eyes lit up at the thought. Now that sounded like real fun.

"Are you guys in?" Juno asked the others who had been silently participating with their eyes.

Hugo got up, dusting off his maroon pants before looking down at Ethera. He offered his hand, which she accepted with a soft smile. "Yeah, I guess," he muttered under his breath. His reputation was precious to him, but here? In a world so far away from responsibilities and his parents, his so-called polished reputation did not exist. Reymond smiled evilly, throwing his hands around his little brother. Hugo attempted to dodge the attack, but Reymond was too quick for his own good. His eyes glared through his specs as he warned, "If you snitch to mom, I'll strangle you in your sleep."

"Done deal, lil bro."

"Ethera?"

"Yeah, I guess I'll give it a try."

They all skipped through the forest in a hurry; the thought had excited every one of them. Back at their campsite, Dilian had already begun preparing the wood, stacking it in the middle. He stopped halfway, his ears twitching when he sensed the presence of mortals inching closer and closer.

His short time of peace and quiet was interrupted too soon for his liking. "Back already?" He asked, irritable brows meeting in the middle without a single glance in their direction.

"Yes, we actually have a great idea-," the elf frowned, "would you like to smoke some magic grass with us? It's from our world, and before you ask—yes, it's completely natural and safe!"

The boy with the slit eyebrow beamed with happiness; he had been waiting for the right time to use them with his friends. After seeing the worrisome expression on the brunette's face for the past few days, he decided that now would be the perfect time to share.

"Mortals," sighed Dilian. "There is no such thing as magic grass in your world."

"How would you know? Are you from there? Nope. This is a different type of magic grass without any magic~."

"Then it is not magic grass if it has no magic. Do what you will, but leave me out of it," he snarled, shutting down the idea completely. He went back to stacking firewood, the loose strands of his hair falling.

The group watched in anticipation, everyone beaming with excitement, but not because they were doing something they shouldn't have, but because the symbolism of it represented home. They had limited things on them, mostly their clothes, phones that were left behind at the Elvenwood, or Rose's lip oil that she tried to use in moderation.

The sun had fully sunk below the horizon, and the sky had begun to dim. Dilian pulled out two rocks from his leather pouch and, with one swift motion, sparked the tinder. The dry leaves and small twigs caught the embers instantly, slowly spreading and tainting the rest of the wood. It transformed into a beautiful, large flame resembling the once setting sun.

They huddled to sit around it, their faces glowing in its light, waiting patiently for what was about to come. The elf disappeared into the forest, instructing the humans to remain within the circle.

"Hey, what happened to 'ladies first'?" Rose wailed, watching Reymond take a hit. He inhaled the soul out of it, keeping it in his mouth for a few seconds before blowing it out.

His eyes closed, his mind getting lost in nostalgia. It felt like it had been twenty years since he had enjoyed the aftertaste in his tongue and mouth. "Girl, please. I've been waiting patiently for this moment, so let me have it," he croaked before letting out a loud groan. "I've been sober long enough."

He proceeded to take another before passing it on. The second one he had given to his brother, who cluelessly held it with all three fingers in the air. He watched patiently for Hugo to take a hit. His inexperienced twin burst into violent coughs that echoed through the forest.

Reymond let out a laugh, muffling the coughs of the mortal boy. "Don't smoke more than you can handle, lil bro."

Hugo cleared his throat, one hand covering his mouth. "Call me lil bro one more time, and I'm throwing it into the pit," he snarled, his brother holding his hands up in defense. Ethera reached out, grabbing the roll from Hugo. Reymond had finally let go of his, passing it to Rose, who stomped the ground excitedly with the soles of her sneakers.

They went around, one by one, chit-chatting among themselves until Dilian returned. His hands gripped six sticks that penetrated dead fish.

"Hmm, salmon! How healthy," cheered Juno.

"God, no wonder their skin is so clear. All they eat is fruit, veggies, and fish!" Complained Rose, her eyes drifting to watch Dilian. He bent down on one knee in front of the pit, his sleeves rolled up as he stuck the sticks into the dirt at an angle, surrounding the fire. His white hair was tied back, and the ponytail rested on his shoulders, running all the way down to his waist.

His hair drowned with light in the dimming sky, a silk so shiny it reminded them of a spider web. Pointy pale ears poked through, he had no use in putting them away. Rose stared at him with jealousy; the elven beauty was truly on another level.

Out of nowhere, Reymond let out a loud groan, tilting his head upwards. "I want a cheeseburger," he announced. They fell silent, imagining the juicy and tender burger. He broke the silence by adding to his order. "And a side of fries. With a sprite, of course."

"I miss orange juice," moaned Rose. Ethera didn't have anything to miss, but her thoughts did drift towards the garden in her backyard. No doubt the sprouting vegetables were half-dead from lack of water. It seemed that the harvest would be late next season.

For the first time in a while, Ethera felt normal. Like a normal rebellious high schooler doing something she should not have, despite their unique circumstances. She could only wish that this moment could last a little bit longer.

Juno flung her black hair out of her face, wishing she had a hair clip to tie the small strands back. "You know, I would have never imagined us getting along like this. I still feel like I might wake up any second and find out this is all a dream," she blurted out. There was truth in that. Rose and Juno belonged in a different hierarchy from the rest. They were known as the 'cool kids' who always had a horde of people surrounding them wherever they went.

Reymond was part of the stoner skater kids, but because of his spot on their football team, he became quite well known, even though he, himself, did not know it. Hugo always surrounded himself with the smartest kids in class, and Ethera was just a loner. Quite the breakfast club mix.

"Not my fault, you guys are total losers."

Hugo tilted his head, rolling his eyes. "We are not losers, your kind just thinks it's better than the rest of us," he snapped.

Rose snorted, her brows pulling upwards. "Please… all your *kind* talks about are test answers and homework sheets during lunch. If I were to hang out with you and your nerdy buddies, I'd be asleep in three minutes."

Ethera nodded. "She's not wrong."

"And you—you walk around like you are a know-it-all and a better version of everyone else. That's why we didn't get along before," Rose pointed at Ethera. The blonde's honesty showed on her face despite the finger disappearing behind the blazing fire.

"She's not wrong. But Ethera is the reason why we got out of that cell, didn't get killed by his people, and figured out how to get to the Pirate King. She is better," admitted Hugo, his glossy eyes looking over everyone's faces. Even Dilian had stopped to listen to the conversation; his hand lingered on one of the sticks with a sizzling fish above. It seemed that human problems were pointless and foolish, but he dared not start an argument with them over that. He immediately continued, realizing he had gotten lost in their conversation again.

"That's true…"

Ethera immediately shook her hands in front of her. "Come on, guys, no one is better than anyone here. I just know more about things like that," she quickly assured.

Dilian scoffed, his ears twitched. "You should write us a ledger on how to anger the Pirate King," the elf chimed in without thinking, his ears turning pink upon realizing.

Ethera dropped her head, resting it on her knees. Her fingers played with the thin fabric of the inner layer of her skirt. "There isn't much of a tutorial for that. People in power always assume they are the strongest in the world. And so, I just focused on threatening his ego, I guess? I don't think a calm and rational approach would have worked on that man." She laughed dryly, forgetting that her next task would be the slaughter of his mother. For a brief couple of minutes, the worries about it had completely faded into the background.

"You got this, Ethera. We believe in you. Even though we won't be there to help you physically, just know that we are waiting for you on the other side," finally, Rose let out the words that were lingering in her throat. She nervously looked away, her ears turning pink.

After a moment of silence, she glanced back to look at Ethera's stunned face that had lifted to face the blonde; the words were like a giant truck ramming itself into her heart. Enough to make her want to cry. She quickly shook off that feeling, not wanting to embarrass herself, but the bitter taste lingered on her tongue.

"We'll be there in spirit. Like ghosts, type shit."

Rose groaned aloud, furious eyes threw daggers at Reymond. "You will be if you don't shut the fuck up for once," she roared in anger, the cute heartfelt moment ruined by the idiotic words of a stoner.

"T-Thanks, guys," Ethera quickly said, not wanting a fight to break out. "This really means a lot."

"Aww, don't go crying on us, Ethy!"

144

"Who's crying? Who made Ethera cry?" Juno finally snapped back to the Thalorin Forest after getting lost in the fire.

"Our Ethy is about to cry. Ooo~."

Ethera's face heated up, her eyes felt dry. "Stop. I'm not crying!"

Reymond pointed at her dramatically. "Then what is that? A tear!"

"That's it, I'm hitting him," Rose groaned, rushing to her feet.

"Enough saying meaningless words and wasting the night's fresh air," Dilian interrupted. He had been watching the food slowly beginning to sizzle in the flame.

"Get a load of this guy, what a party pooper!"

Rose sighed. "Ugh, I'm trying…"

The class fell silent, their eyes hanging on to the blonde.

"What the fuck?"

"What? He's kinda cute. He sorta looks like my ex from freshman year. They have the same forehead, don't you think?" She rambled, drawing everyone's attention to Dilian.

"Whoa! Those things are glowing in the dark!" Reymond pointed again, while the others held on to his stomach for dear life.

Dilian's ears turned a dark shade of pink. "Hold your tongue!" He suddenly yelled out, standing up on his feet. His eyes immediately scanned the dark forest ahead, his arm lifted to silence the humans. "Remain still," he ordered.

They all quietly looked around. Rose's fingers found its way to Juno's. Ethera peeked over Dilian's tall frame, trying to see what he had spotted in the distance.

The forest was quiet, not a single sound emerged from the darkness. They knew that elves had better hearing, vision, and instinct. So, naturally, whatever that was out there, only Dilian would be able to sense.

Slowly, he turned to them. "Do you hear that?"

"No, what is it?" Reymond whisper-yelled, ready to get up on his feet and run.

The elf paused, eyes darting to the human boy. "It's the sound of you shutting the fuck up," Dilian whispered, straightening his proud posture and sitting back down. The smile on his face moved in sync with his ears. Their stiff, frozen bodies melted, their hearts beat to the sound of the school orchestra.

"Jesus…"

Ethera sighed in relief. "Well, he's adapting to our way of speaking…" she pointed out.

"Hardly," he barked back, not liking the sound of that at all.

"Yeah, you are, buddy. We are all friends now," Reymond cooed.

Dilian shook his head, gritting his teeth at Reymond. "I refuse."

"We are like best friends!"

"No, we are not."

"The best of best friends," Reymond continued, teasing the elf whose ears only darkened. The mortal boy continued, wondering if perhaps he could be the next discoverer

146

of a mystical shade of red. "Soul-tied," he continued, ignoring the elf's protests.

"I would rather sever my soul than be friends with you."

The group gasped dramatically.

"Ouch."

Ethera shook her head. "That was too far."

"Oh…I a-apologize."

"God, he takes everything so seriously." Another round of laughs erupted yet again. Dilian had long given up. He sat back down with a face as red as a crab, returning his undivided attention to the fish and wishing that it was him right now.

"We still have some left, you're welcome to take a hit," Reymond reached out, extending his hand and offering a little bit of what was left. The smoke swirled in the air with the scent of damp earth and citrus peel. Dilian's eyes hovered at the offer, battling the urge to try something that did not belong to this world.

His pride held him back. "I refuse."

"Why? Are you scared?" The curly-haired boy taunted.

Dilian's face scrunched in disgust. "Scared? Quit screwing nonsense," the elf denied.

"What? You think you're better than us or something?" Ethera asked, her eyes sparkling with an obvious taunt. Hugo and Juno had caught on immediately, their eyes watching the show unfold before them.

"Were you born with a lousy mouth?"

"Yeah, I got it from my mother. What about yours? Did she warn you to stay far away from the big, bad humans and all of our dangerous little temptations, right? Our way of speaking, our behavior, and let's not forget our scary, corrupting weed," she grinned, leaning forward, voice slowing. "You must be so proud of yourself. Babysitting the naughty sinners, carrying out your noble elf duty. What a good little elf you are——."

"Oh, would you be quiet," shouted Dilian, yanking the bud from Reymond's hand. He mumbled something along with the words of 'how', but the mortal's anticipation completely muffled out his voice. Their smiles grew the closer the elf got. Without much warning, Dilian had placed his lips upon it and almost swallowed the entire bud from the breath that he had inhaled. He coughed out viciously, much louder than Hugo did. It took him a delayed second or two before he spat it out.

It landed in the fire, and Reymond's and Rose's laughter merged into a chorus of no's. "Did you see his face—HA!"

Dilian immediately downed all his water, eyes tearing at what had just happened. Whatever the humans were up to—it was deadly to elves.

The laughter soon faded, replaced by the mouth-watering scent of cooked fish that curled with the smoke from the fire. One by one, they all fell silent, lulled by the crackle of the wood and the melodic sound of crickets in the distance. Teeth bit into the fish's flesh, and the sound of someone chewing filled the air with the occasional sparkle and hiss of the flames.

148

Dilian's ears twitched, hearing the wail of an animal far away. His enhanced sense of hearing was a blessing—and a curse. This meant that the heavy sounds coming from Reymond's mouth in the middle of the night sounded like an alarm blasting on speaker.

Dilian couldn't even count how many times he wished to strangle that mortal boy and dump his corpse elsewhere, away from the camp that had been their temporary home for the past few nights.

He missed his real *home*, not the Thalorin Forest. The home that was taken away by the demons. The bark within the once Enchanted Forest was made of magic. The thickness of the wood could prevent sound from coming in, allowing the elves their rest and peace. The Thalorin Forest did not have such trees, and the ones they used to rebuild their homes acted like a mere sheet over the chaos.

Thus, the elves became weaker. Without the proper rest and the magic of the Enchanted Forest, their bodies became sullen and fragile. The wounds sometimes took weeks to heal, the cells slowly sewing themselves in reverse.

They became *human*.

It was useless to train as much as they used to; their ability to recover fast was reduced the more the body used its supernatural energy. The children grew slower, and the elders could barely walk, forcing their time to draw nearer with every passing day.

They had to rely on medicine made of herbs of all kinds. It relieved illnesses—something that had become new to elves.

The village fell into desperation. The autumn moon-light was only twenty full moons away, and if those born under the leaf did not bask in the night's light within the Enchanted Forest, their bodies would not develop recovery and enhanced abilities.

Their lifespan would be cut short to that of a mayfly. Born only to vanish before the kiss of the next moon. Human or elf, both species, were desperate to find their way home for different reasons.

Hugo swallowed his food, glancing at the elf who had already finished eating. "Dilian, how old are you?" He asked, and the sudden question seemed to take everyone by surprise.

Dilian was shocked; they hadn't asked much about him personally, only about his species. "One hundred and sixty-seven," he said proudly, and everyone's eyes fell out of their sockets.

Ethera was the first to snap out of it, trying to do an impossible math equation in her head. "You're really old!" She gasped, looking over at Rose, who gave her a disgusted look.

The elf reached to toss another log into the fire. Sparks flew upwards into the night's sky. "How long is your lifetime?" Dilian asked, showing interest in human life.

Ethera shrugged, not knowing the answer to his question. "Like anywhere from sixty to ninety." She was sure that their state's average was like seventy-four.

"That's very...little."

"I guess? What is your people's life span?"

"Six hundred," he replied proudly yet again. Ethera didn't know how someone could live for that long and not get bored. She could only guess that maybe in a magical world, it wouldn't have been that bad.

Her eyes widened. "That's a lot. A-And how old is the chief?"

"Chief is five hundred and ninety-three," Dilian's expression lowered, hiding a hint of sadness that Ethera could see all too well.

She shifted uncomfortably, eyes looking at her peers who were having a conversation on their own. "Is he coming to the end of his lifetime?" She asked softly, looking back to the white-haired elf.

He lifted his head, and deep emeralds met hers. "It is the circle of elven life."

He had buried his displeasure and grief. Elves did not fear death—it was simply their way. He had known the chief from the moment Dilian had fallen and sprouted from his autumn leaf. The chief had gifted the child the name *Dilian*, he who walked between dawn and dusk.

At least once in their lifetimes, elves would step in to take care of the little ones born under the autumn moon and present them with their names that defined their character.

The chief was like a father to Dilian, even though the concept of parents did not exist in their world. They were all children of autumn—children of the forest, some older and wiser, others innocent and naive. It was the elven way.

The war had to come to an end, or else his clan would cease to exist. Dilian's desperate gaze fell back to the mortal

151

girl. The ocean and the dirt were set ablaze in the fire that reflected his everything.

CHAPTER 11

By the time the sun rose again, they were gone. The laughter from the night before was nothing more than a fleeting memory, and with every step, Ethera had to remind herself to calm her racing heart.

Her time to shine was coming closer with every passing hour.

She had to kill a sea witch, and then cut out her heart, *no biggie.* The poison that they had acquired was going to do all the work for her; all she had to do was get close enough to prick the witch with the dagger.

The chilling sea witch straight out of the Little Mermaid, a half-woman and half-octopus manifestation had haunted her mind even in her waking hours. But in truth, no one knew what this woman looked like. Even Dilian's limited information provided by the chief was not enough to put everyone's mind at ease. If she was anything like her son, then it would undoubtedly make it harder to kill her.

Ethera didn't think she could kill a human, even if the said human was a witch. The courage vanished, and a siren-like beauty with long black hair lingered in her mind. The mortal's hand twitched, as if the urge to grab the knife that rested against her hip was going to put her own heart at ease.

How inhumane the situation had become. Even as she stood separated from the rest, staring into the distant trees, her eyes widened as her heart sank into the pits of her stomach. Even the cold water could not relieve the dryness of her throat.

The witch's cave was half a day's walk from the Pirate's Lagoon, and much to Dilian's displeasure, the humans were not in the mood to sightsee. But with the sound of their nervous heartbeats and the uncomfortable silence, he began to realize what exactly he preferred more. His ears had twisted themselves, paralleling the ground beneath. He couldn't help but listen to the melody of despair that was orchestrated by their hearts and feet. And even now, when they had arrived, the sound just kept growing louder, making it difficult for him to focus.

Ethera strolled closer to the cliff, staring down at the violent waves crashing below. Somewhere underneath was the entrance to the cave. Too high to reach from the sea and too far to climb from above.

It was impossible to get to. One wrong step and she could fall. Her lifeless body will undoubtedly wash up on the King's ship, as a present from the sea for daring to cross him.

Ethera's brows furrowed. It made sense that the sea witch's whereabouts were unknown to the King, he who had seized control over the ocean. With hollow eyes peering over every nook and cranny, he stood idly, watching every fish and wave that dared to disturb his waters.

His mother had used that knowledge against him, hiding in plain sight away from enemies who roamed the land and the ungrateful son who ruled the one thing she had known her whole life. The sea.

That man's vicious face and coy smile crept up from behind Ethera's pile of worries. His hands had wrapped themselves around her throat, clutching the life out of her.

She suddenly felt faint.

He was watching her right now. There was no way he'd miss out on his all-time favorite show that was now starring, Ethera Heart on 'Self-disposable Sea Waste'. He was certain she would fail, which made her even more eager to prove him wrong.

"Place your leg through here and grip the rope firmly. Distribute your balance, or you'll find yourself swinging when we lower you down," explained Dilian, his fingers interlaced with a rope that he was testing. It was a fifty-foot drop from the edge of the cliff, and they had no choice but to wipe the pirate village clean of rope.

It was sturdy, but the realization of it all had finally settled in. Fear had morphed into anger. Life was not easy for Ethera, even in another world.

Dilian handed the end of the rope to Reymond, who was first in line. Behind him was Hugo, followed by Juno, and Rose. The closest tree was too far, and the only way they could secure Ethera's safety was with their own hands.

The elf had given his hand to Ethera, and the mortal took it without hesitation. She rotated her body, preparing to put her right leg through the loop that Dilian had made.

She quickly stopped, backing away from the edge. "G-Give me your pouch," she demanded, her words stuttering in her mouth.

"What for?" His head cocked to the side, ears twitching to the sound of drums.

"Where else am I going to put the heart? I'm not carrying that shit in my hand!" He sighed; his hand dropped to the side before pulling out a thin cotton-like pouch. He emptied its contents on the ground beside him before passing it on. Her fingers tips shook as she wrapped it around her leather belt, tightening it so it won't meet its doom. Ethera had left her own pouches of food and water behind, along with her cloak and tricorn. She felt lighter despite the drowning pressure. "Alright, let's get this over with."

"Should you fall, rest assured that there are no rocks beneath. Your survival is reasonably high."

She scoffed, holding back the urge to roll her eyes. "My heart might not make it," she breathed out, eyes glued to the waves beneath. "If you guys let go of the rope, *your* survival will be reasonably low," she hissed, looking back at her friends. She tried to smile, but it came out more timid than confident.

Ethera took one look over the cliff, taking a deep breath before squatting down. One hand gripped Dilian's arm, and the other tried to grasp onto any possible dent in the dirt. She swung her right foot through the hole, her left dangled off the cliff, reminding her of the potential death circling her like sharks beneath the surface.

Her only safety harness had just let go of her, and a sharp gust of wind had caused her body to rock. She yelped out, grabbing at the rope with both hands while shutting her eyes. Her fingers gripped each other abnormally tight; the white of her knuckles stained her hands red.

"Are you well?"

"Yep...*just peachy*," she breathed out, voice shaking as much as her body. The elf's worry was making her feel uneasy; the reassurance from a few minutes ago had completely vanished.

"Let's pull her up. I can't do this." It was Rose. Her voice was muffled with the distance, but the concern was more than audible.

"No, no, you're good. I'm good...just lower me down slowly please," she hesitated, her body wanted out, but her mind couldn't. The rope started swaying, dropping her down with slow but sudden movements that caused her to break out in sweat. The wind was howling, with the waves below like beasts waiting to consume her.

Her hands had turned to ice, solid against the rope. The wind sent chills down her spine, and the little droplets of sweat against her forehead felt like they were hardening the lower she went.

Ethera wanted to cry, for the first time in a long time. This was a nightmare; it couldn't have been real. In a second, she would wake up in her cabin, wrapped in fluffy blankets, and pretend that all of this was just something her mind made up to torment her.

But no matter how many seconds she counted as she swung side to side, or how hard she bit her tongue, she did not wake up.

The torture felt like it was never going to end, and her right foot began cramping under the pressure of her weight, reminding her of how real this was. Her other leg felt stiff and numb, much like the rest of her body.

The only warmth was that of her mouth. She huffed at her frozen fingertips just to keep her mind occupied, but the hot air was quick to be swept away by the wind.

Her eyes remained shut for her own peace of mind. The lids fluttered open every few seconds just to make sure that she did not miss the cave's entrance. The moment she spotted it, they stood wide, fixated on the gaping hole in the cliff's side. She feared it would disappear if she stayed cooped up in her dreams of home.

The lowering of the rope came to an abrupt stop. Ethera forced herself to look up, worried that something might have gone wrong on her friends' side. The realization left her feeling powerless; they must have run out of rope to use, leaving her dangling midair.

She glanced back down, her left leg stretched out painfully, trying to reach for the ground below. There was no use, it was too high.

Her inhales caught in her throat; a foolish decision dangled along with her. Ethera used her body weight to swing forward and backward, mustering enough momentum. She scrunched her eyes closed, pushing herself forward as she jumped. Her stiff body crashed to the ground, unable to catch herself quickly enough to break the fall.

A gasp escaped her chapped lips, her lungs overcoming a piercing stab at her side. She lay as rigid as a rock, pain shooting from different parts of her muscles. Pebbles dug at her palms and elbows as they shook with the sudden impact. She pushed from one side, rolling her body onto her back.

The shadows of the cave were reaching overhead, high above from where she could see, reminding her where she was, and how little time she had to mop around. Her tongue swept across her blue lips; a crooked smile tugged at her pale cheeks.

Sitting up was difficult, but the dimness of the cave had no sign of light within and thus frightened her into motion. With a grunt, she pushed herself upwards, stumbling forward as her legs adjusted to her own weight.

This was it. The battle she had to face was consumed by darkness, and it reminded her that there was someone better suited for this.

An elf would have landed on its feet. And Dilian would have already been on his way up.

Her own shadow had stretched short on the dirt in front of her as she wiped bits of blood on the skirt. For once she felt grateful, the layered fabric cushioned her knees and saved her from worse pain.

Little pieces of grass grew between the rocks, and moss sprouted in the most unlikely places across the walls. Dead vines escaped to the edges of the cave, and alive ones lingered within. They stretched out as far as she could see, tempting her to come in.

She took a few steps closer, pausing and waiting for her eyes to adjust to the darkness. Had she known it was going to be this big, she would have borrowed Dilian's rocks to at least start a fire.

Maybe even kill the witch with a good old carbon monoxide poisoning.

She glanced back nervously, making sure that the rope was still there. It swung side to side with an ominous energy surrounding it.

Ethera couldn't possibly see how someone could be living here. There was nothing but rocks inside, and the deeper she walked, the harder it became to breathe. The knife was already gripped by her right hand, and the shaking had long stopped as if her body gave up on warning her.

She had to be careful with it; the blade was already dripping with poison.

There was no way she could sneak in and kill the witch with the amount of noise she had already made no matter how quietly she tried to walk. Her shoes scrunched against the dirt, the sound carried deeper into the cave. The disappearing light played a faulty part in her plan.

It was time for a different approach. *An Ethera approach.*

"Hello? Is there anyone there?" She called out, the knife that had been drawn in front of her now rested at her side, a subtle attempt to conceal her wary demeanor.

No one answered. The mortal's heart began to beat faster with every cautious step she took forward. "My name is Ethera Heart. I am lost, and I'm not from this world. I came here with my friends, and we are trying to find our way back," she began without expecting a reply. The woman was there; Ethera could feel it in the air, just the way the King's aura had dangerously paralyzed everyone's body back in the tavern. This witch hidden within the shadows of the cave was just as sinister as the one she had birthed.

There was no answer for what felt like an excruciating long time. But alas the sea witch made herself known. "I do not have powers anymore, foolish girl," the witch's raspy voice echoed in the cave, not allowing Ethera to pinpoint her location.

"He stole them from you—did the Pirate King stripped you of your powers?" Ethera asked, her mind outracing her heart. A sea witch with no powers, hidden from the King who wants her dead. But the question remained, *why*?

"What do you know of the Pirate King?" She roared, causing Ethera's ears to wince. She could only imagine the cave crumbling above her and crushing her to death from the quake released of the sea witch's anger.

She needed to stop imagining pointless shit before the real deal sneaks up and kills her first. The mortal hesitated, not knowing how to bring forth the truth to this dark place. "I came to make a deal with you that will get you your powers back," she said, confidence echoing in the hollow cave.

The witch fell silent, seemingly contemplating the words of a powerless girl. Shockingly enough, one has shown up on her front porch. "Go on." The witch ordered, intrigued by the words of a human.

"I am part of a prophecy that will stop the war and bring back the Enchanted Forest to its people. I need to sail across the Crimson Waters, but we cannot do that if the water is infested with monsters being controlled by the Pirate King. If I kill the Pirate King, then you can take back your powers and allow us to sail safely. We need to defeat the demons so me and my friends can go home," exclaimed Ethera, her voice almost begging.

The witch scoffed. "The Pirate King will not let you near him."

"He already has, and he's expecting me to return with your heart," Ethera gulped nervously, as if the King could sense her betrayal.

"Are you a fool?" She broke into a dry laugh, her voice sounding as if she hadn't spoken in years.

"I'm just thinking—how can I trust a man who is bound to die soon? What if he drops dead before we even make it halfway through? Then what? We all drown and become monster food?" The mortal rambled; her posture relaxed despite the darkness creeping towards her. The thought of that filthy pirate added fuel to her already existing anger.

"What exactly are you saying? That he's bound to die soon?" The witch's voice had fallen closer, so close that Ethera almost jumped out of her skin.

The sea witch was standing next to her, observing her with eyes of spilled ink. The woman's black hair immediately reminded Ethera of the Pirate King. Her hair was tangled like overused ropes, with cuts and split ends growing in every direction. It looked like seaweed, with not an ounce of volume. And she was wet, dripping salt water from the top to the bottom of her frail body.

Where did the water come from? Ethera tried not to think about the physics of it all as danger stared back at her.

The woman was tall; her genes did not falter. She was draped in a moss-like dress that dragged behind her when she walked closer. The once witch had been transformed into a dying beauty, with her skeleton-like pale body that stretched tight over her bones. Ethera could only imagine how divine she must have been before her son had forced her into hiding, living out her days in a cave that constantly over-looked the sea, which she was not allowed to touch.

Killing this woman somehow seemed impossible now.

Ethera took a deep breath, snapping herself out of her fixated trance. "There is a prophecy that hints at his death but does not tell us how or when. It's only an assumption, but it will happen soon. I just worry he will die before grant-ing us safe passage across the ocean. For all I know, he might be conspiring with the demons behind our backs. But if you had his powers, you could regain your control over the ocean and help us! When all this is over, my friends and I will get to go home, and you'll have your old life back." It was a sweet deal even in the woman's mind, and for a second Ethera caught her gaze shift into the distance behind. The water and the sea whispered for her.

But the woman was no fool to fall prey to another.

Her eyes instantly snapped back. "A daring bluff, mortal, but that knife says otherwise. You've come to kill me, haven't you? All because of that bastard son of mine," the woman inched closer, her eyes and head tilting towards the knife. If Ethera were to swing now, would she miss? Her hand hesitated.

163

"What makes you think I will come down all the way here to talk to a sea witch without a knife? I don't know who you are; for all I know, you could try to kill me if you wanted to."

"And that I shall." Suddenly, the witch leaped at the girl, her skeleton-like gray fingers reaching out towards the live meat. Ethera found herself on the ground, losing balance from the sudden push. The knife had fallen out of her hand, and when she tried to reach for it, the sea witch had grabbed her by the arm, her sharp nails pierced through the skin.

Ethera let out a scream. "I thought we might be able to help each other!"

The woman growled, her mouth opening in a sinister smile. "Nothing personal, dear, I'm just so hungry. And human meat is quite ravishing. And my son…well I can always take my power back after he drops dead. As a thank you for the information, I will make this quick," she licked her lips, eyes growing wide at the temptation. Ethera kicked her legs, trying to get the witch off her, and all while desperately reaching for the knife.

Her wounded arm stretched out, the skin tearing itself with scorching pain. It seemed like Dilian's self-defense class was useless. In the heat of the moment, her brain had completely erased everything that she was taught. It had become instinct rather than strategy.

Ethera dodged another attack, this one directed at her face. A sudden cut split across her cheek, drawing out the crimson color of her blood. With both legs working in sync, the mortal managed to gather just enough force to kick the witch to the side.

Not wasting any time, Ethera dived for the knife with both hands, ignoring the burning sensation in her body and the slight tingle on her cheek. The adrenaline had masked all the pain within and the thoughts in her mind had evaporated into the hot air surrounding them.

The sea witch stumbled up, and before she could gather her strength to attack the girl again, Ethera's knife dug into the side of the witch's back. The mortal's hands immediately let go, stumbling backwards towards the light. Her eyes watched in horror as the woman dug out the dagger, tossing it somewhere behind.

The sound echoed in the cave, overlapping the witch's huffing. "A fool is what you will die as. A blade will not—you cannot kill…" She paused, glancing down at the injury before her trembling gaze landed on the shaking mortal.

The knife had been poisoned; the witch should have known better than to underestimate the insatiable hand of mankind.

With a thud, she had dropped to the ground. Her knees buckled underneath her, fingers clawed at the dirt in an attempt to gather any strength she could muster. She did not dare attack Ethera, instead she inched closer as if she wanted to go back. As if the sea was calling at her return.

The woman's eyes sparkled in what little light was left in them before her heart finally shunned her resistance. Her head slowly dropped against the ground, silence fell inside the cave once again.

The body had gone limp; the witch was dead.

Ethera did it. She had actually *killed* the sea witch.

165

Her body trembled with victory. She turned away, allowing her eyes to be drawn to the light.

It was self-defense, right? The witch had attacked first, and Ethera had to act fast to survive. But she was a fool; in what world was that self-defense? Trespassing into someone else's home with the intent to kill—even someone as sinister as a sea witch, it was still, by all means, murder.

A thief and now a murderer. This was what Ethera Heart had become.

Without allowing herself time to dwell on her misdeeds, she walked back towards the dead body. Dropping down to her knees, her own shaky hands grabbed the frail woman by the shoulders before turning her around.

The woman's eyes were open, staring into the abyss. Death had taken her, and yet her eyes looked no different. Ethera took out another knife, hidden in her skirts, not wanting to make contact with the poison that still lingered on the other.

She raised the blade, stabbing the woman in the middle of her chest. It was easier than she would have thought, cutting out a heart out of flesh that was already half decayed. The horrid smell filled the stuffy cave, not allowing her room to breathe. Forcibly gulping down her stomach, she continued, closing her eyes before digging her hand into the woman's rib cage.

It was not necessary to rob a woman of her heart. And the Pirate King knew that. This was the ultimate price for challenging him.

Her trembling fingers slipped through with ease, swallowed by the cold red blood. Ethera froze, fingers brushing what she assumed was the woman's ribs, and there, beyond the stench, the pus, and the sound that followed, was a rushing rhythm she recognized too well. She flinched away, her eyes clenched as she forced herself to get it over with. Ethera was running out of air, and the body around her hand tightened, not wanting to give away the pulsing muscle. She quickly, yanking it out, a loud crack echoed in the cove.

Her other hand, free of blood and sin, carelessly held the pouch that Dilian had given her. She opened her eyes, trying to see through the tears that threatened to spill. The job was done and the heart was safely secured in the pouch, its crimson color slowly staining it. She took out a piece of cloth that Juno's gave her, and mercilessly, began to wipe her hands.

She couldn't hold it any longer—her body threw up, forcing out the breakfast from earlier. The vivid images flashed through her mind as if she'd watched the whole thing.

Her senses betrayed her, filling out the purposeful holes in her memory. The stench was overwhelming, and it was not just around her; it was on her.

Ethera's fingers were stained a bloody maroon hue, smudged with black dirt and no matter how hard she wiped, it did not fade. After some time, she had finally risen, trailing away from the body and her own breakfast. All the blood rushed to her head, making her stumble deeper into the cave, hands clutched the rocks for support. Her fingers traced them, masking the feel with a new sensation. It had gotten darker; even with her eyes adjusted to its dimness, she could barely see.

The cave had come to a dead end, transforming it into what looked like a home. A bed made of sticks and grass sat in the corner of the tiny opening, a silk blanket hung over it. Different kinds of trinkets were mounted on the rocks above—some she recognized as dream catchers made of corals; others were twigs tied together with string to form tainted sigils.

Glass cans filled with bones, powder, and herbs sat neatly on one of the rocky shelves. Scattered across the table below were numerous torn pages with scribbles in an ancient language. A small collection of books lay next to it, some opened, and others stacked on top of each other, with shell bookmarks sticking out.

Ethera reached out to grab an open one, words were circled all over it with different messy scribbles highlighted on the sides. There was only one word that stood out, something that even a human with no place in this world could understand. Her fingertip traced over it, eyes squinting to get a better confirmation.

Magick.

There could be spells in there, something that might prove to be useful. Ethera ended up stashing two small books in between the corset and the leather belt that sat around her hips. She was in no rush, now that her mind had calmed, and she would have kept exploring if it wasn't for the sudden gush of wind and the smell of seawater that had set off alarms in her head.

She dashed out of the witch's home to get a better look at the situation. The water had begun to fill up the cave, and the witch's body was already coated in the waves of the sea, like blankets trying to comfort the soul of the departed. Ethera could not believe her eyes; the sea had begun to rise, and the thought had not crossed her mind. It couldn't possibly be evening already; she hadn't been here for that long, or had she?

The strength with which the water swept in had almost knocked her off her feet. She pushed through, no time to hesitate. The rope was swinging on the other side, the waves barely missing it as it awaited the mortal's arrival.

She began walking towards it, dragging her feet along the ground as the waves threatened her balance yet again. Another one came in, this one larger than the small ripples that had caused enough trouble as it was.

In a second, Ethera went under. Struggling was pointless; she could not withstand the force of the wave. Her shoulder made contact with something hard, and air bubbles escaped through her teeth.

Finally making it out with a mouth full of seawater, she spat it out, coughing wildly. Her eyes darted back to the water, crawling backwards in an attempt to get away. It had risen to a dangerous level; vicious waves had begun to claw their way towards her. They roared in anger; the sea was disgusted with the mortal's actions and had made it its mission to drown her.

She got up, running back to meet the dead end of the witch's cove. Her dress was soaked with pounds of water, slowing her down. With every step, the resisting force pulled her back towards the waves.

Ethera's eyes squinted, her shaky hands drawn in front of her as if feeling the wall would somehow help her see it better. Bits of light reflected into the cave through the water, but it was no use, she could not see properly. The water was dangerously inching closer with every beat of her heart.

The ceiling of the cave had dissolved into the shadows, but a patch of blackness stood out. The texture caught her eye. It was an opening or a subtle dent in the ceiling but that she could not tell. Her fingers gripped at the rocks and with a quick motion, she leaped towards what she assumed was the exit. The boost did nothing as her shoe pressed on the hem of her skirt causing her to fall forward. Her forehead hit the rock roughly, and her brain froze for a split second.

A sudden yelp left her mouth, feeling startled at the sudden contact of water against her ankle. Her eyes eagerly looked back, scanning through everything but the possibility of survival. Her second attempt was just as bad as the first; her hands slipped against the moss, staining her fingernails green. There was no time to come up with a plan; she'd die by the time she thinks of something.

Rock climbing was definitely not her forte but that seemed to be the only way out.

Ethera tried again, slowly this time. One leg at a time, one hand at a time. It was impossible; she had no grip to support her weight. There was nothing to hold on to. "Shit, shit, shit...FUCK!" She yelled, slamming a fist into the rock dramatically. There was no way she was going to die after doing this. After taking another's life. Was this karma? Had it finally caught up to her.

Pulling away, she shook her hand, ignoring the pain and the rocks that seemed to smile in the darkness. She would have started cussing again if it hadn't been for the sudden figure that appeared behind her. "Need a fin?" The merman asked with a teasing smile, sinking half of his head back into the water to hide the malicious look on his face. It was hard to see; the meek light was of no help, but within the rocks and their shadows was a familiar siren. Ethera's nose crinkled at the thought, turning back around to pay him no mind.

She tried to climb up again, not giving up in the face of danger. That must have been the exit; it *had* to be. Or else the prophecy wouldn't make sense.

Ethera's eyes widened at the realization.

"I shall help you if you answer my question," the merman tried again, already half the previous distance from the mumbling human. He moved with the water that had already reached her waist, slowly eating at her stained clothes.

Ethera shivered from the cold contact of the ocean against her back. The heavy pouch dangled in the water, coloring it darker, and almost erasing its heavy presence. The merman floated beside the human, seemingly curious about the devious thoughts of how one would look drowning.

How *she* would look drowning.

"Answer me, and I will save you." He promised, his words were coated with oil.

With her head half turned, a smile tugged at her lips. "I won't die here. That damned prophecy has other plans for me," she announced confidently despite the nervousness in her eyes. Her voice was loud in what little space the cave had left for her.

Ethera floated with the water, the top of her head pressing against the highest point of the cave. Opening her mouth, she inhaled half of its remaining oxygen before diving deeper into the water.

Her eyes fluttered open, blinking rapidly. The figure loomed over her frail appearance, his tail swayed as it faded against the dark background that cornered him. She hoped, despite her lack of vision, that she would see light, a hint of how she could escape. But there was nothing here, nothing but darkness with the side of fin and tail.

He observed her for a few seconds before making up his mind. "I guess I'll be your knight in shimmering scales for today." He swam towards her with a single motion of his tail, startling the mortal with the sudden loud and clear voice that bubbled in the water. His cold hand grabbed her by the wrist, pulling her floating body towards him, the other had seized her waist. Her body instantly leaned away in the opposite direction towards him, in an attempt to get away from the slimy, fin-like hand that stuck to her arm.

Something cold had pressed itself against her mouth, and she was no fool to know what happened. The merman had kissed her, breathing out the siren's gift.

Frozen from shock, Ethera could not trust her own eyes. Despite the blurry and dark bulb in front of her, there was no doubt in her mind that the fish boy had leaned in and taken a nibble on her lips.

She blinked a few times before the thought finally settled in her mind. Ethera yanked herself from the man, slamming her own back against the hard rocks. She winced in pain, but anger and disgust were stronger than the forming bruises that scattered her beaten body. "Are you mad—," she stated in anger, immediately closing her mouth in realization. With the air bubbles that escaped her lips was her loud voice.

She could breathe underwater.

"Yes, you are very welcome. Now you won't drown, little mortal," he sang sarcastically, throwing his words around as if what he had given her meant nothing.

Ethera's anger had vanished in a second. In her eyes, the vision had slowly begun to present itself before her. The ability to breathe and speak wasn't the only thing that shook her, but the gift of sight left her in awe, paralyzed with this newfound magic.

The water's color was a vibrant blue, the color itself was dancing right before her, like a paintbrush made in contact with a cup of water. It was more than just a mere definition of a pigment created by humankind. It was magic and her eyes gladly accepted the glassy sheen.

The cave had illuminated itself, coming to life with the touch of light that carried from the ocean. Little grass pieces in every corner danced happily with the ripples of the tide that brushed against them. And they glowed too. Ever so brightly, everything around her had come to life, like a vibrant filter washed over a dull image.

Her eyes landed on the merman. It was the first time she had seen him up close; even the sight of him had completely absorbed all her attention. It wasn't until he swam closer with a single wave of his long, seaweed-like tail that she felt a spell being cast over her mind.

A green so rich that even the forest would bow in envy scattered. Lighter scales lined the sides of his magnificent tail, and what looked like bits of grass trailed from the silky fin to the grey bones along his spine.

Ethera was swept by the urge to touch him. She wondered how a siren's tail would feel against her hungry hands. He was much different underwater than when she had met him on the beach. He was beautiful, glowing in the eyes that could see his true form below the surface.

Black hair protectively floated around him, Ethera's hand twitched, wanting to move it out the way. His skin seemed to shimmer, switching from light grey to yellowish white.

"B-Bastard!" The spell cast on her heart had vanished, not strong enough to lure her into the hands of a sea creature. She swung her arms, swimming backwards to put some space between them. Her own hair floated in front of her face, the white and the brown intertwining.

The merman swam closer, as if her reaction had insulted him. "I saved your life, stupid mortal. What would you have done without me?"

"I would have floated up with the water," Ethera pointed upwards. Her feet pressed against the rocks beside her, both hands stretched upwards as she pushed herself. The tunnel was bright with her sudden improved vision, as much to her theory, it had led to land. Bits of light from the blue sky had fallen in, illuminating the little passage. "I would have made it out either way; you didn't have to go out of your way to steal my rescue points," Ethera glanced back, sensing the merman behind her. Now that she saw him properly, it seemed like his sense of boundaries was nonexistent.

He was either a creep or just painfully unaware of how close was *too* close. But one glance at that smug expression and toothy grin had confirmed it—definitely a creep.

Figures.

Even beautiful sea creatures were still *men.*

"W-Well...thank you. I have a delivery to make for his fishiness," Ethera retorted sarcastically, turning her head towards the light coming from above, in all desperation to excuse herself as fast as possible.

Before her thoughts could command her body, he grabbed her arm, pulling her closer before sliding another finned hand down to her waist. The two figures floated so closely to one another, the hem of Ethera's dress tangled around the merman's tail, filling what little space they had in between. Despite being given the ability to breathe, she refused to utilize it.

Some loose black strands of his hair wrapped around her head, harmlessly clawing at her cheeks. His hair was much longer than hers was underwater.

Her eyes did not match one another; and he had never seen anything like it. The merman seemed to inch closer without even realizing it, enchanted by the colors just as she was by his very being. "Your eyes, were they gifted from birth?" He asked lightly, as if this was a perfect time to unravel the mistakes of humankind.

"Y-Yes, it's a medical condition," Ethera responded nervously, slowly attempting to scoot away. This creature wouldn't hurt her, right?

"Okay," He had whispered, but not a single fragment of understanding had crossed his mind. Of course, a merman wouldn't know anything medical. Anything *human*.

"I need to go," She attempted to pull away, the grip on her arm tightened.

"Will you still not tell me the rest of the prophecy? Not even after I so graciously saved your life?"

Ethera paused for a moment before answering. "The prophecy said that he and I would sail across the sea to guide our troops against the demons and the army of the dead. I will give birth to a new world, and he will get what he always wanted."

The merman twitched, loosening his grip on the mortal girl. His eyes zoned out as he tried to decipher the meaning of her fickle words. "I won't mention this to His Majesty, but I will tell him that you successfully obtained the heart. In two days, you will meet him at the brink of dusk on the coast of the Pirate's Lagoon. Understood?" He asked, somehow fanning her with cold water.

Ethera nodded, the word '*yes*' barely escaping her quivering lips. He let go, and it suddenly became twenty degrees warmer.

"Congratulations, Ethera Heart, you have successfully sealed the deal with the Pirate King."

CHAPTER 12

Ethera paddled with her feet, escaping to the surface and leaving the merman behind. Green leaves lay on her hair and clothes the moment she stuck her head out, gasping for breath. Her hands clutched the sides of the dirt, pulling herself out of the water. Her body rolled to the ground; dirt stuck to her soiled hands and clothes.

She immediately sat up, violently attempting to breathe, clawing at her corset and her throat as she gasped and coughed. Her fingers shook against the rough bodice, not enough strength to pull it off. Her vision slowly began to fade but just before she could lose consciousness, her lungs expanded, drawing in an abnormal amount of air. After a tough, long minute, she regained her composure.

Her sight remained blurry as if a pool of tears had masked her vision. But that was not the case. The ability to see underwater could not be used to see through air, just like vice versa applied to water. The aftereffects of the siren's gift were slowly wearing out.

When her vision had returned, she pushed herself off the ground, brushing off the dirt that stuck to her hands and arms. The forest surrounded her and the sun, much to her fear, was nowhere close to the horizon. The wind blew strongly, letting her know she was close to the cliff. She followed the scent of the sea, despite her scrunched expression.

Ethera wanted more than anything to sit down in the sunshine, to allow herself to be warmed by the light, but her mind drifted to her friends and Dilian. They must have assumed that she had drowned to death.

Her eyes dropped down to where the heart was safely secured around her leather waistband. The red dress was stained with something darker that even the water could not wash off. The ocean must have taken the witch's corpse, returning her home. Or the merman, bringing the sea witch back to her son. She thought back to the siren, the merman, whatever that he was. The image of him was as bright as the sun but the chillness reminded her of her brush with death.

Ethera shivered at the thought of what she had done. Of what this identified her as.

The walk back to the cliff was cold but short. The sleeves had stuck to her hands, and her body left a trail of water dripping unto the path of grass that she walked on. By the time she made it back to her friends, her lips had gone blue, and her once rosy cheeks were as cold as ice. It felt like she was still hanging off the cliff, but this time, her friends were nearer.

In the distance, five figures hovered at the edge of the cliff, their heads dangerously leaned over. Their voices overlapped with each other, and the wind was not allowing her to eavesdrop on the chaos displayed. They had pulled the rope up, and Reymond was getting ready to go down there.

Ethera's eyes widened, mouth dropping open. "Hey guys...I'm alive," she waved rigidly once she saw the instant gaze of the elf. Even lifting her right arm felt like a muscle tearing from bone. Her soft voice was caught by Dilian. She already knew by now that there was no use in yelling, he would always hear her.

His expression dropped in relief, but his head tilted upwards as if the worry had taken decades off his lifespan. The mortals had noticed his behavior, turning around and breaking into a run in Ethera's direction. They all collided in a tight hug, their arms warming up not only her body.

Dilian stood on the side, watching them bundled up together with a small smile. She had returned to them in one piece. "You are alive, Ethera."

"You scared the shit out of us!" Rose broke into tears, her warm hands cupping Ethera's cold cheeks. "God, you're freezing."

Reymond had gone whiter than his twin, who was just as pale as the shivering girl. Juno's eyes were red, the tears long wiped on the sleeves of her tunic. "When we saw the water rise up, we thought you were done for!" They all broke into a fit of unsynchronized cries.

Ethera had cried, for the first time in years. But with the saltwater dripping from her face, it all looked the same. "Honestly, I-I really thought I was a goner, too," her bottom lip trembled, stumbling on her words as if the siren's kiss was still in effect.

"He was here," Dilian blurted out, interrupting the happy reunion.

"Who?"

"The Pirate King. There was a reason why I urged us to go through this mission at midday. It is when the waters are neither too high nor too low. All was carefully timed, for when the currents are the calmest, that is when Ethera would go. And yet, the water rose unnaturally, waves stirred out of control. It was his doing, I know so."

"So, he was watching…" Ethera mumbled, confirming her suspicion.

Did that mean that the merman came to save her, knowing this, or did the Pirate King order him to?

Whichever it was, there was something going on between them. Either way, she had to stay away from both, that is, after the heart gets handed over, and the waters will clear for sail.

She sighed heavily, eyes looking away from her comrades. "We are to meet him at dusk in two days," she revealed, leaving out the part about how she knew that. Her teeth clacked in the middle of the sentence.

"Come, let's get you warmed up first." The heat from the sun was not strong enough to dry her clothes, so instead they walked back deeper into the forest to get away from the winds of the sea.

"By the way, why are you guys so dirty?"

"We ate shit when you jumped off."

ᗱᚻᚻᗄ ᗱᚻᚻᗄ ᗱᚻᚻᗄ

The boys had disappeared to gather wood, and the girls had stayed behind to help Ethera take off her drenched clothes.

Five claw marks were visible on her right arm; the thin, torn fabric had stuck itself to her wound as it dried with it. Rose poured some water from her leather flask on the wound. Ethera hissed, her whole arm burst into waves of shocking pain. Juno had rubbed her back, but the comfort could not overpower the agony. The raven-head was quick to disappear, she grabbed the soiled clothes, and walked away towards a stream of water.

If truth be told, Ethera had completely forgotten about her injury, it was lost in the fast-paced course of events that followed. The adrenaline was a toxic rush, blinding her to everything but survival. Her eyes had never strayed, locked on the slimmest chance of victory and the fascinating phenomenon she got to experience.

What human could say they were able to breathe underwater? Even if it was just for a few minutes, a story like this was beyond rare, especially since sirens are known to drown their victims, not save them. She couldn't wait for the right time to share this story with her friends, perhaps after they return to their own world.

Rose waited for a few seconds before attempting to peel the shirt. Slowly, it let go of the dry, bloodied skin. She

181

examined it before pouring more water over it. Ethera felt oddly upset that her favorite tunic—her *only* tunic, was ripped at the sleeve. It seemed that it was the only thing she had grown to like in this world.

"Does it hurt a lot?" Rose's gentle voice appeared beside her, breaking the silence. The blonde had stepped away, preparing some sort of cream, and when she returned, the smell of medicine followed.

Ethera paused, everting her eyes. "Not really, it just stings a little bit."

Rose dropped to her knees beside her, hands cupping a piece of cloth. Inside, moss with crushed herbs, was mushed together into what Ethera assumed was this world's tropical antibiotic. "Oh, that's good to hear. It doesn't look bad enough for stitches, so I'll just apply this and wrap it up," Rose explained briefly, leaning closer. Her finger swiped across the paste, dabbing it on the wound. "Let me know if it hurts." Rose looked up, briefly meeting Ethera's eyes.

She answered with a nod, but even with the blonde's light touch, the skin felt like it was tearing itself. The cream felt cool against the wound, and she winced in pain despite her futile attempts to hide it.

Rose tied a long piece of cotton, wrapping it twice around Ethera's arm before finishing it with a bow. "Thanks," the brunette sighed, happy it was over. Rose reached out again, swiping some paste on Ethera's cheek, startling her. They awkwardly exchanged small smiles before Juno appeared beside them.

Juno walked past the two, hanging the dress, and bodice on the shortest branches she could find. She grabbed the torn tunic before disappearing once again.

Every now and then, the boys would stroll in one by one, turning to look in the opposite direction as they delivered wood before going off once again. Ethera was stripped to her underwear with Juno's cloak hanging over her shoulders as she shivered, and her own, over her bare knees.

Dilian had appeared twice, staying behind the second time to get the fire started as soon as possible now that they had enough wood. Ethera might have looked fine on the outside, but the elf could hear the conflicted war that was stirring inside her heart; after what happened, she needed more rest than anyone. "This should do it. Add a log if you feel the fire weakening. I will take the others to hunt," Dilian announced, his back turned to the girls.

The fire looked odd in the middle of the day, but it was much warmer than the sun. Ethera had wrapped herself in her own arms underneath the cloak, sitting, and rocking closer to the fire. Her toes dug into the cold dirt, and her shoes lay next to the flames along with the two notebooks she had found.

They had completely slipped her mind, and much to her surprise, the damage was minimal. The pages were silky, and not a drop of water stained any part of them. It must have been made of a special material that could survive the touch of water. Did that mean mermaids could read underwater?

Rose had sat next to her, and Juno plopped on the other side with the plan of using their bodies to block off the occasional wind that swept through. The blonde lifted her long, puffy skirt over Ethera's knees, using it like a blanket. "What are those?" she asked curiously, picking up the other one.

Ethera leaned her chin on her knees, eyes darting to the words spilling from the journal. "Not too sure, I think they are magic books. I forgot to mention them to Dilian," she sighed, her body feeling exhausted in the warmth. Her emotional capabilities had been tested today, and reacting under pressure in a situation that was way out of her control seemed to wear her out. She tried not to think of what had happened in the cave, but the thoughts and images flew in by themselves.

The feeling still lingered in her mind, that moment, that wretched second when her mind could not think of a solution, had been frozen in her heart. She had never once doubted her actions until today.

If only she hadn't eaten in the morning. If only she just grabbed the heart. If only she had run towards the rope.

Instead, she explored the cove like an idiot.

Coming to terms with her mistakes was something she had not been taught or had any reason to teach herself.

And death left a lingering salty aftertaste.

The prophecy said that she will give birth to a new era.

New life.

Setting the Enchanted Forest free and saving those who are still alive on the other side will be considered her redemption arc.

Ethera's eyes glanced at her arm, the off-white bow looped perfectly. The injury wasn't deep enough to scar, or so she thought. But Ethera wouldn't have minded even if it did. A scar is nothing but a reminder, and this one she welcomed.

The flames danced in front of her, the heat radiating off her cheeks, burning her tender skin alive. Her eyes soon closed, listening to the sound of the rustling leaves and the bird chirping in the distance. The boys were nowhere to be heard, but she could only imagine Dilian trying to teach a timid Hugo how to catch fish.

"Are you sleepy?" Noticed Rose.

"A little."

She scooted closer. "Rest your head on my shoulder," she suggested gently. Ethera nodded, slowly lowering her head with hesitation. It felt uncomfortable being in such proximity to another person. She didn't think she would be able to calm herself enough to rest, but once her eyes closed again, her consciousness had drifted off.

The clothes had dried out within the two hours that the boys were gone, but the girl never woke up to change into them. Instead, her friends ended up helping her change into the long burgundy skirt and the tunic, before wrapping her with the cloaks.

By the time they realized Ethera had caught a cold, there was only one log left for the fire. Juno had left to scout for more, leaving Rose to take care of Ethera, and tasking her to wipe her forehead with a wet piece of cotton fabric.

Dilian, Reymond, and Hugo returned after a couple of hours, their trousers soaked up to their knees. They made up the missing time with plenty of food for the evening and for the following journey back to the Pirate's Lagoon.

The sun had begun to set in the distance, stretching its shadows over the fire. Ethera did not wake up that evening or throughout the night. Her forehead was drenched with sweat, her head boiling at a dangerously high temperature despite her body shivering and inching closer to the fire.

It had crossed everyone's mind that she had looked too pale that night, almost half dead. They had cooked their food in an uncomfortable silence, their minds drifting back to that cave and the fear she must have felt when the water threatened to end her.

Now and then, she would toss in her sleep, and the damp cloth would slide off her forehead. They all took turns throughout the night, watching her for a few hours, adding wood to the fire to keep it burning.

The humans had it rough. Their bodies would constantly twitch and jump in fright from the noises that emerged in the forest, despite Dilian's magic rune that masked their presence.

When the morning rolled around, Ethera had finally woken up in confusion. Her body was sore and scorching hot; it had been a while since she had fallen sick. The over-the-counter medications that she had stolen had always healed her in a matter of days, sometimes hours, never letting her body temperature rise so high.

Now it was different.

There was no ibuprofen to take the throbbing pain away. Luckily, the soaked cotton cloth seemed to slowly help, but it was all wishful thinking. Every time she stopped to take a few deep breaths, it seemed like the fever just moved to a different part of her body. She could have sworn that the soles of her feet were also burning with fever, or from the long walk that they embarked on.

They had saved her some berries from the night before—and fish, which she rejected. The smell was more than enough to turn her stomach upside down. Food was supposed to help her regain her strength, but it was useless if she didn't have an appetite. Every time they stopped to let her rest, she ate three or four pieces of fruit before wrapping it and tucking it away.

Her weak body was on the verge of fainting every time she pushed herself past her limit. Occasionally, Dilian would carry her on his back, her unconscious head pressed against his shoulder.

The stain of the heart was still on the edge of her skirt that Juno had tried her best to scrub off. It served as a reminder that what happened was no dream. But the fever was a gift in disguise. Her brain was too tired to orchestrate any images or throw her mind into a rollercoaster of memories.

She would sometimes refuse water for that sole reason.

What should have taken them a few hours had stretched out into a full day's journey; they had barely reached their previous familiar campsite spot that overlooked the pirates' village. Pieces of burned wood and ashes remained, and they decided to settle there once again.

The village looked the same, covered in low fog, but this time it was brought to life. Loud instruments played in the distance, and faint yellow lights flickered somewhere beneath that grey cloud that kissed the ground.

But seeing the pirates slip so easily back to their favorite hobbies of looting and drinking told them everything—the King had not returned yet.

"Guys! Check this out!" Rose beamed happily, motioning with her hand for them to come over. Ethera turned on the spot, glancing in their direction while remaining seated. Rose, Juno, and Hugo vanished behind a thick tree. She didn't bother getting up, not like her body would allow it.

Rose bent down in front of a little green bush full of small white flowers. "These are Chamomiles, aren't they?" Her fingers lightly brushed past their little stems. Her eyes sparkled in happiness as she turned back around. "We could make chamomile tea. It's like medicine for the sick, right? It'll help her get better faster!"

Hugo leaned over the blonde's head, eyes squinting to take a better look at the flower. "It appears so."

"We should ask Dilian just in case. Who knows, maybe they are poisonous or something."

Rose tilted her head, examining the flowers yet again. "I don't know…they do smell like chamomiles." She took a handful, ripping them off with ease before heading back. With Juno's glass flask, they were able to figure out how exactly they could bring water to a boil.

"You know, you guys could just go steal a mug or something from the village, right?" Ethera asked dumbfoundedly, seeing how excited her friends had become over some flowers.

Rose's eyes lit up at the idea, while Juno immediately shut it down. "That's too dangerous. We can't go there without Dilian." Both Reymond and Dilian had disappeared into the forest to collect more wood. Hugo organized the small logs he found nearby, lighting them up with the two stones the elf entrusted him to hold on to.

With a clean cloth, they wrapped the flower buds inside before tying a knot and dropping them into the water. It took longer than they anticipated, but eventually it was ready. Rose had tasted it first, making sure that it was safe to drink before handing it to Ethera, who was oblivious that all of this was for her.

She offered the drink to the others first, but they immediately declined. The tea was so gentle against her sore throat, the soothing, earthy taste was easy to swallow, and the warmth had relaxed her from within. Before she knew it, her body dozed off again, making it more difficult for her to be useful and conscious. "She's not dead...is she?" Hugo asked, poking Ethera's cheeks. Rose rolled her eyes, ignoring him as she continued picking more bulbs from their stems to make a fresher batch.

Juno sighed, watching Rose eagerly tear out the poor flowers. "We should have asked Dilian first," she sang, brows rising and lips pursing.

"Dilian this. Dilian that. We can't always rely on him. And they are taking way too long! It doesn't take that long to find some sticks! There are trees literally everywhere." Her head never lifted, but the others could hear the irritation in her voice. Everyone always seemed on edge whenever Dilian would step away. They didn't have it in them to trust this magic rock despite everything that has happened.

Hugo shushed her immediately. "Keep your voice down, she's sleeping," he whispered, getting up to sit closer to the dimming fire.

"Whatever's," Rose scoffed, her head finally lifting. "Why don't you two make yourselves useful and come help me?" She whispered-yelled as she lifted her green-tinted fingertips, tugging the light strands behind her ear.

CHAPTER 13

"Never thought I'd say this, but I miss our bed back in the Elvenwood," Ethera mumbled, a lazy smile on her face. The cocoon-like bed was much softer than the ground, and they all wanted nothing more than to catch a couple of good z's without waking up with knots in their shoulders and unavoidable aches all over their weak, human bodies.

Dilian was the only one who woke up full of energy. They could only assume it was the magic in his blood. Juno had helped them learn a few stretches that helped momentarily, but they were useless against the forming bruises on their hips and backs.

Hugo walked over, squatting down in front of her. "How are you feeling?" He asked, eyes landing on the fresh tea she was drinking. She was holding it close to her nose, not taking a single sip.

"Like I've just been repeatedly hit by a truck."

"She's good to go. Let's get a move on," Dilian declared, sparing no glance in her direction. Ethera's stomach growled in hunger, the sound heard even by human ears. She couldn't recall the last time she had a proper meal. Rose appeared behind them, handing Ethera a cloth with freshly picked berries and, much to her horror, pieces of fish. The brunette's appetite immediately disappeared the moment its smell hit her nose.

Her nose scrunched, and she forced a smile. Rose sighed, catching on. "You'll need your strength so make sure to finish everything." The blonde insisted, ignoring her friend's grim expression. "We're almost there, just hang on a little longer." When she walked away, Ethera looked at Hugo, a smirk tugging on her lips.

"Open up," she whispered, handing him the fish.

"Oh, hell no," he immediately said, getting up to run away.

Ethera was quick to grab him with her left arm. "Finish the fish for me, or else I will tell them that Lacey from second grade rejected you."

"I hate you."

Ethera smiled, watching him anxiously shove the fish into his mouth, all the while shooting familiar daggers her way. "I know."

ᗡ�HᕼO ᗡHᕼO ᗡHᕼO

The Pirate's Lagoon was just up ahead, behind dozens of trees that surrounded their village, which had fallen prey to silence yet again. It seemed that whatever celebration happened yesterday was long put to rest.

Consumed by eternal fog, darkness crept over every moving shadow. The wind howled through the houses, a loud sound banging every two seconds, repeating over and over again, like the thud of a drum sentencing them to their doom.

The breeze felt nice against Ethera's feverish body; her mind could only wish she could rest a little longer. The thought of meeting the Pirate King in this vulnerable state was dangerous. Her mind was not the same, and her reaction time had turned into that of a sloth.

Ever since she arrived in this world, it's been danger after danger chasing her at every turn. She had nearly been eaten alive, *twice*, threatened by every species she'd encountered, nearly died at the hands of a sea witch, faced the risk of drowning in a cave, and now, to top it all off, a fever was threatening to burn her alive.

A vacation to remember. Truly.

If his royal fishiness really was involved in that matter, then the King is lucky that she had fallen ill, after all, she wasn't in her right mind to say anything about it now. What kind of king goes to kill someone who is supposedly helping him?

Her throat had begged for water, the fog making it hard for her to breathe through one nostril. She didn't want to inconvenience her friends by making them stop once again, since time was running short and dusk was approaching fast.

The King was not at the tavern; the familiar man inside directed them to his ship. The town was haunting, the fog only circulating through the roads within. It completely cleared once their shoes had touched the sand as if the village's curse did not dare to cross the borders of the beach.

They strolled through, feet sinking in as they walked towards the wooden port that lined the sea with countless ships. The King's ship was the only one that creaked alone on the right side; all the other pirates had moved theirs to accommodate *His Highness*.

The whispers of the King had knocked on everyone's doors, and they all waited in excitement to find out what exactly was going to happen next. They had already guessed the truth; they just needed confirmation to bring forth their swords and rum.

The colors of orange, red, and pink circled the sky as if congratulating them on the completion of their quest. Ethera had done it. She obtained the heart and will now be granted safe passage across the Crimson Waters. The prophecy was sailing smoothly; it was only a matter of time before the war came to an end.

The singular ship was tied against the dock, growing larger with every step they took. It stretched far into the sky, blocking the sun and casting a long shadow on them. The water splashed loudly underneath, causing the deck to creak. The scent of seawater circulated the air around them.

A man stood at the bottom of the plank as if waiting for their arrival. There were holes in the knees of his pants, and the ends were ripped right above his shins, showing his bare tan ankles. The dark brown hair was combed backwards neatly, but it didn't make up for his messy appearance.

Ethera didn't judge; she knew that she smelled and looked like she had rolled over a pound of dirt.

The man shifted uncomfortably, nervously picking at his black nails. It was clear that he was there against his will, tied as a servant to the king he could not refuse. "Only she can meet with the King," the pirate said, his raspy voice coated with fear and nervousness. They followed the direction of his finger that landed on Ethera.

She rolled her eyes. "Are you kidding me?" Breathing out in annoyance, her voice was hoarse, barely escaping her throat. As if anything in this world was easy. Sighing deeply, she extended her arm towards Dilian, palm facing up, without meeting his eyes. Ethera's sharp gaze pierced the pirate, as if somehow her anger would make it to its rightful recipient.

The light muscle dropped onto her hand. Her eyes lingered on the pouch, her fingers twitching as if the urge to squeeze it was enticing. It was cold, and it stank; the smell drifted faintly past her scrunched nose. "Let's make this fast," The human mumbled, following the pirate up the slanted wooden plank. Her other hand hovered over the wooden post to ensure she would not fall or roll back down. It was her first time boarding a ship, and a slight tingle of excitement washed over her worn body.

The ship's flag stood high, fluttering in the air above her head as if it was getting ready to depart any minute now. The ship was known to be the only one that cut through the sea like a blade through flesh—its once pearly white sails had turned a light hue of gray, tied against the poles with brown rope. They swayed with the wind, a hollow yellow glow on one side was illuminated by the sun behind, threatening to unleash sail onto the impatient ship.

The body was made out of scorched wood that looked black on one side and a tainted brown on the other. Her hand reached out to touch its sacred body. When else would she get the opportunity to touch a *real* pirate ship? And that of a king, no less.

Towering masts had disappeared into the clouds, twisting downwards into the middle of the deck. Ropes flung from above, swaying with the wind. The chains rattled suddenly, startling her as she looked up.

Something white poked out. There was no doubt that those were bones, as if a dead body had recently been hung by its ankles. Ethera shuddered at the vivid image. The light from the setting sun was making it hard for her to observe the other fascinating details.

There was so much to see, but time was not on her side. She didn't want to get caught gawking at something that belonged to *him*.

Others were moving through the ship, and she twitched in their direction, not being able to tell shadow from crew. The pirates had stopped to watch; a few of them had their hands on mops and cloths, scrubbing and polishing the sides of the spiked railings that were stained with rust and what looked like blood.

There was a filthy smell in the air, something almost fishy.

The pirate had led her through the ship. It flinched with every wave that bumped into it, and Ethera was feeling the berries on the edge of her throat. The pirate paused in front of a wooden door and knocked.

After a moment with no reply, he gently opened it, one hand on the golden knob and the other on the door itself, as if it could somehow muffle the creaking sound.

He stood idly on the side. Ethera's eyes curiously scanned the room ahead, not seeing a single sign of the Pirate King. Her eyes looked back at his servant, waiting for an answer that never came. He did not dare to speak to her or even look in her direction.

She clutched the pouch before walking through the door. It immediately closed behind her. Her throat was itchy, threatening to break into a fit of coughs. Her legs wobbled to the side as she strolled in while taking a gentle deep breath.

Following through the unfamiliar hallway, she came across an opening, a room with him in it.

Act normal.

"A heart cut out by yours truly," Ethera snarled sarcastically, announcing her arrival as if he did not hear her hesitant footsteps. She tossed it on the table before the king, who didn't make any moves to stand up or greet her. It was dim in the room, and the lanterns mounted on the sides of the wooden walls were fighting for their lives to stay alive.

The King looked different; his tunic was the same color as his hair, a black so dark it blended in with the color of his ship. It wasn't tucked in the leather belt of his brown pants, making him look unpredictable and relaxed.

His hair was tied with the same golden skull hairpin, and the rings on his sturdy fingers were reduced to only one, a golden round signet on the index of his right hand.

Less flashy, but twice as scary.

A smile crept on his face, eyes never looking away from her. The mortal was the first to turn, finding his stare uncomfortable well beyond words. There was one window behind him, the glass so blurry that it was pointless to even try to look through it. It glowed a bright red, pointing towards the setting sun.

It was a study. A table sat in the middle, surrounded by countless chairs despite his lack of company. There was food on one side: cherries, grapes, apples, bread, a steaming hot meat, and most likely served with dark wine. The other side had maps, different figures, trinkets, coins, and other things that were pushed to the side in a hurry. Some had even fallen on the wooden floor, and rolled underneath the table. The walls were covered with books, stones, seashells, and paintings.

The lack of light was killing Ethera's curiosity. She wanted to walk closer to the paintings, examine them as if they were literal photographs of this world. A sort of proof she would love to bring back home. "I'll be taking my leave now, *your highness*," she sighed in exhaustion, eyes still fixated on the covered paintings as her body got ready to turn. His silent stare down was not how she thought this conversation was going to begin. Or end.

He sighed. "What's the rush?" He asked coldly. "I want to hear all about my dear mother." The screech of the chair and a few shuffled footsteps brought the King danger-ously closer. The girl almost jumped out of her skin.

Ethera's memory had been unlocked with a single sentence; the sea witch's face flashed before her; from the way her son had just appeared right beside her in a split sec-ond.

She tried to regain her composure, but the heat within the room was making it difficult to breathe. "You are sick in the head." She turned to leave, but he grabbed her by her right hand, his grip purposely over the injury.

She hissed in pain, trying to shake off him off. The King strolled back towards the table, dragging the mortal be-hind him. He pulled out a chair in front of the mountains of food, shoving her to take a seat. Ethera stumbled towards it, somehow her body exquisite at the thought of resting. She didn't hesitate to sit down, her hazy eyes peering over the King, who had taken a seat next to her. Despite the delicious aroma in the room, she could only smell the sea.

It was a bit brighter on the other side, the bits of light flickered, illuminating what she most wanted to see. She blinked rapidly in an attempt to adjust her vision faster. The pirate's eyes scanned the girl's face, his eyebrows dropping.

This wasn't as fun as he had imagined it to be. After all, he went out of his way to prepare all this for her. "What is the matter?" He asked, his hand reaching to touch a loose strand that hung in front of her eyes. A white strand that did not follow the curl pattern of the rest of her hair.

Ethera pulled away, her reaction delayed. "How about next time you kill your own damned mother?" She bit back, glaring in his direction and wanting nothing more than to leave. The pirate smiled, his finger tracing her burning forehead.

The metal ring brushed over her skin, bringing instant relief. She found her body leaning into the touch despite her realization. His finger tickled her face, brushing over the healing scab on her cheek.

It was cold like the sea that haunted her dreams. "I could have drowned," Ethera breathed out, her eyes long closed in a daze. The image of the water poured itself through the cracks of her mind.

Consuming her whole being in a single swoop.

How easy would it have been for her to perish in that cave? To drown in agony.

Cold and alone

The Pirate King remained quiet, both his eyes and hands observing the mortal before him. His dark orbs fell to her neck. Desire darkened his soulless eyes.

It would have been as easy as taking a deep breath of air. Snapping her neck in an instant, erasing the disturbance of his waveless life.

With control over the winds and the water, the sea had fallen at his mercy. He had the power to do whatever he wished. And yet, the thought of drifting along the sea alone had begun to repulse him. It had been long since the last time someone had called him back ashore, and now a lingering prophecy of this mortal involved him.

She had caused a ripple in the steady waters, and more than anything, he wanted to let it die. To kill her, display her body as an example to those who thought they could challenge him.

Or he could wait. See what else this tide changing ripple would bring. The prophecy was not what she made it out to be, he knew that much. "You're not as weak as I thought you were, Ethera Heart." Upon hearing her name, the mortal's eyes popped open, and she momentarily woke up from the sour daydream that consumed her.

Her eyes shot in the King's direction, her body shot up and got ready to bounce. The wooden chair screeched as her red dress caught in the way of her sudden escape. The rush of movement sent her blood flowing to her head, her vision turning black.

Her body had gone limp as the Pirate King caught her by her arm. He chucked before bending his legs, and with one swift motion, he picked her up.

The mortal had fallen unconscious in the hands of the most dangerous man alive. Her body was weightless in his arms as his mind contemplated what to do. She burned in his hands, like a fire created to consume him.

Get rid of her, a part of him whispered.

Keep her, the other collided.

His eyes glistened in the dying light. He carried her through the narrow corridor; the wood creaked under the weight of the two of them. The heel of his black boot kicked the door open, the smell of salt and rust filling his nose.

The sun had already disappeared, hiding from his cold eyes. The breeze perked up as if excitement stirred in the air. The mortal's hair swayed in the current, a pleasant scent disappearing just as soon as he caught on to it. His body slowed deliberately, and he couldn't hide the sinister smile that crept across his face, fully aware of her comrades'

201

prying eyes. He came to a halt in front of the plank that connected his home to land.

The horrified faces of her friends painted their thoughts aloud. He hid the urge to laugh, as two of them dashed towards him, instantly tearing Ethera away from his arms. He raised his hands in defense, feeling a slight chill sensation now that the furnace was no longer in his hold.

The ship creaked loudly, and waves roared below at his command. "We will set sail in ten days on the brink of dawn. Ready your little herd, elf, and sharpen your spear. I will take you across the Crimson Waters."

CHAPTER 14

Ethera had safely returned to them in the hands of a pirate. Her body lay unconscious in his arms, almost as if he had got rid of her himself. But when the corner of his lips twitched upwards, and his malicious gaze looked down at the defenseless girl, Reymond and Rose had gotten the reassurance that she was still alive. For now.

They broke into a sprint, thuds echoing below the plank as it shook with the hearty steps of their weight. Hugo fell behind, consumed by his own thoughts and the guilty feeling that scratched the back of his mind. He should have followed after them—after her but fear had paralyzed him once again.

Reymond immediately snatched Ethera, his eyes dangerously meeting that of the pirate. Rose followed closely behind, her hands hovering in front of her, not knowing how to help.

They rejoined the rest of their friends, who formed a circle around their passed-out friend. "She's okay, she's just sleeping," Rose reassured Hugo after seeing the look on his face.

Her own heart couldn't calm down upon the scare. Rose took a deep breath, her hands instinctively reaching for Ethera, shaking against her warm forehead.

Dilian's eyes lingered on the Pirate King, his words ringing loud in his pointy ears, ignoring the bickering of the mortals. Ten days to prepare for a war was not enough time at all. But it was a generous amount coming from the King. The elf was half-heartedly expecting to be ordered to be here the following day.

His people were already ahead; they had begun their preparations after receiving a note from the elf that marked the completion of the bargain. Everything was moving according to plan, and the words of the Wishing Well were not just a song of hope.

The pirate glanced back to Ethera, his black orbs seemingly mesmerized by her appearance once more before turning around and leaving. Dilian glared suspiciously at the captain until his silhouette was swallowed by the grand ship.

The elf's ears shivered at the thought. Perhaps the days granted were all because of Ethera. After all, the King would not be entertained if it meant the mortal was lying lifelessly, breaking out with fever all over. Perhaps, his fascination with her was shared with the elven clan.

Why was she chosen? A human, no less, brought to a world she was never to be part of.

Rose interrupted his thoughts, appearing beside him. "We must head back. She's too exhausted to walk, and her fever keeps coming back." The mortals nodded, looking back at Dilian to make the final decision.

The elf, surprised by their obedience, nodded quickly. "Let's rest here for the night and resume our journey in the morning."

A good night's sleep was hard to find in a world where everything was trying to kill them. Drenched with anxiety from head to toe, even the mortal boy, whom they called Reymond, didn't have it in him to crack a joke.

Dilian felt aggravated at the feeling of worry that clawed at the back of his mind. He exhaled sharply, dark green eyes pulling away from his new human friends, and with a single turn of his body, he left those meaningless feelings on the boarding dock of the Pirate King's ship.

The group dragged themselves towards the tavern. The lone face of the innkeeper greeted them at the door with eagerness, welcoming the first customers that he had received in days. For the first time in a long while, the owner missed the busy boom of angry pirates that daily tore his tavern upside down. Or at least—the gold that they carried.

It seemed that his good old friend, the Pirate King, had a talent for killing business. No one dared to come to the inn, knowing that the King enjoyed his drink just as much as the rest of them.

And there was no better place than the Gal's pub.

No one knew why the King had reappeared after all these years. But one thing was certain, everyone who misspoke always ended up dead. That was more than enough to keep business nonexistent.

The elf paused in front of the pirate, taking out a small cotton pouch. It clattered against the dark wood. "We shall stay here for the night." He could almost hear the shock radiating behind him.

The mortals exploded in synchronized cheers. "Wait, so we are sleeping on real beds tonight?" Reymond questioned with happiness, twirling the knocked-out Ethera. The girls cheered, relief washing over them. Their backs ached from the ruthless grounds of the Thalorin Forest and even the sparse patches of grass offered little relief.

Even Hugo flashed a small smile of excitement. "I didn't know that taverns had rooms."

The pirate snatched the money almost immediately. "The rooms here are accommodating...if one can sleep through the ruckus."

"We won't be here long, just for tonight. Prepare yourself. Once word spreads, you shall find no shortage of unexpected guests. We sail with the King in ten moons, to bring the war to the demons and reclaim the lands that were once ours."

The tattoo pirate snickered, a wide, toothy grin revealing his golden tooth. "Good," he began, "—ye folk brought quite the hassle to our land."

"Apologies, we don't get along well with the faerie folk, but that's common knowledge."

"Aye, aye, that much I know. Three rooms?" The pirate asked, glancing over at the mortals. The elf nodded, looking over at them, too.

They had fallen quiet as they listened to the conversation, unaware of this newfound knowledge. The pirate turned around, pulling open a drawer that scraped the wooden cupboard. He grabbed a set of keys, turned around, and tossed them at the elf.

Dilian caught it with ease. He glanced back, briefly meeting the curious eyes of the humans. "The elves are warriors who bring honor and wisdom to the battlefield. The faeries are trickster folk. Mischievous and lazy things," he explained, his voice led them to the back of the tavern, through to the stairs that revealed a second floor.

The elf couldn't understand why he had the need to keep the mortals informed; they would never know the history that went back centuries. And they'll be long gone by the time the autumn eclipse washes over.

There was no need for them to know this information. But their eyes reminded him of the young elf kin, and it seemed to get the better of him; after all, he was sort of like their guardian.

What was the word they used? Babysitter?

In their eyes, he was nothing more than a story that had come to life. A work of fantasy.

They hurried up the stairs, following after the elf, who oddly took the lead as if he had stayed here before.

"Wow, that's really cool! Do they have wings? Are they pretty?" Questioned Rose, her eyes lighting up the dim hallway. The words—mischievous, lazy and trickster folk—completely flew over her head. The keys clacked as they paused in front of each door, attempting to match the numbers on the keys to the ones on the doors.

"What other species exist here?" Next was Hugo, whose mind couldn't really grasp the concept of flying people.

"If you're that curious, I shall tell you after we settle down."

Reymond had carefully laid Ethera on the bed, her eyes still closed, and her forehead reflected the limited light in the room. Juno agreed to stay behind while the others got ready to hunt. She took off Ethera's sneakers before wrapping her in a blanket, its edges torn.

Dilian nodded at Juno, his green eyes briefly fell to Ethera before he left the room.

The elves had knowledge beyond the lifespan of a pirate, along with sharper survival instincts. While pirates indulged in alcohol, violence, and the small pleasures of life, the elf clan strove to learn and better understand what their existence brought to the world.

They were the sole protectors of the Enchanted Forest, and they failed.

It was the only battle that they couldn't win. A traitor had turned against them and disappeared instantly after unleashing the wrath of the demon clan.

Dilian's brows furrowed at the thought; his grip on the spear tightened. The carving on the wood was barely visible with the dimming light that entered through the small window. His eyes were lost in the scene that played loudly in his head.

The scene in which he could not kill the traitor. The traitor who was of fae origin.

Reymon appeared through the open doorway, cracking his knuckles, which startled the elf. "We're ready. We also have to get some cold water for Ethera on our way back," he announced. Dilian nodded, following the mortal boy down the stairs.

With this opportunity, he couldn't let the written victory fall through his stained fingers. He was restless to end the war, for everything to return to its rightful place and to forget the mistake that cost his people their lives.

꼬HH◊ 꼬HH◊ 꼬HH◊

It felt weird not being surrounded by trees and dirt, something that they had all become accustomed to. Their eyes peered into every visible corner. They hadn't been in a mortal-made establishment in what felt like forever. The structures that the pirates had built were haggard in comparison, as if the idea of maintenance had never crossed their minds.

Much to their surprise, when the four of them stepped outside, the fog had begun to clear. The King's ship stood far ahead on the boarding deck, her white sails loose, fluttering in the wind and ready to take to the ocean. If it weren't for their tired eyes, one could have assumed that it glowed; a dark red, ominous energy that hovered around it like a warning. Like a red-eyed crow lurking in the trees in the early hours of dawn.

They still couldn't understand how a man could single-handedly sail a ship that size. Their eyes, like magnets, tore away from it.

The streets remained empty, all doors and windows shut. No one was planning on opening them anytime soon, as long as the King's ship haunted their dock. There was barely any light; even the pub beside them had dimmed its fire from within.

The forest was just as quiet as the village, and Dilian didn't waste any time on what remained of the bright sky. "Gather the wood and start a fire," he instructed while he tossed the rocks to Hugo, "I'll go find us some food." He adjusted the hold on his spear before disappearing into the woods.

The humans didn't spread out; instead, they all stuck together, quietly picking up logs and dry sticks they found on the ground. "You know, I could write a book about our adventures. It'll sell well, and we'll become hella rich," said Rose, trying to lift the heavy mood that dangled in the air.

Hugo let out a snort. "How are you going to write a book if you can't even pass English?" he joked, making her face flush a bright red.

She lifted a stick with two fingers, not wanting to soil her hands. "It's not my fault she makes us read such big books."

They all paused, remembering their English class. "What do you mean? The Great Gatsby was like this thick." Reymond lifted his pinky finger. Hugo flinched. "I bet you were one of those students who would just Google everything, am I wrong?"

"Listen here, smartass, at least I made an effort to learn about the book. You didn't even open it," she turned her face away, not wanting to confirm his assumptions. Despite cheating her way through, she still ended up failing the class. "We can always study during spring break," she quickly added, tossing the twigs into a pile. Worrying about English class was pointless; either way, they had a lot to catch up on if they returned on time to pass junior year.

"Imagine we all get held back for another year," Reymond burst out laughing at the thought, while Rose's face morphed into horror.

"Nope, not going to happen! We have Ethera and Hugo, they'll help us study. Right?"

Rose's pleading eyes caught Hugo's. He let out a bitter laugh. "Didn't you say something along the lines of 'you're unbearable to hang out with because all you talk about is school and homework,' or am I mistaken?" He taunted, mimicking Rose's voice.

Her face flushed a bright red. "I don't sound like that! A-And that was way before when I was immature!" She yelled, defending the only thing that stood between her and failure. The blonde didn't want to be held back, especially not with Reymond, who was her only equal when it came to grades. Her best friend, Juno, was smart and no doubt would catch up with the rest of them in a matter of days.

They continued making light jokes until Dilian came back, and only then did everyone fall into silence. Hugo had started his first fire, and soon enough, much to Rose's displeasure, they were frying two abnormally big rabbits.

211

"So, how is mortal school?" Dilian asked curiously, having heard most of their conversation. His ears were sharp and long for a reason.

"Terrible!" The two slackers yelled in unison.

Hugo shook his head, adjusting his glasses. "Very educational, they teach us a lot about different subjects like math, English, science, history, politics, and economics," he began rambling, "but those are all mandatory. There are other classes you can take, too; they are called electives. Rey is going to be taking art next year while I enrolled in psychology."

"Art?" Dilian repeated, somehow finding that awfully surprising.

"Yep, I chose it because it's easy!"

Rose stood up, one arm on her hip while the other, which held a stick, pointed at the boy. "No, you only chose it because of Melissa." Reymond looked away, eyes wide and cheeks pink. He was lacking in the visual art aspect and had no creative juices whatsoever, so it was quite a shock when they found out he had enrolled in that class for the next semester. One could only assume why.

"How do you even know that?"

"Dude...*everyone* knows."

Dilian, confused as an elf would be, was trying to catch on to their conversation. "Is that his lover?" Reymond had covered his face with both hands, but the red illuminated color on his ears told a different story.

His twin smiled evilly. "No, it's this poor girl he had a crush on since middle school."

Reymond sighed, turning back to face Dilian. "Can we stop talking about this? You said you were going to tell us more about the other species," he quickly changed the subject, in hopes of getting the attention away from his burning ears. The sky had turned pitch black, and the skinned rabbits were only halfway cooked.

Dilian's green eyes looked up, and with each name, a different story was brought to life. "Elves, faeries, mermaids, goblins, unicorns—but they haven't been sighted in two hundred years— there are also nymphs, but they barely show themselves. Sprites were quite common—they make talking mushrooms to lure other creatures to their death—."

Rose raised her hands to pause the conversation. "Wait, wait, wait. Slow down a little. There are unicorns here?" She squealed loudly in excitement.

"Yes, although the last of them might have perished in the Enchanted For—."

"Did you say Sprite? Like the drink?"

"How do talking mushrooms kill you?" Hugo asked, somehow wishing he had a pen and paper to write all this down. Ethera would have been pleased to hear about this; she couldn't stand the taste of mushrooms when they were younger.

Dilian sighed before continuing. "They speak until your mind is at their disposal. They mock your voice, echoing it with twisted delight, until you can no longer resist replying. And once you do, the enchantment binds your tongue until death claims you," he simply told of the common tale but the mortal's faces threw him off guard. His fingers wrapped around a necklace, pulling it out from underneath his tunic. "Why else would we wear the glow-berries around our necks? The sprites had created those monstrosities as a means to prank us. A cruel prank, but there is no humor in a corpse," he remarked in a matter-of-fact tone. The berries in question were nothing more than shriveled-up blobs, tied with a single string around the elves' necks.

No one would have guessed those were berries. Sometimes the elf forgot that the mortals—his new friends—knew nothing of this world.

"Talking mushrooms, huh?" Reymond paused, thinking out loud. "Now that's a first."

Dilian continued, keeping an eye on the food as well. He told them stories of other creatures that resided here, and others that lived far. Like people made entirely of lava. It was a myth of the north mountains that was said to be covered by fire even in the dead of winter.

He told them other things. The healers in the west and the demons in the east that had conquered the Enchanted Forest that stood in the south. But even with this small bit of information, Hugo's mind was trying its best to envision it on his map. He would often occupy himself with theories about where they might be on the human scale, but after what the elf had revealed, it seemed that this world existed separately from the plane of Earth.

The sun rose in the east and set in the west, but the moon never waned. It hung forever full in the dark sky through the many days that had passed since their arrival.

It made no sense. Even more so than before.

CHAPTER 15

The following morning, everyone woke up bright and early, preparing for the long journey ahead of them. The walk back to the Elvenwood took an entire day, but the thought of curling up again in those comfy cocoons gave them a newfound determination.

The beds in the tavern were not as comforting as they had hoped they would be, but anything was better than the cold, hard ground of the forest. Even Ethera, who had woken up confused, felt somewhat refreshed. Hugo and Rose sat beside her on the edge of the bed, ready to catch her up to speed on everything she'd missed.

Before they could get far, Reymond burst in excitedly, interrupting with dramatic tales of evil mushrooms that talk you to death. "Huh, kind of sounds like Mr. Harris," laughed Ethera. She could only imagine him trying to talk himself out of the trouble of losing five students in the school library. Her laugh soon turned into a fit of vicious coughs. Hugo's hand patted her on the back, but the girl continued coughing.

Rose instantly jumped off the bed, already through the doorway. "I'll go get you some water," she yelled out, running in the hallway and quickly down the stairs.

"Ah," said a voice so cold it froze up the entire room with a single breath. "I've been patiently waiting until one of you decided to come down." Sitting on one of the high chairs was the Pirate King. He didn't turn to look who it was that made their way down those stairs; any of them would have sufficed for his questioning. His hand held a glass, its contents a deep marrow that swirled around in the morning light that entered through the cracks of the windows. He kept tilting it gently, watching the liquid shift from side to side.

It made no sense to drink this early, but he was the Pirate King. Sense had never been his master, and so he did so as he pleased.

He continued with no answer. "Please, do take a seat."

"I'm afraid we'll be departing soon, so I really should head back——."

"Please, I do insist," the man interrupted, his dark eyes finally meeting hers. The little hairs on the back of her neck stood up, pulling her away from the dangerous man. Despite the urge to run back upstairs, her legs did the opposite. She dragged herself towards him, eyes narrowed with caution, observing him as he did with her.

He didn't speak until she had sat down, leaving a chair in between them. "A friend of Ethera's?" He asked despite knowing the answer. He seemed slightly less intimidating by the mention of Rose's friend, but the odd smile on his face said otherwise. The Pirate King had come with no sword again. He was defenseless.

Or was he?

No one had ever dared to try to kill him and take his place as the next Sea King. Everyone hid the moment he came ashore. Rose could only assume he had some strange power that made him powerful and invincible. He could not be underestimated, and the mortal knew to finish this conversation as fast as possible. Oddly enough, he seemed intrigued with Ethera, and Rose was desperate to find out why.

His eyes reeked of evil. And for once she felt fear. Fear for her friend's life.

Rose took a quiet breath in. "Yes, I am," she stated, forcing her voice to remain steady. She was determined not to let him hear her fear, and yet she didn't quite know how to conceal it.

He averted his gaze back to his own glass. "Do have a drink with me." The innkeeper poured another drink of the same kind before sliding it in front of Rose, who cautiously looked at it. He wouldn't poison her, right?

The deal has been completed; a pirate's word is absolute. But who is to say that this man, who does whatever he pleases and lives solely on the sea, will abide by the pirate's code?

He didn't follow the rules—he wrote them.

Rose's eyes lingered on the glass, watching the liquid go still. "I don't drink," she lied, not in the mood for anything unless it was served with music, lights, and a crowd.

"Hmm."

"What do you want?" She asked, perhaps too directly. Rose tried to be brave, but her nerves were desperately trying to keep her lips shut. She envied Ethera for always being so fearless.

The Pirate's eyes glanced back at the girl. "No need to be so wary, I just came to talk to someone who knows her best." He was here because of Ethera; it seemed like she had made a foe out of the wrong enemy.

Rose felt his piercing gaze; she tried her best to refrain from turning. "I'm afraid you're talking to the wrong person. Hugo was the one who grew up with her," she responded, trying to understand where this conversation was leading and if it was okay to reveal such information to the likes of a pirate.

"Hugo," the King whispered to himself, the air drawing colder as if his thoughts had frozen it. Rose gulped nervously, and the palms of her hands began to sweat. When she remained quiet, the pirate continued. "I couldn't sleep all night, a question on my mind. Why are her eyes two different colors?"

She fiddled with the fabric of her skirt. "It's something she was born with."

"Even in a world full of magic, I've never seen anything quite like it. She looks like she belongs here, doesn't she?"

The blonde spun around, instantly meeting his cold gaze. "Of course not!" She bit back, losing her cool at the pirate's audacity to spout rubbish. Ethera belonged at home, back on Earth with everyone else. What was he trying to achieve by asking her such a one-sided question?

But he had gotten what he wanted, for the eyes never lie. "I want to know her weakness," he persisted, placing his drink down. The black soulless eyes watched Rose's trembling ones, and only then did she realize that he was analyzing her every answer. The air shifted, and it felt dangerous; for whatever reason, he was out to hurt Ethera.

"Like hell, I'd tell you."

"So loyal, such a bittersweet friendship you have. But I am not asking, I'm demanding."

Rose narrowed her eyes, her fists bawling around the fabric as she strengthened her back. "Over my dead body," she spat angrily. The tavern keeper took a few steps back, not wanting to get caught in the crossfire.

The pirate got up, appearing right in front of the mortal. Rose's mind could not process what had happened, but one thing was for sure: the fear had frozen her before him. "That could be arranged," he whispered coldly, appearing next to her, and grabbing at her neck without hesitation. Coldness clutched at her skin, but before he could squeeze and snap it in two, something had hit the back of his head, bouncing off and falling back to the ground with a thud.

Ethera stood there, her eyes wide and her hand extended towards where she had just thrown her sneaker. Her other hand shook against the wooden handrail, clutching it for dear life as if, without her shoe, she would fall.

Her breath tore through her chest, ragged like a storm tossed in the sea. "Y-You let go of her right now," the mortal demanded, her voice hoarse from dryness. Her throat itched, and the desire to claw at it never faltered; a cough was threatening to break free. She pushed it down, halting her breathing to keep it at bay, and in return, her eyes began to water. "Are you not ashamed of yourself? Where is your honor? How dare you come in here and threaten us after striking a deal?"

His head turned around, a smile returning to his lips. Rose could see it as plain as day, his eyes did not match the look on his face. "Apologies," he uttered, letting go of Rose's throat. She quickly got up, chair creaking against the wooden floor. Her own hand reached towards her throat, shaking at the thought alone.

The captain straightened himself to get a better look at Ethera, the sole object of his sleepless night. She stood in the middle of the stairs with one foot, the other hovering in the air, her body leaning over the hand railing for balance.

Rose choked back her tears that were threatening to stain her cheeks. She blinked them away, carefully watching the dangerous man in front of her. No one made any sound or movement, even the innkeeper was paralyzed, watching the movie pause momentarily in front of him. And just as suddenly as it stopped, it resumed.

The Pirate King had bent down, picking up the lost shoe that dared to hit him in the back of his head.

Such force, such precise aim. It took him by surprise from thought alone. The heels of his boots made the ground tremble as he inched closer towards the frozen Ethera. Fear had tied its hands around her body, rooting her in place. The image of Rose's lifeless corpse, lying still across the cold ground, had enchanted her mind, unraveling what little strength she had to fight the man before her.

She didn't run as he inched closer towards her; her body was unprepared for the stress and the thoughts that haunted her mind. The pirate stood at the bottom of the steps, only four small wooden planks separating them. He did the unexpected, putting one foot out, as he had gotten down on one knee right before the stunned mortal.

The shoe rested on his thigh, the heel pointing towards him. She blinked dumbfoundedly, knowing exactly what he was waiting for. The raging look on her face could not be controlled, and her robot-like body moved by itself. Lifting her leg, she slid her foot inside the shoe that had long gone cold. Her bare skin slid between the cut of her burgundy skirt. Her white breeches peeked through, and the place where her knife should have been, stared back at her, bare.

His head dropped, tying the shoelaces right before her eyes. He took his time too, as if making sure that the scene before her was going to burn into her memory for eternity.

He then spoke softly and slowly. "I apologize for trying to kill your friend, Ethera Heart." His cold hand rested against her ankle as he looked up, a sinister smile on his face. Ethera attempted to pull away, but the hold was too strong. There was no doubt Dilian heard him—so where was he?

The pirate was making a point; she understood it all too well, and he dragged on the seconds to also burn the image before him. His dark eyes twinkled just like the rings on his fingers, reflecting her astonished expression.

She had never felt this way before. The burning urge expanded through every vein in her body—her heart tensed at the mere image her mind cultivated.

To kill him would have been mercy. Fulfillment beyond words. And for the first time in her life, she never wanted anything more.

The moment his grip loosened, she pulled away, the leg stepping back instantly. He got up, his eyes leveling up to hers, despite being two steps below. With a soft, dangerous tone, he said, "I'll see you soon, Ethera Heart."

The man left just as suddenly as he had appeared, letting the room finally catch a break. The innkeeper's eyes followed Rose as she dashed across towards her friend. Without hesitation, she pulled on the girl's wrist and led her upstairs back to their room.

The boys were ready, chatting among themselves, when they noticed the grim expressions on the girls' faces.

Before they could say anything, Ethera broke down. "We need to do something about him," she began, biting down on the corner of her nails as the wheels in her head began to turn. Rose remained quiet, hands shaking, but her eyes never left Ethera. "This won't do. He's going to get in the way; we have to do something!"

"Ethera, take a deep breath. Speak clearly, what has happened?"

"That fucking son of a bitch tried to kill Rose! If he so much as looks in her direction, I'll take care of him myself." Rose wasn't the only one shaking; Ethera was, too.

But she boiled with a dangerous temperature, *rage*.

The audacity of that man to do as he pleased had snapped all of the strings that she had sewn to keep her sanity. She absolutely hated that. She hated *him*.

"Who? What are you talking about?"

"The Pirate King!" Rose snapped, her tear-stained eyes looking in their direction. Juno threw her arms around Rose, attempting to calm her down.

Dilian's face had gone cold. He had not sensed him— or heard him at all, as if the captain had somehow masked his presence.

"Oh my god, we need to figure something out. He's up to something, I can just feel it! He's not going to let the prophecy come true," Ethera's voice cracked, her eyes refusing to look at Rose.

"It's okay, Ethera. Don't worry, we still have time. We'll come up with something."

CHAPTER 16

Three days had passed since Dilian's letter arrived, tied to a bird's leg. A single word had been enough to turn all one hundred and fifty-seven of them into tireless working machines. From sewing armor, preparing medicine, cooking food, sharpening spears, knives, and every tool imaginable that would soon taste battle.

This wasn't just a charge into war. They were going back home. Loss was not written in their future; the prophecy had told them so. The once enchanted forest will bloom new life into their world. Trust was placed into the mortal's hands, the mortal whom they called Ethera Heart.

It had been predestined, and fate had brought her to them. Truly a miracle worth nothing. And they believed it, more than anything.

However, due to the happenings of the last couple of days, she lay alone in the infirmary as the elves celebrated her accomplishments every night, dancing and singing song of a new life. They waited in anticipation until the day she would wake up to lead their people across the sea and take back what rightfully belonged to them.

A loud sound disturbed the mortal's sleep, causing her to stir awake. Without much thought, she forced herself to sit up almost at the same moment her heart had pounded the shock through her veins.

Another thud echoed from the outside, mushing through the numerous sounds she heard all around. A herbal, medical scent filled the room she sat in. She inhaled it deeply, spiraling her brain into action as its fuel had entered her system.

Ethera's throat was hoarse yet again, that was the first thing she had noticed. It seemed that the scratchy feeling refused to let her go. The next was the overwhelming darkness. She almost panicked, but her body moved before her mind, pulling off a blindfold that was lightly wrapped around her head.

She freed her vision, wincing at the impact that the light had made. The infirmary looked as if the tree itself was growing from above it, with every root coming down and hugging the round walls. Roots within roots braided themselves around before disappearing from underneath. Clover leaves sprouted on every side, and the smell of dirt and rain mixed itself in when a gush of wind blew through the vines of what she assumed was a door.

A small dancing fire was mounted on a stick, surrounding a shiny liquid in a metal container. It resembled an extra-large candle, which was something that Ethera had seen before. Right beside it were tools, herbs, bandages, leather pouches, flowers, and more metallic containers with their contents unknown.

The vines rustled again, and this time, an older woman walked in. Ethera glanced in her direction, and a small ray of outdoor light followed the elf through until the vines settled back next to each other.

This elder was dressed much differently from her fellow people. Without being draped with tunics and leather pants decorated with knives of all sizes, she looked rather plain. Instead, her braided hair had grown way beyond her ankles, brushing the ground ever so slightly wherever she went.

She wore a dress, a long-sleeved tunic that had been tied at the waist with a brown rope. It stretched all the way to the bottom of her feet, and decorative flowers were embedded on the hem. Over it, a moss green cape fell to her thighs. Her eyes were a much darker green than what Ethera was used to seeing, and the deep lines at their corners softened when she smiled at the mortal. "How are you feeling, child?" She asked, her voice was like the sound of waves crashing into the sides of an empty oak log.

Ethera felt overwhelmed in her presence. It was clear this woman was powerful, but with something that stretched beyond mere strength. "I-I'm alright," the mortal stuttered, she cleared her throat, attempting to hide her flushed face with her bed hair.

The elder walked closer, standing beside the girl. "Let me have a look at thee," she exclaimed softly, her hands reaching out to touch Ethera's forehead. The elf's hand was cold against the girl's face. A lingering sensation of rain tapping on her skin washed over her, much different from the dangerous coldness that froze over her when the King touched her cheek.

Deliberately, the mortal reached out to the cup that very spot, as though this motion might overshadow the memory that remained. His touch felt like ice water being dumped on her naked, exposed body, and yet somehow, she felt very affected by it. The thought of that very hand grasping the neck of her friend crossed her mind, the room and the expression on her face darkened dangerously.

The elder woman let go, noticing this change in her mind. "Oh, ho! Child, calm thyself. It seems that our fighting spirit has rubbed off on thee."

"Sorry...I'm just tired," sighed Ethera, her hand dragging up to her head as if relieving a future headache. The war was just nine days away...that was barely enough time to prepare *anything*.

"Thou art not alone; your friends have been quite busy whilst you were recovering," she began. "That large one wields the sword admirably. The young lady, with hair as dark as night, shoots with grace most elegant. And the other young child hath rendered considerable aid to this poor, decaying elf."

Ethera gasped in shock at the old elf's honesty. Not literally, but figuratively.

"I have lived a long life, child, yet I am glad to still breathe, to witness the birth of a new world."

Ethera did not want to think of the prophecy. "W-What about Hugo? Is he also doing well?" She quickly asked before the conversation could drift further away.

The elf nodded, a pleased smile appearing. "Ah, yes, that one. A most diligent young child, working earnestly upon that journal." Ethera sighed in relief. He was doing well, and that's all that mattered.

She couldn't seem to remember even arriving at the elves' village or how many days she had been out. "How long have I been—*sleeping*?"

"Three days hence, but I insist you rest two more–."

"THREE DAYS?" Ethera exploded in shock, quickly getting to her feet and searching for her shoes. She had spent so much time lying bedridden, unable to move, think, or plan her next move. But now that she had fully recovered, with no lingering headache or body chills, she had to get to work as soon as possible. The preparations for the war, not to mention finding something on the Pirate King, will not be solved in one day, and there wasn't any time to spare.

"Child-." Ethera hadn't let the elf finish, she grabbed the shoes and ran out in her socks, her feet stepping on little pebbles and roots. She skipped halfway, slipping on one shoe and then the other before breaking into another jog. Her eyes flicked back to her loose laces, and the man's hands flashing in her memory—the way his fingers moved, the glint of his rings as he tied them for her. A nasty scrawl formed on her face as she ran harder, trying to get as far away from that memory.

Yes, it might have been quite romantic to have a man down on one knee, tying the laces of a lady's shoes. And Ethera, just like any other girl, had dreamed of romance and love. But this man was a psychopath, just like the other one who had kissed her underwater in that cursed cave. It seemed that insanity had manifested itself in the form of men, and they haunted her everywhere she went in this world.

"Whoa, slow down there, Ethera!" Reymond called, startled when she almost ran through him. The sun was shining brightly behind as he stood between her and the exit. She squinted slightly, adjusting to the light, and making sure that it was really her friend she was seeing.

His hair was slick with oil and sweat, and so was his body. He looked different, as if life itself had been poured over him. His hands were loosely on his side, and little calluses had already begun forming from the labor of the past few days. A surprisingly long metallic sword hung from his leather belt, secured carefully against his hip. It was new, much different from his rusted pirate decoration.

Ethera was stunned, as if she were asleep for a very, *very* long time. "Whoa, Reymond?"

"Yeah…what can I say? I got an upgrade," He smugly puffed his chest upwards, and Ethera rolled her eyes, forcing back a smile.

He opened his mouth to say something, but the voice of the elder followed behind. "Eeek! The old hag is coming, let's go!" Reymond yelped, grabbing Ethera by her left arm and dragging her away. The elder was strict, and Reymond couldn't remember how many times she had kicked him out of the infirmary and Hugo's temporary study. "That one is crazy! She tried to throw rocks at me once!"

"Did she now?" Ethera asked sarcastically, knowing well that there was a good reason behind that. They both ran through the elf village that was brought to life with more elves than Ethera could count. Where had all of them been hiding? It felt like it was reborn with lots of foot traffic, sounds, conversations, and life.

Reymond had dragged her down to another elf-made cave, this one lit up with natural light that slipped through the roots down towards the inside of another root-made cocoon.

The tunnel was surrounded by shelves, books of all kinds scattered all throughout, pulling them deeper underground into an opening. Ethera wanted to stop to take a look, but Reymond's hand dragged her away. The passageway led to a grand room, and right in the middle of this small study sat a large rectangular table made of polished oak. Its legs were like roots; they dug their clutches into the ground below.

Piles of books, papers, quills, and candles followed, spread all around in every corner. Hugo's back was turned towards them, he shuffled about, hands digging through multiples papers, as if he was looking for something he just had. The loud footsteps of his brother went all over his head as his concentration was unwavering.

Hugo quickly scribbled something down, a grand black quill in one hand and the other gripped the dirty blonde curls of his head.

"Oh, brother~."

The boy sighed heavily, his hand dropping towards his face. "Fuck off," he grunted, taking Ethera slightly by surprise.

Reymond let go of her arm, strolling inside like he owned the place. He raised his hand and, with a wide grin, hit the back of his brother's neck. Hugo got up, his expression dark, and his eyes were ready to drag his brother by the neck and drown him in the Pirate's Lagoon. When his eyes landed on Ethera, his expression softened.

Dark circles shadowed his big brown eyes. "Ethera, you're awake…" His voice was low, surprised, but relief was written all over. Ethera gave him a small smile in return, feeling slightly lightheaded after running so much.

She strolled deeper inside, her eyes running over the table before them. "Whatcha working on?" She asked softly, not wanting to irritate him like his twin did.

He immediately spun around to face the papers on the table, hands resting on the wood. "I'm learning magic," Hugo exclaimed, although the tone in his voice did not match the desperation in his eyes. Ethera was taken aback.

Magic?

Her brows furrowed in confusion. "As in like magical powers and stuff? Like the elves have?"

"Well, yes. You see, the books that you brought back are magic books, but they are encrypted in another language. So, by learning that language, I'm deciphering the journals that the witch left. No doubt there will be something useful in it, maybe something that could even help us stop the…Pirate King," He finished, glancing back at Ethera at the last few words.

Her eyes widened further before being replaced with a smile. "Perfect! That makes sense. Maybe his dear old mother had already come up with something? Anything useful so far?" She questioned, her eyes skimming through the English words that darted across numerous separate papers, thicker and darker in hue compared to the underwater journals. The original books were in another language, a language even elves did not speak. It made sense for Hugo to tackle this, after all, studying and learning was always right up his alley.

Hugo's eyes landed on them, drilling holes through the pages. He shook his head with disappointment. "Not much, just some defense spells and curses. We can't really curse him, can we? I mean, the guy would drop dead for sure, but…" Hugo's voice trailed at the thought.

"I mean, I've already got one body, so what's another on my list?" Ethera joked darkly, but the room went oddly quiet. Nervously, she added, "I'm kidding."

"No shit."

Reymond walked closer to the table, lifting one of Hugo's notes. "I mean, she's not wrong," he shrugged, eyes squinting. The messy scribbles were unreadable, so he tossed them back onto the table before pulling out a chair.

"We can't just go around killing people because they are the bad guys!"

Reymond took a seat, throwing his feet up on the table. "I'm just saying, he threatened to kill Rose."

"Rey's right. But I also agree with what you said. Let's just leave the curse as a last resort. And how would you even be able to cast a spell to begin with? You're a human, last time I checked, we don't have magic in our blood."

Hugo inched closer, shoving his brother's feet off the table. "When we arrived back here, I felt very much useless because I'm not as strong as Reymond or as fast as Juno. I wasn't good with my hands and so I decided to see what these journals were all about. Turns out that the witch was studying magic. It made no sense for her to study it unless she had something that could manifest her lost magic—or at least replicate it. So, I asked around, and Elder Alfar told me of magic stones that can be used to cast spells," he explained carefully, showing a drawn picture of these stones to Ethera, who was the only one who hadn't seen them.

Her eyes widened in realization. The drawing was sloppy, but there was no doubt about it. "I've seen those before," she exhaled, pointing her finger at them excitedly. The excitement didn't last long, and soon her expression darkened against the opposing light. These stones were scattered in the Pirate King's study, all over the shelves and even on his grand table. The thought of that pirate was enough to cast her into a terrible mood. She spat out sourly, "They are in the Pirate King's ship."

"Of-*fucking*-course."

The boys groaned, their excitement evaporating. "Well, we have already sent a few elves to bargain with the goblins. There is a slim chance that they possess some, but from what the elves said, goblins are a greedy bunch. They won't trade anything for the stones unless it's something brighter and shinier. So, we are kind of fucked," Reymond muttered sadly.

Ethera paused, weighing their options. "I could try to steal them. It'll be easier if I just sneak into the ship and take the stones," she suggested, her hand scratching the back of her head.

The twins immediately shook their heads in disapproval. "That's too risky. He already tried to kill Rose, and he might kill you this time."

Ethera knew deep inside her mind that the pirate would not harm her—at least not in any ordinary way. Just the way he looked at her promised something more sinister than death itself.

Death would be a mercy, a release from the suffering he intended to unleash upon her. What he desired the most was to ruin her; to let her pain scar her soul for eternity and through her, the very fabric of the world itself.

It made sense now. His desperate need to uncover her weakness, and the way he had left with a grin twisted with hunger. Yet the thought of breaking into his ship lingered heavily in her chest, refusing to loosen its grip.

Was it fear she felt? Is that why she was hesitating?

"We'll figure something out," Hugo reassured them before kicking both of them out of his private study. There was no peace with Reymond around, and Ethera would only make him anxious rather than focused. He was desperate to impress her, to make himself useful even if it took days or weeks.

Reymond had taken Ethera to see Juno, who was practicing on an empty field alongside other elves, bows swung over their shoulders or pulled in a steady aim. It was Juno's turn, and Ethera hurried forward for a better view.

Juno's short hair was pulled into a bun, a small braid crowning her head. Dark strands escaped from underneath, stirring in the wind. A yellow flower was tucked into the bun, secured by a small wooden pin.

Juno pulled back her bow, raising her chin. The arrow rested on her index finger; a matching yellow feather attached to the end of it, tickled at her cheek, right below her beauty mark. Her shoulders rose as she took a deep breath before letting go. A short swoosh, and it hit its target with perfect precision. Despite the light wind, Juno's arrow did not sway.

The elves clapped their hands in excitement, and some even whistled. Juno turned around, a big, toothy grin on her face. It fell when her eyes landed on the other mortal girl watching from the crowd. The raven head broke into a jog, tossing the bow over her shoulder. Her hands extended, embracing her friend. "Ethera!" Without much thought, she hugged Juno back. "Good to see you looking so healthy!"

"Thanks, and since when did you know how to shoot a bow?" Ethera questioned curiously, eyes peering over her dark green, awfully long, weapon.

Reymond appeared beside them, wrapping his hands around the two girls. "Since like two days ago, she's a natural, I'd say!" He butted in, embracing them for a short second before pulling away.

Juno smirked proudly. "I knew how to shoot when I was a little girl, but I stopped practicing. I'm glad I still remember. My grams would have been so happy to see her lessons pay off so well!"

"You know, this has been quite fun. Swinging swords, shooting arrows, we are like the unstoppable, wreaking force of good. We should have like a team name or something," Reymond joked, throwing a hand over their shoulders and dragging them on a walk.

"Team name? Are you serious, Reymond?" Juno kicked his hand off her and walked a little faster. Ethera had no strength to shoot the boy away, but he was adding a tiresome couple of pounds to her sore body.

"Yeah, I'm thinking 'The Ghoul Busters' since we are going to kick some demonic ass. Or—what about 'The Chosen Delinquents', Wait! No, I got more—."

"How about Team Mouthy Mortals?" Dilian asked, all of a sudden, appearing next to them.

"No, shut up, we're talking."

"That could work too," Dilian shrugged.

"You know, you're kinda part of the group. So how about Team Awesome plus an *Extra*?" Dilian gasped at Reymond's provocation. They have been more at each other's throats ever since they started training together, it was refreshing to see.

Dilian shook his head immediately. The thought of being part of their team was somehow insulting. "How about Team Extra Baggage?" He rhetorically asked, a smirk curling upwards on his pale face. Ethera watched the two bickering as she pulled away to walk alongside Juno. This was a new sight, much different from the silence that she was used to. A lot happened in just a span of three days; everyone seemed to put in their all while she was sleeping like a fool.

"Quit yapping about this and that. Technically, we are the endangered species here," Reymond's loud voice broke any form of thought in Ethera's head; she had long stopped following their conversation. She stayed silent along with Juno, who seemed lost in thought.

"Ah, yes, the lifespan of a fly and the intelligence of a rock. Your kind would disappear so fast, it wouldn't even be considered as an endangered species."

"Oh, please, like you'd survive in the real world, buddy. Your tall ego will get crushed by our skyscrapers in an instant."

"What the hell does that even mean?"

Ethera sighed, rubbing her temples. "Reymond…we don't even have skyscrapers." The tallest building in their town was a church.

"For someone so old, you almost got beat by mighty little me!" Reymond said proudly, a smug smile tugging on his cheeks. Ethera sighed in defeat, there was no getting through Reymond.

Dilian's nose scrunched up. "That's because you kept pointing out how my ears twitch every time I fling my spear!"

"They do! It's so cute, you guys should definitely swing by tomorrow during practice and see it for yourselves. Totally adorable," Reymond giggled like a little girl, curling his bottom lip and batting his eyelashes at Dilian. The elf's ears turned pink, and he shoved Reymond to the side in a strong, non-playful manner. The mortal boy stumbled back but didn't fall; a taunting laugh followed.

"I already told you, they react to sound!" Dilian had the urge to pull his spear and challenge him to another round of combat.

Rose appeared from beside the girls; her hands and clothes stained with white powder. Elven attire was draped around her body, a long, yellowish tunic that extended towards her ankles. "Gosh, you two are still at it?" She asked, the smudges on her cheeks lifted with her smile as she watched the boys fooling around.

Her blue eyes landed on Ethera, the smile deepening. "Wakie wakie, sleeping beauty. Quite the long nap you had, huh? How are you feeling?" She slowed down her steps to match her friends.

Ethera greeted her with a nod. Her hand lifted upwards, wiping the white powder off the blonde's nose and cheeks. "I feel much better, thanks. What have you been up to?"

"Oh, just helping out here and there, I'm not much of a fighter, and background work is good enough for me," She insisted before her eyes glanced down to Juno's hands. She lifted Juno's right arm, twisting it around. A nasty mark accompanied by a few calluses had reddened her olive skin. Ethera winced upon seeing that, immediately looking away after a nasty feeling stirred up in her stomach. Her mind was at it again, playing gross flashbacks as she tried to find the switch.

They came to a stop; Rose quickly stuck her hands into a deep pocket made of loose green fabric that she draped around her waist. "Here, I got you some of this. When will those gloves be ready?" she asked, pulling out a little cotton ball. She unwrapped it carefully, revealing some kind of cream. The strong herbal scent immediately hit their noses.

She applied the medicine to Juno's hand before Reymond jumped in. "What about me? I also have some!" He whined, showing the calluses on both his hands.

Rose gave him a nasty look before closing her cotton handkerchief. "Suck it up, that's for Juno only."

"The gloves should be ready tomorrow, they will definitely help," Juno answered her friend, ignoring the complaints from Reymond.

"Oh, come on, why are you guys always so mean to me!"

They all soon split apart, going back to their designated tasks. Ethera was told to take it easy, so she joined Rose in the back, stocking medical herbs, both freshly harvested and those older ones that were already dried.

She smashed a few with a flat rock and glanced back at a young elven maiden, who nodded in satisfaction. The sound echoed in their cocoon as Ethera repeated the process, passing the mixture to the elf, who simply mixed it with other ingredients and added a hint of a water-like liquid. It felt like chemistry class all over again.

The sun had begun to sink after two hours of honest work, and they kept cleaning until everything was neatly put away. Rose and Ethera walked in silence to the lake to wash up. It didn't grow any less uncomfortable being naked around others—female elves or humans alike. Ethera made a conscious effort not to stare whenever an elf passed by in all her naked glory.

After a quick wash in the cold water, they dressed and returned to find Reymond crouched over an empty fire pit. The rocks were stacked around dry leaves and logs as the mortal boy tried his best to start the fire. Rose squatted beside him, patiently trying to teach him.

Ethera's eyes drifted past them, staring out far ahead into the tall trees looming in the background. A soft swish caught her attention. She looked down just in time to see a small flame catch onto the dry leaves. They all hurriedly sat around it, hands warming up by the heat. Most of the elves had dispersed, leaving behind only a few to tend to the fires or clean up the mess of the busy day.

Now all that remained was for Dilian to return with their dinner. Their stomachs rumbled together out of sequence while in the distance, Hugo broke into an urgent run, the journal pressed tightly to his chest as he skipped over exposed roots in the dimly lit tunnel.

His eyes had long since adjusted to the darkness, despite the faint glow of scattered candles in his temporary dim study. The sun had fully disappeared, and the sky shifted into deep blues and greys.

A grin broke out across his face when he spotted Ethera with Reymond and Rose, gathered around a fire that was barely starting to grow.

He paused before them, catching his breath as he pushed the glasses up the bridge of his nose. "I found it! The answer, the magic that will help us get an upper hand on the Pirate King!" They all sat up, eager to hear what the boy had to say. "We'll bind him. We'll bind his magic so he won't be able to use it!"

"Wait— that's smart! If we bind his magic, he won't be able to control the sea monsters and will be left defenseless," Rose nodded excitedly, jumping to hug Ethera, who sat there stunned by the information.

"W-Well…what do we need for it?"

"Nothing much. Some string, and well, obviously a magic stone. I think the witch was going to use this spell herself, it has been reworded like five times," Hugo pointed out, opening the book. His fingers traced over the words once again. "And, I'm pretty sure this drawing is of him." He turned the book around, and a drawing of an angry fish with arms and legs was drawn on the bottom. The fish had black hair tied into a messy bun. The group burst into laughter, imagining that as the Pirate King. "I'm pretty sure she called him a few fish-slurs. I couldn't translate them properly, but I think one of them means gill brains?"

Ethera snorted, trying to hide her laugh. "Well, now that it's figured out, we can sorta relax." The thought of having the upper hand gave birth to a new thrill in her stomach, an itch for dangerous excitement.

"We should bring that book home with us so we can print that image on a shirt or something."

Rose shook her head, lifting a palm in protest. "Yeah, and match in our yearbook photos? No, thanks!"

"Oh, come on, that'll be so funny!"

CHAPTER 17

By the time morning rolled around, Ethera had a plan. She would steal the stones that would tip the balance of power against the Pirate King. It was a dangerous move, but she felt confident in her ability. After all, this was her specialty. To move within the shadows, taking what wasn't hers and vanishing before anyone could notice.

She was filled to the brim with lies, deception, trickery, murder, and theft. When had she become all the things that she had grown up to despise? Ethera was no better than a villain in her own eyes. The more good she tried to do, the further off course she strayed.

But breaking into the Pirate King's ship and stealing a few of his rocks would be a piece of cake for her. Hugo had been against the idea from the moment she had mentioned it yesterday. It was out of the question, especially given the obvious threat that the King had delivered.

But Hugo was not a part of her plan.

Reymond and Dilian were the ones she needed to ensure that everything would go smoothly. Dilian was a skilled scout and a mighty warrior; he could see well in the dark and knew the woods better than anyone in her party. Reymond was also a capable fighter—at least from the praise she had recently heard. Two were better than one, and Ethera simply identified herself as the cunning brain. Hugo would get those stupid rocks even if it meant it would be the last thing she does.

She quickly packed a few essentials, fastening pouches around her waist before throwing a cape over her shoulders that she had borrowed from Juno when the raven-head had left for practice. Ethera had left the skirt behind, not wanting it to get in the way of the midnight marathon that they were about to participate in.

The night air would only grow colder the closer they get to the open sea, but she was bound to be sweating by the time they reached the coast. She double-checked her pouches, making sure they were empty and open. The act of stealing something so small had to be flawless and unno-ticed. If worse came to worst, she'd talk her way out of trou-ble. But based on the information acquired during the day, that would not be necessary.

"Ready?" A voice called out, suddenly behind her. Reymond wore a short, tunic-like cape; his hood was already pulled over his head. It was one of the elf's signature pieces, and it looked like he had taken a piece from their handbook of stealth. A sword hung at his hip on one side, a smaller knife on the other. The light struck half his face, making him look like a vigilante.

Dilian emerged behind him, his tall frame filling the doorway to the infirmary. He was dressed similarly, though without the need for warmer layers. Elves were a wild folk of nature—extreme temperatures, whether the freezing winter or the scorching summer, rarely affected them. "Let's move while everyone's still distracted," Dilian commanded. The chief was already made aware of their so-called mission, so his words were directed at the mortals who had been left in the dark.

"Hugo and Rose would lose it if they found out, so let's make this quick."

Dilian disappeared, and Reymond followed. "I guess we're not sleeping much tonight," Reymond sighed, weariness heard in his voice. His training had started at first light and stretched well into the afternoon. His body craved rest just as much as his mind, but this mission was worth the sacrifice. "I don't think I'll show up tomorrow," he spoke again, his head tilting towards the elf.

Dilian smacked him on the shoulder almost instantly. "Nice try."

"Come on, guys, save the bickering for later," Ethera ordered, exiting the room. Her eyes glanced around, making sure that none of the others were walking by.

"Fuck off, you can't stop me," Reymond spoke, deliberately ignoring Ethera. "I doubt you'll be able to wake me up, even my mom has a hard time." He did not heed Ethera's warning of silence.

Dilian paused, his mind coming up with all sorts of answers. "Maybe I will lure a beast into your chambers, and have it drag you by your leg," the elf snickered.

"We sleep in the air, genius."

"There are all sorts of beasts, some even take to the air."

"Holy shit, like dragons or something?"

"No, you fool. Dragons have long gone extinct. But perhaps birds—."

"Don't you fucking dare—."

"Where the hell are you three going?" A loud voice yelled out from behind them. Juno had casually caught up, a small smile on her face. It vanished immediately; the garments of their clothes had told her that this was not just a light stroll before dinner.

"Well—."

Before anyone could come up with something smart, the mortal boy interrupted. "We are going to steal a few magic stones from the Mr. High and Mighty King," He answered casually, forgetting all about the definition of a lie. Ethera and Dilian exchanged irritated looks.

Juno raised her eyebrows. "Oh? Are you now?" Her almond eyes glanced at the other two for confirmation. The silence had told her everything.

Reymond had finally caught on to his mistake. "So, we will need you to keep the other two busy. Tell them we are going on a night watch or something. We are counting on you!" He grabbed Juno by the shoulders, turning her around to walk away. He flashed a smile and a quick thumb to Dilian and Ethera, his face read: See? I'm Reliable.

She fought viciously, but his grip was too strong. "Idiot, we don't even have night watches!"

"I don't know Juno—you're smart, so think of something...*smart*."

"We really need those stones, Juno. Hugo knows what he's doing, and there is no guarantee that the elves will be able to bargain with the goblins. If we can just sneak in, grab the rocks, and dip, then we'll really stand a chance against this guy. You weren't there, but…he was really going to kill her. We can't just stand by. What if one of us really gets hurt?"

The sincerity in Ethera's eyes was something unbecoming. Juno nodded, letting go of Reymond's arm. They all exchanged grateful smiles before disappearing into the dark woods.

It was hard to maneuver through once they were deep inside, away from the comforting glow of the village fires. Dilian had no trouble taking the lead. Every few minutes, he would raise a hand, his ears attuned to the forest's subtle sounds.

"It's kind of creepy walking through here," the mortal boy whispered. "At least during the day, you can hear things. Right now…it's just quiet."

They fell silent, listening. Only their footsteps echoed softly through the undergrowth. No crickets. No owls. No life. Did this world even have such obvious animals?

Worry crashed through Ethera; the stillness was agonizing. "Yeah, and let's keep it that way," she whispered back, praying they would not bump into something sinister. The growing uneasiness settled in her chest, and the moment they stepped onto a narrow path that curved to the right, the feeling intensified. She couldn't shake the sensation that the forest had grown a pair of eyes—and all of them were watching them.

She wasn't entirely wrong.

The forest *was* watching. From the camouflaged frog clinging to the bark of a tree, to the one-eyed birds that perched high in the branches. Their single, unblinking gazes pierced through the dense fog that hovered above the ground. Their wings lifted slowly, silently preparing to dive at the intruders—two mortals and one elf.

No one thought to look up, and even if they had, their eyes would have been useless against the falling clouds. Dilian sensed the danger anyway, though he couldn't pinpoint its source. There were too many. Dozens, if not more creatures clinging to every tree. His right hand slid towards the knife on his hip, his left reaching for the staff.

A sharp, unnatural birdcall rang in the air.

The flock dove at the tree in a fit of starvation.

Ethera screamed, the sound tearing through the forest, loud enough to surely alert other predators. Dilian was immediately surrounded, the birds clawing at his face, aiming for his eyes. He fought back with controlled swings, but there were too many.

Ethera panicked, swinging her pocketknife wildly. She took a few stumbling steps backwards, shielding her eyes. Her heel caught on a rock, slamming hard against the ground.

Reymond fought with precision. His sword gleamed as he slashed at the attackers, cutting through them mid-air. Their bodies evaporated into sprinkles of black mist as they fell towards the ground. Ethera could only watch, wishing she could be more like him—more useful when it came to a fight.

He had grown. A lot.

Despite his clumsy demeanor, he had managed to take control of the situation. Determination surged through her at the sight. Gritting her teeth, she stood up and began slashing, landing enough blows to slow them down. Even a little bit was better than nothing.

Through the chaos, Dilian suddenly reappeared in front of them, swinging a long wooden stick lit with flames. The firelight seared through the descending flock. The one-eyed birds screeched in agony, catching flame and retreating to the trees. Some evaporated into black mist that sizzled as it slowly crept towards the ground.

"Jesus…" Reymond muttered, breathless, putting his sword away. "I fucking *hate* birds."

The sounds disappeared almost instantly, but Dilian never let his guard down. "Let's go before they call rein-forcements." No one needed convincing; they all took off running, silent and bursting with adrenaline. Dilian and Reymond were covered in small scratches from the vicious claws of birds they had never seen before. The elf's wounds had already begun to heal in the darkness, unknown to the mortals who could not see. Ethera managed to survive un-scratched, but her lack of aid showed.

The forest felt like a trap—the twigs bent inwards, and the darkness pressed closer in on them. It was odd how safe the Elvenwood had become, while everything around it was poisoned with all sort of creatures. "That won't be the last of the monsters," Dilian warned in a low voice once they were far enough. He paused, scanning the path ahead. His ears twitched, turning around sharply. "Run," he ordered.

Without a word, Ethera and Reymond bolted. Tears blurred their vision from the fear that clutched at their chests. "Oh my god, we are so going to die!" Reymond cried out, glancing back.

A beast was hot on their tail.

A low growl vibrated through the air as if confirming that their eyes were in fact, seeing the truth. The creature was long and lanky; it was hunched over the ground, its long limbs digging into the dirt as it inched closer. Its skin shimmered in the moonlight, mottled with patches of moss like strange, wet, rotting bark. With each step it took, it left behind a trail of blackened earth as if its presence poisoned the ground.

"Mama bird?" Ethera couldn't imagine how Reymond had the time to comment on everything, even in the heat of the moment. The air pierced her limbs in excruciating pain, making even her brain unable to think.

The creature did not look like a bird; it was featherless, but the resemblance was uncanny. Its long beak stretched too wide across its head, the three red eyes shook between the two mortals, undecided on which one to gobble up first.

Ethera glanced back, trying to spot Dilian, who disappeared within the trees. The creature was catching up to them. It was like a cat chasing mice—except the cat was a magical monstrosity and the mice were very, *very* frail.

Dilian had completely concealed his presence, only to appear above the beast, slicing through the air like a fallen leaf. Soundless and quick.

He landed squarely on the beast's back, driving his long spear down with a forceful strike. A deafening shriek ripped through the forest, a warning sent to every other creature lurking in the shadows. He pulled his spear out, jumped off, and landed beside the beast, making sure to finish the job. Dark crimson blood gushed out, making the mortals shriek in disgust.

Dilian didn't wait to celebrate his victory; he broke into another run. The mortals caught the hint a few seconds later, not getting the opportunity to admire the elf's handiwork.

Dash and dip.

"That. Was. Horrifying! I loved it, but let's never do it again," Reymond exclaimed, adrenaline rushing through his legs. Seeing the elf flying around in action was nothing more than watching a 4D movie on the biggest screen imaginable. It was spectacular the way he wielded the spear with such ease. Almost as if they were one.

But it had become clear that without Dilian, they were as good as dead. Reymond's eyes watched the retreating back of the elf, envious of the skill to cut through air like that. No matter how many days or years of practice, he would never be able to do what someone with magic can.

They continued running toward the Pirate's Lagoon. What should have taken them half the day took only two hours with their steady speed. Reymond and Dilian were in excellent shape for long-distance running, and Ethera managed to keep pace well enough to not fall completely behind. Occasionally, they stopped to rest, sip water, and catch their breath before pushing forward. It was easier to outrun danger than to wander slowly and risk another surprise attack.

"It's way scarier at night," Reymond whispered, eyes jumping from every shadow between the trees. He wasn't the only one who was on edge. "At this rate," he added, "the forest might finish us off before we even make it to that ship."

"Don't be foolish," Dilian snapped, his ears focused on the mortal's voice rather than the possible danger ahead. "The only thing that shall finish you mortals is me if you don't shut up."

His tone left no room for argument. They had learned to understand that the hard way; his command was absolute. Dilian was the only reason they were still alive, and for the first time, Reymond was starting to understand the meaning of silence.

The forest eventually cleared, revealing the destination that they had been running to. It was as deserted as before. The fog had become unbearably thick; it crept in from the village and now clung all around them, making it harder to navigate without tripping over the roots and unevenness of the earth.

What was it with pirates and fog? It seemed that even this village did not know what it looked like on a clear day.

As they neared the ship, the group slowed and dropped into a crouch, huddling together as they tried to form a plan. There wasn't much to discuss.

In and out. As quickly as possible.

Dilian straightened out, staring into the distance. His sharp eyes picked up what the mortals could not. "Do you see him? Is he on the ship?" Ethera whispered urgently, firing questions Dilian couldn't yet answer.

He narrowed his eyes, scanning the enormous boat with unnerving focus. But the King was nowhere to be seen. "I don't see anyone," he said at last. "He could be resting in his quarters."

"Okay…okay. Here goes nothing," Ethera murmured to herself. She took a deep breath and looked at her comrades. Reymond offered her a thumbs-up. Dilian gave her a nod of acknowledgement, although his eyes clearly said, 'get caught, and we're all dead'.

"I'll reflect the light if I see anyone coming your way," the elf added, pulling out a small pocketknife. He angled the blade to catch the moonlight, tilting it side to side until it flashed like a silent signal.

Ethera nodded, hoping that it would be noticeable from that distance. She rose carefully and broke into a light jog, keeping low as she moved. Her body ached, and the muscles in her calf pulsed in agony. The boys watched her closely as she ducked behind every obstacle—rocks, barrels, tall weeds—anything she could use to stay hidden from any lurking eyes.

But then her breath caught in her throat. Her body went rigid at the sight.

Much to her horror, the Pirate King appeared at the ship's entrance. His silhouette loomed on the deck, eyes sweeping across the shoreline. Ethera dropped down behind a stack of wooden crates lining the boarding deck, heart pounding in her ears. She held her breath, frozen in place, praying he hadn't seen her.

Ethera tried her best not to peek, half-expecting him to address her the moment she did. Her hands clutched her cape, throwing the hood over her head as if that was going to help her blend in.

She cursed him about a dozen times in her head; he always seemed to have eyes and ears everywhere, shadows in every corner that obeyed his every wish. His grip over this entire world was absolute—it threatened any chance she had of making it home in one piece.

After a tense minute, he began descending the long ramp to the deck, each footstep echoing above her. She watched him as he strolled across the beach toward the only building still lit in the distance: the tavern.

Ethera waited for a few minutes, making sure that the man had made it inside and not deliberately turned around. She broke into a run, her feet pounding against the log ramp, louder than she wanted and heavier than planned. But there was no turning back. Each step carried her desperation, her racing heart, and the narrow window she'd given herself to pull off this mission.

The ship swayed and crept with every movement, chains rattling in the distance as if trying to call for the captain. 'IMPOSTER' was being shouted to the whole Pirate's Lagoon, with the sounds of the waves below that seemed to fall quiet just to eavesdrop.

She had about five to ten minutes before the man could return, that is, if he wasn't staying for a friendly chat.

But Ethera only needed two.

The ship looked even more menacing in the moonlight; the sails were tied up, revealing the long poles that reached high into the night sky. The ropes swayed in the gust of wind. It had become colder, and Ethera felt a nasty chill spread down her back as she tried not to pay attention to it.

She yanked at the handle of the familiar door, only for it to stay still, causing her to stumble back. Frustrated, she rattled the knob a few times, twisting it in every direction before her eyes widened with realization.

Of course, the bloody pirate would have locked it.

Without hesitation, she pulled out her knife, crouching before the door.

Her fingers were clumsy, shaky even as she tried to work some sort of magic. The bulky tip of the blade's end wasn't small enough to fit through the hole, causing her to groan with frustration. If only she had something smaller. If only she had a hairpin.

"I didn't think I'd find a rat aboard my ship; however, the audacity is admirable," A cold voice suddenly spoke behind her, startling her.

Ethera froze, the knife still halted in the door. The grip on the handle tightened as she slowly stood up, attempting her best to pull it out.

It was stuck.

She placed her hand on the door, using it to support herself as she pulled with all her might. The heat on her neck and cheeks opposed the cold night's air as she struggled for a few long, painful seconds. "W-Well, hello there, Your Majesty," Ethera quickly muttered, turning around to face the Pirate King, expecting nothing less than fury. But instead, the same unsettling smile stretched across his face. Was he capable of any other expression?

How did he make it back from the tavern so quickly? She was sure she had seen him walk in. But now, here was, standing right in front of her. His long coat waved behind him, mirroring her own much shorter one. "What brings you to my ship so late? I don't reckon it's because you've missed me?" he asked, stepping closer.

Ethera stepped back, trying to keep a distance, but the locked door behind her left no way out. She was cornered—boxed between two towering walls with no escape in sight. "W-Well, I just thought we should talk about what happened four days ago, don't you think?" The mortal stuttered in the King's presence. His shadow loomed above her, swallowing her from head to toe.

Without a word, he leaned in, and Ethera instinctively closed her eyes, bracing herself for the impact. He didn't strike her; instead, he pulled out the knife, and with a soft click, the door creaked open.

She stumbled back from the surprise, nearly tripping over her own feet. An unyielding grip caught her arm, his wide black eyes locked onto hers, seemingly pale in comparison to the darkness of the room. He was drowning in her scent—freshly bathed sunlight, pine trees, and crushed grass—much like the stench of an elf.

He smiled. "Do come inside."

Ethera quickly brushed his hand off her arm, stepping aside to let the man lead her in. There was no way she would let this beast walk behind her. This beast in the shape of a man. "So…how did you know I snuck in?" Ethera asked casually, trying to take the lead in the conversation.

The urge to clear her throat shook her. There was something about him that made her uneasy—her thoughts dried up, the blood in her veins would pop, and when she would try to speak, her voice would come out hoarse.

He fell silent, weighing the answer in his head. The lights suddenly flickered on. "This ship is a part of me, I know when something washes over here, and I am surprised that this time the waves have brought you."

They certainly did not!

"Well, yes. You see, we are still concerned about what happened last time, and we think it'll be better if we sail on our own ships," Ethera suggested quickly, motioning with her hands. "Nothing personal, of course!" She slowly circled the room like a nervous animal ready to bounce the moment an opportunity presents itself. The elves were preparing their own ships, but from what the elves told her, she was to sail with the King.

To hell with the prophecy.

There was nothing in the books about them having to share a boat.

The stones were still there, sitting still and collecting dust. There was absolutely nothing magical about them, so she could only hope that they were the ones Hugo needed.

The Pirate King had fallen quiet, and for a second, Ethera forgot he was there. "No."

She turned around instantly; her curls flipped over her shoulder. "No?" Shock flashed across her face as she repeated his answer. In the same motion, the hand that brushed past the cupboard closed around the stone, slipping it into her palm as she moved away, stepping toward him. The rock felt hard and cold beneath her touch. She bit back boldly, "Then behave yourself. You threatened us after striking a deal. No one believes for a second that you will stay true to your word."

His smile vanished. "I do plan to stay true to my word," he echoed, repeating her last words. His sudden seriousness almost made Ethera believe him. But just as quickly as it appeared, it vanished. That sweet, poisonous smile curled back onto his face. Ethera looked away, her eyes already in search of another target.

"I don't think you even realize how hard it is for your own people with all these magical folk infesting every corner of your island?"

"No, do tell me," He lied. Her voice was like a seashell, hollow and everlasting.

"That's what I've been hearing. Either way, you will have a war on your hands—whether it be with the demons or the elves. Which brings me to my next point—," she slipped another stone into her pouch, "—I don't quite trust the elves. But to be fair, I don't trust anyone."

"And why is that?"

"Do you think so little of humans? We aren't dumb enough to walk into this war blindly. We are mortals, yes, but not fools. I know we don't belong here. It'd be so easy to get rid of us if they so much as wanted to. And don't you think the prophecy's a little strange? Why must we sail together, of all things? I don't think it really matters which ship we board. And how will our temporary unison play into the birth of a new world, anyway?" Ethera mumbled aloud, hoping to force him into thinking, to draw his focus elsewhere.

It didn't work. His eyes never left her. If not for the darkness of the room, she would have long been caught.

Or perhaps… she already was?

"Sounds to me like we are to give birth to a child," his smile darkened at the sound of his own words. Ethera spun around in the blink of an eye, ready to raise her voice, only to find him already standing beside her.

How long had he been there? Did he *see*?

He leaned closer with every blink of her eye. "Shark caught your tongue, little pebble?" He taunted, taking the breath out of her lungs. She felt small in his presence. Her eyes couldn't hold their own—even his boots were enormous in comparison to her shoes.

She took a sharp breath, hoping it might steady her. "D-Don't be stupid. The prophecy means a new world—a new beginning. Plus, you're not exactly my type," Ethera snapped, thrusting a hand between them, urging him to back away.

He misunderstood the gesture.

With a firm grasp, he caught her hand and pressed it to his chest with his own hand closing over hers. Her fingertips brushed past the golden pendant sleeping there.

The Pirate King was cold, like the seawater beneath the moon. "What are you trying to say?" He asked like a clueless child.

Ethera shuddered, her mind going blank. "I'm gay. I'm *GAY*!" She blurted, mortified to find her hand glued to some random man's solid chest. The thin black tunic rose and fell beneath her palm with every slow breath he took. She couldn't feel the beat of his heart, only the thunder of her own. His eyes had become dangerous, the smile fading as the beast in him paced unpredictably.

Silence had befallen them while Ethera struggled to free her hand. "I beg your pardon?" Questioned the Pirate King. There was a deep vibration in his chest when he exhaled, it created a rippling effect that washed over her like chills that sank their teeth deep into her chest.

"I-I like women. No—I *love* women!" It seemed the more nonsense she poured into the situation, the redder her face became.

His chest shook beneath her touch—he laughed. A low, deep chuckle echoed through the study, ringing in her ears. Suddenly, a wave struck the side of the ship, causing her to stumble back against the cabinet. Her hand reached out, feeling for something she could use to help her get away from him.

If need be, she'd gladly cut her own hand off.

Ethera groaned from frustration, her face practically lighting up the room. She had shouted the first thing that came to mind, and now he wouldn't let it go.

Or her.

She absolutely could not stand him. "Women?"

"Yes! *Women!*" She snapped. "So, respectfully let go of me! Aren't you supposed to be a gentleman, or were the rumors fake?"

Of course, they were lies. Ethera was the sole inventor of those so-called rumors. They had spread far and wide—from her left ear to her right.

The Pirate King had let go, smiling yet again as if he had adopted this new persona of a so-called gentleman. He gripped her hand, pulling it to his lips. "As you wish, my lady," he said, bowing low, his dark orbs never leaving her face as he placed a cold kiss on her knuckles. Only then did he finally let his eyes trail to different parts of her odd features. White strips of her eyelashes, her two-toned brows and eyes, and such strange features. The peculiarity pulled him in.

"If that's all," Ethera began, still dazed as she tried to regain her composure, "I'll take my leave." The mortal had totally forgotten her mission with the distracting close presence of the King that seemed to rattle her more than she was willing to admit. Still, she'd managed to snag two stones, only making it halfway to her original goal.

"Do you want them?"

She froze. "Want what?"

"The magic stones," he noted casually. "Isn't that why you're here? You kept staring at them. If you want it, then just take it."

Ethera raised her chin to meet his eyes. "I was just staring at them because they are pretty. W-What would I even need a rock for?" Playing dumb was not her forte.

His head tilted slightly to get a better look at her unraveled expression. "I think you know the answer to that better than I do." Her eyes darkened, but she made no effort to hide the way she reached for one. She lifted it closer to her face, twirling the stone and examining it.

His face glistened in the light. "Do you really think I'll let you take it for free?"

Ethera scoffed, her eyes shot sparks at him. "Think of it as compensation for the days I had fallen ill. I did just

take care of your problem with my own two *pebble* hands,"
She bit back, stuffing the stone into her side pouch before he
could change his mind.

"You are a funny little pebble. Fine…take it and more
if you so wish," his tone was light, but his next words
dropped like a playful warning. He stepped in front of her,
blocking her path. He added, "—but use them wrong, and
there will be consequences." His cold breath fanned the side
of her cheek. It was unnatural, and she shivered at the sensation, the hairs on the back of her neck rose.

He was dangerous, an entirely different species. It
was easy to forget that, considering how human he looked.

He stood there in his untied black tunic, the lower
half of his tall frame draped with fine coral and blue silks
that hung loosely, some even dragging across the wooden
floor. Jewelry glinted at his fingers and rested carelessly on
his neck. At a glance, he looked nothing less than a man.

A dangerous—*rich* man.

The contrast between one of the most powerful beings in this world compared to the elves was grand. The pirate, for once, feared nothing. He sat comfortably at the top
of the food chain, untouched, unrivaled. No one came close
to even threatening his position.

She could only question why he was so lenient with
her. He turned a blind eye to her foul language, her defiance,
and her lack of respect for him.

"Do you want it?" He asked, drawing her gaze to his.
"It's all yours."

Her eyes had landed on his necklace. The old, weathered piece of bronze rested like a charm against his chest. A

skull carved into a large coin-shaped pendant with a single ruby embedded in its right eye.

Ethera blinked, snapping herself out of it. Every time she was near him, her thoughts would slip out of her control. Lost to distraction—to danger, to something she didn't yet understand.

And it *always* caused her problems.

"What? Are you interested in me or something?"

"I do find you fascinating to watch," he replied vaguely. To him, she was like a fancy new object that washed off on the shore of his beach. A toy, perhaps. One he hadn't yet figured out how to use.

Her skin crawled. "Get in line, fish stick."

CHAPTER 18

The Pirate's Lagoon bustled with life. Both pirates and elves ran amok in every direction, filling the air with unsettling energy and chaos. The pirates, armed with long, pointed swords and brown hats riddled with dark holes, were thrilled more than anyone else to be able to sail the waters without fear of being devoured by the monsters that lurked below.

For the first time in years, the legendary Pirate King had returned, commanding vast armies and permitting sailors to board the great ships that once thrived in these waters.

But unknown to many, their King was no ordinary man—he who had dabbled in dark magic, commanded not only them but the monsters that terrorized the sea. Their relentless violence was no accident—it was under his command, orchestrated to keep everyone off the sea that he had desperately adored.

The Pirate King showed no mercy, not even to his own kind.

Crates overflowing with booze, meat, and exotic fruits lined every ship, tempting the pirates to the everlasting feast despite the time of war. Their ships were massive, far outmatching the ones crafted by the elves—not just in size, but in presence. The pirate ships, were made from dark oak, loomed with towering cabins and three masts clawing the sky above, each draped in black or white sails worn thin by years of violent winds. Their decks creaked with every wave, threatening to hit the others that lined the boarding decks.

The lead ship, the one that belonged to no one other than their king, bore a carved serpent that twisted along the bow, flashing its fangs in a silent, eternal snarl.

On the shoreline, a lone figure of a woman with dual-colored hair and mismatched eyes watched the scene unfold. The air was thick with an overwhelming stench of fish, sweat, dust, and rust. But as she moved closer to the elven ships, the atmosphere shifted. She could finally breathe with ease.

Sculpted from enchanted trees of the Thalorin Forest, the elven ships seemed almost alive. Blessed by ancient spirits for the long voyage ahead, they radiated good fortune and grace. Delicate sails flowed like silk banners in the wind, and green vines traced their way along the railings. A soothing aroma drifted through the air, the blooming scent of soft blue flowers that shimmered in the sunlight enchanted the scene into something peaceful and bearable.

Ethera could only assume that the flowers were enchanted, too, just as much as the elven people were. With their large presence about, it seemed like the fog would not dare to descend upon them.

The mortal hadn't realized she was holding her breath until she stood beside the elegant ships, surrounded by more elves than she had seen in the village. Their tall figures cast shielded her from the scorching sun, and their eyes peered at her for a moment before drifting back to their current tasks of sharpening weapons, loading supplies, and hauling massive number of hand-made arrows. Compared to the mannerless pirates—grimy, wild, and loud—the elves painted a refreshing picture.

It was a strange sight, seeing two different species working together in unison. The elves were ready for war. The pirates, giddy with anticipation, were eager to be part of the battle of the century. Together, they would march to take back the Enchanted Forest from the horrors haunting it, each for their own reasons.

Skeletons—was that what they were?

Ethera was thrilled to be able to witness something so unthinkable. Demons and walking skeletons seemed to shock her more than Hugo conjuring magic with a rock.

Magic or not, Reymond had taken naturally to the sword. As if he were born to wield it. He complained often about his sore muscles from swinging the heavy blade around every morning, but everyone was so surprised that he could even lift it at all. The sword was massive—so heavy that none of the three girls could even budge it.

Reymond had referred to himself as Thor, the only 'worthy' one in their group to be able to wield the ridiculous thing. His remark earned him an arrow whistling past his head, missing by only an inch.

Juno, of course. She never missed unless she intended to. Archery came naturally to her, and much to everyone's surprise, she had carried the gift with her from childhood. The movements weren't easy to get used to; her own body had forgotten how it felt, and much like Reymond, with practice, she got the hang of it. Only recently, she'd confessed that she was considering entering the Olympic archery team—assuming they all made it back alive.

Ethera didn't have any special gifts and, much by contrast, felt useless. Her only talents were talking her way out of trouble—which worked most of the time, and stealing—neither of which felt like she could use out there. And her fists were useless against the supernatural.

Rose wasn't much help in battle either, spending most of her time with the elves, packing food and creating medicine.

Still, Ethera was grateful to be walking again without the nagging fatigue that had plagued her. Not long ago, she'd fallen ill after taking a late afternoon swim in the ocean. She'd walked the way back, soaked to the bone, the midsummer wind slicing through her clothes like knives. And then there was the cursed heart—hanging in a pouch—dangling from the side of her hip.

She could still feel the sickening weight of it, the way it pulsed unnaturally, trying not to think about what she had done. Her regret fell upon provoking the Pirate King.

Everything might have turned out differently if she had just kept her mouth shut. Dilian would have killed the sea witch, and Ethera wouldn't be haunted by nightmares every other night. It always felt like she was running from something, creatures of some kind, that had the intent to kill.

Chills crawled up her spine, clawing at her corset. It has been a while since she had such vivid nightmares. And her own hand tingled with numbness. Even now she could feel it, the dying warmth, and the sound of cracking bones.

A voice rose faintly from the sea, interrupting her thoughts.

She came to a halt, her gaze falling over the calm waves washing over the beach, uncertain whether she had imagined it or if this, too, was part of the strange reality that became her life.

Ethera Heart

She let out a loud groan before making up her mind. With one last glance over her shoulder, she slipped out of view and made her way towards the far side of the water—away from the crowd and the ships. The scent of salt and fish grew stronger with each step, mingling with the gentle sound of easy waves that scattered the shore.

Kicking off the sneakers with her feet, she then peeled off her damp socks and tossed them aside behind her. The warm sand stung slightly underneath her bare feet. Gathering the sides of her skirt, she lifted it slightly and continued toward the water, half-expecting the woman siren to appear again.

But it wasn't her.

Instead, it was him—the man with pitch-black seaweed hair and pale blue skin, his head broke the surface of the still water ahead. The sunlight fell upon his complexion, making the droplets on his forehead and the bridge of his nose shimmer like tiny gems. His two yellow orbs locked in with hers.

He had appeared before her just as suddenly as in the sea witch's cave. He, who had stolen her first kiss to save her life. A shiver ran down Ethera's arms, raising visible chills along her skin.

The merman looked just as enchanting in the sunlight as he did under the water. The water barely moved, clashing against her shins as the mysterious man slowly inched closer. She had no intention of going any deeper than necessary, causing him to take the initiative.

Five feet.

Four.

Three

She stopped before him. "What brings you here, sea-weed?" She called out, her voice strong and sharp. His eyes burned her skin—under different circumstances, they would have equaled the warmth of the sun.

He raised his head higher above water, baring his teeth in a slow, amused smile. There was no doubt in her mind that he could tear flesh with ease with those sharp fangs. He didn't answer right away—pausing deliberately, as if savoring the tension of her fear and interest in him. "I come bearing interesting news that you would love to hear," he spoke at last. His voice sounded deeper above water, more grounded than she remembered from the witch's cavern.

Clearly, this was a trap but intrigued she was. "News?" she asked, drawn by the curiosity tugging at her legs. "What kind of news?"

"For the right price," he paused smoothly, "I'll tell you everything."

Ethera's eyes almost rolled to the back of her skull. Of course, there was a catch. Nothing came for free—not on Earth and especially not here, not in the Pirate's Lagoon.

"And what do you want seaweed?"

His gaze darkened, dropping to her lips. He didn't need to say a word—it seemed Ethera spoke *creep* fluently.

She clenched her jaw. There was no way she was going to prostitute herself for some half-baked piece of information that might not even be worth it. His patience for her answer was refreshing, and it was almost enough to convince her.

"Coming back for more already?" She laughed coldly, tilting her head. "One wasn't enough for you? What a greedy fish." The merman had drifted closer until she stood hovering over him, watching as the sunlight caught on the sharp definition of his broad shoulders. His hair swayed with the little waves, floating towards her.

Ethera towered high above him, and a fragile illusion of control washed over her. She knew full well that he could easily grab her ankles and pull her under, somehow trusting that he wouldn't stoop so low.

"That was underwater," He muttered like a spoiled child, his voice barely louder than the sound of the water. "I want one here." His voice was nothing more than a whisper, laced with such fear, as if even a fish might hear his tide-stirring request.

Ethera's eyes narrowed. Her mind was already working, turning over the situation and cooking up a solution that would still give her what she wanted. She smiled, biting the corner of her mouth and restraining her malicious thoughts. "Fine, close your eyes."

The merman listened without hesitation. Little droplets sat on his long lashes, sparkling like sea treasures in the sun. Ethera leaned in, her eyes never closed, fearing that the man might attack and swallow her entire existence. She tilted her head, brows furrowing in slight embarrassment as her lips made contact with his cold cheek for an excruciatingly long two seconds. She pulled away, forcing herself to look at him. A sudden urge to lick her lips crossed her mind.

Startled, the merman's hand reached out to grab the spot she kissed, eyes fluttering open. The mortal couldn't hide her creeping smile; the bewildered look on his face bore an unforgettable hole in her memory. "Well, a deal is a deal. Now then, what is this information you have for me?" She acted smug, but the whales in her stomach were doing back-flips.

"What was that?" His words bubbled in his mouth like a fish trying to talk out of water.

"A kiss, duh. You didn't specify what kind you wanted so—."

His hand finally dropped back into the water; face scrunched with impatience. "Must I teach you everything?" His arm shot out, pale fin-like fingers curled around the back of her neck, pulling her small frame closer to the water.

Ethera swayed, her hands slipped from her skirt at the sudden pull as she struggled to keep her balance. One of her knees went down, along with an arm, soaking the dress she tried so hard to keep dry.

The merman had gotten what he came for; her lips were now fully his to claim and do as he pleased—along with her mouth. The shock of the cold water lapped against her thighs and waist, making Ethera gasp against his lips. He seized this opportunity; his tongue explored boldly, fighting for what he thought was his rightful place.

Inside of her.

Her fingers dug into the sand below the water, anchoring herself, while her other hand trembled against his solid chest. He had his clutches in her, his fingers interlaced with her hair, seizing her body from any movement. His other hand secured her waist, pinning her in place and sealing off any hope of escape.

She didn't struggle to free herself; her body seemed to fall into a temporary state of shock. Her breath was caught in her throat; every inhale was stolen by his relentless hold on her lips as he took every ounce of oxygen within her body. Ethera's stomach twisted in knots, and her cheeks flushed the color of the setting sun, mirroring the dark and burning depth of his eyes.

It frightened her. She was the one who provoked him, and yet she found herself unable to resist the consequences. A dark thrill stirred beneath her fear, and a sudden urge to keep going overlapped her ability to think. The tips of her fingers traced his collarbone, and the grip on her hair tightened. A sharp tooth grazed her bottom lip, biting down just enough to draw blood. His tongue traced the fresh wound, swirling with possessive insistence.

Ethera's eyes flew open, summoning the courage to pull away. No matter how fiercely she shoved or struck, he wouldn't let go. Instead, he tightened his hold, drawing her even closer—her waist pressed firmly against his chest, her skirts dancing along his scales against the rising sand.

Without thinking, her hand shot up and grabbed his hair, yanking him away from her. "Shameless bastard! How dare you bite me, *again*?" She squealed, stumbling to her feet, her hands releasing his hair. His fin gripped her soaking arm, helping her up despite her frantic attempts to shake him off. It reminded him of a fish fighting a shark; the resistance was laughable, and it made the corner of his mouth twitch upward.

She had caught on to his smirk. Her eyes flickered to his bare chest, and instinctively, she raised an arm to shield her eyes while still trying to tug her wrist free. His half-naked presence seemed to bother her more than before, her face flushing a million different colors, each one hotter than the last.

She had momentarily lost her senses; his words must have cast a spell on her. "Crazy fish bastard!" She shouted, her legs shuffling awkwardly in place. Ethera's eyes widened in realization. With one quick motion, she drew her dagger, the blade gleaming from the water, the end pointing viciously at the merman before her. "Let go of me right now before I turn you into fish dinner!"

He chuckled, his hand immediately letting go. "Easy there, crabkin."

"Crabkin? What the fuck is that supposed to mean?"

He bared his teeth in amusement, leaning into the blade without hesitation. He knew she wouldn't use it on him. "Your face resembles that of a crab. And since we're apparently close enough to give each other nicknames—."

"We are NOT close, seaweed. These are insults! *Insults*!"

He laughed darkly, catching the hand that held the knife and twisting it with ease. Ethera stumbled backwards, her skirts tangling around her legs. Her toes dug into the sand, trying to bring back the lost balance. Her back landed against his chest, and his fingers slithered toward her corset once more.

"The Pirate King has betrayed you," he murmured, his voice dropping to a serious whisper. "The demons and their army are waiting to ambush you the moment you arrive on the other side."

Ethera froze, her strength immediately drained from her limbs through the sound of his voice. Her hand fell to her side, the dagger almost slipped out.

"How do you know this?"

"I just do. He'll lead you through the waters, straight into a trap. Your elf friends will die. The pirates join the winning side and the Enchanted Forest? Gone. Your mortal friends will vanish too; all will be over in a snap of his finger."

"W-Why are you telling me this? Why betray *your king*?"

He leaned closer, his pale lips nearly brushing her ear. "Let's just say I've found something worth the price. So, what will you do, Ethera Heart? Will you take advantage of this newfound truth…or will you and your friends fall prey to the demons?"

The sound of her name on his lips sent an involuntary shiver down her spine. His grip softened, becoming no more than a light graze of fingertips, tracing the sides of her bare hands and wrists. He lingered like that, enjoying the close proximity and taking advantage of Ethera's mind, which had fallen victim to the new dilemma.

The hair that fell loosely against her ears tickled with every purposeful breath he blew her way as if daring her to move.

And so, she did.

Snapping from her trance, Ethera broke away and dove for the shore, putting as much distance as she could between herself and this dangerous sea creature. She gripped her wrists protectively, her back turned to him. The warm sand glued to her legs, the light wind barely budging her drenched skirt.

She didn't dare look back. But, nevertheless, she stayed and listened. He hadn't moved. The only sign of life was the slow sweep of his tail in the water that occasionally broke the surface.

"Ethera Heart," He called, voice low and sweet like a siren's song. "Just know that if you ever jump in the water, I will keep you."

Silence fell like a stone, forgotten, sinking deep and sending slow, unseen ripples through her heart.

Ethera didn't turn around, not until the sound of water shifting signaled the creature's departure. Only then did she finally let herself breathe. "What the hell does that even mean?"

She hurried back, breaking out into a sprint. There was no time to lose. The entire island made her sick with fury, and the desperation to escape was suffocating. The merman's words echoed in her mind.

What was she supposed to do now?

If she warned the elves about the ambush, they'd never board those ships. And without the ships, there would be no way of getting across the Crimson Waters. They will be stuck here longer…if not forever.

But if she kept her mouth shut…

The casualties would haunt her. Their blood would stain her conscience; a wound carved with a poisonous blade. But what did it matter?

This war was not hers to fight to begin with. It had started as someone else's problem, and it would end that way, too. She had already taken a life with her own two hands.

She had done more than enough for these people. Her hands were forever red. Ethera came to a halt, looking down at her trembling fingers. Confusion had transformed into rage. The truth had made her blood boil; it was worth the icy tingle that still clung to her bruised lips.

What would she even tell the others? It's not like she'd ever mentioned the first meeting with the merman, or second, for that matter. Her arms dropped to her sides, two balls of fists forming, one against the body of the blade.

A dark thought slithered into her mind.

Revenge.

She will flip the cards until they favor her—and her only. After all, that's what she was best at. The dirtier the game, the more she craved to sink her teeth in. She wanted, more than anything, to make the Pirate King pay for doing this to her.

"Ethera? What are you doing here? Hurry up, we're leaving soon!" Juno's voice broke through Ethera's thoughts. The dual-haired girl turned to see her friend approaching, a bow slung over her shoulder and a quiver strapped across her back. The familiar pirate attire was long gone. Instead, she resembled an elf. An elf in Doc Martens.

Juno immediately took notice of Ethera's sluggish gaze and smiled warmly. "I tried scrubbing off the mud. This looks better than before, right? Oh, and check this out—."

She spun in place, twirling with ease in the sand and gesturing proudly at her new outfit. The leather pants hugged her frame perfectly, tailored by skilled elven hands. Her tunic remained the same, simple with visible torn sleeves that were stitched back together. A leather glove draped her right hand, its strings hanging loose, making it easy to adjust or take off with ease.

"Oh, and this right here—" she lifted her hand, wiggling her fingers. "—one of the elf girls made it for me. I told them all about these gloves. They help relieve the tension on the fingers when you shoot, y'know? The elves absolutely loved it! For a second, they thought I was this really cool genius, but I had to break the ice. It was nice being praised for something so small, even if it only lasted a minute. What about you? Where have you been?"

Ethera forced a smile. Juno's enthusiasm felt like a heavy weight pressing down on her chest, making it unbearable to take a breath. Juno's eyes drifted off to Ethera, her face soon morphing into confusion.

"I, uh…took a tumble in the water. Actually—that reminds me—I kind of left my shoes. Walk with me?" Her expression shifted, guilt vanishing behind a carefully practiced mask. The sand clung stubbornly to the hem of her skirt. And it pissed her off.

"Oh gosh, you're soaked! And your lips—you're bleeding," Ethera's hand shot up to cover her mouth. She had forgotten all about the cut. The mark that he maliciously left behind. Her tongue traced the visible raw skin.

It burned.

She could taste the sea on her lips.

Ethera looked away, her stomach knotting. "Yeah, I tripped and hit a rock on the way down," she lied. "But anyways...are my pants ready? I can't bear another second dragging this skirt around." She was afraid to meet Juno's eyes, for all the right reasons. The girl was highly perceptive.

Juno laughed. "Almost, don't worry. You shall look like elven kin in no time."

Ethera looked away quickly, afraid that her abused lips would reveal the truth that she was desperately trying to hide. Her ears burned with heat—whether from her own frustration or the sun above. Only then did the realization hit her how absolutely lewd it had been to kiss a half-naked stranger. A magical sea creature, sure, but no less a man.

"Come on," Ethera urged quickly, putting on her socks and sneakers. "Let's have some fish for lunch before we leave."

"Oh—I should probably warn you," Juno added casually. "They actually showed up."

"Who did?"

"The others."

Ethera paused, swallowing hard. That was going to be quite a sight.

"Don't worry," Juno reassured, tugging her gently forward. "They're boarding separate ships. I'm assuming their kind doesn't like to mingle with elves or pirates. Try not to stare too much, it makes them *grumpier*."

As the two girls walked closer, Ethera began noticing unfamiliar figures moving across the shore—smaller, round-bodied people that hadn't been there before. Their heads were disproportionately large, and thick stones sat on top of their even rounder shoulders. Their necks were barely visible beneath the layers of dark, hard skin, and their short legs carried them with a hurried, swayed walk. Compared to the tall, elegant elves, these newcomers looked like oversized mushrooms with arms. But Ethera found it hard to look away.

The goblins had finally arrived.

Despite their late and comical appearance, they were anything but harmless. The skin, as thick as stone, acted as natural armor, making it difficult to be injured by blades or arrows unless struck in the precise spot. Warts and jagged scars covered their exposed limbs like battle medals.

Their clothes were nothing more than a messy patchwork of different fabrics they could get their greedy hands on. Scraps of leather stitched with bones draped their short legs, belts dangling with mismatched tools and trinkets.

Their little feet shuffled in a hurry, kicking up puffs of sand. Eagerness and jagged rows of cracked teeth glinted in anticipation for the war to come. They weren't just ready to fight; they were eager to bleed their enemies dry, to soak their own hardened skin in blood.

The elven soldiers whispered of an old superstition that warned them so—it softened the goblin's tormented flesh.

Ethera, however, wasn't so sure there would be any blood to spill. At least on the enemy's side. As far as she knew. skeletons did not bleed.

Demons might. And if they did, she would imagine it to be ink so dark and taunting that even a single glance could put a stain on ones soul for eternity. Just thinking about the idea of cutting something open again sent a shiver down her neck and arms. She scratched them with her chipped nails, trying to chase the sensation away.

A sudden voice chased her away. "What are yee lookin' at?" One of the goblins growled, nostrils flaring beneath its round nose. Ethera and Juno ducked their heads in a hurry, picking up their pace with their hands interlaced as they passed the creature. That was enough to shake the nerves off; instead, a few short steps later, they both burst out laughing.

"Oh my god—." Juno wheezed.

"I don't think I'll ever forget this," Ethera murmured, breathless.

But forgetting it felt impossible. This journey had shaped her into someone new, someone even she had a hard time getting to know. And it wasn't over. The final chapter was yet to come.

Things were different. She had friends, she had a purpose. For the first time in her life, she felt like she belonged somewhere. They had started as strangers, clashing in pointless arguments. But every fight, every vulnerable moment they shared had made them stronger together.

There were still things Ethera hadn't said. Things she feared might push them away. But deep down, she knew her new family wouldn't reject her. Not for flaws that were not of her own doing.

Juno gasped. "Oh god, we are boarding *the* Black Pearl?" Her eyes fixed straight ahead. Her tone was light, but her face was dead serious.

Ethera followed her gaze.

The Pirate King's ship loomed in the clearing ahead, a monstrous beauty had been revealed. A sleek beast was stained with wood so dark it almost seemed black. The sun had pierced through, casting light on its true color. A dried bloody brown. Shells clung stubbornly along the sides of the ship and the body of the woman, looking like scales of a sea serpent.

The ship looked alive. Hungry, even.

Before Ethera could ask what Juno meant, they spotted their friends standing by a group of elves. They were no longer dressed in their usual green leather. Instead, the elves' garments were replaced with combat gear. Blackened armor that blended with the shadows that they knew awaited them on the other side. Their boots were heavy, thick with knives. Their dark olive tunics were tucked in the black leather gloves that were coated with a thick layer of tree bark, visible only upon closer inspection. Other parts of their garments concealed the bark, reinforcing their bodies like second skins of durable protection.

Belts tied around their waists, little pockets, and small visible daggers lined them. Spears flung over their shoulders, each one unique to every elf, though only the top ends were visible. The tips glowed in the light, their shapes and metals subtly different from their neighbors. White hair was braided and tied tightly at the crowns; it looked like pale silks in the sunlight. Even the mortals hadn't noticed their color beneath the rustling leaves of the Thalorin Forest.

Reymond was the first to spot them. He waved at them, breaking from his group. "There you guys are!" He wore the same leather trousers and boots that looked twice his size despite the perfect, comfortable fit. His shirt was a relic of their old world, recalling the good days of the detention before the storm. The color was faded and cracked, and the once-black fabric had faded out into a brownish gray. Across his chest, *Not Dead Yet* was written in bold, faded letters, the Es replaced with wide, star-shaped eyes. His arms flexed as he spun his sword lazily, a smug grin plastered on his face.

Rose was still a pirate queen on a full scale. Her side braid mirrored the elven tradition, but her human ears peeked through, betraying her origins. She had long lost the pirate hat, but her dark eyeshadow made up for the lack of accessories.

Ashadow, she had called it. Made from the leftover ash of their fires. Her blue eyes appeared bolder under the sunlight, leaving Juno and Ethera stunned from the impeccable blending. Her rosy lips sparkled from her lip gloss; after all, she had saved it for this specific day.

Hugo arrived last; his mortal shirt bore an animated character that no one seemed to recognize. His brown trousers were rolled up to his shins, and his checker vans were desperately crying to be put down. A large bag hung over his shoulder, its contents known to everyone in their group. He had a larger pouch on his hips, unzipped, and a corner of the transcribed book peeked out. His gaze found Ethera. They shared a wordless look, a silent acknowledgement. Half wet and soiled, Ethera greeted them with an encouraging smile.

Rose immediately bubbled up with joy. "Look, they made me a small sword!" She announced to the two, turning dramatically to show off the slender, long blade on her hip. The handle was freshly polished, blinding them.

Reymond snorted. "Girl, I told you, that's a toothpick."

"Ready?" Hugo asked quietly, eyes still on Ethera as the quarrel of their friends faded in the background.

"Let's save the world and go home," his twin grinned, "I'm itching to test out my skills on someone smaller than my sensei."

Together, they all boarded the Pirate King's ship.

CHAPTER 19

The cold winds weren't the only thing sending a hive of chills down Ethera's spine. The thought that the man inside the ship's cabin had betrayed them was far more unsettling.

She had taken a risk. A calculated one. But the angry waves crashing against the side of the ship felt like a sign of something worse.

The sun blazed overhead, yet Ethera shivered, wrapping her arms around her. She tried to focus on the future; on the life she was returning to—a better one at that. The third year of high school had reshaped her completely, and she could only hope they would be back in time to finish it.

Risks must be taken, she reminded herself. It was a dangerous game, and the pieces were their lives. Her eyes drifted to Hugo, who sat still, head resting against the wall, eyes closed. His hair fluttered in the wind, fluffy and wild. He looked more like his twin now, especially with the new freckles that touched his cheekbones.

He wasn't asleep but deep in thought, much like Ethera. She was easy to read, or as she let herself, and he already had a sense of what was about to happen. Still, he made no move to stop it.

This little adventure had confirmed what his ego had long suspected: Ethera was just better than him. In every thought, shape, and form. Brilliant, fast-thinking, and fearless when it came to making decisions. She never hesitated when she believed she could control the outcome.

And she *always* knew she could.

To Hugo, she was extraordinary. It was why he tried so hard to catch up to her. But the more he ran, the faster she moved—flawlessly, always a step ahead, always bending the world to her will. Even now, he waited on standby, ready to run to her side the moment she gave the signal.

It was her plan. Not his. But what did it matter? She needed his ability—the skill he had acquired just for her, and he was willing to face the consequences to make sure she could use it. Deep down, he knew that if she truly set her mind to it, Ethera could also learn to wield magic just as he did.

With the elves' guidance and the help of that book she had found, he had learned to manifest magic. To turn thought into reality. Whether levitating a leaf or binding the power of the Pirate King, it was now possible.

With training, prayer, and practice that the elven people were kind enough to share. The learning process was an adventure of its own.

As the voyage neared its midpoint, Hugo found himself drowning in a pool of anxiety. He repeated the words of the spell in his mind. Over and over again, as if a single stray thought would erase hours' worth of practice.

The creak of the cabin door was masked by the loud clashes of the waves that carried the enormous boat. The captain slipped out, the hem of his black coat barely brushing the spotless deck.

The Pirate King dabbled in luxury. He adorned himself with jewelry, gold rings on almost every finger, and draped himself with the finest of silks.

His dark eyes locked on the only figure standing before him—the mortal's face was turned away, her eyes fixated on the horizon. With the wind between them, it was easy for him to catch her scent—the stretch of salt and sea, laced with the sweet, poisonous aroma of some exotic flower. Much different from his, that of nothingness. The woman didn't notice his presence until the edge of his coat brushed against her moss green trousers. She flinched slightly and turned at once, her hands still gripping the wooden railing.

Her palms were slick with sudden sweat as she offered a forced smile. "Cold at sea, huh?"

The captain answered with a slow, knowing grin. "As always."

"What brings you out here? Ready to take the wheel, Captain?" she asked, sarcasm crawling from the depths of her throat. She was yet to see him take the helm. In fact, much to her surprise, no one has touched the polished spokes since their departure.

The displeasure in her tone was obvious, but the pirate was already used to it. "I'm in need of some company. Come have a drink with me," he ordered, his voice deepening into a growl. He didn't wait for an answer—just hovered a moment, then turned on his heel. This time, his footsteps were deliberate, loud against the wood below as if to ensure she noticed his retreat.

A lump caught in her throat. She swallowed it, masking her uneasiness. "O-Okay," she stammered, unintentionally. She followed, but not before glancing back and meeting Hugo's gaze across the deck. His expression was unreadable. Ethera knew one wrong move could drown them all in the middle of the ocean. No amount of clever words could save their feeble mortal lives.

"It's dark in here. More than usual," she said, more to herself than him, trying to act normal.

He walked ahead, unbothered by the darkness, as if he could see right through it. She quickened her pace behind him as her eyes adjusted to the dim interior. "My pixies all died," he crooned, his voice echoing with dark amusement. "They get seasick when we slice through the winds at such speeds."

The cabin windows rattled with the ship's motion and Ethera flinched, having the urge to grab on to something. Her gaze drifted to the large table in the center—the map's contents had been adjusted to reflect the coming war. A compass, scattered stones, miniature ships, weathered coins, and bright red apples were stacked on top of each other with uncanny precision in a shallow golden dish.

"So...you wanted to talk about something?" Ethera ventured freely once the ship's movement settled. She felt nervous standing about, and she couldn't quite figure out how to steer this conversation to her advantage because this time, she already had everything she needed from him. The memory of what happened last time flashed in her mind and she shivered.

Behind her, he rustled through something. Her eyes wondered around again, concealing the urge to kill with curiosity. Each visit revealed something new—today, it was a painting lying on the ground in the corner, partly hidden under a draped red velvet cloth. From beneath it, a child's painted eyes peeked through. The thought struck her, was that the captain as a child? He must have been one once. She turned quickly as his footsteps came to a halt.

"Let's have a toast," he began, his teeth gleaming in the low light. "To a successful victory."

"We've still got a long way to go," Ethera replied, carefully calculating what someone clueless about the future might say. She almost tripped over her own words with each sentence the man threw at her.

"We're nearly there." He stepped closer, a loose strand of his raven hair fell over his pale forehead, his smile curling upwards.

Her eyes caught sight of two golden goblets cradled in his hands, fingers painted white and gold. The embedded gems didn't sparkle—they stared back at her with a captivating dullness.

She rubbed her forearms. "I don't drink. I'm not even eighteen yet." Her voice was polite but steady.

"Oh?" The surprise flickered in his smile. Then, without hesitation, he clicked the goblets together and drowned them both in one fluid motion.

Ethera couldn't help but watch. Was that real gold? She could only imagine how much one of those cups might fetch back home.

"What a gentleman," she cooed, flashing a fake smile.

The Pirate King didn't flinch as the alcohol slid down his throat, but its warmth spread slowly through his body, lingering in his veins. He loved rum—a sweet, caramelized flavor that left just the right burning sensation in his mouth.

"Since you've got nothing else to say," Ethera continued, her voice cool, "I'll be taking my leave."

He turned around, placing the goblets down. "You are so quick to escape me."

"I mean—who wouldn't? You're quite a dangerous breed to hang around with."

His back was turned to face her, his expression hidden. "You would make a fine pirate," he suddenly imagined. The comment was unsolicited and unwelcome.

Ethera, though fond of the feel and flair of pirate garments and the freedom that came with them, would rather drop dead than be called one. The constant stench of fish alone would be more than enough to drive her mad. "Funny joke," she muttered, forcing a short laugh. Her weight shifted to her left foot, ready to run.

He rested his hands on the table, fingers tapping against the map. The goblets cast deep shadows across it. Her eyes fell to it, widening slightly, her head tilted to get a better look. The inked land beneath the cups, once known as the Enchanted Forest, sparked a sudden thought that momentarily dulled her awareness.

She looked up and froze. He had turned, the dark orbs watching her intensely.

Sharp and predatory.

It was *thrilling*.

A rush surged through her fingertips, racing to her heart. This was a game. And this…or rather *he*, was the final obstacle. Acting on impulse, she stepped forward and gave him a light push towards the table. The unexpected contact made him stumble slightly, his hand gripping the edges of the wood to steady himself. Ethera stood tall, trying to project confidence and intimidation.

It wasn't the same with someone like the Pirate King. A warning was what she wanted to get across the table. She wasn't trying to corner him, only to let him know that she wasn't a pawn to be used and discarded.

She paused for effect, making sure he took notice of their close proximity. "Watch yourself, *Your Majesty*," she hissed coldly. "If you even think about betraying me, I won't take it lightly."

He didn't react. Didn't even blink. As if he'd expected nothing less from her. As if she reminded him of himself.

A past he was trying to drown.

Ethera turned to leave, then paused. With a subtle flick, she tossed something over her shoulder. The golden goblet he had drunk from landed in his hands, a clunk echoed in his study as it rang against his rings. His eyes widened at the realization—he hadn't even noticed her take it. Not in the moment and not in the aftermath.

Despite her racing heartbeat, Ethera smiled. A soft, steady glow lit her striking white strands as she watched him. "I'm not afraid to get my hands dirty. But you already knew that, huh?" she whispered, then slipped out of the cabin and into the sun's warm embrace.

The wind hit her instantly, cutting through the heat that still had its hold around her body. Threatening the Pirate King—that was exactly what a reckless, *clueless,* Ethera would've done.

And so, she did just that. Even if her heart still thundered from the rush.

Hugo stood where she'd been not long ago, his back to her, stiff and silent. His loose shirt flickered in the wind as he massaged his knuckles, nervous energy seeping through his fingertips.

"We're good, for now," she spoke softly, voice as mellow as a midsummers rain. Her eyes flickered toward the deck, scanning for any watching crew. Their ragged faces buzzed with excitement. To be able to sail under His Majesty was honor beyond belief. "We'll be arriving soon. Get ready."

Hugo nodded but didn't look at her. He swallowed hard, his thoughts as dry as his throat. Ethera turned to him, sensing something wrong. The corners of her mouth tugged upwards. "Trust me," she added shortly.

The words made his eyes widen. He turned, studying her expression. She was planning something, just as she always did. And if it was to work, his trust was much needed. He nodded again, tight-lipped, worry etched into his face.

Trust her? *Always.*

The two of them straightened, tension replaced by anticipation as the island finally came into view—at first just a dot on the horizon. But with every wave the ship cut through, it grew, slowly but steadily.

The island was enormous. Much larger than the one they had departed. But even with all that space, it felt lifeless. The trees stood wilted and rotten, the grass had turned into a yellow crusty color, and every flower decayed where it once bloomed. The only thing that stood out was the crystal castle at the island's heart, once a beacon of pure white light, and now darkened like a shadow cast across a heart.

It was a warning flashing them to turn back.

Black clouds hovered all around; the blue sky that joined them in their sails had turned deep gray. Jagged rocks lined the right side of the island, clustered at the steep base of a cliff. In the middle, a long pale beach curved westward, disappearing from view. A low fog crept over the dead forest, weaving the ghostly veil and shielding the enemy hidden from view. The ships all came to a halt, as if they too fell into shock at what had become of the place they once called home.

They deployed smaller boats. The Pirate King's first boat boarded about twenty soldiers, a mix between pirate and elf. The goblins had boarded their own boats that gave up under their crushing weight.

They paddled in silence, holding their breath in fear that the island was watching and would react to their intrusion in a second. Quietly but quickly, their forces moved in as close to the shore as possible. Hoping off the boats, their leather boots landed in the cold water with a splash. The elves moved first, slowly crawling close to the ground and awaiting the rest of their unordinary allies to fall in.

The air was heavier on land than it was on sea. Still and suffocating. Every sound was muffled, and even the wind seemed to hold its breath. Ethera's eyes locked on the forest, and her heart dropped. Something was moving ahead, the darkness multiplying and spreading towards the shore, contaminating the only color this island had.

The restless army of the dead had awakened.

What began as a scattered few turned into a horde in a matter of seconds. Corpses rose from the ground unnaturally, tripping over their own comrades in an uncoordinated fit of hunger. They dragged their bodies across the sand. Some had begun to sprint, while others limped or crawled. But all had one goal in common. To kill the impostors.

The army of the dead was not something Ethera had prepared for. She assumed zombies—but instead, the skeletons had no physical body mass. They wore bits of old armor, ripped pieces of fabric that clung to their bones, and rusted weapons that were glued to their fingers. Their skeletons seemed to take the shape of many different species, some that she didn't recognize. But without a doubt, some of them were fallen elves.

There was no life in their eyes, but a faint, ghostly glow flickered within.

And so it was true.

The Pirate King had betrayed them.

CHAPTER 20

Shock infected the elves, along with the pirates. But they didn't waste time to speculate, instead, unleashed a furious cry and charged forward, swords and spears drawn. None of them questioned how the skeletons knew of their arrival. It did not matter. The moment steel clashed with bone, the war bloomed on the once enchanted land.

The clatter of the blades, the screams of the dying, and the roar of battle swallowed everything but the footsteps behind Ethera and Hugo stood out the loudest.

The Pirate King appeared behind them, his smile wide at this sight. "Are you disappointed?" he asked, his voice smooth yet mocking. His eyes naturally went to Ethera.

Her expression remained cold. "I'm not surprised," she replied. In a sudden motion, she reached out and grabbed his wrist, wrapping something around it with practiced precision.

Her eyes locked with Hugo's. "Now!" she cried, desperation flashing through her calm facade.

Hugo didn't hesitate. He spoke quickly—words Ethera didn't recognize. The rhyme of an ancient music box twisted by magic spilled through the palm of Hugo's hand that clutched a rock. The Pirate King stumbled back, his smile faltering. The dark chant rang through the air like a curse reborn, freezing his body in place before he could react. It stuck to his skin, twisting within his limbs and through his blood.

The beads glowed brighter, the ends connecting together. It had been a long time since someone used black magic on him—and succeeded. He started at his hand, where the binding now pulsed faintly in the form of a ragged string against his skin. He flexed his fingers, brows furrowing.

Hugo stood firm, the spellbook open in one hand despite the chant being permanently carved into his soul. In the other, he held a crystal—the very same one Ethera had borrowed from the captain's quarters. Its glow dimmed faintly as the magic settled. Hugo's eyes widened through his glasses, focused on the pirate before them. Another spell threatened to escape his lips as his stomach dropped into uncomfortable loops.

Did it work? Or had he failed her?

The battle raged behind them, but for a moment, the world had narrowed down to this highlighted scene. Two mortals, one spell, and a sea god—the Pirate King, caught like a fish in a net.

The mana around the pirate had taken the form of wind, swirling tightly around its user and marking the completion of a difficult spell.

Hugo had bound the Pirate King's magic, cutting off all communication with his sea pets. On top of that, his movement had been restricted, reflecting the command of his mind. "What the bloody hell is this?" he growled, jerking the bracelet from his wrist. The amusement had drained from his face, and the black and brown string of beads shrank tightly around his hand, burning into his pale complexion.

"A gift. Since you like jewelry so much," Ethera teased, stealing a smug smile directly from the pirate's book.

He let out a cold, dry laugh. "What makes you think—" He stopped, paralyzed from his own thoughts. The moment he imagined doing something violent—like grabbing the mortal by her throat, the spell had caught him, binding the intent before the action.

Ethera let out a dry laugh. "I warned you," she scoffed, satisfaction lit up her two-colored eyes. The battlefield only grown in size, allies and enemies clashed on the beach. "Looks to me like you tipped us off to your little demon friends, you sly bastard."

"I warned you not to cross me, *human*." His voice was low, bitter, and Ethera couldn't believe his nerve. Even now, with no power left, he still thought he had control. The game was hers. It has always been hers.

"I'm not letting you and your crew of hobos get in the way of me and my friends going home." Her eyes locked with his, sharp and unflinching. He was harmless now, and whatever cold, dangerous aura he once carried had been sealed away along with his magic.

"And what's your plan now that you've captured the big, bad fish?" He asked with a crooked smile, completely concealing his fury.

Ethera cringed at the phrasing but tried her best not to let it show. She turned towards the fog-covered battlefield, where their allies danced with death. The demons were there—somewhere behind the action, sitting and watching. "I'm going to use you as fish bait and get us home," she smiled as she drew her small knife from her hip. In one swift motion, she grabbed him by the arm and yanked him off balance, closing the distance between them. He remained silent, his eyes darkening with rage. Being manhandled by a mortal girl was not how he had imagined the war would go.

The blade pressed cold and steady beneath his jaw. His eyes flicked between the knife and Ethera's hostility.

He had completely fallen at her mercy. The pirate shifted away from the blade, a single finger brushing against its edge. "You need me. Do you really think you'll be able to get home without finishing the prophecy?" he snickered, testing her patience like he always did.

To Ethera, his words were nothing more than background noise. Empty threats from a man who had already lost.

Hugo quietly closed his book, slipping it back into his leather pouch after reassuring himself that his specs were not fooling his vision. He took out a rope from his bag, stepping closer to the King as he tied his wrists together.

The spell had been cast successfully. The book was no longer needed, despite the urge to hold on to it for a bit longer. Still, he kept the mana stones, ready to defend his friends if things went sideways. The binding spell was just one of the few that he had managed to transcribe.

Hugo caught himself smiling, watching in anticipation of the way Ethera continued to torment the defenseless pirate. "I wonder what the demons will do once they realize you're powerless," she taunted, tugging on the black sleeve of his tunic. She hadn't changed—he was reminded of the fights she would get into at school and of the gossip that would spread shortly after.

But now, she looked like a real villain. Her anger was justified, after all, the pirate did threaten their escape. He had brought his own men here to die. He was no better than she was—but the difference was vast.

Her eyes gleamed with a fierce satisfaction as the three of them made their way down to the edge of the ship. The pirates who had stayed behind were already waiting with their swords drawn, sharp blades pointed upwards with a booming cheer. When their eyes landed on their captain, they turned, taking a step towards him.

Ethera immediately stopped, eyes narrowing. "Stay back or he dies," she threatened, the knife resting still against her prisoner's skin.

Reymond, Rose, and Juno appeared at their sides, weapons instantly drawn. Their shocked faces dared not look away from the trouble that stirred on the ship.

The tension cut through the air, eyes narrowed in distrust from both sides. The pirates were frozen in shock; no one dared to move. They couldn't understand how the most powerful man alive was dragged away by a bunch of human kids.

Reymond and Juno urged Rose to climb over the deck, down the wooden stairs, and into an empty small boat waiting at the bottom. Ethera pushed the King to go first, quickly following after him. Once he was on board, he extended his hand to help her down. She ignored it, jumping instead, and landing against the wood with a thud. It swayed from side to side as Rose tried to stabilize it with the paddle.

The others followed suit. Once everyone was in, they paddled quickly toward the beach where the battle was already spiraling out of control. Goblins splashed color across the black and white ball, their skin rolling like moss over the sand.

Countess bodies littered the ground, bleeding it red and purple. Bones of every shape and size lay littered, turning the beach into a graveyard. As Reymond and Hugo paddled through the water, they all watched in horror at the scene ahead.

The safety of the ship had vanished, replaced by the reality of war. The thought of death—their own death hadn't really crossed their minds until now. They'd been so swept up in magic and fantasy, in the fairy tale of it all, that they'd forgotten this wasn't a dream.

This was the real world. And real rules still apply.

Only Ethera and the Pirate King were left unfazed.

The water splashed against their boat, making them all jittery. "What's the plan, guys? We're getting kinda close…" Reymond asked nervously. Ethera motioned for them to stop paddling as she tried to think fast.

They were originally supposed to remain on board and to obey Dilian's pleas to stay put. But alas, with the betrayal of the King, Ethera had decided to take the leverage onto land.

There was no way to cross through without getting involved. "We need to go around them—into the forest," she quickly decided, and everyone nodded in reply.

They backpedaled clumsily then redirected the boat toward the far edge of the battlefield, trying to put as much distance as possible between themselves and the worst of the fighting. But even there, more skeletons appeared, charging straight at them from the tree line.

"Incoming customer service," Reymond breathed out, jumping off the boat into the water. He took three steps before swinging his sword. With one clean strike, the skeleton dropped to the water, its bony body severed. His eyes widened in disbelief. "Did you guys see that? Woah! I'm so good—I cut his ass in half!"

Juno was right behind him; her socks soaked through the cold. "Behind you!" she shouted, quickly drawing her bow. The arrow pierced through the air, striking another skeleton in the skull. They fell silent, watching it as it plopped on the damp sand.

Ethera leaned against the boat, impressed at Juno's precision. She had only seen her shoot once, and the praises she heard were high, but seeing it firsthand had left her astonished. The speed and precision were perfect.

The Pirate King jumped off the boat, and his boots landed in the water with a splash. He offered his bound hand again, a smile on his face directed at Ethera. The rope swung with the light wind and her eyes glanced down at it, making sure he was still restricted.

Her nose scrunched, the awe from Juno's shot was replaced by disgust. "Stop it."

"But I'm not doing anything."

"I know what you're up to—."

"Quit fooling around. We gotta go!" Juno yelled out after Reymond, whose sword poked at the skeleton's corpse.

He shoved his golden hair out of his face. "You'd think these guys would be unstoppable, but they're actually kind of weak."

"You do realize that the magic in your sword is doing the job for you, right?"

He rolled his eyes, swinging the sword over his shoulder. "Please—it's my strength and talent, not the magic."

Juno didn't want to argue despite being right. If it weren't for the magic embedded in their weapons, they would not be able to put the skeletons down with such ease.

They fought off two more before bolting into the dark forest. Everyone lined up behind each other, stepping over the dead bushes, going around the decaying trees, and through dark grey mist. Their footsteps surely echoed through the stillness of the forest; the silence had become deafening and the ocean's wind did not dare set foot on the dead land.

The Pirate King, breathless from the run, was clearly out of shape. He couldn't remember the last time he'd had to flee like this. Unlike the rest of them, he was almost wheezing from lack of oxygen. The mortals weren't that far off; they, too, found it hard to breathe in the fog. Ethera's grip was still tight on his arm, her other hand clenching the knife, half-expecting something to sneak up behind her.

"So," the King began between gulps of air, "where exactly are we running off to? Because if it's the castle you're looking for…it's that way." He lifted a finger—the shiny gold ring took the shape of a lion's face as it pointed to their right.

"Fuck," Reymond swore, his breathing unsteady. It didn't help that their hearts were running marathons on their own. Everyone had paused, out of rhythm and out of breath; they all looked in the direction the pirate had pointed.

"We could go around," Juno suggested.

"That'll take too long."

"Then we better make it fast."

"Guys…I can't do this anymore. I don't even run in *PE*!" Rose whined, sweat dripping down her forehead. She was in worse shape than the captain.

"We need to keep moving," Hugo urged. "We're making too much noise." He motioned in the direction that the Pirate King had pointed.

"I've got an idea," Ethera's eyes lit up, taking an un-steady, quick breath. "But it's risky," she quickly added.

"Go on".

"We go straight to them. If we get caught, we'll use *him*. I've got a bargain that I know they won't refuse."

"I am quite expensive, darling—."

Ethera yanked on the pirate's arm so roughly that he nearly fell. "Oh god, do you ever just shut up?" she snapped. Her shorter frame fought to keep the tall pirate in check, pull-ing him as if he were an unruly beast on a leash.

It was clear to everyone that he enjoyed taking a piss in her litter.

They moved forward in silence, the smell of rot growing stronger as they neared the battle. Every few steps, they paused, doing their best to evade detection. Just when the tension became unbearable, they nearly screamed as a figure charged at them from the mist—shouting a loud elvish battle cry.

"Dilian!" Ethera gasped, relief falling over her. The elf was stained with blood—but not his own. His hair had already turned into a bird's nest in such a short time. Bits of dirt stuck to one side of his face and clothes.

"What are you guys doing here?" Dilian hissed, furious at the sight before him. "You were supposed to stay on the ship!"

"Sorry, change of plans."

"There is no change of plans!" He shouted, eyes locking onto the hunched Pirate King. "And what the hell are you doing with him?"

A few skeletons stumbled out of the fog, interrupting the argument. Reymond and Dilian moved fast, slicing them down without missing a beat.

"This kinda just hap—."

"Well, well, well. What do we have here? The sea king, five humans, and an elf, what a bittersweet alliance," came a sickening voice that pierced through the air like knife. It echoed from every direction, making the mortals stumble, their heads turning in an attempt to pinpoint the intruder. A deeper, fouler presence than the rot of the dead emerged. It was unmistakably a demon.

302

Ethera stood firm, eyes scanning the shadows. "I want to make a deal with the Demon King. I have something of great value that he will love," she spoke loudly, head turning in every direction. Dilian fell silent; he clutched his spear.

The voice chuckled. "And what do you have that His Majesty doesn't already own?"

"How about a powerless Pirate King, ready for the taking?"

"Ouch," the pirate muttered, pressing a dramatic hand to his chest.

The voice went silent for a moment, as if acknowledging the sight displayed before him. Then a figure suddenly materialized from swirling black smoke. The demon did not look like a monster or a beast. He had no purple skin, no spots, no pitch-black eyes as they had expected. Instead, he took the shape of a man—a human form molded from darkness, horns curling upwards from his skull, and vanished into the fog above.

Where his face should have been, there was nothing but hollow emptiness. His limbs were unnaturally long, fingertips extending like claws of a wild beast. His lower half twisted like a slow-moving tornado of smoke, never quite touching the ground.

The demon floated closer, his face, or where one might have been, turned towards the pirate. "And what is it you want in return?"

"Safe passage home," Ethera answered, "for me and my friends."

The demon paused again. His face stretched out, mouth opening up as if he had smiled. Something red glowed from within, unnervingly bright against the darkness. "I'm sure he can make that happen. Please, follow me."

Dilian stood frozen, unsure of what to say. Finally, he stepped forward, blocking Ethera's path. "Wh-What are you doing? We could've used him to win—!"

"This is *your* war, Dilian," Ethera interrupted, stepping around him. "I brought you here, and now your people can finish it. No harm done."

Rose and Juno exchanged anxious glances. Ethera wasn't wrong, not exactly, but the coldness in her voice made their stomachs turn.

Her eyes shifted to her friends, noticing their uncomfortable faces. "I just—I just want to go home," she sighed, almost to herself.

The elf fell silent, his ears dropping despite the furious expression in his eyes. "Fine. Be it. We don't need you," he whispered, eyes cast downward. He walked past them without saying another word and disappeared into the woods.

The humans remained quiet.

"How does it feel to betray the elven clan? Your good little friends?" The Pirate King taunted by her side.

Ethera yanked on his arm, pulling him to keep moving. "It's not a betrayal," she noted, tightening her grip. "We're just leaving the party early."

CHAPTER 21

Ethera's stomach knotted at the thought as she fought the urge to glance back to where Dilian had disappeared. Doubt flooded her thoughts; a question hung in the air like a storm cloud—was this really the right way to go about things?

More than anything, they all wanted to get home as soon as possible. But sneaking around, going behind the elves' backs…it felt wrong.

Especially after all the hospitality they'd been shown these past few days—the training, the food, the magic they shared with them, the history they learned… And this was how they repaid that kindness? By turning tail at the first chance they got?

But who was to say the elves would even survive this war? Let alone win it. The prophecy left too many questions unanswered, and Ethera wasn't going to waste their best shot at getting home by second-guessing herself.

She was no hero. Fighting a war she was not part of was laughable. Her friends seemed to have realized the same. One by one, they had caught her eye, their faces full of fear but also filled with blind trust. They didn't know if this was the right path, but right now it was their only one— and they believed her enough to follow her.

The demon drifted through the fog that seemed to part for them, letting them pass. He moved like a silent guide, and his presence seemed to ward off any potential threats.

Finally, the fog began to thin, giving way to a forest that stretched for miles. Ethera could only imagine what beauty this place once had. The Enchanted Forest was once full of life and color before it rotted under the demon's influence. Now, the trees were stripped bare, their limbs twisted like skeletal fingers reaching for the dull and grey sky.

Every so often, Ethera swore she saw one twitch despite the lack of wind. The soft crunch of dead leaves soon gave way to dry, hardened soil as they neared the blood-stained crystal palace.

The air grew heavier. Everyone was breathing harder now, clutching their bags, weapons, or, in Ethera's case, the Pirate King's arm. He followed with a quiet intensity, reduced to little more than a prisoner.

An important prisoner. Still, his eyes glinted with something unreadable. He'd been watching them. Watching Hugo, especially.

The spell that the young mortal boy had cast was no small feat, even with the use of a mana stone. The pirate knew magic, knew how much willpower it took to bend the world like that. Desperation wasn't enough; you needed something more. Something more valuable. And Hugo had it.

That made the boy dangerous. The King's gaze lingered on Hugo longer than necessary.

Ethera noticed.

She yanked his arm hard, and he turned his eyes to her. Something dark passed through them. She couldn't tell if he was angry, amused, or just curious. It was like he didn't have normal emotions, just mere shadows of them. She could only recognize malice, amusement, or temptation.

He suddenly leaned closer, whispering so only she could hear. "Are you excited to go home, pebble?" His voice was velvet-soft, coated in venom.

Ethera looked straight ahead. "Be quiet," she snapped loud enough for the group to hear. He straightened, but his gaze didn't leave her.

The path widened, the trees thinned and began to line up along the dirt road that pointed directly at the palace. From afar, it still looked magical. Massive, gleaming crystals stabbed into the dark sky above. The crimson color swirled like thousand dancing leaves, each flicker reflecting the light from within.

The group's pace slowed as the gravity of it all hit them. If the glow on the castle was caused by demon energy, then it only meant that there were hundreds inside.

The closer they got to the palace, the colder the air turned. Ethera's breath caught in her throat. The chill in the air was more than just weather; it was the kind of cold that reached inside your bones and freaked you solid from within. It reminded Ethera of the sea witch. At that exact moment when her blade slid through something once alive.

Her hand tightened on the King's arm, enough to catch his attention. "Scared?" He asked with false concern. She didn't respond and just kept walking, dragging him with her.

They finally reached the bridge. It was long, thin, and barely held together. Several planks were missing. The railing was cracked and splintered, and below, the dry riverbed had turned into a jagged pit of stone. One misstep and it was game over.

The demon glided over the bridge without hesitation.

Reymond stepped forward first, testing the first plank, then slowly shifting his weight onto it. It was sturdy. One by one, the others followed, stepping carefully and avoiding the loose boards. No one spoke, no one dared to even breathe.

Below them, only death stared up.

"Want me to hold your hand?" The pirate whispered, leaning closer. Her eyes darted down at the rope that tied his wrists, with his hands that already began to reach towards her, slow and steady. The red on his fingers glowed, and every word of his courtesy was laced with scorn.

She ignored him, trying to stay in control of her emotions. But somehow, he had already sensed it. Somewhere between the fog and the cliffs, he noticed her fear—and a dark realization clawed at her back.

He wasn't just watching. He was waiting for something.

The man seemed to take notice of every little thing. As if he could read her thoughts just by staring and observing her movements, the rapid blink of her eye, the flare of her nose. Even now, as Ethera slowly turned her head, his eyes were already locked on her. Not once had he looked down on where he stepped; he only ever watched her.

In a heartbeat, one of the wooden planks snapped beneath Ethera's foot. She let out a sharp yelp as her leg plunged through the hole. It wasn't wide enough to swallow her whole, but the shock sent her into a momentary panic.

The Pirate King raised his hands mockingly, eyes flicking toward her friends. "Is this the part where I help her and get shot by an arrow?"

Ethera grunted, forcing herself up with shaky arms. "I'm okay, I'm okay," she muttered between shaky breaths, waving Rose off before shooting a nasty glare at the pirate. He only smirked, nudging his arm and allowing it to get captured again. With her footing regained, they pressed onward across the bridge.

Inside the palace, everything sparked a shimmering crimson. It was exactly as they imagined. A castle that looked like it was made out of ice. A crystal so polished and smooth that its own reflections followed them from every angle. Light danced off hallways, rooms, and doorways that twisted deeper into the structure like a maze.

The only thing out of place were the skeletons. Some stood as if on guard, others crumpled across the marbled floor, surrounded by dirt, dead twigs, moss, vines, and dried blood. A thin veil of decay hung in the air.

There were no decorations, no other sign of life. She half expected it to be filled with velvet carpets or carved white walls. Perhaps even paintings of others who had lived in these walls once before.

Much to her disappointment, it looked less like a fairy tale, and more like a prison.

She couldn't stop glancing at the reflections. No matter where she turned, they followed—*his eyes followed.*

The pirate's black tunic hung open at the collar, revealing the sharp line of his collarbone and the broad slope of his shoulders beneath. One shoulder was armored with a lightweight piece of blackened steel, engraved with ancient black runes as if he were ready to take to the battlefield anytime. His close-cut pants, made from thick black cloth, were reinforced with soft leather at the thighs and knees. Shin-high, soft-soled black boots stomped against the marble floor, each step echoing louder than those of humans.

His eyes promised revenge. Ethera could feel it through the air, his dread and his desire for it. This time, he might actually kill her if he gets a chance.

His bun had fallen loose, strands brushing the back of his neck. In the mirrored walls, he didn't wear his usual grin. His lips were neutral, but his eyes—they smiled a black so dark they almost swallowed her.

She turned away quickly, refocusing on the smoky figure ahead. The demon guide glided soundlessly through the air, barely in touch with the physical reality. Ethera couldn't help but wonder, what would happen if something like that crossed into their world?

Will a war break out? Will everything fall prey to the hands of demons and the army of the dead? If portals existed, could these monsters come through whenever they pleased?

The questions buzzed in her skull, crowding her thoughts. She forced them down; the final battle was yet to come. They weren't on the front stage anymore—they were playing a quieter role, something more predictable, and controlled.

As if they were backstage, trying to find the exit.

"We have arrived," The demon said, stopping in front of two towering crystal doors. They reached high, nearly touching the slanted ceiling. Each door had its own oval crystal knob that retained the once-bright light blue color. The demon turned around, flashing his glowing red eyes before his entire body vanished into a thin black mist.

No one moved.

The doors weren't transparent, and whatever was beyond them radiated with something terrible. The air here was heavier, thicker, steeper in a fear that crawled beneath their skin.

"L-Let's go," Juno whispered bravely, stepping forward. Her hand never even touched the knob, but both doors opened silently inward on their own.

Inside sat the Demon King.

His throne was forged from glass and bone, perched in the center of the chamber. His form was a dense swirl of smoke, sharper and more solid than that of his underling. Long horns curled from his head, blending into the mist behind him like roots. Covering the top half of his face was the skull of some great beast that resembled the carving of a dragon. The lower half bore the human jawline of a man.

When he exhaled, grey mist spilled from his mouth, still floating beside him. His claws were as long as his raw presence. The man was a perfect manifestation of death. Even the Pirate King's face scrunched in disgust.

The man-like demon tilted his head. "What a curious bunch," he said, voice low and static. "Five mortals…and a fish."

The Pirate King chuckled under his breath. Ethera sucked in whatever oxygen her lungs could grasp. "We've come to make a deal," she abruptly declared, taking the initiative. She took a step forward, walking alongside Juno and leading the others into the throne room.

Behind the demon was what looked like a massive crystal clock embedded in the wall. But its hands were motionless. The room itself was simple—empty—but the demon's presence filled every corner with dread beyond words.

"We want safe passage home," the mortal announced, carefully choosing her words. "In exchange, we offer you the Pirate King, stripped of all power."

The demon tilted his head, sitting up, his red eyes drifted towards the pirate. A slow, rumbling laugh escaped him. "Oh, well, this is just delicious," he laughed and more smoke filled the air around him. "Hello, old friend. Quite the hole you've sank yourself in."

The Pirate King scoffed. "It was built around me. I see you still enjoy stealing things that don't belong to you."

The room fell quiet as the Demon King ignored the pirate, weighing the offer. "And where is this…home?" he asked, claws twitching slightly.

"It's through a portal bound to a book, and we believe that book is in the palace. Perhaps in the library?" Ethera replied, her voice softening, almost flattering.

Maybe they shouldn't have left Dilian behind. He would've known what to say. What to ask and what to look for. But the mortals found comfort in the mere thought of chance.

They found a book once—they will find it again.

The Demon King remained quiet, his glowing red eyes watched. Ethera's eyes flicked to the crystal clock again, feeling uncomfortable by his peering gaze. It had no hands, no numbers. How was she so sure it was a clock?

Then, in the mirrored wall beside the throne, she noticed something. A glimmer just beyond the smoke trailing from the demon's body. Something bright, nearly hidden behind his shifting mass.

It was a crystal-like sphere, an orb glowing faintly and floating behind the throne. There were no chains, no stand beneath it. It simply hovered in the air, pulsing brightly, half-hidden in shadow and yet still making itself known.

Before Ethera could get a better look, the demon's swirling mist shifted, completely obscuring the object. "Fine," he finally answered, a smile curling his lips. "You shall have your book—after you give me the fish on the leash."

"No," Ethera answered immediately. "We want to see the book first. If you don't have it, then this whole transaction is worthless to us."

A tense silence followed. The mortals waited for the Demon King to lash out, to snatch the pirate by force, but instead, he let out a cold chuckle. "Smart mortal," he said, voice slithering and carrying the heavy weight of approval. "I suppose I can wait."

He lifted one smoke-dripping hand, and with a wave, three demons materialized in front of his throne. They weren't as imposing as their master but still took an unsettling shape. "Take them to the library. Find the book they need and come back."

The words carried order, and the command soaked with power. Then the Demon King leaned back, utterly relaxed. The tension lifted slightly the moment they stepped out of the throne room. Everyone let out a breath they hadn't realized they were holding. These demons, though scary, weren't as suffocating as their master.

Ethera kept track of their route. Every hallway. Every turn. Every oddly shaped door. If things went south, they'd need a quick way out. Everything about this felt too easy.

Reymond didn't relax for a second, walking just behind Juno, who clutched her bow with a white-knuckled hand. Her free hand held an arrow, ready to blindly shoot if the demons took the wrong step.

But how does one kill a creature made of smoke? Dilian had not shared this important piece of information and they were too preoccupied to ask beforehand.

They reached another set of doors, wider and shorter than before, etched with swirling patterns that slid outwards onto the walls like living dead vines. The doors creaked open, revealing chaos.

The library was a battlefield of paper and ink. Shelves were knocked over. Books were thrown across the ground, some torn, others still intact. Triangles of long shelves leaned on each other, the weight barely enough to hold them upright. The smell of dust, old pages, and forgotten knowledge hung thick in the air, untouched and undisturbed for what must have been months.

Hugo's eyes sparkled. So much knowledge. So much power. A single day in this room could change the course of one's life.

As the demons slithered in, the room dimmed further. Books shrank from their presence, literally curling inward on the shelves or folding shut like frightened animals. Even books in this world had life and magic.

Finding the right one would be difficult. The letters on the spines twisted, skipped, and rearranged, not wanting anyone to read them. Some books barely resembled English at all. The air seemed to distract the mortals' vision, making it almost unbearable to focus. "Just remember," Juno whispered. "It should be black, with golden carvings. Something like that."

They spread out quickly, and the demons followed suit.

It was Reymond who found it. Tucked between bright-colored tones, as if it were hiding in plain sight for him to grab. The book seemed to pull at him, not the other way. His hands closed around it, but the moment he opened the cover, his heart sank.

It was empty. Weightless. Lifeless. "Son of a bitch..." he cursed, closing it and stuffing it under his tunic.

Ethera, meanwhile, was doing her best to search the shelves, despite the Pirate King's constant tugging on her sore arm. "Will you quit it?" She snapped under her breath.

"Maybe you should've used a chain. Your grip's so weak I could've escaped ten minutes ago."

"I'll keep that in mind next time."

"Will there be a next time?" He asked, leaning dangerously close. Always too damn close.

Ethera instantly scooted away, almost letting go. "You reek," she snapped, suppressing a shudder.

He tilted his head as if genuinely considering her words. He sniffed himself but did not smell a thing. "Like the sea with a dash of handsome?"

Before Ethera could respond, Rose appeared, breathless and whispering. "Ethera—we have a problem..."

Reymond stepped out from behind her, holding up the book with a grim expression. "So, I opened it to see if it works, but I don't know. I think the battery is dead or something, I'm like seventy-five percent sure it's this one."

Ethera took it into her hands, opening it. The empty pages fluttered, and particles of dust flew outwards. "Fuck..." she whispered. "Hugo. We need Hugo. Maybe he knows how to charge it or something."

Then, the Pirate King laughed. Loudly. The group whipped around to shush him from drawing the demon's attention. "Shut up!" Rose hissed, not fearing him despite their last meeting.

"Oops," he said, unapologetically. "It must have slipped through my mind because of the excruciating pain in my hand but—you need to destroy the Demon King's spell to be able to use magic from this island. Here's a hint: it's in the throne room. You've seen it, haven't you? The little white orb he tried to hide?"

Ethera stiffened.

"That orb is a spell?" Reymond asked, eyes wide. "You're saying…we have to destroy…*that*?"

"Destroy it," The pirate responded, voice low now. "Do it fast, and the magic will flood back into the land. All demons will be cast out. The Enchanted Forest will be reborn. And you? You get your little portal."

"No way," Reymond shook his head. "You're insane. That guy could kill us!"

"What orb?" Rose asked, confused. Ethera's mind relapsed.

The orb…the light behind the throne. It was never just a decoration. It was the key.

The Pirate King leaned closer, smirking. "Do it quickly, and you won't even have to fight him."

Reymond turned away, taking a deep breath. "Oh, for fuck's sake."

No one answered. None of them trusted a single word that came out of his devious mouth. But they felt the weight of his truth.

Hugo might be able to protect them or buy time with the magic from those mana stones. Maybe even help them figure out a way to destroy that orb. It seemed like the prophecy wasn't done with Ethera yet.

"Okay," the girl finally snapped from her thoughts. "We split up. Get Hugo and Juno up to speed. See if he can charge this book. If not, then we are heading straight for that orb. Either way, we need a plan."

Then she turned, jabbing a finger at the Pirate King.

"And you—stay quiet. One more word and I'll feed you to your own pets."

He only grinned, tilting forward towards the excitement. "You're starting to think like someone I know too well."

"And who's that?"

"Myself."

CHAPTER 22

The plan was self-explanatory. Gather the three demons in one place and momentarily freeze them. It was one of Hugo's favorite self-defense spells; his twin, Reymond, had fallen victim to it a few times too many

Three minutes—that was all the time they had to find their way back, freeze the Demon King, and destroy the orb. Everything depended on how fast they could run and the memory that stirred within Ethera's mind.

She was confident that her childhood friend would succeed, and yet nerves pulled at her heartstrings. She listened quietly, silently praying for her friends. It had gone quiet with no sound for her to emerge from hiding. Perhaps too soon?

The Pirate King stood beside her, his arms crossed in a relaxed manner, his boring gaze falling over the titles of different books.

Ethera scoffed, *as if* he knew how to read.

She didn't trust him enough to let him take part in the plan, which meant she had to remain hidden on the sidelines, babysitting a pirate.

The book felt oddly light in her hands, as if it didn't contain a single sheet of paper. Instead of standing idly, staring at the thug, she kept flipping through the pages, hoping it would suddenly activate.

It didn't.

But the sharp, venomous tongue of the sea scoundrel did. "Nervous?" He asked, his voice slithered its way into her mind like a parasite. Ethera's eyes remained on the empty pages of the book before closing it with a thump.

Her eyes scanned the cryptic text written in a foreign language, something ancient beyond belief. "No…they got this. I know it," she whispered, her finger tracing the carved sigil.

Reymond had long disappeared, getting lost in the long aisles of the library as his eyes searched for his brother. His loud steps crunched the dry leaves, making it impossible to quietly sneak around freely. But even with the gruesome amount of sound he was making, the demons did not suspect a thing.

Hugo was on the second floor with a demon that suspiciously followed him, and *only* him. It had flown past him a few shelves down, but every so often, it peaked through the aisles. The thought of such a creature being that close was dreadful beyond measure. He could only pray that one of his friends had better luck with finding the book. Doubt settled in, twisting with anxiety at the thought of hiding the book god knows where—if he were lucky enough to find it first.

He had not seen anything that remotely looked similar to a book of golden letters. There were countless dark books; the thought of looking through every single one would surely take days, if not weeks.

And time was the only thing not on their side.

The air was thick and cold, purposefully forcing his heartbeat to pound louder in his ears. When Reymond came up the stairs, his footsteps were drowned out by the whirlwind of thoughts in Hugo's head. He didn't notice his own brother until a hand tapped his shoulder, startling him and snapping him back to reality.

Hugo spun around, getting ready to curse, until he saw the serious look on his twin's face. Reymond quickly put a finger to his lips, signaling for silence. He glanced towards the stairs, and the two of them carefully began descending, eyes alert for any signs of the demons.

Hugo immediately sensed its unsettling presence, following a few paces away. Halfway through the steps, Reymond paused, leaning closer to his brother. "We found it—but there are some complications," he whispered. "We need you to use your anti-me special."

Hugo's head tilted slightly, signaling his brother of the entity that had descended with them. Before Hugo could respond, Reymond nodded his head, understanding everything as if twin telepathy had for the first time connected.

They had the book, but clearly something must have been wrong. Dripping with sweat from nerves and adrenaline, Hugo spun around, his expression morphing into something along the lines of excitement and desperation.

Indeed, the demon hovered a few steps away. "They had found the book," the human yelled out, nodding his head. "We are ready to head back." The demon's expression did not change, but it followed Hugo, who led it down the spiral stairs, meeting up with the rest in the middle.

He ran down in a hurry, his loud footsteps pounding on the wood in hopes of sending a signal to his friends. The demon was surely fooled by the mortal's urgency, despite it all being an act and a terrible one at that. Hugo was anything but a liar; his facial expression often revealed what his words did not.

But he was ecstatic to finally be able to use the spell on something other than his brother. Something not human. The perk was that even their mouths froze shut in a terrifying stale state of quiet that lasted for three whole minutes.

Across the library, he spotted Juno, followed closely by another demon. Her nervous gaze flicked between the hovering entities before she bolted toward the far side of the room, where Rose stood holding a dark, old-looking book that bore a faint resemblance to the original.

A demon loomed beside her, speaking in a voice too distant to make out, though the body language and its demand for the book were unmistakable. Hugo and Reymond moved quickly, trailing behind the other two demons, sweat sparkling on their foreheads.

Rose, being *the* dramatic high-school girl, let out a frightened squeak and dropped the book before diving out of the way. All three demons were lured together, surrounding the book on the ground. They paused, looking down, afraid to make contact with it in case it was dangerous.

322

But the real danger stood right behind them. Hugo raised his arm, eyes closing as his other hand gripped a glowing magic stone. He whispered words in a language foreign to his friends, with the familiar words that some of them had heard before. The bright light that flared through his palm indicated the successful completion of the spell.

When he opened his eyes, they glowed faintly gold for a moment before fading back to his usual humane brown. "Let's go!" Hugo shouted, his voice sharp with determination. He threw his hands in the air with a clenched fist.

His confidence returned—the spell had worked with ease. Just for a brief moment, hesitation did cross his mind, considering the subject's body was that of mist.

The worry crumbled under the weight of reality. He didn't want to admit it, but the surge of power that briefly ignited in his veins was intoxicating.

Reymond popped out from behind a nearby shelf, his eyes wide with surprise and excitement. For the first time, it wasn't him on the receiving end of that god awful spell. He approached the demons, waving his hand carelessly. The shock was visible on their dark, faceless appearances.

The plan had worked well. Ethera and the Pirate King sprinted into the center of the room; their eyes immediately locked onto the demons.

Frozen in a statue-like state, they couldn't do anything but shift their glowing, scorching red eyes from one mortal to the next. "Come on!" Reymond urged, taking initiative. "We don't have much time." They bolted from the library, turning left and allowing Ethera to lead.

The Pirate King ran alongside them, impressed by the mortal girl's sharp sense of direction. Strangely, they barely seemed to notice him—he was reduced to nothing in their minds.

Not a priority and not a threat. And he was desperate to remind them otherwise.

The Demon King was on a whole other level, but only the pirate knew the real extent of his *true* power.

Sabotaging the human's plan had crossed his mind more than once, but the mischievous glint in Ethera's eyes had thrown him off guard. Now it was mere curiosity that haunted him, the urge to find out if she would see it through.

Would the prophecy come true? And if so—what will it gift him? There was nothing in this world that he truly desired.

Now, despite the chaos, the mortals were inching closer to their goal with the help of a little bit of burrowed magic and the trust they had between each other. Somehow that fickle realization had begun to irritate him more than he cared to admit. No number of cunning words could ever break the trust that they had built out of nothing.

They reached the towering doors of the Demon King's throne room and came to a hard stop, each of them panting, eyes darting between one another.

This was it. The final act.

And yet, no one dared to move despite the clock ticking in their heads.

Time was running thin. All eyes turned to Hugo, his hand clenched tightly around the glowing stone. Both his palm and the magic crystal were coated in sweat.

With a single nod, he stepped forward and reached for the doorknob only to be stopped by the Pirate King. "I didn't mean for things to come this far, so don't take it personally, pebble," he suddenly said, drawing everyone's attention. In one swift motion, he grabbed Ethera and yanked her into a chokehold. His cold hand gripped her angrily by the throat. The rope rested against her chest, scratching at her skin. She struggled to breathe, and her eyes went wide in shock.

She hadn't seen it coming, feeling so comfortable in Hugo's spell that should have prevented the pirate from doing anything foolish. And yet there she was, clawing at his arm with one hand, gasping, trying to set herself free.

She had leaned on magic too comfortably, forgetting that not all spells last forever. The Pirate King's power was still bound—but like an overfilled glass, it had started to spill over.

Her other hand, the one holding a knife, had been twisted behind her back, pressing into her hair. She attempted to kick him away, but he left no opening for her sly tactics. "Set me free, and I'll let her go," the Pirate King demanded, voice calm but loaded with threat. The order was simple, yet it put everyone at a sharp disadvantage.

His grip on her wrist tightened, and Ethera gulped against his palm. "Don't do it! Forget about me! You need to freeze the demon and break the orb. GO!" She shouted, eyes meeting Hugo's.

With all her strength to back her words, she threw her head backward, smashing it into the pirate's nose. A scratching pain shot through his skull as the impact landed, causing his grip on her to loosen for just a split moment.

Without much hesitation, Ethera swung her right leg, trying to trip him. Hugo didn't hesitate; he trusted Ethera's judgement without question. He sprinted through the towering doors, his hand outstretched in desperation and lips pronouncing the words of the spell. Loud and clear, just like he practiced. Within seconds, the Demon King was captured.

Back in the corridor, the others stayed behind with Ethera, desperately trying to help her without risking her further harm from the pirate's grasp. They had barely taken a step when the ground beneath them began to shake. Slick black liquid began seeping through the cracks of the marble floor, bubbling around them, forming oval pools. From the puddles, skeletal hands clawed their way to the surface, dragging their grey, white bones and rotting limbs onto the floor.

The mortals watched in horror, bodies paralyzed as the magic had spawned more of the dead than what they had fought on the beach. Without warning, the skeletons charged forward.

Reymond swung his sword, steel clashing loudly with brittle bone. Juno fired arrow after arrow, each one finding its mark with precision. Rose stumbled back, her hands shaking against her own thin sword, caught in chaos. Her eyes darted back and forth, torn between helping Ethera, or fighting off the undead.

Ethera rolled across the cold ground, grunting and struggling to gain control over the massive man above her.

The Pirate King, much to his surprise, was enjoying this more than he had thought he would.

With her friends out of the way, he had as much time as he wanted to cozily roll around the dirt with the one person he wanted to rip to shreds. The mortal wasn't giving up, swinging her knife recklessly in an attempt to injure him, or worse, *kill him*. He twisted, flipping them both and pinning her hands behind her back as he held her neck firmly against the cold marble.

Her face flushed in anger. The floor felt strangely comforting against Ethera's burning cheeks, offering a fleeting moment of cool relief. Her eyebrows furrowed, trying to wiggle out of the man's hold.

She was immobilized yet again, with half of his body weight pressing her down. Struggling was useless. No amount of energy, tricks, or screams would change that.

Her friends were lost in a battle; there was no one who could help her now. And then, the manifestation of her negative thoughts had turned pitch black. The floor beneath them bubbled, close enough to soak in Ethera's face.

A skeleton's head was the first thing to appear. The gruesome details hit her all at once, from the cracked bone, dried mud, and the overwhelming stench of decay. She screamed louder than ever, jerking her head away. The pirate's grip tightened, holding her in one spot.

This was it. She was bound to meet her doom sooner or later. Her eyes squeezed shut. But then, suddenly, the Pirate King released her neck. Only to seize the skull beside her. Her eyes shot open, nose wrinkling at the scene.

His ring fingers drove into the eye sockets of the skull and crushed it before the rest of it could rise. Bone shards scattered across the marble floor, the black faintly disappearing. Purple goo tainted her pale cheek, her body wet, rigid with shock. She could barely turn her head, but it was just enough to meet his malicious gaze.

He had just crushed a skull with his bare hand.

That could have been *her* head.

Still could be.

She screamed again, twisting violently, trying to roll away even if it meant dragging him with her. But he only smirked wider, his eyes glittering with dark amusement and a storm of tempting ideas brewing behind them. His head inched closer, fingers brushing her hair out of her face and smearing the skeleton's blood across her cheek.

She flinched away, but there was nowhere to go. "W-We'll let you go!" She shouted, voice cracking. "The moment we break the orb, we will release you—so please, until then, help us!"

She couldn't bear to meet his gaze, her eyes squeezed shut yet again. His breath tickled her ear as he laughed. His grip was still hard, but it began to loosen; she could finally breathe better.

"Do you promise to play nice?"

"Yes, I promise! Hurry!" Ethera shouted, surprised at his sudden obedience. But time was running dangerously short—no one knew how long it had been since the spell was cast, or how soon it might wear off. The appearance of the skeletons had jolted everyone into action, and the looming threat of hundreds of demons flying in pushed their adrenaline into overdrive.

The Pirate King released Ethera and began to rise to his feet, grabbing a rusty old sword that had fallen beside a skeleton's corpse. She stared, bewildered, as he twirled effortlessly, slicing through the undead with ruthless power, not wasting any time.

He moved as light as a feather, as if gravity itself had feared him. The stage was crafted in his honor, with or without his sealed powers. He was still just as dangerous. But it was the serious expression on his face that caught Ethera off guard.

That look...focused and cold. It was like a glimpse into the true extent of his powers and of *him*. Something she should have never laid her eyes on.

Snapping back to reality, she scrambled to her feet and sprinted toward Hugo. The Demon King stood locked in a fearsome, mid-roar expression. Behind him hovered a glowing orb—radiating the light that had been stolen from the Enchanted Forest. Magic pulsed from it like a living heartbeat, warm hues of yellow and white swirled inside, begging to be set free.

If what the Pirate King said was true, then destroying this would bring magic back into this land. The demons would perish, and so will their control.

But the question remained. How were they supposed to destroy it?

Hugo was already standing next to it, the wheels in his head turning in every direction. His hands flickered through the small book, looking for something useful.

Ethera scanned the room, desperate to find a hint.

Her eyes flickered to the door, just in time to see the three demons materialize out of the air.

Then a fourth…a fifth…a sixth.

Their time was up.

The others rushed deeper into the room, breathless, fatigued, but alive. They circled instinctively, backs pressed to one another, guarding their blind spots. The Pirate King had joined them, sweat gleaming on his forehead and brow, his chest rising and falling as he tried to steady himself. His lips were parted, eyebrows furrowed with frustration.

He looked odd standing among the mortals.

Hugo and Ethera pressed into the group. The orb still hovered untouched. The demons were closing in, there was no time, and no one knew what to do.

"Free me, and this will all be over!" The Pirate King shouted, inhaling a sharp breath. He was surprisingly concerned, and he hated it. A weak being was a dead one, and right now, he felt very, *very* weak.

Ethera looked at Hugo. They locked eyes, pondering to themselves. If the spell wore off, the Demon King would be unleashed—and with him, the fury of his rage.

They had to act soon, or else they would all die.

"Fine—." Ethera began but was cut off by a sudden whoosh and the sound of metal piercing flesh.

CHAPTER 23

A spear shot through the demon's chest. The creature looked down in disbelief, its red eyes widening before its body evaporated into ashes. The spike clattered to the ground, surrounded by a swirl of glowing dark dust.

At the doors, Dilian and several elves stood, bows and spears drawn, unleashing hell with their advancing forces. Ethera broke into a relieved smile. The mortals stood with their eyes wide and mouths agape, and a new feeling surged through their bodies.

Hope

Their graves were not set in stone.

"Surprised?" Dilian called out, a grin on his face as his ears stretched proudly outward. "Like hell I'd leave you, weaklings alone."

The battle continued. Ethera motioned frantically for Dilian to make his way across the chaos that spilled inside the throne room. He retrieved his spear and darted through the battlefield, skeletons and demon dust piling around him. He was impressed that the mortals lasted this long. Clearly, they had learned more from the elves than he'd expected. They were no longer scared little kids he had found in the Thalorin Forest.

Ethera didn't hesitate to get to the point as soon as the elf appeared beside her. "Do you know how to destroy this?" She shouted over the noise, pointing at the orb as it pulsed.

Dilian didn't answer at first. His eyes locked onto it, his mind racing. He knew exactly what it was, perhaps even how to destroy it. In the corner of her eye, she noticed the Pirate King still locked in combat, too distracted to help.

Dilian's gaze dropped to his spear.

Without a word, he lifted it high above his head— and brought it down in a powerful swing, aiming directly for the middle of the glowing orb.

In an instant, everyone was thrown backward. Demons, skeletons, elves, and mortals were taken by the force. It took a second to understand what had just happened, and a few more to even begin to recover from the impact.

Ethera groaned as she pushed herself upright, her knife lost somewhere. Bones rattled beside her as the skeletons tried to reassemble themselves, clattering piece by piece. Her eyes darted back to the orb—it remained intact. Disappointment sank within her.

Dilian lay a few feet ahead, groaning, curled on his side. His normally fair complexion had gone worryingly pale blue. A rare sight for an elf.

Ethera crawled toward him, placing trembling hands on his shoulders. "Shit…are you okay?"

"That hurts…like hell," he muttered and Ethera smiled with relief. The once well-spoken elf had already picked up some habits from his mortal companions. Ethera gave a breathy, nervous laugh, relieved he could still speak at all.

Behind her, Juno and Reymond had already bounced back, faster than lightning as if the unknown force did not affect them. Their blades and arrows tore through the scrambling undead like they were born to fight evil. It was almost unsettling how natural they looked. Like warriors, not students who used to sit in classrooms solving math equations and writing essays they never proofread.

They didn't belong in school. They belonged in a war. They had a frightening natural talent, or perhaps their foes were too weak.

A low, deep roar echoed through the throne room, shaking the ground, the windows, and even the ceiling with chilling force.

The Demon King had finally broken free.

His eyes glowed with pure rage, scanning the throne room with the fury of a god watching ants disturb his temple. One flick of his arm could end it all—wipe them all from existence in a flash.

But before he could, the Pirate King stepped into view.

Smug, blood-splattered, and unbothered.

His tunic had been stained in purple and brown goo—not his own but that of his enemies. And most notably, the one-shoulder armor was missing, along with the red string that had once sealed his powers.

Ethera's stomach dropped. She turned quickly, searching for Hugo and praying he was still alive.

There, his terrified brown eyes stared across the throne room, locked on the Pirate King's back. When Hugo released the binding spell, an overwhelming surge crashed through him like a vicious wave. That power locked within—it had been too much, causing his own body to tremble from the aftereffects. And the power—so terrifying and desiring, flowed freely back to its rightful owner.

The Pirate King's eyes had flickered crimson for a second before returning to its usual black color. In his hand, a sphere of water formed, floating above his palm and dripping little droplets onto the marble ground. They, too, froze in the air surrounding him. His long hair was loose, floating unnaturally as the power within surged like water on a stove.

Ethera felt it in her bones—a realization so deep it struck her like lightning. This wasn't just a pirate. This was a force of nature. A wild, unnatural force that had taken the shape of a man.

"What do you think?" The pirate asked, strolling casually towards the Demon King. "Care for a rematch?"

The Demon King did not move. Not even when the breath of grey smoke emerged from the corner of his mouth. For a second, it looked like he had remembered—something painful and humiliating.

The pirate was stalling, giving his magic time to settle, to flood back into his limbs.

The Demon King hesitated. "Is this really necessary?" He growled; voice laced with venom. "We had a deal.

You stay in the sea. I take the land." He suddenly did not sound like the most powerful being in the room.

Ethera flinched as cold water touched her hand. Strings of it were crawling along the ground, pulled like puppet threads towards the Pirate King. Water slithered below him from every corner of the room, ripping through the cracks in the walls, the floor, and the ceiling.

He didn't move. He didn't need to; the storm was rattling up and forming from behind him. His eyes were calm; his infamous faint smile curled on his lips. Water spiraled in perfect circles around him, faster and faster. Power pulsed in every drop.

Then, with a single sweep of his arm, a gust of wind blew through the room. A wave rose behind him, crashing forward. Water exploded outwards, droplets staining his shirt and soaking his skin. His complexion darkened to a stormy gray as the sea itself seemed to answer his call. The dark abyss in his eyes swirled, its edges bleeding blue, like a storm-whirlpool set loose.

The Demon King's eyes widened as the attack flew at him. With a roar so loud, he summoned fire—but not flame. A thick, shadowy darkness bled across the air like spilled ink. At his command, a barrier formed just in the nick of time.

But it couldn't stop the pirate's raw power. The water slipped through the tiniest cracks in the shadow-wall, threading between the weaknesses of the Demon King's shield. Some of it evaporated on contact, hissing into steam. The rest punched through, striking the demon with a force that sent him staggering backward.

The Pirate King moved like a wave crashing against a cliff.

One moment, he stood still before the throne, and the next, he was right in front of the demon with arms extended and his hand locked around the demon's throat.

He sliced through the darkness that surrounded the demon as if it were nothing more than child's play. The Demon King raised his hand, controlling the darkness surrounding him; it lifted and swallowed them both. They vanished into a swirling cloud of black mist, the air thickening with pressure and energy as it spread, swallowing the throne. It felt draining with every breath and heartbeat.

Ethera couldn't move. She sat frozen on the floor, eyes wide, her body paralyzed by more than fear. The Pirate King wasn't merely wielding water.

He *was* water.

Fluid and furious, vicious and untamable. A living current of unstoppable force. And suddenly, it all made sense.

The cave, the waves that dragged her under. The helplessness she felt…the panic. The way her lungs had burned as she sank, over and over again, in that suffocating darkness. The moment she was cursed to relive in every dream, over and over again. The fear clung to her in silence when night fell. That drowning feeling had never been just the ocean.

It had always been *him*.

And now, she finally understood why the water haunted her so. And why she loathed it.

Her eyes scanned the tiled floor, spotting the silver of her knife. Ethera crawled towards it, getting up halfway and grabbing it in a fit of rage. She sprinted towards Rose, grabbing the blonde's hand and pulling her away from two skeletons that threatened her frozen state.

Rose had not learned combat. And even with Ethera's limited knowledge, it was better for them to stick together than separately. It was no surprise when Ethera's movements came out sloppy; she swung her knife, using it as if it were an extension of her fist.

The rattling pile of bones charged at them. At the last second, Ethera had jumped out of the way. It tripped over something, its sword clacking on the ground as it lost its balance and fell. His bony fingers inched to grab it, but Rose's fast thinking enabled her to step on its hand. It was crushed underneath, her converse against the sword.

Ethera appeared above him, lifting her dagger next to her head and colliding it with eyes closed. Her heart pounded with dark thoughts. It proved easier to kill something that was already dead.

A moment of silence followed, the numb body flinched against the floor. "Behind you!" Rose screamed, her voice sharp with panic. Without hesitation, she threw herself at the approaching skeleton, tackling it to the ground before it could reach her friend. They rolled across the marble floor, limbs and bones thrashing as they fought for dominance over the other. "Get off, damnit!" She yelled at him, as if it understood human speech.

Ethera jumped to her feet, still breathless as she lunged forward. She grabbed onto the skeleton's back, wrapping her arms around it and using her body weight to try and pull it off her friend.

It didn't move; it felt like its bones were forged from steel. Without thinking, she raised her dagger and drove it down into the skeleton's skull. There was a crack, followed by an unsettling sound of purple goo erupting from the inside of the shattered bone, splashing across Rose's clothes.

Rose froze in horror; goo dripped from her chin as she attempted to wipe it off. It smeared across her lips. Her eyes widened in shock as she scrambled out from beneath the corpse, frantically wiping her mouth with the torn sleeves of her tunic. Terror flashed in her eyes. "I'm about to throw up," she announced, one hand clutching her stomach as she tried to regain composure through hollow breaths.

Ethera rushed to her side, kneeling beside her and gently patting the blonde's back. "You're okay. Just breathe, breathe."

Across the battlefield, Hugo had joined his brother and Juno, forming a tight triangle as they fought side by side. Despite the fatigue growing on their faces, they continued at it. Reymond didn't seem as hesitant as before; his brain had convinced him to think of this less as life-or-death and more as a video game.

A point for every skeleton. Two if he gets a straight headshot.

He used the heel of his foot to kick the skeleton away. Purple blood rolled down the silver blade of his sword as he shoved his hair away from his face that was obstructing his vision. The blonde curls had grown out way too much.

Juno was getting tired, slowing down with every skeleton she shot. The constant motion of reaching over her shoulder had begun to tense her muscles. A possible cramp was overdue. Her short raven hair had stuck to the sweat that piled on her forehead and cheeks.

The elves fought further back, holding the demons from going after the mortals. Shadows crawled along the edges of the room, and the clash of steel echoed off the walls.

The momentum of the battle was slowing. Everyone's movements were heavier, their breaths shorter. The adrenaline was fading, and the exhaustion was catching up. The enemies only grew in number. "Fuck—they just keep on coming!" Reymond muttered angrily, his eyes scanning for the next attack while giving himself time to catch his breath.

"We need to destroy the orb, like right now!" Juno backed him up, motioning for Hugo to go figure it out. He nodded frantically, clutching a random sword he picked off the ground. He dashed across the room, jumping over bones and all.

Rose was throwing up in the corner. Ethera had long moved away, afraid she too might be next.

"Right now, is not a good time, Rose!" Hugo yelled, panic flooding his voice. Rose glared at him, eyes watery and wild. If she still had her sword, she would've thrown it at his face without hesitation. Unfortunately, it was lost somewhere in the sea of disaster that was once the throne room.

"We can't hold them off much longer," Hugo continued, turning to Ethera. "Everyone's exhausted." She glanced around, her friends, some bruised, some bleeding, but all were still fighting. Their strength was fading as they pushed past their own limits. Every movement was slower than the last; they couldn't hold out much longer.

She followed Hugo's gaze to the glowing orb and then to the pitch-black bubble that had swallowed the Pirate King. The prophecy had said that *she* would bring victory to the Enchanted Forest. But standing here, surrounded by chaos and despair, it felt like death was the only fate waiting for them.

Her grip tightened around her knife.

Maybe…just maybe it had to be *her.* The prophecy had hinted at a new world—maybe it was just a riddle for unleashing magic? Setting it free? Letting the world return to how it has always been.

She charged towards the orb, heart hammering.

Ethera stopped just a few inches away, raising her knife, and with one breathless motion, she stabbed it. The blade passed through. Light exploded from the orb, blinding her in the process as it blasted in every direction. It was working, she could feel it. Cracks splintered along the surface like a spider's web.

A smile tugged at her lips.

And then pain. Her body slammed into the cold floor as something snatched at her leg and yanked her back. She hit the ground hard; air knocked from her lungs.

A thin, black rope-like string had attached itself to her ankle. Her eyes hazily followed its source as it dragged her closer and closer towards the shadow bubble that led to the Demon King. She screamed, scrambling for anything to hold on but her fingers slipped past everything they touched.

Rose and Hugo had appeared at her sides, grabbing her hands and trying to pull her towards them. More dark vines lashed out, wrapping themselves around them, binding the mortals together. They fell, unable to move as the shadow gripped them tighter with every struggle.

Ethera's shirt rode up as she was dragged, marble floor scraping at her arms and back, leaving raw burns on her elbows. There was nothing she could hold; her feet kicked wildly, but the darkness swallowed everything.

She couldn't stop it.

And she didn't want to.

Maybe Dilian hadn't struck the orb right. Or maybe the prophecy was cruelly literal—*she* had to be the one to break it. Her, of all people.

But Ethera was no hero. She never was.

She had killed. Lied. Stolen. She was selfish. She didn't care about this world—not until it affected her plan. To her, all of it had been fake. A dream where she could pretend nothing mattered and that all of this would somehow work out in the end. Everything would reset after the war, and she would be back in the comfort of her home.

But that was no home. No one was waiting for her.

So why did the prophecy pick her?

It should have been Reymond. Or Juno. A warrior. A real leader. Someone who belonged, not a wannabe hero.

The shadows closed around her, pulling her body and her soul into the abyss. And with it, her will to live.

Ethera stopped fighting, going limp.

CHAPTER 24

Ethera's head struck the stone steps leading up to the throne. The world had turned pitch black. Darkness had swallowed everything—her sight, her breath, and even her mind. She could not tell whether this void was something she saw or something she felt.

She failed, didn't she?

The darkness was by no means comforting. It was cold and reminded her of a lonely winter. A sudden gust of wind swept past, lifting strands of her hair, carrying with it the sharp string of ocean salt.

It was suffocating. Her nose burned from each breath.

Somewhere in that endless dark void, two kings fought. One for the throne and the other for fun. The thought was absurd; she couldn't even see her own hands, let alone the battlefield.

With no light, there was nothing to hold onto. Nothing to aim for, nothing to *want*. She had long since forgotten what it felt like to not chase anything.

Then, in the distance, a figure broke through the darkness. The Pirate King stumbled forward, eyes scanning the surrounding area as if he knew he'd find her sooner or later. Once his eyes landed on the mortal, he broke into a limping jog. His skin was as dark as his eyes, which glittered like pieces of obsidian, staring off into a flame.

Ethera didn't bother to move. Her limbs were glued to the marble ground, her head sagged back, and her eyes slipped shut helplessly.

The man knelt beside her, his hands hesitated. "What are you lying there for? Get up!" He barked, his voice cutting through the haze. Finally, his arms had seized her by the shoulders and hauled her upright. She groaned as a sudden pain shot through her skull and down her spine.

Her eyelids fluttered open. Through the fog, her vision landed on a golden skull with a single ruby eye that stared back at her. The necklace hanging from his neck was too familiar—so familiar that she could no longer trust if she imagined it. The scale between memory and hallucination tipped dangerously.

She squinted, trying not to lose her focus again.

The pirate brushed his fingers across her forehead. Blood. Warm drops pooled and slid down her face despite the coldness that had its clutches on her. He sighed and glanced into the darkness that stretched endlessly around them.

The Demon King had swallowed him whole, and he was yet to find a way out. This mortal was his only hope…but she was reduced to nothing. The blood loss was pulling her under. He had to save her to save himself.

His hand lifted towards her injury, the palm an inch away. With closed eyes, he took a deep breath, focusing on the sound of a rapid heartbeat. One by one, droplets of blood froze midair. With a sharp gesture, he drew them back towards her wound as though dragging time in reverse.

The blood re-entered her skin, settling beneath the scab. He pressed his finger into it, and the blood beneath it hardened, sealing the injury. The thin layer of magic acted as nothing more than a band-aid, but it was more than enough to bring her back.

Ethera's eyebrows furrowed, her hands instantly pushing the man away from the sudden piercing headache. "Hey, hey! Wake up!" He slapped her cheeks lightly. The mortal groaned, her head swinging to the other side, away from the pirate. He cast a glance over his shoulder, half expecting the Demon King to emerge from the void at any given moment.

His suspicion only arose. Either the demon was playing mind tricks, or his own magic did not let him locate his lost toys within the void. The Pirate King glanced back, giving the girl another shake. "I need you to get me out of here, mortal," he urged, voice low and strained.

"…What do you mean?" Ethera croaked, her voice falling halfway through.

The pounding in her skull echoed through her ears, reducing the words of the pirate to mere muffles. She felt submerged underwater, only granted the cruel mercy of breathing. Her eyes blinked open again, her head threatening to drop back.

He scanned the shadows with sharp, anxious eyes. If they didn't escape soon, this pool of infinite abyss would become their tomb. "This magic. I can't break through it," the man growled with irritation. "Which means we're stuck. You need to snap out of it—think of your friends. They might be dying on the other side. Can you hear me? Your friends—dead!"

Ethera's eyes instantly opened. "What? They're dead?"

"No, you fool!" he snapped, losing his patience. "They *might* die, unless you get us out of here."

The pirate shook her fickle body with urgency. It seemed that the unnecessary roughness somehow worked; her mind fell into place, jolting her body into motion. "How the hell am I supposed to do that, you bastard? Get off me!" She yelled out, shoving his arms off her.

"I don't know. Figure it out, *mortal*." He scoffed, getting up.

"Listen here, you dimwit. I don't have any magical powers like you. So why don't *you* hurry up and get us out of here!" She staggered to her feet, her eyes getting lost in the surrounding void. Faint dizziness washed over her.

There was absolutely nothing out there. Not even a sound. Even her own voice echoed back at her. The abyss stretched for what looked like forever, and yet even within the darkness, only she and the pirate glowed ever so faintly—just enough for them to see each other.

She raised her hand, as if sheer will might light the path ahead.

There had to be a way out. There *had* to be.

Otherwise, all of this…all of the suffering…would be for nothing. Guilt slammed into her, the thought of her friends bleeding out somewhere, calling her name, dying alone—

It was unbearable.

"Didn't your parents teach you to mind your words?" The pirate muttered after a moment of silence, as if the lack of conversation was making him nervous.

She didn't look at him, though she felt how close he stood. "No. They taught me to cuss at traitors."

He let out a low, bitter laugh. She turned toward him and shoved him hard into the fog. He stumbled, startled at her sudden action. The blackness parted slightly around him, reacting to his presence. The void bulged outward as if accommodating the space for the big fish.

"…Well, that didn't quite work," she said dryly, turning away, and ignoring the fussy pirate. She bit the nail of her thumb, hoping to trigger some kind of idea—a solution to this mess.

The abyss pulsed like a living creature, its heart a suffocating mass that smeared despair over everything it touched. Ethera and the pirate walked side by side, arms brushing. For once, she didn't pull away. It reminded her that she wasn't alone despite not being able to hear his footsteps.

The Pirate King's breath suddenly trembled. The darkness crept closer—not just around them but now within him. The crushing weight tugged at his chest, fogging his mind. He staggered, clutching the temples on his head.

But her presence, even with a simple touch, seemed to anchor him. A desperation to resist the dark magic that took on many useless forms in his mind.

He reached out blindly. His fingers caught her arm as his knees buckled. He collapsed, panting, his vision blending with the background.

Ethera knelt beside him, eyes flickering with worry. Concern—not fear. And for once, not hate.

She remained untouched. The fog simply recoiled from her, bouncing harmlessly off her skin, unable to dig its claws inside her mind.

The Demon King's spell could not harm her.

Perhaps it was the reason why it made her so important to the prophecy. As the burden of the abyss crushed him down towards the ground, the mortal called out to the man, only to realize that she did not know his name.

He was the Pirate King. A beast the world feared. But the man beneath was nameless.

Ethera hesitated. "Hey… what's wrong with you?" She shook him by the shoulders, carefully, as if touching him would drown her.

He couldn't answer. His chest rose and fell, ragged and weak. His eyes were shut tight, shielding himself from something only he could see. He struggled beneath; a war had broken out in his head. Inner demons dragged him into a place she could only hope to reach.

Ethera sat there frozen, unsure of what to do. His skin had lost all its color—he looked as pale as a corpse. She couldn't leave him like that, not with the monster that waited for them out there. "Come on," she whispered shakily, throwing his arm over her shoulder and struggling to lift him. "Bear with it for a bit more. I'll get us out of here."

Another promise she made with no clue of how to keep it. How was a powerless human supposed to fight an eternal abyss created by an enemy so powerful that the dead had escaped its salvation? It was a cruel joke. Destiny handed her a broken sword and told her to fight a god.

Still, she walked forward, one step at a time, dragging his heavy frame with her. He was dead weight, a heavy sack of meat. Ethera grunted under her breath.

She could have left him—she *should* have left him. But the thought of walking through this void alone chilled her more than the darkness could ever hope to.

It felt as though she had been walking for hours, accompanied by only the sound of her own struggles. But in reality, it was mere seconds. Occasionally, the man would twitch, groan, or whine. Sweat pooled along his forehead, soon mirrored by her own.

She couldn't hold him anymore; her hands began tingling with numbness. There was nothing in front of her, nothing behind her, and yet with a single spec of hope, she managed to find a breakthrough.

Against all odds, she hit something solid. Her body bounced back from the impact. The Pirate King fell from her grasp, thudding against the invisible floor next to her.

Ethera stumbled forward, shaky hands extended. Her palms touched something cold and firm. A slight electric chill traveled from her fingertips to her shoulders, causing her lips to tuck in an encouraging smile.

It was a wall of some kind. She was sure of it despite her lack of vision. She pounded her fists against it, unable to even put a dent. She threw her body next, bouncing right off it.

The mortal turned desperately, her eyes landing on the pirate curled up on the ground. His brow furrowed, face twisted in pain as his lids flickered with distress.

The nightmares had begun. He looked just like her—helpless and useless. His magic, his power…it meant nothing here.

"Hey!" Ethera barked, lunging towards him desperately. She tugged on his shoulders and shook him violently. "Make me a weapon! Like a sword out of water or something—*anything*!"

He groaned, eyes barely fluttering open. Her voice had pierced through the haunting void in his mind, louder than the chilling whispers of the voices and the memories clawing at him.

She helped him sit up. His hands trembled, but he raised them, palms upwards. Water began to swirl between them, faint but gathering, shaped by sheer will.

The abyss would not have him. It hadn't beaten him, not yet. The air around them grew crispy and cold. A wave of the sea had stung her nostrils yet again as it coiled between her and the Pirate King, taking the form of a sword. Without hesitation, Ethera seized it. A few droplets splashed onto the pirate's palms, darkening them in the dim light.

With one swoosh, she struck the barrier. Cracks spread instantly—thin white lines scattered all around the water sword, racing across the black shadow wall and creating a disturbance in the abyss. The darkness shook in rage, howling in the distance, and she was sure the Demon King felt it.

Ethera swung the sword again—this time harder with the strength of her whole body. The invisible glass shattered, tiny pieces falling down towards the ground as the sound echoed through the mountain of black fog.

It was still dark. But something surely broke.

She went back for the pirate, drunk on the uncontrollable dark memories. Ethera grabbed him by the arm, helping him up, and dragged him with all her might as her free hand grasped at the sword's spine.

A soft sound could be heard from within the sword, the melody of little ripples clashing with one another, sprinkling little mists all around.

Ethera let out a yelp when they stepped through the broken wall, falling down the stairs of the throne as light poured from all over. They were back, lying on the ground weakly and aching in different parts of their bodies.

The light had temporarily blinded them, and the clutches of the darkness were retreating. The scene before them remained the same. Rose and Hugo were still tied to each other on the floor, rolling around trying to break free. Reymond and Juno fought—although Juno was completely out of arrows. The elves were at war with the demons, and some were down on their knees, heavily injured.

Ethera twitched weakly against the ground, turning her body to glance back at the once pit of eternal darkness. The Demon King was gone, and the shadows had completely evaporated.

But he was still here. She felt him. And so did everyone else. He was in the air, hiding somewhere in the shadows, drifting and watching, planning his next attack.

The pirate was first to recover, much faster than Ethera. He quickly got up on his feet and brushed off his clothes as if that was going to completely dry them of filth. Ethera got up too, slowly stumbling towards her two tied friends. She used the water sword in her hand to cut them free, and they all scattered away from each other like magnets before tackling her in a hug.

Rose wailed loudly upon seeing Ethera. "We thought you were gone!" She yelped out, her eyes already puffy from previous tears. Her body shook against Ethera's frozen one, it seemed that the blonde cried a lot.

It was like a fever dream to be here with them instead of lost in *there*. She did not move to hug Rose, but instead, turned her head to glance back at the orb.

The sudden overwhelming feeling to destroy it washed over her. Rose had let go, sensing Hugo's hand on her shoulder. They watched Ethera walk towards the glowing sphere, the sword in hand and fury in her eyes. But before she could put an end to it, the water had flown away from her hand and back to its master.

She spun around, eyes glaring at the pirate. "Are you kidding me?" She hissed. A smug smile danced on his face as Ethera cursed about. The Demon King appeared between them, his horns dancing with rage at the betrayal and trickery used on him. His red orbs landed on Ethera, who stood the closest to the orb, and with the blink of an eye, he appeared right in front of her.

The shadows had swirled all around her, gripping at her body as she stared back. He grabbed her by the throat, swinging her across the room. Another move of his arms had sent her friends flying backwards. No one was going to stand between him and his victory. It was time for them all to die.

The mortals had long infested his throne room with their mindless games of trickery. The demon had been enraged; his shout had rattled the ceiling above. Little cracks had formed, and debris sprinkled down on them. Bigger pieces had begun to fall, squishing, whoever was not fortunate enough to move in time.

Ethera's body was drenched in water; nothing had been broken upon the impact. She quickly rolled over to the side, getting up, and ignoring the aches. Both she and her friends were bruised, beaten, and had numerous cuts all over. Reymond's shoulder felt like it was going to pop out any minute now. The fight had been going on for quite some time, and it seemed that only their side started giving up.

The Pirate King had jumped into action, summoning another water ball and throwing it at the demon. A shadow appeared, but the water flew through it, hitting the demon and causing him to fly backwards.

The final battle had begun.

The two powerful beings fought at each other's throats while the background characters scurried around with their limited ability to survive.

Another water ball was thrown without a hesitation. Seconds before contact, it opened up like a net and threw itself against the demon, temporarily restraining him. The demon whispered something in another language, and the water loosened, evaporating into thin air.

The pirate shrugged, half expecting his attack not to land. "Well," the man began, almost cheerfully, "somebody finally picked up new tricks." The throne room was nothing more than a playground for him.

"You are a fool if you think that you can get me with that cheap trick twice."

"Worth a shot," the pirate mumbled, extending his hand again. Behind him, a large wall of water rushed forward, swallowing the demon. The water immediately collapsed and sank back towards the pirate.

Another wave followed shortly after.

The pirate didn't attack the way everyone in the room hoped he would. Instead, he waited. Smiled, even. Let the water toy with its prey, like an inescapable current, all the while its vicious waves caused more damage to the room.

With a loud roar, the demon screamed in fury, "I'm going to end you!"

The pirate glanced at Ethera, and for a brief moment, their eyes locked on. It was obvious that this was his plan. A distraction, he was giving her some time to finish off that orb.

She got up, getting ready to run. The ground below her was covered in obstacles, collapsed ceilings, rock, and bones. She waited for the right moment, while also memorizing the fastest way to the orb that didn't involve jumping. The demon charged at the pirate, this time bringing the fight closer. Ethera seized the opportunity, breaking into a sprint.

It was more difficult than she had thought. The demon had not once let his guard down when it came to the orb; the black restrains had knocked her body down yet again. She was so close when she had collapsed again. Her body struggled against the crushing force; her eyes locked on the orb. Her knife was missing. There was nothing near her that she could use.

The Demon King laughed as he blocked the pirate's attack. The water hissed with contact with the black mist. The pirate's boots splashed against the water on the marble ground, echoing through the battle with every heavy step. He appeared before the demon, swinging his hands that were drenched with force. The demon dodged, stumbling backwards as if not expecting to be on the receiving end of the short-range attack.

Ethera continued struggling, her hands unwrapping the binds on her legs. The energy from the orb pulled her. It felt like the lost white magic of this land was begging to be set free. `

If she doesn't destroy it soon, they just might be toast.

The pirate jumped to the side, flickering his wrist as the water swirled in the air before him. He pushed his hand toward the demon, throwing him backwards against a wall. The magic on Ethera had loosened, allowing her to break free. "You're still as weak as ever. Some things don't change," the pirate taunted. The wall had cracked in front of him, and with a deep breath, the water surged upwards, ripping through the marble tiles.

The demon growled, extending his hand as dark energy shot right towards him. The demons that were fighting Dilian and the other elves were suddenly sucked into the Demon King, disappearing as they blended in with his magic.

Ethera could only imagine how much stronger it made him. He let out a wild roar, struggling to contain that power. Wings tore from behind his body, claws stretched out from his long limbs, tearing at the ground he stood against. But the water kept coming—denser and colder. The smell of the sea filtered through the air as if the King of the Sea was pulling water straight from the ocean.

The pirate raised his hands a split second before the demon, shooting out water with such speed and pressure that it would have been impossible to survive such an attack if his foe was a human. The water made contact with the black demonic energy, thickened with an unknown force. It repelled outwards, briefly hovering before morphing into about two dozen sharp spears. The man flicked his wrist, shooting the demon in all directions.

The demon's own energy shot at the pirate, and smoke filled the air when it made contact with the ground and the wall. Ethera could not see the Pirate King; the smoke had completely hidden him from her view.

Was he dead? Did he lose?

Everyone had gone quiet, trying to make out what had happened after the loud booming sound that appeared on the other side of the throne. Smoke filtered through the air, and little droplets fell from the broken ceiling. They couldn't tell if it was rain or the repelling water of the Pirate King's power.

The demon had gotten up, struggling as the energy around him scattered uncertainly. More of his soldiers appeared before him, realizing how serious the injury had looked. They surrounded their master, preparing to defend him.

Somewhere closer to the crowd of elves, the pirate had appeared. One of his knees rested against the ground, and his hand grabbed hold of a long spear. Blood gushed through the side of his cheek, turning the surrounding skin into a darker shade of pale blue.

CHAPTER 25

"Catch!" The Pirate King shouted, throwing Dilian's spear through the chaos. Ethera reached up with both hands, barely managing to grab the weapon. She spun around, her body turning desperately towards the floating orb. Without hesitation, she drove the elf's spear through it.

The orb cracked under the pressure, and thin fractures fell across its surface. Ethera clenched the spear tighter, afraid it was going to jerk backward. Her hands held it at bay, pushing her entire body weight into it.

A skeleton slammed into her from the side, knocking her hard to the floor. Its rotten jaw snapped wildly, teeth clacking inches from her face. Her fingers trembled against its torn armor, but her eyes never left the floating orb. Light began spilling from its visible wounds.

It pulsed abnormally, with each growing crack, the light escaped its prison, and the shards fell away—disintegrating before they could even hit the ground. The skeleton on top of her began to weaken. Its grip slacked, and the weight grew limp against her arms.

With a grunt, Ethera kicked it off and scrambled up, only to be thrown back by a sudden burst of wind. A soft warmth consumed her, sweating over her like sunlight breaking through mountains of stormy clouds. It was gentle against her bruised body, so full of peace that it sent chills up her spine.

It felt like hands were pulling her away from death's front door.

The orb exploded into a storm of wind and power. Magic danced in the air like dust on fire—spinning and then vanishing into the air. Across the room, skeletons dropped like puppets with their strings cut, one collapsing right on top of Rose, who let out a shriek of disgust.

The demons fled, flying through the shattered windows and the cracks in the ceiling, as they attempted to escape. Before they could make it far, their bodies dissolved into ash, falling through the air like snow.

Ethera groaned, forcing herself to sit up. Her ribs ached, and her limbs throbbed.

She must have broken a bone. Or something. There was no way she was going to leave this world unscratched after being thrown around in every possible direction.

Around her, the others were also getting up, stopping midway to catch their breath. It seemed she wasn't the only one who was sent flying. Juno lay on her back, knees slightly raised. Her pants were ripped, and her tunic was colored gray and purple. The bow that she grew so accustomed to was lost in the pools of rotten corpses and rusty weapons.

Rose had thrown up again, and Hugo patted her on the back with a scrunched nose. Dilian was nowhere to be seen, hidden behind a group of his own people.

Reymond stood up, placing a boot against a fallen skeleton's ribcage as he yanked his sword free. He let out a nervous chuckle, trying to ease his own tension as he swung the sword over his shoulder. "Well, miraculously, we all survived. *Again.*"

Ethera wasn't in the mood to make jokes. She was tired, hungry, and could barely stand upright. The adrenaline felt deadly, consuming every part of her shaky body.

The Pirate King appeared next to her with a wide, malicious smile on his face. Ethera flinched, preparing herself for any incoming tricks. He bent down in front of her. "I understand the prophecy now. You really did give me something I've always wanted, and I will be back to collect it when it finally hatches," He announced, leaning over to make sure she was the only one that could hear him. His hair had fallen loosely on the sides of his face, spilling over her. A nasty smile pulled on his cheeks; the threat flew right through the mortal's ears.

Ethera's body leaned back, her brows furrowing with confusion at the pirate's words. "Wait a second...you——." He raised his hand, interrupting her, and in the blink of an eye, he turned into a body of water. It fell on the ground with a splash, slithering through the cracks in the marble floor until there was no trace of it left.

Ethera sat there, her mind seemingly going black. It seemed that no one had heard him, but his missing presence lifted the invisible weight in the room.

She finally got up, legs trembling, eyes glued to the ground where he suddenly disappeared. "It's over. We won," she breathed out after a moment of silence.

The pirate was gone. The demons and skeletons were no more. The prophecy had finally come true. A breath of relief slipped past her chapped lips, and a small smile lifted her cheeks.

They did it—they made it back alive in one piece.

The Enchanted Forest was once again under elven care, though Ethera was sure it would be years before it regained its former glory.

"We survived, again. Man...I do wish this could go on my college essay."

Rose and Hugo helped Juno to her feet, and together they met Reymond and Ethera in the middle of the clearing. "We did it!" Juno and Rose jumped with excitement, crashing into a hug before pulling the others in. The rest joined without hesitation. They stayed wrapped in each other's arms. Comfortable, exhausted, and more than a little sweaty, but thankfully, with no major injuries. They glanced back to find Dilian standing beside them.

The elf lingered at the edge of the group, one eyebrow lifted as he watched the humans with a peculiar look on his face. They shifted aside to make space for him. He instantly declined with a single flick of his wrist.

Reymond did not accept the refusal. The mortal jumped out of the huddle, seized the elf in one swift motion, and gestured for the rest to join in. Dilian struggled to pry the leech off, but it was useless once the other humans joined.

In a moment, he was swallowed by a cluster of little humans hugging and squeezing the rainbow out of him. Receiving such affection after a battle was unheard of. For the mortals, it was their first battle and their first victory. As for the elves…it was merely one among hundreds that followed their life paths.

Breathless and worn from the fight, they walked quietly back to the library. The urge to go home had pulled them forward despite their tired bodies that begged for a moment's rest.

Only Ethera knew where the book was hidden. Thankfully, she'd had the foresight to stash it behind the first shelf of the seemingly endless enchanted library.

It still looked the same, except this time it felt different. Less suffocating and freer, without the cursed energy of the demons. The door they'd left open had let fresh air seep in. The musky scent of old paper still lingered in the air, but now it brought forth comfort.

Sunlight streamed through the windows that lined the far wall—golden rays cast long beams of light across the dusty marble floors. It seemed like even the sun had come out to congratulate them.

Ethera quickly separated from the group, disappearing down an aisle.

Hugo stood by the window, his eyes glancing down at the destroyed forest. No ounce of life was visible, and yet he could almost picture the beauty of it.

Perhaps one day they could all come back and visit, cast their eyes upon the land that they had saved with their sweat, tears, blood, and vomit.

A comforting silence filled the air before all their ears twitched with fear. Something was making its way towards them. The faint sound of footsteps echoed in the corridor beyond, and everyone froze in anticipation. They drew their weapons; sore posture shifted towards the door as their hearts pounded in their ears.

To their relief, the chief and five elves rushed in, their weapons stained with purple goo. The chief glanced around the room, his eyes wide with surprise.

Silence fell before them.

Ethera appeared behind, awkwardly clearing her throat as she clutched the book close to her chest. "Well? The prophecy is complete. The demons are gone, and your land has been taken back." Her voice echoed through the room, breaking the suspicious silence.

Did the chief not expect them to destroy the orb and win the war?

"Yeah, no need to thank us or anything. Hero is kind of our middle name," Reymond butted in. The mortals all exchanged looks before breaking into a lighthearted laugh.

The events of a single day flashed in their heads. "Wait a minute—you used me as bait back there!" Hugo exclaimed angrily, suddenly remembering being tossed by his brother. His fists bawled as he inched closer to grab him.

Reymond took a step back, bringing forth his sharp, long sword. "Watch yourself, lil bro. I'm dangerously armed," he threatened, tilting his head with a smile. Hugo huffed and narrowed his eyes, warning his brother to put the sword down. "This kind of grew on me, I'd love to take it back, but I think mom will faint if she sees me with it."

Reymond walked over to Dilian, twisting the sword and handing it back to its original wielder. The elf looked down at it, the weight resting in his hands. A sudden empty feeling washed over him as the realization sank in. His days of babysitting were over; the humans were finally free to go home.

Hugo followed his brother, walking over to the chief and handing him the journal in his pouch, along with a few magic stones. They held eye contact longer than necessary, as if exchanging some silent dialogue unknown to the others.

"I gotta admit, I had fun beating your ass," Reymond cockily stated, putting his hand on the elf's shoulder. Dilian rolled his eyes, flicking the hand off.

"And here I thought the skeletons hit some sense into you."

"Never," he smiled widely, pulling the elf into a hug. Dilian froze but relaxed soon enough, his ears dropping. Reymond pulled away, his lips curling and his eyes sparkling in a taunting way. "Aww, are we finally friends now?"

"Piss off already! And do not set foot here ever again," Dilian muttered, shoving the boy away. Rose looked inside her pockets, trying to decide if there was anything she wanted to leave behind.

Her eyes lit up in excitement as she skipped towards the elf. "Here, have my lip gloss to remember me by!" She said excitedly before handing over her E.L.F lip oil. It barely had any product left, after all, she was giddily using and abusing it throughout their little 'vacation'. Dilian's eyes widened as he stared at the logo with confusion.

It was Juno's turn, she shifted uncomfortably, her fingers refusing to let go. "I don't think I'm leaving this behind, sorry," the raven-head announced, motioning to her bow and some stray arrows she picked up. It had become something entirely special to her, and she felt the need to preserve it. The elves didn't protest; they had hundreds of those. She only had four arrows, stained with skeleton goo, but each was just as special.

Ethera nodded, agreeing with her. "I-I think I'll hang on to the dagger too," she muttered, wanting something physical to remember the trip of her lifetime. She had picked it up earlier, just in case. Despite the war being over, a heavy feeling still stirred in her heart. Was it because of the Pirate King's words?

"We ought to thank you for everything! You took care of us and kept us alive and well...so thank you!" Rose cheered, her hands clasped together.

The chief smiled in return with a single nod of acknowledgment. "All is thanks to thee for the prophecy now stands complete." His green orbs scanned everyone's faces. Ethera's eyelids dropped, and a bitter taste clung to the back of her throat.

Guilt

In her eyes, they didn't deserve the word heroes. *She* didn't deserve it. After all, if things were even *slightly* different, then she wouldn't have finished off the orb and stopped the war.

But no one had to know that. They were heroes in the elves' eyes, and that's all that mattered.

"I must confess, we did once underestimate mortals, yet it has been an honor to make acquaintance with thee," The chief continued, bowing his head with thanks. In the background, Rose and Juno snatched the book from Ethera, fiddling with it as they searched for a way to activate it, mindful of the last time it had drawn them inside painfully.

Rose opened it in the middle, and the pages rustled on their own, turning by themselves until it found what it was looking for. A sudden blue light burst from the paper, spilling into the air before her. The wind chimed in, brushing her strawberry hair out of her face. From the yellow-inked words rose a delicate haze of pale blue, forming an oval, mirror-like circle.

Startled by the sudden electric feeling that zigged through her fingertips, Rose dropped the book; its spine struck the ground with a thud. The mist expanded upon the impact, rising towards the ceiling above her, while the blinding light softened into a warm, gentle glow.

Before them, now stood a portal.

Juno sighed. "Oh, thank god." This time, the book chose to treat them good.

"Wow, it's like this world is trying to say 'get the fuck out' nicely," Reymond snorted sarcastically. He glanced back at everyone, flashing them with an encouraging smile and a little wave of his hand. "Don't need to tell me twice."

He skipped through it, disappearing within and causing a little ripple in the blue mist-like glow. He was gone, and the rest of the mortals stood around, gawking at the portal. Juno followed next, waving her gloved hand as a bright smile crossed her face before she too disappeared.

"Come on, Ethera! I'm dying for a hot shower," Rose whined before jumping through as well. Ethera laughed at how fearlessly her friends had leaped through without even knowing where the other side would lead. She turned around, nodding at Dilian before walking towards the portal without hesitation.

By reflex, her hand reached out first. "Huh?" Ethera breathed, dumbfounded. Her fingers pressed against something hard. An invincible barrier stopped her from passing through. She exchanged a glance with Hugo, confusion drawing on her face before trying again, this time pressing both hands forward.

It didn't budge. The more she pushed, the hotter it felt. Pain seared through her fingers. She quickly pulled away, wiping her hands on her trousers.

Hugo appeared beside her, slipping his hand through the portal with ease. It fell through, a tingling effect tickled at his arm before he pulled it back, eyes wide. "W-What does that mean?" He asked aloud, yanking at Ethera's hand and reaching toward the blue light. Her fingers halted, blocked again. Desperation darkened his gaze as it landed on the chief. The elf's expression remained calm, ears twitching slightly.

Ethera was not allowed to go through. Her body froze with horror.

She was trapped here.

It was exactly what the Elder Alfada had warned Hugo: meddle too much with this world's magic, and one could become bound to it. He had been ready to pay that price himself—but why Ethera? She hadn't cast a single spell.

The thought darkened Hugo's heart. What if the magic had chosen her deliberately as the ultimate price for the caster?

Ethera couldn't believe it. She began banging on the portal in frustration, tears blurring her vision as she attempted to force herself through. The portal did not crack.

Hugo took a shaky breath in. "There must be something that can be done…" His voice trailed, hopeless even to his own ears.

The chief's head lowered. "I-I'm afraid there is nothing thee could do," he began. "Too much has been taken. And to restore the balance, it has taken her."

Ethera spun toward the elder, overwhelmed by fury and disbelief. She grabbed him by the tunic, pulling his frail body to meet her eye. The elves around them drawn their spears, threatening the hero if she did not release the chief.

Dilian appeared beside her. "Ethera, calm down—." He urged, placing a hand on her shoulders while holding the elves at bay with the other.

"You! I did everything you wanted—EVERYTHING the prophecy demanded! Why can I not go through?" Her voice broke under the weight of her words. She had given everything and received nothing in return, and yet this was how the world repaid her.

The elf's eyes remained emotionless, her own reflection staring back at her. Her arms dropped to her sides like a wilting flower. "It's magic," she muttered, shoulders shaking. "Of course…it rejects magic. That's why Dilian could not destroy the orb. That's why…that bastard threw me the spear. I destroyed the magic and it has taken me." Her tears brutally rolled down her cheeks; the elf's ears twitched at the sound of her sobs.

Her plan had backfired. It failed her. This world has conspired against her. It plotted traps and lay in wait until she had fallen.

She was to stay, never to return home.

Hugo regained his composure, trying to sound uplifting. "Alright, well, it's decided then. I'll stay. I'll find a way to break whatever is keeping you here."

Ethera froze, wiping her nose. He going to stay here? For *her*?

"Thee was warned that meddling with magic would bind the caster. It is a miracle thy soul remains free, but if you keep this pretense up, there won't be a second chance," the chief warned. The spears finally lowered, and Ethera looked at Hugo's guilty expression, which confirmed the chief's words.

Her eyes widened. "Y-You—why didn't you say anything?" She whispered, her voice breaking. Then, without thinking, she threw herself into his arms. He hugged her tightly, patting her back, grounding her shaking body. She held him for the first time in what felt like an alternative lifetime.

"It was the only way a-and it doesn't matter now. I'm staying, and we'll get through this together."

"I can't let you do that, Hugo. Your family…Rey…they are all waiting for you," she muttered into his chest, her voice sounding forcefully soft.

His chin rested atop her head, eyes closed. "Don't be foolish. Your family is waiting for you, too. And your friends," he replied. She clutched his shirt, tears staining the worn fabric.

She took a deep breath in, memorizing his familiar scent. He smelled like *home*. "I—I have no family. My mom ran off years ago. I've been alone…And friends? I—," her voice cut off into an uncontrollable sob. Pulling back, she wiped her tears on her sleeve, holding her breath to stop herself from crying, from looking *weak*.

Her eyes felt distant, or maybe it was because Hugo was finally seeing her. The real her that she was trying hard to hide.

He froze, realizing things that he never would have guessed. Ethera couldn't bear to look at him; he was the first and the only one who finally knew the truth.

It was too late now—she was never to come back.

She forced a smile through the tears that blurred his face. "I'll see you around, pipsqueak," she struggled to say as she lifted her pinky finger. But before he could respond, her hands pushed him through the portal. He fell, disappearing into the swirling blue light.

Ethera's eyes widened, her arms stood in shock, eyes staring off into the fake life that she deluded herself with. She stumbled toward the book, dropping down to her knees. She could not feel the coldness of the ground.

The book slammed shut, and the portal instantly vanished. Then, in a fit of despair, she tore the pages apart, sobbing violently, severing the portal forever. The sound echoed in the silent library.

Dilian appeared beside her, unsure how to comfort a girl.

"Don't fucking touch me!" She shouted, sensing his presence near. She continued ripping the pages relentlessly, tears blurring her vision until there was nothing else to rip.

Nothing mattered anymore.

Hugo was *meant* to go back. He had friends. He had a family, a future.

While she had nothing. No one waited for her. Maybe that was the reason why the prophecy chose her. Unlike everyone else, she was...*nothing*. She was a sacrifice that the world would not care for.

Soon, even her friends would move on—Rose would go off to fashion school. Juno will take over her parents' restaurant and become an Olympian. Reymond will become the football captain and go off to play in college. And Hugo...

Hugo will never know how much she had cared, how much their childhood had meant to her. He will forever remain oblivious.

Finally, her body gave out, and her hands let go of the book. She pressed her face into her palms, wishing she could drown in them. Dilian held her trembling form, guilt flooding his every thought. She cried in his arms, attempting to shove him away but falling weak after some time.

Her cries shook the room, and a light breeze stirred the palace as a soft glow began to rise from within her.

The elf let go abruptly, stumbling back onto the ground, eyes wide with awe as the white light spread slowly at first, brushing against the ground beneath the mortal to every bookshelf and wall of the library.

Ethera paused, lifting her head to examine her own hands. The glow only grew under her watch, intensifying until it escaped through every window and door, spilling into the surrounding trees.

Everyone but her had closed their eyes, shielding themselves from its brilliance.

The pirates, goblins, and elves who had celebrated the victory on the beach froze, shielding their eyes as the radiant light stretched beyond the palace walls.

Even the Pirate King, sailing on his empty ship, turned to look—instantly drawn to the warmth, as a smile perked up on his lips.

The world itself shifted, for the birth of a new world had begun.

SEQUEL

"Are you feeling alright, dear?" A hand brushed against the forehead of a blonde girl. The sudden contact startled her, almost knocking her from the chair. She regained her composure quickly. Her mother stared, eyes narrowed in displeasure, her rejected arm still hovering in the air.

The girl looked away, shrinking away from her mother's concern. Her own hand instinctively wiped the spot where her mother's love dared to linger. "I-I'm fine," she said coldly. Her lack of appetite had infected her words. She twirled the warm silver fork against the bowl, stabbing at a blueberry until the vanilla yogurt bled a rich purple. Though her eyes lingered on the untouched breakfast, her mind had drifted elsewhere again.

The woman in front of her sat back against the wooden chair, sighing heavily without saying a word. Her eyes flicked between her spouse and her only child. The man cleared his throat, wiping the corner of his mouth with a white napkin. He scrunched it and tossed it atop his empty plate.

372

With his brows raised, he took a deep breath in, mustering the courage to pierce through the tension. "It's time to go, or you'll be late to school, Rose," he spoke softly, rising from the chair. It screeched against the dark grey floor, making Rose flinch. Not even the sound of her own name drew her back to earth, and her parents were beginning to notice.

Her mother rose; lips pressed into a thin line. "Don't forget your sweater, honey," she whispered gently, brushing the girl's head once more. The girl nodded briefly, too weary to push her mother away.

Rose left the dining room, steps muffled, leaving the lingering whispers behind her. She passed through the living room, up the stairs, into her room. Snatching her school bag, she swung it over her shoulder, phone sliding into her jeans pocket. Her eyes lingered aimlessly on the converse at the bottom of her open closet.

She walked towards them, reaching behind the dirty pair and grabbing a pair of white boots. Her hand rested on the back cushion of the velvet chair, slipping on one foot at a time.

Rose stumbled towards the door, pausing in the doorway. With a deep breath, she retraced her steps back to the closet before grabbing the shoes. She dashed down the stairs, emerging in the kitchen where the sound of a fork scraping leftover food hovered in the air.

She paused beside her mother, tossing the worn Converse into the trash. Her blue eyes hovered on the uneasy sight as if saying a wordless goodbye. "They don't fit me anymore," she muttered before her mother could get a chance to comment.

Her father waited in the black SUV, engine rumbling as the car warmed from within. Rose opened the door, jumping in. She dropped her bag beside her feet, jacket in her lap as she pulled the seatbelt over her chest.

The car rolled backward, out of the driveway. The radio softly played classical music—her father's favorite. She found comfort in the soft melody, her eyes instantly closed, almost fading into a distant daydream.

He stayed quiet, unsure whether she needed the comfort of space. But even silence began to tear at his mind until he had no choice but to let it out. "Your mother and I are worried about you," he began, not knowing how to approach his daughter with ease. "If you need help, we're here for you, okay?"

Rose didn't answer, but her eyes fluttered open. Her own thoughts felt like an everlasting fog, but her father's voice seemed to dispel the curse momentarily. She lifted her head, finally turning to look at him. "I-I lost something, and I don't know where to find it," her voice felt strange even in her own ears, as if she has not spoken in a long time.

He thought for a minute, his hands gripped the steering wheel despite the red light. He didn't need to look at her to understand how she felt. "Have you looked everywhere?"

Rose's eyebrows knitted, and she looked away with confusion. The people crossing the road shone brightly, their big smiles bloomed with the spring flowers above them. The season's warmth seemed unable to reach her, no matter how much she wanted it to. "B-But what if I don't know where to look…" her voice was barely audible against her fingers, the warm breath fanning her worn spring set.

Her father's chest shook with laughter. "Silly girl, if you don't go out there to try, then how will you ever find it?"

꙳꙳꙳ ꙳꙳꙳ ꙳꙳꙳

The door slammed open, striking the wall beside it. Juno burst in, sweat drenching her frizzy black hair. Rose lifted her head, startled—her father's conversation instantly dominated by the disturbing presence of her best friend. "Jeez, what's with you today?" The blonde smiled, faint but trying. Juno didn't greet her as she pushed through a group of students who gathered before the first bell. Her heart pounded loudly against her lungs, and a sudden dizzy feeling shot through her vision.

Rose readjusted her posture, leaning her cheeks against the palms of her hands. Without warning, Juno shoved the bright screen of her phone in the blonde's face. It brushed past Rose's nose, causing her to squint her eyes.

She pulled back, leaning against the chair. "What the hell is wrong with you?" She snapped, hands gripping the sides of her small table.

Juno ignored the irritated snare, shoving the phone closer. "Look closely," she urged, shaking the phone. Rose snatched it to get a proper look. Faces stared back at her.

"What the hell is this?" she asked, her fingers zooming on the picture. Her blue eyes widened, heart dropping down to the cold ground.

375

"I found it on my phone. I took this on Friday…four weeks ago."

Rose tossed the phone onto the wooden table, her arms crossing in front of her chest. Her blue eyes looked away from the unsettling image. "I'm afraid your prank came too early, April is not until next week."

Juno grabbed the phone, and her own fingers moved to zoom in on the picture. "This is not a prank. I don't remember taking this, like at all! S-Seriously, I stayed up all night searching—this is…it's Ethera Heart, right?" She declared, flipping the screen once again. It shook in her hand, but the confident expression didn't waver.

The unknown face with dyed white stripes stared back at her. "Who's Ethera Heart?" Rose asked, her tongue carried the name with a sense of comfort.

"T-That I don't know…"

www.ingramcontent.com/pod-product-compliance
Lightning Source LLC
Chambersburg PA
CBHW030550260626
47157CB00006B/2251